Henry Vizetelly, Marius Topin

The Wan With the Iron Mask

Henry Vizetelly, Marius Topin

The Wan With the Iron Mask

ISBN/EAN: 9783337178659

Printed in Europe, USA, Canada, Australia, Japan

Cover: Foto ©Andreas Hilbeck / pixelio.de

More available books at **www.hansebooks.com**

THE
MAN WITH THE IRON MASK.

BY MARIUS TOPIN.

TRANSLATED AND EDITED

BY HENRY VIZETELLY,

AUTHOR OF
"THE STORY OF THE DIAMOND NECKLACE."

"No one must know what has become of this man."
Order of Louis XIV.

LONDON:
SMITH, ELDER AND CO., 15, WATERLOO PLACE.
1870.

TRANSLATOR'S PREFACE.

M. TOPIN'S *L'Homme au Masque de Fer*, of which the present volume is a translation, has met with considerable attention in France, on the part both of historical students and the reading public; several editions of it having been called for in the course of a few months.

That a work which professes to give an authentic account of this almost legendary character, after having discussed in an exhaustive fashion the various theories that have been broached during a century and a quarter respecting his mysterious identity, should have been received with so large an amount of favour, is not surprising, for the story forms perhaps the most romantic episode of a reign more than ordinarily rich in dramatic incidents. But the extent of M. Topin's historical knowledge, the painstaking nature of his researches, the subtlety of his reasoning, the skill which he has displayed in the grouping of his materials, combined with his life-like pictures of events far from commonly familiar, not only render his work highly amusing reading, but entitle it to take its place in the library, both as an historical study which has resolved beyond all doubt a problem that had long perplexed some of the acutest minds, and as a valuable contribution towards the history of Europe during the latter part of the seventeenth century.

During the progress of the translation M. Topin's text has been carefully revised, and a few errors have been corrected. Additional notes, too, have been given whenever the subject-matter seemed to require elucidation, or where individuals little known to English readers make their appearance on the scene.

H. V.

Paris, April, 1870.

AUTHOR'S PREFACE.

If this book had been intended merely to satisfy a vulgar and commonplace curiosity, it would only have consisted of a few pages. My aim has been a loftier one. I have endeavoured, while concerning myself with the most famous and romantic of State-prisoners, to write the history of the principal individuals in whom people have beheld the Man with the Iron Mask. As regards some of these I have been compelled to lay bare the private life of Louis XIII. and Anne of Austria, and in order to refute the accusations with which the memory of this princess has been sullied, I have not hesitated to touch upon certain delicate points, and to follow her accusers on to the ground on which they have carried the discussion. But I have imposed upon myself the obligation of always respecting my readers, and of influencing their judgment without offending their taste. I have traced the others throughout their adventurous careers and agitated existences, and some of them even through their captivity, spent, sometimes in the monotonous inaction of solitude, sometimes with the resignation of the sage, or animated more frequently still by daring attempts at flight which the incessant vigilance of the most scrupulous of gaolers always foiled. Thus there will be found grouped together in this work Louis XIII. and Anne of Austria, the seductive Buckingham and the affecting Vermandois, the versatile Monmouth and the adventurous Beaufort, Lauzun the rash, and Fouquet, rendered admirable by his resignation and Christian virtues, the unfortunate Matthioly, and Saint-Mars, whose memory, and even existence, is inseparable from that of his prisoners.

The sole and firm ground-work of this book are the materials, for the most part unpublished, to be found in our Archives. For the space of two years I have been collecting them in the different depositories of manuscripts ; and at the Ministries as at the Archives of the Empire, at the Imperial Library as well as at the Arsenal, at the Institute as at the Hôtel de Ville, I have everywhere met with the most cordial reception, the most unreserved liberality, and the most invaluable courtesy. It is my duty, and at the same time my pleasure, to testify my gratitude to MM. Camille

Rousset, Gallet de Kulture, Margry, de Beauchesne, Lacroix, Ravaisson, Sage, Aude, and Read. The treasures of our Archives are not only rendered accessible by the goodwill of their Keepers, but are also made easy of consultation by the order which these gentlemen have introduced among the profusion of documents by means of classifications as clear as they are ingenious.

I have given in the text the more important documents of which I have made use, and in the notes those which are of less consequence, whilst I have contented myself with indicating the collections where those materials are to be found which are altogether of a secondary character. By this means the reader will have a complete check upon me. Without sacrificing anything of the strictest exactitude I have endeavoured to introduce into my account the spirit and the action proper to the individuals brought on to the scene, and, in a subject at once legendary and historical, to represent the faithful drawing of history under the seductive colouring of fiction.

Paris, November 8, 1869.

CONTENTS.

Page

CHAPTER III.

CHAPTER IV.

CHAPTER V.

CHAPTER VI.

CHAPTER XI.

CHAPTER XII.

CHAPTER XIII.

CHAPTER XIV.

CHAPTER XXIV.

THE
MAN WITH THE IRON MASK.

INTRODUCTION.

Arrival of the Man with the Iron Mask at the Bastille—His Death—
General Reflections on this celebrated Prisoner—Motives which
determined the present Writer to make fresh Researches concerning him—Plan and Object of the Work.

ABOUT three o'clock in the afternoon of September 18,
1698, the Sieur de Saint-Mars, coming from the Isles Sainte-
Marguerite, made his entry into the château of the Bastille,
of which fortress he had just been appointed governor.
Accompanying him, and borne along in his litter, was a
prisoner, whose face was covered with a black velvet mask,
and of whom Saint-Mars, with an escort of several mounted
men-at-arms, had been the inseparable and vigilant gaoler,
throughout the long journey from Provence. Saint-Mars
had halted at Palteau, an estate situated between Joigny
and Villeneuve-le-Roi, which belonged to him, and for a
long time the old inhabitants of Villeneuve used to recall
having seen the mysterious litter traversing in the evening
the principal street of their town. The remembrance of

this apparition has been perpetuated in the district, and the singular incidents characterizing it, related by the former to each new generation, have been handed down to our own days. The care taken by Saint-Mars at meal-times to keep his prisoner with his back to the windows, the pistols which were always to be seen within reach of the suspicious gaoler, the two beds which he caused to be placed side by side, so many precautions, so much mystery, excited the lively curiosity of the assembled peasants, and formed an incessant subject of conversation among them. At the Bastille, the prisoner was placed in the third room south of the Tower of La Bertaudière, prepared for him by the turnkey Dujonca, who, some days previous to his arrival, had received a written order to that effect from Saint-Mars.[1]

Five years afterwards, on Tuesday, November 20, 1703, at four o'clock in the afternoon, the drawbridge of the formidable fortress was lowered and gave passage to a sad and mournful train. A few men, bearing a dead body, having for sole escort two subordinate employés of the Bastille, silently issued forth and directed their steps towards the cemetery of the Church of Saint-Paul. Nothing could be more thrilling than the sight of this group gliding along furtively under shadow of the falling night. Nothing could be more

---

[1] *Estat de Prisonnies qui sont envoies par l'Ordre du Roy à la Bastille, à commenser du mescredy honsiesme du mois d'Octobre que je suis entré en possession de la charge de Lieutenant du Roy, en l'année* 1690, by Dujonca, fol. 37, verso :—Archives of the Arsenal. Letter from Barbézieux, Minister of War, to Saint-Mars, dated July 19, 1698 : —"You can write in advance to His Majesty's lieutenant of this château to have a chamber ready to receive this prisoner on your arrival." —Unpublished despatch from the Archives of the Ministry of War. Traditions collected at Villeneuve-le-Roi. Registers of the Secretary's Office of the King's Household.

utterly abandoned, and, in appearance, more obscure, than these unknown remains followed by two strangers, in a hurry to fulfil their task. Around the grave as, the evening before, around the bed of the dying man, there were no signs of sorrow or of regret. The prisoner of Provence had fallen ill on the Sunday. His illness having suddenly increased during the following day, the chaplain of the Bastille had been sent for; too late, however, to allow him time to go in quest of the last sacraments, yet still sufficiently early to enable him to address some rapid and common-place exhortations to the dying man. On the register of the Church of Saint-Paul he was inscribed under the name of Marchialy. At the Bastille he had always been known as the Prisoner of Provence.[2]

Such is the mysterious personage who, unknown and abandoned to the obscurity of a prison during the latter part of his existence, became, a few years after his death, celebrated throughout the entire world, and the romantic and piquant remembrance of whom has, for more than a century, charmed the imagination of all, attracted universal attention, and exercised uselessly the patience and sagacity of so many minds. Become the hero of the most famous of legends, he has had the rare privilege of everywhere exciting the curiosity of the public, without ever either wearying or satiating it. At all epochs and among all classes, in England, Germany, Italy, as well as France, in our own

---

[2] *Estat de Prisonnies qui sortet de la Bastille à commenser de housiesme du mois d'Octobre que je suis entré en possession, en l'année* 1690, by Dujonca, fol. 80, verso :—Archives of the Arsenal. *Registre des Baptêmes, Mariages, et Sépultures de la Paroisse de Saint-Paul,* s. 1703–1705, vol. ii. No. 166 :—Archives of the Hôtel de Ville. Registers of the Secretary's Office of the King's Household. Imperial Archives.

days, as in the time of Voltaire, people have manifested the utmost anxiety to penetrate the secret of this long imprisonment. Napoleon I. greatly regretted not being able to satisfy this desire.[3] Louis Philippe, too, discussed this problem, the solution of which he acknowledged himself ignorant of ;[4] and, if other sovereigns [5] have pretended they were acquainted with it, their contradictory statements lead us to believe that they were no better informed, but that in their eyes the knowledge and transmission of the dark secret ought to be counted among the prerogatives of the crown.

In the long list of writers whom the Man with the Iron Mask, the sphinx of our history, has attracted and tempted, are many illustrious names, as well as some less known now-a-days. During thirty years, Voltaire, Fréron, Saint-Foix, Lagrange-Chancel, and Father Griffet took part in a brilliant joust, in which each of the adversaries succeeded a great deal better in overthrowing his opponent's opinions than in securing the triumph of his own.

Many times, and in our own days even, has the debate been resumed, then momentarily abandoned, then recommenced again. Far and near new theories have been broached, invariably supported by vague and weak proofs, and soon overthrown by strong and valid objections. Fifty-two writers [6] have by turns endeavoured to throw light upon

---

[3] *Souvenirs de la Duchesse d'Abrantès*, recueillis par M. Paul Lacroix (Bibliophile Jacob).

[4] I am indebted for this information to the kindness of M. Guizot.

[5] Especially Louis XVIII., whose language is in complete disaccord with that of Louis XV. But I shall refer to this point of debate hereafter.

[6] Voltaire, Prosper Marchand, Baron de Crunyngen, Armand de la Chapelle, Chevalier de Mouhy, Duke de Nivernais, La Beaumelle, Lenglet-Dufresnoy, Lagrange-Chancel, Fréron, Saint-Foix, Father Griffet, Hume, De Palteau, Sandraz de Courtilz, Constantin de Renne-

this question, but without success; and it can be affirmed that a century of controversy and of exertion has not yet dissipated the mysterious gloom in which Saint-Mars' celebrated prisoner is enveloped.

So many successive checks, by still further stimulating curiosity, have caused it to be believed that it was impossible to arrive at an incontestable and definitive result. Every new explanation having been victoriously repelled almost as soon as started, people have despaired of ever attaining the truth, and some have even gone so far as to proclaim it as being beyond human reach. "The story of the Iron Mask," says M. Michelet,[7] "will probably for ever remain obscure," "The Man with the Iron Mask will very likely always be an insoluble problem," has been said elsewhere;[8] and M. Henri Martin declares that "history has not the right of pronouncing an opinion on what will never emerge from the domain of conjecture."[9]

If different methods of procedure had been adopted by the numerous writers who have attempted the solution of this problem, I should not have had the temerity to have added to their number; but an attentive study of their

---

ville, Baron d'Heiss, Sénac de Meilhan, De la Borde, Soulavie, Linguet, Marquis de Luchet, Anquetil, Father Papon, Malesherbes, Dulaure, Chevalier de Taulès, Chevalier de Cubières, Carra, Louis Dutens, Abbé Barthélemy, Quintin Craufurd, De Saint Mihiel, Bouche, Champfort, Millin, Spittler, Roux-Fazillac, Regnault-Warin, Weiss, Delort, George Agar Ellis, Gibbon, Auguste Billiard, Dufay, Bibliophile Jacob, Paul Lecointre, Letourneur, Jules Loiseleur, De Bellecombe, Mérimée, Sardou; without counting the writers of general history, such as S. Sismondi, Henri Martin, Michelet, Camille Rousset, Depping, and all who have written articles on this question in cyclopædias.

[7] *Histoire de France*, vol. xii. p. 435.

[8] *Art de Vérifier les Dates*, vol. vi. p. 292.

[9] *Histoire de France*, vol. xiv. p. 564.

writings shows that they have all taken the same point of departure, and that they have all given themselves up to a single idea. All have kept fixed in their minds this observation of Voltaire's :—" What redoubles one's astonishment is, that at the time when this prisoner was sent to the Isles Sainte-Marguerite, no important personage had disappeared from Europe." [10]

All have asked themselves if there really did not disappear from Europe some important personage, and they have immediately set themselves to discover some person of consideration, no matter who, that had disappeared during the period extending from 1662 to 1703. When by the aid of the very faintest resemblance they have fancied they have found their hero, they have forthwith adapted the mask of black velvet to him, and have seen in him the famous dead of November 20, 1703. Erecting their conjecture into a theory, they have become ardent propagators of it, and have adopted all that told in its favour with the same readiness with which they have energetically denied all that happened to be opposed to it. When the list of missing illustrious men belonging to this period was exhausted, certain writers, sooner than renounce seeing the Man with the Iron Mask in some person still alive in 1706, have had no other expedient than to delay for several years the death of Saint-Mars' prisoner, in order not to abandon so dear a discovery." [11]

But many of these ingenious and inventive writers acted in good faith. Not perceiving the defects in their pleading,

---

[10] Voltaire, *Siècle de Louis XIV.*, p. 289.

[11] M. de Taulès, for instance, a partisan of the theory which makes Avedick, the patriarch of Constantinople, the Man with the Iron Mask, and to which I shall refer in the after-part of this book.

they only considered its feeblest parts, and in default of making a great number of converts, they invariably ended, as is easy enough, by convincing themselves.

Persuaded of the unsatisfactory nature of a method of procedure which had always produced such ephemeral results, I have thought that, extraordinary means having proved so inefficacious, more simple ones might perhaps lead to a new solution, (yet one hardly dared hope for it, when twenty-five hypotheses had already been put forward) —to a solution at once decisive, to an absolute conviction, to the certainty of not having to apprehend from the reader either doubt or objection. Commencing the study of this question without any fixed opinion, and with the firm resolution of seeking only the truth, I set about collecting from the whole of our archives authentic despatches relating to the State prisoners under Louis XIV. from the year 1660 to 1710. Without pre-occupying myself with the Ministers who signed them, or the prisoners whom they concerned; without limiting my researches to· Saint-Mars, Pignerol, the Isles Sainte-Marguerite, or the Bastille, I arranged these despatches, of which more than three hundred are unpublished, in order of their dates. They then lent a material assistance; some explained others, and from this long and minute inquiry, slowly pursued through heaps of documents, has resulted, I hope, a definitive solution.

It was expedient this solution should be obtained.[12] In

----

[12] About a year ago (*Moniteur* of September 30, 1868) *àpropos* of the fine collection of unpublished documents given to the world by M. Ravaisson, under the title of '*Archives de la Bastille*, M. de Lescure expressed a wish to see this question definitively settled. I had been occupying myself with it for a considerable period, though not without having satisfied myself that the learned conservator of the Arsenal

this century, when the historian's resources are increased by the progress in certain sciences, by so many spectacles offered as an instruction to his fruitful meditations, by a more complete knowledge of institutions and facts, by the facility afforded of penetrating into collections which it had been believed would remain for ever inaccessible to investigators—in this century, which is literally the century of history, it behoved us not to leave in our annals, without solving it, a problem which had so frequently attracted the attention of foreigners. It is this which determined me to undertake a task which some may consider more curious than important. But to the interest peculiar to this subject has to be added that which is attached to the principal persons in whom by turns people have seen the prisoner of Saint-Mars. Before bringing on the scene the true Man with the Iron Mask, I shall examine rapidly, and with the aid of unpublished documents, the illustrious usurpers of this romantic title, so that this work may serve, not only to satisfy a trivial curiosity, but also to throw a new light upon some of the most singular points of the inner history of our country.

Archives contemplated no work on the Man with the Iron Mask, in continuation of his publication, not yet brought down to the epoch of the entry into the Bastille of this famous prisoner. Among contemporary authors, besides M. Paul Lacroix (Bibliophile Jacob), who in 1840 supported the theory that made Fouquet the celebrated prisoner, M. Jules Loiseleur, in the *Revue Contemporaine* of July 31, 1867, and M. de Bellecombe, in the *Investigateur* of May, 1868, have maintained, as the result of their labours, that the Man with the Iron Mask was an unknown and obscure spy, whose name would never be ascertained. We shall recur to the two studies of MM. Lacroix and Loiseleur, of which one is very ingenious, and the other exhibits a penetrating sagacity, while both display a varied and trustworthy erudition.

CHAPTER I.

Theory which supposes the Man with the Iron Mask to have been a
Brother of Louis XIV.—Voltaire the first to support this Theory
in his *Siècle de Louis XIV.*, and in the *Dictionnaire Philosophique*
—Certain Improbabilities in his Story—Account of the Man with
the Iron Mask introduced by Soulavie into the *Mémoires Apocryphes
du Maréchal de Richelieu*—The three different Hypotheses of the
Theory which makes the Man with the Iron Mask a Brother of
Louis XIV.

AMONG the numerous theories which attempt to explain the
existence of the Man with the Iron Mask,[1] some have been

---

[1] We shall speak of these briefly further on. We believe it useless
to mention, otherwise than in a short note, the opinion of those who,
despairing of finding the solution of the Man with the Iron Mask,
have taken upon themselves to deny his existence. All the documents
which we have just cited (official despatches of the Ministry of War,
Dujonca's *Journal*, &c. &c.) clearly establish the fact that a prisoner
was sent with Saint-Mars to the Bastille in 1698, and that he died there
in 1703, without any one ever having known his name. The silence of
the *Mémoires de Saint-Simon*, which is very thoughtlessly evoked in
support of the theory in question, will be explained very naturally in the
course of this work. Neither is there any need to enlarge upon an opinion
put forward a short time since in certain journals, which makes the
Man with the Iron Mask a son of Louis XIV. and the Duchess of
Orléans. This opinion, which there is nothing whatever to prove,
which rests upon no document, nor even upon any historical fact, is,
moreover, set forth in an article filled with errors. The only cause of
the disgrace of the Marquis de Vardes, exiled to his government of
Aigues-Mortes, was an intrigue in which he played an important part,

imagined so carelessly, conceived with so much haste, and supported in so loose a manner, that they are not worthy of a serious examination, and simply to mention them will suffice to do them justice. But there are others, due to an ingenious inspiration, and sustained with incontestable talent, which, without being true, have at least many appearances of being so. Among others, the most devoid of proofs, but also the most romantic, is that which makes the Man with the Iron Mask a brother of Louis XIV. " There are many things which everybody says because they have been said once," remarks Montesquieu.[2] This is especially true of things which border on the extraordinary and the marvellous. So, there are few persons who, on hearing the Man with the Iron Mask mentioned, do not immediately evoke a brother of Louis XIV. Whether the result of an intrigue between· Anne of Austria and the Duke of Buckingham,[3] or a legitimate son of Louis XIII.

---

and which had for its object the overthrow of Mademoiselle de la Vallière and the substitution of another mistress for her. As to the death of the Duchess of Orléans, it is now demonstrated that it was not due to poison. M. Mignet, in his *Négociations Relatives.à la Succession d'Espagne* (vol. iii. p. 206), was the first to deny this poisoning, relying principally on a very conclusive despatch from Lionne to Colbert, of the 1st July, 1670. Since then, M. Littré, in the second number of *La Philosophie Positive,* has incontestably established by the examination of the *procès-verbaux,* and of all the circumstances relating to the death of Henrietta of England, that it must be attributed to an internal disease, unknown to the physicians of that period. [The Duchess of Orléans here referred to is Henrietta-Maria, youngest daughter of Charles I. of England, who married Philip, younger brother of Louis XIV., and first Duke of the existing branch of the House of Orléans.—*Trans.*]

[2] *Grandeur et Décadence des Romains,* chap. iv.

[3] The grave English historian, David Hume, has re-echoed this theory, supported also by the Marquis de Luchet, in his *Remarques sur le Masque de Fer,* 1783.

and twin brother of Louis XIV., matters little to popular imagination. These are but different branches of a system which is profoundly engrafted in the public mind, and which it will not be unprofitable to overthrow separately, since it has still innumerable partisans, and touches upon the rights, moreover, the Bourbons have had to the throne of France.

By whom was this widely-spread opinion first put forward? And by whom has it been revived in our own days? What proofs, or, at least, what probabilities are invoked in its support? On what recollections, on what writings, is such a supposition based? Does it agree with official documents? Is it in accord with the character of Anne of Austria or with that of Louis XIII? Is it founded on reason?

First Voltaire,[4] in his *Siècle de Louis XIV.*, published in 1751, wrote the following lines, destined to excite a lively attention and to start a theory which he only completed in his *Dictionnaire Philosophique :—*

"Some months after the death of Mazarin," he says, "an event occurred which has no parallel, and what is no less strange, all the historians have ignored it. There was sent with the greatest secresy to the château of the Isle Sainte-Marguerite, in the Sea of Provence, an unknown prisoner, above the average height, and of a most handsome and noble countenance. This prisoner, on the journey,

---

[4] The *Mémoires Secrets pour servir à l'Histoire de Perse*, Amsterdam, 1745, had already revealed the existence of Saint-Mars' prisoner, and maintained that he was the Duke de Vermandois, a natural son of Louis XIV. and Mademoiselle de la Vallière. We shall recur to them when considering this theory, in the same way as we shall speak, with reference to the principal theories put forward, of the works which have discussed them, without regard to the period at which they have appeared.

wore a mask, the chin-piece of which was furnished with steel springs, which left him free to eat with the mask covering his face. Orders had been given to kill him if he should remove it. He remained in the island till a confidential officer, named Saint-Mars, governor of Pignerol, having been appointed governor of the Bastille in 1690, went to fetch him in the Isle Sainte-Marguerite and conducted him to the Bastille, always masked. The Marquis de Louvois went to see him in this island before his removal, and spoke to him standing, and with a consideration which betokened respect. This unknown individual was taken to the Bastille, where he was lodged as well as he could be in the château. Nothing that he asked for was refused him. His greatest liking was for linen of an extraordinary fineness and for lace; he played on the guitar. He had the very best of everything, and the governor rarely sat down in his presence. An old doctor of the Bastille, who had often attended this singular man in his illnesses, has stated that he never saw his face, although he had examined his tongue and the rest of his body. He was admirably made, said this doctor; his skin was rather brown : he interested one by the mere tone of his voice, never complaining of his state, and not letting it be understood who he could be. This stranger died in 1703, and was interred during the night in the parish church of Saint-Paul. What redoubles one's astonishment is that at the period when he was sent to the Isle Sainte-Marguerite, there had disappeared from Europe no important personage. This prisoner was without doubt one, since this is what occurred shortly after his arrival in the island :—The governor himself used to place the dishes on the table, and then to withdraw after having locked him in. One day, the prisoner wrote with a knife on a silver plate, and threw the plate out of the window towards a boat which was on the shore, almost at the foot of the tower. A fisherman, to whom the boat belonged, picked up the plate and carried it to the governor. He, astonished, asked the fisherman : ' Have you read what is written on this plate, and has any one seen it in your possession ?' ' I do not know how to read,' answered the fisherman ; ' I have just found it, and nobody has seen it.' The peasant was detained until the governor had ascertained that he could not read, and that the plate had been seen by nobody. ' Go,' he then said to him, ' you are very lucky not to know how to read !' " [5]

The following is the explanation by which, in his *Dictionnaire Philosophique*, Voltaire, under his editor's name, afterwards completed this first story : " The Man with the Iron Mask was doubtless a brother, and an elder brother of Louis XIV., whose mother had that taste for fine linen on which M. de Voltaire relies. It was from reading the *Mémoires* of the period which relate this anecdote concerning the Queen, that, recollecting this very taste of the Man with the Iron Mask, I no longer doubted that he was her son, of which all the other circumstances had already convinced me. It is known that Louis XIII. had not lived with the Queen for a considerable time, and that the birth of Louis XIV. was only due to a lucky chance." Voltaire proceeds to relate that previous to the birth of Louis XIV., Anne of Austria had been delivered of a son of whom Louis XIII. was not the

---

[5] *Siècle de Louis XIV.*, chap. xxv.

father, and that she had confided the secret of his birth
to Richelieu : he then goes on to say,—" But the Queen
and the Cardinal, equally penetrated with the necessity
of hiding the existence of the Man with the Iron Mask
from Louis XIII., had him brought up in secresy.
This was unknown to Louis XIV. until the death of the
Cardinal de Mazarin. But this monarch, learning then
that he had a brother, and an elder brother, whom his
mother could not disavow, who, moreover, perhaps had
characteristic features which betokened his origin, and
reflecting that this child, born during marriage, could not,
without great inconvenience and a horrible scandal, be
declared illegitimate after Louis XIII.'s death, may have
considered that he could not make use of wiser and better
means to assure his own security and the tranquillity of the
State than those which he employed, means which dispensed with his committing a cruelty which policy would
have represented as being necessary to a monarch less
conscientious and less magnanimous than Louis XIV." [6]

What improbabilities, what contradictions, what errors
accumulated in a few pages ! This unknown, whom no
one, not even his doctor, has ever seen unmasked, has his
face described as " handsome and noble ; " Saint-Mars,
named governor of the Bastille in 1690, and traversing the
whole of France in order to fetch a prisoner, for whom
during eight-and-twenty years another gaoler had sufficed ;
this mask with steel springs covering day and night the
face of the unknown without affecting his health ; this
resignation which prevented his complaining of his position

---

[6] Voltaire, *Dictionnaire Philosophique*, vol. i. p. 375, 376. Edition of
1771.

and which did not allow him to give any one a glimmering as to who he was, and this eagerness to throw out of his window silver plates on which he had written his name; this peculiar taste for fine linen, which Anne of Austria also possessed, and which revealed his origin; this haste on her part to confess her adultery to her enemy, the Cardinal de Richelieu; the Queen of France making only the Prime Minister the confidant of her confinement; and these two events, the birth and the abduction of a royal child, so well concealed that no contemporary memoir makes mention of them : such are the reflections which immediately suggest themselves on reading this story.

No less improbable, and more romantic still, is the fictitious account given by the governor himself of the Man with the Iron Mask, and which Soulavie has introduced into the apocryphal memoirs of the Marshal de Richelieu.[7] "The unfortunate prince whom I have brought up and guarded to the end of my days," says the governor,[8] "was born 5th September, 1638, at half-past eight in the evening, while the King was at supper. His brother, now reigning (Louis XIV.), was born at twelve in the morning, during his father's dinner. But while the birth of the King was splendid and brilliant, that of his brother was sad and care-

---

[7] London, 1790. It is known that Soulavie used the notes and papers of the Marshal de Richelieu with such bad faith, that the Duke de Fronsac launched an energetic protest against his father's ex-secretary.

[8] "Account of the birth and education of the unfortunate prince removed by the Cardinals Richelieu and Mazarin from society, and imprisoned by order of Louis XIV., composed by the governor of the prince on his deathbed." (*Mémoires du Maréchal de Richelieu*, vol. iii. chap. 4.)

fully concealed. Louis XIII. was warned by the midwife that the Queen would have a second delivery, and this double birth had been announced to him a long time previously by two herdsmen, who asserted in Paris that if the Queen was brought to bed of two Dauphins, it would be the consummation of the State's misfortune. The Cardinal de Richelieu, consulted by the King, replied that, if the Queen should bring twin sons into the world it would be necessary to carefully hide the second, because he might one day wish to be King. Louis XIII. was consequently patient in his uncertainty. When the pains of the second labour commenced, he was overwhelmed with emotion." The Queen is delivered of a second child "more delicate and more handsome than the first." The midwife is charged with him, " and the Cardinal afterwards took upon himself the education of this Prince who was destined to replace the Dauphin if the latter should die. As for the shepherds who prophesied on the subject of Anne of Austria's confinement, the governor did not hear them spoken of any more, whence he concludes that the Cardinal found a means of sending them away."

"Dame Péronnette, the midwife, brought the Prince up as her own son, and he passed for being the bastard of some great lord of the time. The Cardinal confided him later to the governor to educate him as a King's son, and this governor took him into Burgundy to his own house. The Queen-mother seemed to fear that if the birth of this young Dauphin should be discovered, the malcontents would revolt, because many doctors think that the last-born of twin brothers is really the elder, and therefore King by right. Nevertheless, Anne of Austria could not prevail upon herself to destroy the documents which established this birth. The Prince, at the age of nineteen, became acquainted with this State secret by searching in a casket belonging to his governor, in which he discovered letters from the Queen and the Cardinals de Richelieu and Mazarin. But, in order better to assure himself of his true condition, he asked for portraits of the late and present Kings. The governor replied that what he had were so bad that he was waiting for better ones to be painted, in order to place them in his apartment. The young man proposed to go to Saint-Jean de Luz, where the court was staying, on account of the King's marriage with the Spanish Infanta, and compare himself with his brother. His governor detained him, and no longer quitted his side.

" The young Prince was then handsome as Cupid, and Cupid was very useful to him in getting him a portrait of his brother, for a servant with whom he had an intrigue procured him one. The Prince recognized himself, and rushed to his governor, exclaiming, ' This is my brother, and here is what I am !' The governor despatched a messenger to court to ask for fresh instructions. The order came to imprison them both together." [9]

" It is at last known, this secret which has excited so lively and so general a curiosity ! " [10] says Champfort, in

---

[9] This story is closely reproduced in Grimm's Correspondence, on the assumed authority of an original letter from the Duchess de Modena, daughter of the Regent d'Orléans, said to have been found by M. de la Borde, a former valet-de-chambre of Louis XV., among the papers of Marshal Richelieu, who was the Duchess's lover.—See *Correspondance Littéraire, Philosophique, &c., de Grimm et de Diderot,* vol. xiv., pp. 419-23. Paris, 1831.—*Trans.*

[10] *Mercure de France.*

noticing these fictitious *Mémoires du Maréchal de Richelieu.* This implacable and sceptic railer allowed himself to be really seduced by this interpretation. Many others were convinced with him, which exonerates them ; and the version given by Voltaire was rather neglected for that of Soulavie.

In our own days, the theory which makes the Man with the Iron Mask a brother of Louis XIV. has been supported by four writers, who have powerfully contributed to revive it, and render it more popular still. The first two, by transferring to the stage,[11] and the third, by weaving into the plot of one of his most ingenious romances [12] the pathetic fate of the mysterious prisoner, have sought less to instruct than to interest their readers, and have completely succeeded in the purpose they had in view. The fourth writer, who, with MM. Fournier, Arnould, and Alexandre Dumas, has adopted the romantic theory, is an historian, M. Michelet.[13]

Before showing that this pretended brother of Louis XIV. could not be the unknown prisoner brought by Saint-Mars to the Bastille in 1698, let us seek when and how this theory could have been started, and, to the end that the refutation may be complete and definitive, let us see if his birth is not

---

[11] *Le Masque de Fer* of MM. Arnould and Fournier, played with great success at the Odéon Theatre in 1831.

[12] *Le Vicomte de Bragelonne,* by Alexander Dumas.

[13] *Histoire de France,* vol. xii. p. 435. "If Louis XVI. told Marie-Antoinette that nothing was any longer known about him, it is because, understanding her well, he had little desire of this secret being sent to Vienna. Very probably the child was an *elder* brother of Louis XIV., and his birth obscured the question (important to them) of knowing if their ancestor, Louis XIV., had reigned legitimately."

as imaginary as his adventures. There are three dates assigned for this birth—in 1625, after the visit to France of the Duke of Buckingham, who has been considered as the father of the Man with the Iron Mask; in 1631, a few months after the grave illness of Louis XIII., which caused the accession to the throne of his brother, Gaston of Orléans, to be feared; and lastly, September 5, 1638, a few hours after Louis XIV. came into the world. [14]

If, in this searching examination, we touch upon delicate points—if, in order to destroy the unjust accusations with which the memory of Anne of Austria has been defaced, we penetrate deeply into the details of her private life and that of her royal husband—we are drawn thither by those who, by carrying the debate on to this ground, compel us to follow them. We shall unhesitatingly touch upon each of the memories which they have not feared to recall, and nothing will be omitted that can throw light upon our proof. We shall, nevertheless, strive not to forget what is due to our readers, and the necessity of convincing them will not make us negligent of the obligation we are under of respecting them.

---

[14] I shall not examine in detail the hypothesis which makes him a child of Anne of Austria and Mazarin, since it is abandoned even by those who are the most eager to see a brother of Louis XIV. in the prisoner. "It is doubtful," says M. Michelet, "if the prisoner had been a younger brother of Louis XIV., a son of the Queen and Mazarin, whether the succeeding kings would have kept the secret so well." Moreover, the general arguments which I shall advance in Chapter V. will apply equally to a son of Mazarin, of Buckingham, or of Louis XIII.

CHAPTER II.

First Hypothesis—Portrait of Buckingham—Causes of his Visit to
France—Ardour with which he was received—His Passion for Anne
of Austria—Character of this Princess—Journey to Amiens—Scene
in the Garden—The Remembrance that Anne of Austria preserved
of it.

THE Duke of Buckingham, charged by Charles I. with
conducting Henrietta-Maria, the new Queen of England,
to London, arrived in Paris, May 24, 1625.[1] This brilliant
and audacious nobleman, who had known how to become
and to remain the ruling favourite of two kings utterly different in character and mind, and who, from a very humble
position, had raised himself to the highest posts in the
State, enjoyed throughout the whole of Europe the most
striking renown. He owed it, however, less to the favours
with which James I. had loaded him, and which his son
had continued, than to his attractive qualities and his
romantic adventures. All that Nature could bestow of
grace, charm, and the power of pleasing, he had received
in profusion. Deficient in the more precious gifts which
retain, he possessed all those which attract. He was well
made, had a very handsome countenance,[2] was of a proud

---

[1] *Mercure Français,* 1625, pp. 365, 366.
[2] *Mémoires de Madame de Mott-ville,* p. 15.

bearing without being haughty, and knew how to affect, according to circumstances, the emotion which he wished to communicate to others, but did not feel himself. During a long stay in France, he had succeeded in rendering exquisite those manners which were naturally delicate, and had become accomplished in all the arts which display the elegance of the body. He excelled in arms, showed himself a clever horseman, and danced with a rare perfection. The adventurous visit to Spain which he had made with the Prince of Wales [3] had increased his reputation for elegant frivolity, and the successes which his good looks and audacity had secured him made people forget the defects of the incautious negotiator. Already extravagant during his early poverty, he dissipated his fortune as if he had always lived in the opulence for which he seemed born, displaying a magnificence and a pomp unknown in a like degree before his time. Moreover, volatile and presumptuous, as inconstant as pliant, without profundity in his views, without connection in his projects, clever in maintaining himself in power, but disastrous to the sovereigns whom he governed, by turns insolently familiar and irresistibly attractive, sometimes admired by the crowd for his supreme distinction, at others execrated for his fatal authority, not low but impetuous in his caprices, not knowing either how to foresee or to accept an obstacle, and sacrificing everything to his fancy, he possessed none of the qualities of

---

[3] The Prince of Wales had been on the point of espousing the Infanta Maria, Anne of Austria's sister, and had proceeded to Spain with Buckingham, in order to hasten the conclusion of this project. See the very interesting Story of this negotiation in M. Guizot's *Un Projet de Mariage Royal.*

the statesman although he may have had all those which characterize the courtier.

He was expected, and was received in Paris with the most eager curiosity. "M. de Buckingham," wrote Richelieu to the Marquis d'Effiat, "will find in me the friendship which he might expect from a true brother who will render him all the services which he could desire of any one in the world,"[4] and Louis XIII. caused to be said to him, "I assure you that you will not be considered a stranger here, but a true Frenchman, since you are óne in heart, and have shown in this marriage negotiation such uniform affection for the welfare and service of the two crowns, that I think as much of it, so far as I am concerned, as the King your master. You will be very welcome here, and you will have access to me on all occasions."[5]

From the day of his arrival, Buckingham really showed himself "a true Frenchman" by his manner of behaving, by the ease and freedom of his movements. "He entered the court," says La Rochefoucauld, "with more splendour, grandeur, and magnificence than if he were King."[6] Eight great lords and four-and-twenty knights accompanied him. Twenty gentlemen and twelve pages were attached to his person, and his entire suite was composed of six or seven hundred pages or attendants.[7] "He had all the treasures

---

[4] Collection of Unpublished Documents concerning the History of France. *Lettres et Papiers d'État du Cardinal de Richelieu*, published by M. Avenel, vol. ii. p. 55.

[5] *Ibid.* vol. ii. p. 71.

[6] *Mémoires de la Rochefoucauld*, p. 340.

[7] Hardwicke (*State Papers*), vol. i. p. 571. Documents quoted in M. Guizot's work already cited, p. 332.

of the Crown of England to expend, and all its jewels to wear."[8]   He alighted at the splendid Hôtel de Luynes in the Rue Saint-Thomas-du-Louvre, which was then called the Hôtel de Chevreuse, "the most richly furnished hotel which France at present possesses," says the *Mercure*, and for several days the people of Paris were dazzled by the extraordinary luxury displayed by the ostentatious foreigner.[9]   The admiration at the court was quite as lively, and Buckingham there pushed liberality to extravagance.   Each of his sumptuous costumes was covered with pearls and diamonds intentionally fastened on so badly that a great number fell off, which the duke refused to receive when they were brought to him.   His prodigality, the importance of his mission, the seductiveness which enveloped his past life, and the amiability which he invariably displayed, his title of foreigner which rendered his perfectly French manners more piquant, that art of pleasing which was so easy to him, all contributed to make him alike the hero both of the town and of the court.

Giddy with a success which surpassed even his expectations, and dazzled by the splendour which he shed around him, he saw only the Queen of France worthy of his homage, and suddenly conceived for her the most vehement passion.   Too frivolous to bury this sentiment in his heart, he displayed it with complacency, and his temerity increased with his ostentation.   Anne of Austria was a Spaniard and a coquette.   She understood gallantry such as her countrywomen had learned it from the Moors—that gallantry

---

[8] *Mémoires de Madame de Motteville*, p. 16.   *Mercure Français*, 1625, p. 366.
[9] *Mercure Français, ibid.*

"which permits men to entertain without criminal intentions tender sentiments for women ; which inspires in them
fine actions, liberality, and all kinds of virtue." [10]   " She
did not consider," says one who best knew Anne of Austria,
" that the fine talk, which is ordinarily called honest gallantry, where no particular engagement is entered into, could
ever be blamable." [11]

So she tolerated with indulgence and without astonishment a passion congenial to her recollections of her country
and her youth, and which, while flattering her self-esteem,
did not at all shock her virtue. She received this homage
of vanity with the complacency of coquetry, knowing
herself to be most beautiful, most powerful, and most
worthy of being loved. On Buckingham's side there was
indiscreet persistence, multiplied signs of being in love,
and eagerness to be near her ; on hers, timid encouragement,
gentle sternness, severity and pardon by turns in her looks
appeared to Anne of Austria the natural and ordinary incidents of a gallantry where neither her honour nor even
her reputation seemed exposed to any peril. Moreover,
if numerous festivities gave them frequent opportunities
of seeing one another, the court being always present at
the many interviews of the Ambassador with the Queen,
restrained and embarrassed the enterprising audacity of
the one, but entirely justified the confidence of the
other.

---

[10] *Mémoires de Madame de Motteville*, p. 18. "In our time," adds
Madame de Motteville, "there has existed what the Spaniards call
fucezas." "This word," remarks the commentator on these Memoirs,
" appears to come from *huso*, a distaff. It seems to express the idea of
spinning love."

[11] *Ibid.*

After a week devoted to ballets, banquets, and feats of horsemanship, the wife of Charles I. set out on June 2 for England, conducted by the Duke of Buckingham, the Earls of Holland and Carlisle, and the Duke and Duchess de Chevreuse. Louis XIII., who was ill, remained at Compiègne ; but Anne of Austria, as well as Marie de Medicis, accompanied by a great number of French lords, proceeded to Amiens. There the brilliant assemblies recommenced, and the Duke de Chaulnes, governor of the province, gave the three Queens a most magnificent reception. During several days the whole of the nobility of the neighbourhood came to offer their homage and augment the brilliancy of the pleasure-parties and fêtes given by the governor. The town not containing a palace sufficiently large to receive the three Queens, they were lodged separately, each being accompanied by a train of intimates and lords, who formed a little court for her. Buckingham almost constantly deserted his new sovereign in order to show himself wherever Anne of Austria was. Attached to the abode of the latter was a large garden, near the banks of the Somme. The Queen and her court were fond of walking in it. One evening, attracted, as usual, by the beauty of the place, and tempted by the mildness of the weather, Anne of Austria, accompanied by Buckingham, the Duchess de Chevreuse, Lord Holland, and all the ladies of her suite, prolonged her promenade later than usual. Violently enamoured, and arrived at such a pitch of self-conceit that everything seemed possible, the Duke was very tender, and even dared to be importunate. The early departure of Henrietta Maria rendered their separation imminent. Favoured by the falling night, and taking advantage of a moment of isolation due to the winding of a path, he threw himself at the Queen's feet, and wished to give way to the transports of his passion. But Anne, alarmed, and perceiving the danger that she ran, uttered a loud cry, and Putange, her equerry, who was walking a few steps behind her, rushed forward and seized the Duke. All the suite arrived in turn, and Buckingham managed to get away in the midst of the crowd.[12]

Two days afterwards Henrietta Maria quitted Amiens for Boulogne; Marie de Medicis and Anne of Austria accompanied her to the gates of the town. Anne of Austria was in a carriage with the Princess de Conti. It was there that Buckingham took leave of her. Bending down to bid her adieu, he covered himself with the window-curtain, in order to hide his tears, which fell profusely. The Queen was moved at this display of grief, and the Princess de Conti, " who gracefully rallied her, told her that she could answer to the King for her virtue, but that she would not do as much for her cruelty, as she suspected her eyes of having regarded this lover with some degree of pity." [13]

Too passionately enamoured for separation to be able to cure him of his love, and excited still more to see Anne of Austria again by the recollection of his gross rashness, the Duke of Buckingham, whom unfavourable winds detained at Boulogne, returned suddenly to Amiens with Lord Holland, under pretence of having an important letter to deliver to Marie de Medicis, who, owing to a

---

[12] *Mémoires de La Porte. Mémoires de Madame de Motteville*, p. 16. *Mémoires de la Rochefoucauld*, p. 340.

[13] *Mémoires de Madame de Motteville.*

slight illness, had not quitted this town. " Returned again !" said Anne of Austria to Nogent-Bautru, on learning this news; " I thought that we were delivered from him." [14] She had been bled that morning, and was in bed when the two English noblemen entered her chamber. Buckingham, blinded by his passion, threw himself on his knees before the Queen's bed, embracing the coverings with ecstasy, and exhibiting, to the great scandal of the ladies of honour, the impetuous sentiments which agitated him. The Countess de Lannoi wished to force him to rise, telling him, with severity, that such behaviour was not according to French customs. " I am not French," replied the Duke, and he continued, but always in the presence of several witnesses, to eloquently express his tenderness for the Queen. The latter, being very much embarrassed, could not at first say anything; then she complained of such boldness, but without a great deal of indignation ; and it is probable that her heart took no part in the reproaches which she addressed to the duke. The next day he departed a second time for Boulogne, and never again saw the Queen of France.

Such is the famous scene at Amiens, which furnished · opportunities for the gross liveliness of Tallemant des Réaux and the libertine imagination of the Cardinal de

---

[14] *Mémoires de La Porte*, pp. 8, 9. Madame de Motteville assures us that her mistress was informed of this visit by Madame de Chevreuse, which is possible. It is the only point, and moreover, a very secondary one, in which La Porte's account differs from Madame de Motteville's. But we must not forget that the former was an eye-witness, whilst the latter, who entered the service of Anne of Austria afterwards, learnt the events, which she describes at the commencement of her Memoirs, long subsequent to their occurrence.

Retz.[15] The statements of La Porte, who was present, of Madame de Motteville, who collected her information from eye-witnesses, and of La Rochefoucauld, less likely to show partiality, leave no doubt of Anne of Austria's innocence. Marie de Medicis, whose interest it then was to injure her with Louis XIII., and who often did so without scruple, could not on this occasion, says La Porte,[16] "avoid bearing witness to the truth, and telling the King that there was nothing in it; that if the Queen might have been willing to act wrongly, it would have been impossible, with so many people about her who were watching her, and that she could not prevent the Duke of Buckingham having esteem or even love for her. She related also a number of things of this kind which had happened to herself in her youth."

Marie de Medicis might also have quoted examples from the life of Anne of Austria herself, who had previously loved the Duke de Montmorency and the Duke de Bellegarde without her honour having been tarnished by so doing.[17] The recollection of Buckingham's love dwelt more profoundly in the memory of all, because his passion had been more fiery and had been manifested by incautious acts. But to the end of the Queen's life, even after the death of Louis XIII., and during the regency, it was in her presence a subject of conversation which she listened to complacently, because it flattered her self-esteem, and which she would certainly not have tolerated, had any one

---

[15] Retz places the Amiens scene at the Louvre, and does not neglect the opportunity of blackening the Queen's honour.

[16] *Mémoires de La Porte,* p. 10.

[17] *Mémoires de Madame de Motteville,* p. 18.

dared to start it, if this recollection had been to her a cause for remorse. Far from this, people familiarly jested with her about it with grace, and without offending her, since they could thus remind her of a liking which had been sufficiently strong, but had not led her to commit any fault. Richelieu, presenting Mazarin to the Queen, said, "You will like him, madam, he has Buckingham's manner."[18] Much later Anne of Austria, when Regent, meeting Voiture walking along in a dreamy state, in her garden of Ruel, and asking him what he was thinking of, received in reply these verses, which did not at all offend her :—

> "Je pensais que la destinée,
> Après tant d'injustes malheurs,
> Vous a justement couronnée
> De gloire, d'éclat et d'honneurs ;
> Mais que vous étiez plus heureuse
> Lorsque vous étiez autrefois,
> Je ne veux pas dire amoureuse,
> La rime le veut toutefois.
>
> Je pensais (que nos autres poëtes
> Nous pensons extravagamment)
> Ce que, dans l'humeur où vous êtes,
> Vous feriez si, dans ce moment,
> Vous avisiez en cette place
> Venir le Duc de Buckingham,
> Et lequel serait en disgrâce,
> De lui ou du père Vincent." [19]

Everything combines to absolve Anne of Austria from the crime of which she was accused during the troubles of the Fronde, and in the midst of the unjust passions aroused by civil war. Louis XIII.'s conduct with respect

---

[18] *Mémoires de Tallemant des Réaux*, vol. i. p. 422.

[19] Père Vincent was the Queen's confessor.—*Mémoires de Madame de Motteville*, vol. i. pp. 81, 82.

to her, and his persistent coldness, alone seemed to condemn her. But does this coldness date from Buckingham's stay in Paris? Were the isolation in which Louis XIII. often remained and his neglect of the Queen such as people have believed up to the present time? Must we admit, as has been maintained, the proof of a criminal infidelity on the part of this Princess, deliberately committed either with Buckingham in 1625, or with an unknown individual, in 1630, with the view of being able, at the instant of Louis XIII.'s death, which then seemed imminent, to reign in the name of a child of whom she should be *enceinte*, and who, after the unexpected recovery of the King, became the Man with the Iron Mask?

CHAPTER III.

THE political story of Louis XIII.'s marriage with Anne of Austria has been told; the motives which determined this union, the negotiations which preceded it, the great interests connected with it, and the powerful springs which put it in action, have all been set forth and weighed in a decisive manner.[1]

If, neglecting this grave examination, which is entirely foreign to our work, we occupy ourselves solely with the character and secret thoughts of the persons thus tied to one another, and whose private life has been ransacked in order to give a solution to the problem of the Man with the Iron Mask, we see that a very strong liking for France and for her King, on Anne of Austria's part, was in accord

---

[1] *Les Mariages espagnols sous le règne d'Henri IV. et la Régence de Marie de Medicis*, by M. Perrens, Professor at the Lycée Bonaparte.

with the necessities of policy.   Contrary to what frequently happens in the case of royal marriages, the obligations imposed on the Infanta by her rank were not repugnant to the sentiments of the woman, and when she crossed the French frontier for the first time, she realized a hope long since conceived and dearly cherished in her heart.   With only eight days between their births and at once betrothed to one another in public opinion, the Infanta and the Dauphin had been the object of the researches and predictions of all the astrologers of the time,[2] who proclaimed that, having come into the world under the same sign, they were destined to love each other, even though they might not be united.   The Infanta had believed in this augury. She had early liked to hear the young King spoken of, she sought after his portraits, she preferred garments of French cut, she willingly wore ear-rings formed of fleurs-de-lis, and, the changes of the negotiation having for a moment fixed the choice of the two Governments on her sister Doña Maria,[3] Anne, then nine years old, declared, "that if it was to be thus, she was resolved to pass her life in a monastery without ever marrying."[4]   When, three years afterwards, the Duke de Mayenne, on quitting Madrid, whither he had come to sign the marriage contract of Anne and Louis XIII., asked the former what she wished him to

---

[2] Manuscripts of the Imperial Library, *fonds Harlay*, 228, Nos. 14, 15 ; Court of Spain, Embassy of M. de Vaucellas, already quoted by M. Armand Baschet in his amusing work, very rich in rare documents, *Le Roi chez la Reine.*

[3] The Infanta Maria, married to Ferdinand III., King of Hungary, afterwards Emperor.

[4] Despatch from M. de Vaucellas, November 20, 1610.   Manuscripts quoted above.

say on her behalf to the King of France, she replied : "That I am extremely impatient to see him." This answer having shocked the austere Countess d'Altamira, her governess, who exclaimed — "What! madam, what will the King of France think when M. de Mayenne tells him that you have made such a speech?"—the Infanta rejoined, "Madam, you have taught me that one should always be sincere; you should not be surprised then if I speak the truth."[5]

The two years which elapsed before her departure saw no change in these sentiments. The 9th November, 1615, she parted at Fontarabia from her father, Philip III., with less sorrow than he showed in allowing her at length to leave, and it was with pride and contentment that the new Queen, radiant with youth and beauty,[6] crossed the Bidassoa, on her way to Bordeaux, where the French court was stopping. What kind of husband was she about to meet there?

Very different from those of the Princess Anne were the impressions of Louis XIII., concerning the marriage and the family to which he was going to unite himself. People had frequently, and at an early age, conversed with him about the project. The first replies of the Dauphin, questioned from his most tender infancy, would have no significance.[7]

---

[5] *Mercure Français,* vol. ii. p. 549.

[6] Manuscripts of the Imperial Library, *fonds Dupuy,* 76, p. 145, and Archives of the Château of Mouchy-Noailles, No. 1706. *Mariages des Rois et Reines,* by M. Baschet in his book already quoted.

[7] *Journal de Jean Héroard sur l'Enfance et la Jeunesse de Louis XIII.* Manuscripts of the Imperial Library. It has just been published by Didot, having been edited by MM. Eud. de Soulié and Ed. de Barthélemy, with an intelligence, a carefulness, and an erudition on which they cannot be too strongly felicitated.

But as he advanced in age, his aversion to everything Spanish manifested itself with characteristic energy. Twice he replied in the negative to Henri IV., when the latter spoke to him of the Infanta as his future wife.[8] One day, on M. de Ventelet asking him if he liked the Spaniards, he answered, "No." "And why, sir?" "Because they are papa's enemies." "And the Infanta?" added De Ventelet, "do you love her, sir?" "No." "Why, sir?" "I don't want any Spanish love."[9] Later, when his chaplain was making him recite the Commandments, on coming to "Thou shalt not kill," the Dauphin exclaimed: "What, not the Spaniards? Oh, yes, I shall kill the Spaniards, because they are papa's enemies! I will beat them well!" And on his chaplain observing that they were Christians, he replied: "May I only kill Turks then?"[10]

To this aversion, a great deal more significant since it was contrary to a project generally acquiesced in by those about him, soon came to be added a certain distaste for marriage. Born with the ardent and lascivious temperament of his father, impelled to follow his example by conversations often loose, sometimes obscene, Louis XIII. succeeded in modifying these early tendencies by a force of will and a power of reflection truly rare. He was naturally an observer, he spoke little and laughed still less. He was usually serious and grave at times when his pages found cause for great merriment. All that he remarked became profoundly engraved on his mind, and enabled him years afterwards to reply with marvellous pertinency to questions which were

---

[8] *Journal d'Héroard*, November 3, 1604, and March 2, 1605.
[9] *Ibid.*, April 4, 1605.
[10] *Ibid.*, January 29, 1607.

sometimes embarrassing. His young imagination was early struck by the singular effects which the King's conduct produced at the court. In his cradle he received frequent visits, not only from his mother, but also from Henri IV.'s repudiated wife,[11] and from his numerous mistresses. They all sometimes found themselves assembled around him, the latter proud of their master's affection, Marie de Medecis irritated, jealous, and showing it. The issue of these very open intrigues, were the Dauphin's companions; but he instinctively abhorred them. He struck them without motive; would not have them at his table; absolutely refused to call them brothers; and when Henri IV., after having beaten him without overcoming this insurmountable repugnance, asked him the reason of it, he answered, "Because they are not mamma's sons."[12]

This hatred for everything connected with illegitimacy was certainly the origin of the chaste reserve which was to characterize so particularly him who was the son of Henri IV. and the father of Louis XIV. From his illegitimate brothers, this aversion extended to their mothers, whom he qualified in very contemptuous terms, and to the intrigues in which they were engaged. "Shall you be as ribald as the King?" said his nurse to him one day. "No," he answered, after a moment's reflection. And on her asking him if he was in love, he replied, "No, I avoid love."[13]

It was especially after Henri IV.'s death that the tendencies of the young king revealed themselves. He loved his father tenderly, a great deal more than Marie de Medicis

---

11 Marguerite de Navarre.

12 *Journal d'Héroard, passim.*

13 *Ibid.,* June 9, 1604, and October 21, 1608.

did, who, moreover, never showed much affection for her elder son.   He worthily wept his violent death,[14] and long afterwards, hearing at the Louvre, one of the late King's songs, he went aside to sob.[15]   But if, while yet a child, he had appreciated the glory of Henri IV., if he had shared his patriotic sentiments, if he was proud of his victories, he had silently blamed the licence which, in acts, and still more in language, then rendered the French Court one of the most gross in Europe.   As King, he would not tolerate these excesses.   He showed himself openly austere in his speech, and modest in his actions, forbade in his presence obscene songs and scandalous conversations, and in order to avoid any pretext for them, replied sharply to M. de Souvré, his governor, when he wished to talk with him about marriage : " Do not let us speak of that, sir ; do not let us speak of that."

It was nevertheless necessary to speak of it, and to set out for Bordeaux.   Louis XIII., then in his fifteenth year, still possessed, and was to preserve for a long time, the tastes and predilections of his infancy.   He gave himself up to them in order to divert his mind from the marriage festivities.   He kept birds, armed his gentlemen, and enrolled them in a vigilant and disciplined troop ; then he assisted at the Council, replied pertinently to the

---

[14] "Ha!" he said, when he was told of Ravaillac's act, "if I had been there with my sword, I would have killed him."—*Journal d'Héroard*, May 14, 1610.

[15] Another day, November 14, 1611, he proceeded to St. Germain. "He went there to visit his brother, who was ill of an *endormissement*, accompanied with slight convulsions.   He awoke, and Louis XIII. said to him, 'Bonsoir, mon frère.'   He replied, ' Bonsoir, *mon petit papa.*' At these words Louis XIII. commenced to weep, went away, and was not seen for the whole of the day."—*Journal d'Héroard*, Nov. 14, 1611.

deputations presented to him, and thus mingled the simple amusements of the child with the grave accomplishment of his business as King.[16]   Much less desirous of fulfilling his duties as husband, he nevertheless affected towards the Infanta, either from self-esteem, or from a sense of propriety towards the strangers who were bringing her to him, an attention which surprised and charmed the court.   He went to meet the train which accompanied her, showed himself curious and pleased to see her, and was timid, but attentive and courteous, in the first interviews which he had with her.[17]   This was all; and, if for an instant, he possessed the manners of a gallant and attentive cavalier, he by no means exhibited the behaviour of a lover. During the evening after the celebration of the ceremony, he remained insensible to the encouragements of M. de Grammont,[18] and Marie de Médicis had to exert her authority in order to induce him to go to Anne of Austria.   Four years afterwards the marriage was not yet consummated; and this event, ardently desired by the Court of France, disconsolate at the King's coldness; by the Court of Spain, which saw an insult in this disdain; by the Pope's nuncio, and by the Court of Tuscany, which had so much contributed towards the union, became in some degree an affair of State.

Many efforts, many attempts were necessary to induce Louis XIII. to change his course of behaviour, of which the remote cause may be ascribed to his early impressions as Dauphin, and of which a more immediate one has been

---

16 *Mémoires du Maréchal de Bassompierre.—Journal d'Héroard.*

17 Despatch from the ambassador of the Grand Duke of Tuscany, Matteo Bartolini, December 4, 1615, quoted by M. A. Baschet. *Journal d'Héroard,* November 21, 1615.

18 *Journal d'Héroard,* November 25, 1615.

discovered by the Nuncio Bentivoglio.[19] Sometimes the King's pride was attempted to be touched, and the politic Nuncio, availing himself of the marriage of the Princess Christine with the Duke of Savoy, asked Louis XIII., " If he wished to have the shame of seeing his sister have a son before he had a Dauphin." [20] Sometimes recourse was had to influences still more direct.[21] At length, January 25, 1619, Albert de Luynes, after vainly begging him to cede to the wishes of his subjects, carried him by force into the Queen's chamber.[22] The following day, all the ambassadors announced this event to their respective governments.

From that time, Louis XIII. was less scared, but almost as timid [23] as ever, and though, preserving all his repugnances, he sometimes overcame them as a matter of duty, and showed himself a tolerably ardent, but never very tender husband. In the month of December, 1619, there were

---

[19] Despatch of the Nuncio Bentivoglio, January 30, 1619.

[20] *Ibid.*, January 16, 1619.

[21] Despatch of Contarini, ambassador from Venice, Jan. 27, 1619.

[22] Despatches of the Nuncio Bentivoglio, vol. i. pp. 157, 240, 300; and vol. ii. pp. 10, 31, 39, 40, 44, 80, 82, and 84. Despatch of Bentivoglio, January 30, 1619. See also despatches from the Venetian ambassador, January 27, and February 5, 1619; the *Journal d'Héroard*, January 25, 1619 ; Letter from Father Joseph to the Minister of Spain, February 14, 1619 ; and, lastly, the *Mémoires de Bassompierre*, vol. ii. p. 147.

[23] To the causes of Louis XIII.'s reserve, which we have just cited, may be added another, which the duty of not omitting anything causes us to indicate. According to the *Rélation de Don Fernando Giron* (Archives of Simancas), Louis XIII. held aloof from Anne of Austria "because he had been persuaded that if he had a son, while yet so young, it would cause a civil war in the kingdom." Nothing, however, confirms this supposition, or renders it likely.

reasons for hoping that the Queen was pregnant.[24] This hope, which soon vanished, was renewed at the commencement of 1622, but was again destroyed by a fall, which Anne of Austria had while playing with the Duchess de Chevreuse.[25] Buckingham's rapid visit to France, if it left a profound remembrance in the Queen's heart, certainly had no influence upon the King's conduct. Nothing was changed in the intercourse of the two spouses, which was neither more frequent, nor ever entirely interrupted.[26] After, as before this visit, Louis XIII. almost invariably saw in the Queen the Spaniard in blood and affection; and when in May, 1621, he had to announce to her the death of her father, he did it in this wise: " Madam," said he, " I have just now received letters from Spain, in which they write me word for certain, that the King your father is dead." Then, mounting his horse, he set out for the chase.[27] It is undoubtedly true, moreover, that Anne of Austria, who was, to her eternal glory, to become thoroughly French on assuming the Regency, and perceiving the true interests of her young son, to serve them with patriotism, intelligence, and firmness, even in opposition to her old friends, was, during the life-time of Louis XIII., the natural centre of a secret but constant and implacable opposition to the system which Richelieu supported. Good, but proud, she had been galled by her

---

[24] Despatch of the Nuncio Bentivoglio, December 4, 1619.

[25] *Mémoires de Bassompierre*, confirmed by the *Journal d'Héroard*, March 26, 1622.

[26] *Journal d'Héroard, passim*, and especially June 8, and August 21, 1626.

[27] *Ibid.*, May 10, 1621.

husband's indifference, humiliated by Richelieu's chicanery and mistrust, and irritated at not possessing any influence, so that, in the midst of the war which divided Spain and France, she had not wished to dissimulate the attachment which she preserved for her own family and for her country. Badly advised by the frivolous and restless Duchess de Chevreuse, she had engaged in different enterprises by which, without betraying France, she had furnished her enemies with arms sufficiently powerful for them to be able to maintain her in disgrace with Louis XIII.

This Prince, who during his whole life longed for the moment when he should quit his state of tutelage,[28] and who, from being under the control of his governor, was to pass under his mother's, then under Albert de Luynes', and lastly, under Richelieu's, joined to rather a fierce pride a true and just sense and exact knowledge of his inferiority. He detested the yoke, but he felt that it was necessary. Destined by his own incapacity to be for ever accomplishing the designs of others, he submitted to constraint, although constantly disposed to revolt. But he loved neither his mother, whom he discarded, nor De Luynes, whose death he did not regret. Richelieu alone, not only by the vast superiority of his genius, but especially by the obsequiousness of his language, by incessant precautions, by continually new artifices of humility, succeeded in seducing that unquiet and distrustful

---

[28] "He was playing with some little balls, rolling them along his taper stand, and calling them soldiers. M. de Souvré reproved him, and told him that he was always amusing himself at childish games. 'But, Monsieur de Souvré, these are soldiers; this is not a child's game!' 'Sir, you will always be a child.' 'It is you who keep me one!'" —*Journal d'Héroard*, February 21, 1610.

spirit, over which flattery had no power.[29] He ended by even attaching the King to himself, whatever may have been said about it, and by inspiring in him an affection which was bestowed quite as much upon the man as upon the indispensable Minister. Louis XIII. had the greatest solicitude for Richelieu, and paid him the most delicate attentions; and it can be affirmed, after a perusal of his letters, as yet unpublished, that these marks of lively friendship were not merely the result of self-interest.[30] Moreover, even when he was in possession of supreme authority, Richelieu, ever on the alert, showed himself to the last as studious in preserving it as he had been ingenious and supple in acquiring it. His efforts were constantly exerted to neutralize the influence of a Spanish Queen over a King whom he wished to maintain in the glorious policy of Henri IV. But he did not content himself with depriving the legitimate wife of his King of the whole of her power, which was a matter of no difficulty. Although incapable of criminal desires, since he could abstain from lawful pleasures, Louis XIII., sickly and morose as he was, reaping from love only jealousy and trouble, devoured by inquietudes and cares, had need of pouring out his complaints, of exposing his griefs, of unbosoming himself to a friendly heart, away from the pomp and noise which he fled. Richelieu always directed this inclination; and if he subjugated the King's mind by the force of his own genius, if he fascinated him by the seductive power of

---

[29] Several facts cited by Héroard prove that Louis XIII. was not at all sensible to flattery. (See particularly Oct 8, and Dec. 3, 1610.)

[30] Archives of the Ministry of Foreign Affairs. Manuscripts. Original Letters of Louis XIII. Section France, 5.

his words, he watched over all his actions by means of spies, with whom he surrounded him, and governed even his soul through his confessors.[31] When the Prince's affections, " purely spiritual, and enjoyments always chaste," as says a contemporary, were bestowed on instruments, indocile to the directions of the ruling Minister, the latter knew how to conjure up scruples in the King's mind, even for these pure connections, and which triumphed over his inclinations. To Madame de Hautefort succeeded, in the royal affections, Mademoiselle de la Fayette, to her Cinq-Mars, and these three individuals, whose relations with the King always continued perfectly irreproachable, but who rebelled against Richelieu's imperious will, expiated their resistance—one in exile, another in a convent, and the third on the scaffold.

If, then, it was true that Anne of Austria had, in 1630, committed adultery in order to give an heir to her dying husband, how are we to admit that a Minister so suspicious and vigilant would not have been cognisant of it, and knowing it, would not, by informing the convalescent King of this crime, have brought about the ruin of a Queen whom he detested, and who, in union with Marie de Medicis, was then plotting his downfall? It is in vain to object that a feeling of propriety would have restrained the Cardinal :[32] he was incapable of any such sentiment. Inflexible towards

---

[31] Archives of the Ministry of Foreign Affairs. Manuscripts. Section France, vol. lxxxviii. fol. 99, and lxxxix. fols. 3, 23, 67, 78, and 103.

[32] M. Michelet indicates another motive which it is only necessary to cite in order to show its improbability. " Richelieu," he says, " trusted in the weakness of the Queen's nature, and, consequently, that one day or other she would be involved in some embarrassment or thoughtlessness which would leave her at his mercy."

his enemies, because he regarded them, with reason, as the enemies of the State, to unmask and ruin them he employed a stubbornness and a persistence which nothing could overcome. When it was necessary to persuade Louis XIII. of the communication which the Queen kept up with Spain, the implacable Minister could make the most minute search and put the most humiliating questions. He could cause her dearest servants to be arrested; he could confront her with spies; he could treat her as an obscure criminal; and the admirable devotion of Madame de Hautefort[33] could alone enable the Queen, very strongly suspected, but not entirely convicted, to escape from this grave danger. And yet people desire to maintain that Richelieu would have left Louis XIII. ignorant of a much greater crime, and one which touched more immediately the King's honour! Moreover, where, when, how, and in what interest would this crime have been committed? To conjectures and vague insinuations let us oppose positive facts, which prove that Richelieu did not acquaint Louis XIII., because Anne of Austria had never ceased to be innocent.

The King fell ill at Lyons, not during the early part of August, as has been said, but on September 22, and here especially dates are of the utmost importance.[34] He was seized with a fever, which consumed him. The seventh day—the 29th—it was complicated by a dysentery, which exhausted him. The attack of this last complaint, produced by one of those medicines then much in vogue, was

---

[33] *Mémoires de La Porte*, p. 370.

[34] Letter from Richelieu to Marshal de Schonberg, September 25, 1630; Letter from Father Suffren, Louis XIII.'s confessor, to Father Jacquinot, October 1, 1630.

so violent, and its consequences so rapid, that by midnight
the doctors despaired of saving him. Marie de Medicis
had retired. Anne of Austria, who did not leave the royal
patient, resolved to have him warned by his confessor of
the danger he was in. But, at the first cautiously spoken
words, Louis XIII. conjured Father Suffren, and those
who surrounded him, not to hide the truth from him. He
learned it with calmness and courage, confessed, communicated, and asked pardon of all for any wrong he might
have done them; then, calling the Queen, he embraced her
tenderly, and addressed to her a touching farewell. As she
retired on one side in order to weep freely, the King prayed
Father Suffren to go and find her, and again beg her from
him "to pardon him all the unpleasantnesses he might have
caused her the whole time of their married life." He afterwards conversed with Richelieu, and offered a spectacle of
the most edifying resignation. Towards the middle of the
day, the Archbishop of Lyons was preparing himself to
bring in the extreme unction, when the doctors, who had
already bled this exhausted body six times in succession,
ordered a seventh bleeding.[35] But then the true cause of
the illness, which was unknown to them, was made clear;
an internal abscess broke, and nature saved the patient
at the moment when the intervention of his physicians
promised to be fatal.[36] Louis XIII., soon re-established

---

[35] Letter from Father Suffren, already quoted. In one year Bouvart,
Louis XIII.'s doctor, had him bled 47 times, made him take 212
medicines and 215 injections.—*Archives Curieuses de l'Histoire de France,*
by Cimber and Danjou, 2nd series, vol. v. p. 63.

[36] Letter from Richelieu to Schonberg, September 30, 1630;
Letter from Richelieu to d'Effiat, October 1, 1630.—*Mémoires de
Richelieu,* book xi. vol vi. p. 296. Letter from Father Suffren, already
quoted.

in health, left Lyons with the Queen, who did not cease to lavish on him the most tender cares, and whose sincere grief had touched him. In this crisis the two spouses had forgotten the past. [37] The repugnance and the coldness of the one, the wounded pride of the other, had disappeared, and they were naturally led to appreciate whatever goodness and amiability were to be found in each other's natures. [38]

Strong in the unaccustomed sway which she exercised, but exaggerating its extent, Anne of Austria was not content with holding in the King's heart the place which properly belonged to her. Aided by the ambitious and vindictive Marie de Medicis, after having occupied herself with her griefs as a wife, she desired to extend her censure to affairs of State, and to attack, in Richelieu, not only one who had kept alive the mistrust of herself, who had called suspicion into existence, and had separated King and Queen, mother and son, but also the stubborn pursuer of the great policy of Henri IV., who maintained abroad the pre-eminence of France over Spain, and the abasement of the House of Austria. We know how Louis XIII., who was incapable of vast projects, but who understood their value, was re-

---

[37] A similar and as perfect return of lively affection and reciprocal tenderness was produced anew on the occasion of the illness of February, 1643, to which Louis XIII. succumbed. See the *Mémoire fidèle des choses qui se sont passées à la mort de Louis XIII.*, written by Dubois, his valet-de-chambre. The ingenuousness and the precision in details which it exhibits does not permit us to doubt the exactitude and authenticity of this account. See also Archives of the Ministry of Foreign Affairs: *Mémoires Manuscrits de Lamothe-Goulas, Secrétaire des Commandements du Duc d'Orléans*, vol. ii. p. 368.

[38] Archives of the Ministry of Foreign Affairs: *Mémoires Manuscrits de Lamothe-Goulas, Secrétaire des Commandements du Duc d'Orléans*, vol. ii. p. 367.

called by reasons of State to Richelieu, and, on a famous day, confirmed his authority at the very instant that it seemed annihilated.[39]

To what period are we to assign the commission of the fault resulting in Anne's pregnancy of January, 1631 ? It cannot have been on September 30, 1630, when Louis XIII.'s life was in danger, for the Queen was delivered during the first five days of April, 1631.[40] Was it on the arrival of Louis XIII. at Lyons, at the commencement of August, 1630 ?   But Anne of Austria did not then have the same interest in being a mother, which, according to her accusers, she would have on September 30, when the King was dying.   Either the child was still-born, or else its conception dates from a period when Louis XIII. was its father.   The origin of this pregnancy is suspected because Richelieu, in a journal attributed to him, and of which it has been said "that it lent to Voltaire's supposition rather a serious ground of argument," [41] was pleased to note the

---

[39] November 11, 1630—known in French history as "the Day of the Dupes"—when the Duke de Saint-Simon, father of the famous memoir writer, brought about a secret interview between Richelieu, who, in disgrace, was on the eve of retiring to Havre, and Louis XIII., then at his hunting-seat of Versailles.   At the moment when every one believed the downfall of the once all-powerful Minister to be complete, the latter succeeded in recovering his lost influence over the King, of which he had been deprived through the intrigues of Marie de Medicis, who had demanded of her son whether he was " so unnatural as to prefer a valet to his mother."   Richelieu, when firmly reinstated in power, did not spare the queen-mother's partisans, upon several of whom he avenged himself with his accustomed severity.—*Trans.*

[40] This date is given in Richelieu's Journal, of which we are about to speak.

[41] M. Jules Loiseleur, *Revue Contemporaine*, of July 31, 1867, p. 223.   This Journal has been published in the *Archives Curieuses de l'Histoire de France*, of Cimber and Danjou, 2nd series, vol. v.

progress of the Queen's condition, often sent to inquire after her health, carried off her apothecary, then returned him to her, forbade the Spanish ambassador to make too frequent visits to the Louvre, and, in a word, exercised over Anne of Austria a suspicious and unceasing vigilance. But if we admit the authenticity of this journal, which, probable enough in certain details, is much less so when taken as a whole, all the facts which it relates, the espionage which it chronicles, the suspicions which it insinuates, concern the Spaniard, irritated at Richelieu's unexpected triumph and dreaming of overthrowing him, not the guilty spouse whose crime it is desired to prove. Accepting this last theory, why should Richelieu have restored to the Queen the medical attendant who could have aided her in concealing the consequences of her fault? Why was she not entirely separated from all her confidants? Why were not the visits of the Spanish ambassador altogether forbidden? Richelieu, it is true, caused the Countess de Fargis to be dismissed. But it was only because she had advised the Queen to espouse her brother-in-law, Gaston d'Orléans, if she became a widow, because she had inflamed Anne of Austria's resentment, and because she was the soul of the opposition, of the political intrigues, and of the secret plots against the Cardinal. If everything in her long correspondence seized by the latter, and existing in the archives,[42] justifies him for having exiled the dangerous Countess, if we find in it traces of the hopes of the two Queens, of the affections which bind them to Spain, of the successes they desire, of the reverses they hope for, nothing can be discovered that sullies Anne

---

[42] Imperial Library. Manuscripts, *ancien fonds Français*, No. 9241.

of Austria's honour.   The Countess de Fargis appears in it
as the active instigator of cabals, but not as the complacent
accomplice and the confidant of a crime.

The truth is that *enceinte* for the third time, and fearing a
third accident, Anne of Austria did not wish the news of her
condition to be spread abroad, or to arouse in the minds
of the people a hope which the remembrance of the past
rendered very uncertain of fulfilment.   That this pregnancy
was due to the reconciliation arising from the King's illness,
Richelieu himself attests, not as the doubtful author of a
journal which, however, does not contain a single line
really accusing the Queen, but as the indisputable writer of
those innumerable letters, papers, and authentic documents,
which have passed from the hands of the Duchess d'Aiguillon,
his niece, into the archives of the State.[43]   "It is suspected,
not without good reason, that the Queen is *enceinte*," he
writes.   "If this happiness befalls France, it ought to receive it as a fruit of the blessing of God and of the good
understanding which has existed between the King and the
Queen, his wife, for some time past." [44]   The same care
which Anne of Austria took to conceal a third miscarriage,
she had already shown with regard to a second, which
occurred March 16, 1622, and at that time "they had
hidden from the King as long as possible the destruction of
his hopes." [45]   But from the first day that Richelieu entered

---

[43] *Lettres et Papiers de Richelieu*, published in the collection of
Documents inédits de l'Histoire de France, by M. Avenel, Conservator
of the Bibliothèque Sainte-Geneviève, with a profound knowledge of the
period with which he is concerned, and an exactitude, an intelligence
and a care for which one cannot too highly praise him.

[44] *Lettres et Papiers de Richelieu*, vol. iv. p. 115.

[45] *Mémoires de Bassompierre.*

upon power, nothing escaped the penetrating regard of the attentive Minister. He watched, he observed, he knew everything. Every member of the royal family was surrounded by some of his agents. If from this incessant surveillance, and from the written evidence in which it stands revealed, springs the proof that the Queen had coquetted with Buckingham, been swayed by the counsels of the Duchess de Chevreuse,[46] and faithful to the last recommendations of her father, Philip III., had been always ready to support the Spanish interest near the King; if, in a word, Richelieu represents her as a Queen but little French, he never insinuates that she has been a guilty spouse; and history can scarcely hope to be better informed, and certainly ought not to show itself more rigorous than the clear-sighted and pitiless Minister.

---

[46] Marie de Rohan, Duchess de Chevreuse, who possessed so great an influence over Anne of Austria, was the daughter of Hercule de Rohan, Duke de Montbazon, Governor of Paris, and one of the first noblemen of France. In 1617, she espoused Albert de Luynes, favourite of Louis XIII., who on the occasion of the marriage created his confidant a duke and appointed his wife Superintendent of the Queen's Household. Shortly after the death of her husband, in 1621, from fever caught at the siege of Montauban, she married Claude de Lorraine, Duke de Chevreuse, the son of that Duke de Guise whom Henry III. caused to be assassinated at Blois. The Duchess de Chevreuse was a charming and beautiful woman, gifted with extraordinary powers of intellect and proud of her high lineage, but incorrigibly given to intrigue.—*Trans.*

CHAPTER IV.

Third Hypothesis—Reconciliation of Louis XIII. and Anne of Austria—
The Queen *enceinte* for the Fourth Time—Suspicions with which
Royal Births have sometimes been received—Precautions adopted
in France for the Purpose of avoiding these Suspicions—Story
of Louis XIV.'s Birth—Impossibility of admitting the Birth of
a Twin-brother—Richelieu's Absence—Uselessness of abducting
and concealing this pretended Twin-brother.

SEVEN years were to elapse before the realization of the
wishes of the nation, which ardently desired a Dauphin,
and was alarmed at the prospect of seeing the little-loved
brother of Louis XIII. ascend the throne of France. Anne
of Austria was *enceinte* anew, in January, 1638 : not, as
Voltaire has said, and as people have so frequently repeated
after him, "in consequence of a reconciliation brought about
by chance between the two spouses, who had lived separately for a long time."[1] There was no longer any need
either of a storm surprising Louis XIII., ready to set out for
the chase, or the pressing entreaties of Mademoiselle de la
Fayette, or the supplications of the Captain of his Guards,
in order to induce the King to visit the Queen. Unquestionable documents[2] show that long before the month of

---

[1] Voltaire, *Dictionnaire Philosophique*, vol. i. p. 375.

[2] Archives of the Ministry of Foreign Affairs, section France, 5.
There exists, amongst others, a letter of January 10, 1637, in which

December, 1637, Louis XIII. knew how to reconcile his duties as a husband with his ever-increasing passion for the chase, and that when this sport kept him away from the Louvre for too long a time, his habit was to send for the Queen. On September 5, 1638, the latter brought into the world a prince, who was afterwards Louis XIV. It is upon this day that the birth of the Man with the Iron Mask is fixed by those[3] who recognise in this personage not an adulterine son of Anne of Austria, but a legitimate twin-brother of Louis XIV., born some hours after him, and condemned, for his late arrival in the world, to a perpetual imprisonment.

There are few royal births that have not been the object of malevolent insinuations, and often of very plain accusations of criminal fraud. Such an event almost always destroys the right of some collateral heir, who has perhaps long coveted the crown. Sometimes even it ruins the projects of a whole party; and whilst it confirms the position of some, it suddenly throws down a hundred ambitions, and exposes those who are disappointed in their expectations to the temptation of gainsaying that which destroys their hopes. When, on June 21, 1688, Marie d'Este, second wife of James II., rendered him the father of a son,[4] William of Orange, then long married to the Princess Mary, the eldest daughter of the King of England, seeing his wife's rights annihilated by this unexpected birth, refused to admit as real an event so fatal

---

Louis XIII. writes to Richelieu " that he will have the Queen come to Saint-Germain, the evenings there being very long without company."

[3] Dulaure, *Histoire de Paris;* Simonde Sismondi, *Histoire des Français;* Dufey de l'Yonne, *Histoire de la Bastille;* The Chevalier de Cubières, *Voyage à la Bastille.*

[4] The Old Pretender.—*Trans.*

to him.   He caused accusatory libels to be spread throughout Holland, and even in England,[5] in which it was represented that the Queen's pregnancy was feigned, that
the birth was imaginary, and that an unknown child,
picked up at hazard, had been furtively introduced into the
bed of its pretended mother.[6]   Several English writers, and,
at their head, the ardent Burnet, welcomed this opinion, and
the scandal which they raised contributed, some months
afterwards, to the success of the attempt made by William
of Orange to seize on the throne at the very moment when
he seemed to have been excluded from it for ever.

In France, doubts of this nature being rendered still more
easy by the sceptical and fault-finding spirit of the nation,
care has been taken at all times to avoid even a pretext for
them, by infinite precautions and excellent customs.   Not
only had the birth of a prince the greatest personages of the
State for obligatory witnesses, but the people themselves were
also invited to be present at the advent to life of him whom
a very old tradition happily designates as the Child of France.
The doors were opened to the public, who penetrated freely
into the royal dwelling at the solemn moment when the
family of their rulers was perpetuated.   They also entered
there on certain occasions when the King allowed himself to be seen at table by his subjects.   These two
privileges were the only ones granted to them at that time,
and, reasonably enough, they were not disposed to rest content with them for ever.   The first, however, at least, offered

---

[5] M. Topin is in error.   William was, in fact, remonstrated with by
the Whigs for having publicly acknowledged a birth which the great
majority of the English people at that time believed to be a feigned
one. — *Trans.*

[6] The child was said to have been brought in in a warming-pan.

the advantage of making them forget for an instant that they were nothing, and of associating them in some way with the greatest event connected with the reigning family. When Marie Antoinette gave birth to her first child, the concourse of people in her chamber was such that Louis XVI. broke a window to give air more quickly to the Queen, who was on the point of losing consciousness. From that day the people ceased to be admitted to the birth of the King's children. But long before Louis XIV. came into the world, nothing was neglected that could give the greatest authenticity to this event, and the accurate Héroard[7] shows us the chamber of Marie de Medicis filled with spectators at the moment of the birth of Louis XIII.

It was the same at the birth of Louis XIV. The first signs of an approaching accouchement showed themselves on September 4, 1638, at eleven o'clock in the evening.[8] The next day, at five o'clock in the morning, Louis XIII., learning that the pains are increasing, visits the Queen, whom he does not quit till her delivery.[9] At six o'clock

---

[7] *Journal d'Héroard*, September 26, 27, 1601.

. [8] *Corps Universel Diplomatique du Droit des Gens*, of Dumont, Supplement, vol. iv. p. 176. Letter from Chavigny to the Cardinal de Richelieu, September 6, 1638. Despatch from Louis XIII. to M. de Bellièvre, his ambassador in England, September 5, 1638.— Manuscripts of the Imperial Library, *fonds Saint-Germain*, *Harlay*, 364[27], fol. 170.

[9] " The King was present all the time, and his two attacks of fever have not in any way diminished his strength," writes Chavigny in the letter in which he relates to Richelieu, then absent from the court, the birth of the Dauphin. This precise statement destroys that of M. Michelet, who, from an anonymous Life of Madame de Hautefort, says that " Louis XIII. would have consoled himself without difficulty at seeing his Spaniard die, and that during the pains he had history read to him to find an example of a King of France having married his subject."—M. Michelet, *Histoire de France*, vol. xii. p. 211.

arrive successively at Saint-Germain, Gaston d'Orléans, so interested in watching the issue of an event which is, perhaps,
to put him aside from the throne for ever; the Princess de
Condé, Madame de Vendôme, the Chancellor, Madame de
Lansac, the future governess of the royal child, and Mesdames
de Senecey and de la Flotte, ladies of honour. Behind the
canopy of the bed occupied by the Queen, is erected an
altar, at which the Bishops of Lisieux, of Meaux, and of
Beauvais, say mass in turns. Near the altar, and even in
the adjoining room, press Mesdames de la Ville-aux-Clercs,
de Liancourt, and de Mortemart; the Princess de Guéméné;
the Duchesses de la Trémouille and de Bouillon; the Dukes
de Vendôme, de Chevreuse, and de Montbazon; Messieurs
de Souvré, de Liancourt, de Mortemart, de la Ville-aux-
Clercs, de ·Brion, and de Chavigny; the Archbishop of
Bourges; the Bishops of Metz, Châlons, Dardanie, and
Mans; and, finally, an enormous crowd which invades the
palace at an early hour, and soon completely fills it.[10] At
eleven o'clock precisely Anne of Austria brings into the
world a child, the sex of which the midwife at once causes
to be verified by the princes of the royal family, and particularly by Gaston d'Orléans. This latter remains quite
stunned at the sight, and cannot hide his vexation;[11] still
the very visible signs of his discontent are almost unperceived
in the general gladness, and amidst the noisy acclamations
that arise on all sides. The joy of Louis XIII. is as lively
as his melancholy and dreamy nature allows. He admires

---

[10] Dumont, *Corps Diplomatique du Droit des Gens,* vol. iv. p. 176.

[11] Letter from Chavigny to the Cardinal de Richelieu, September 6,
1638. Louis XIII. made his brother a present of six thousand crowns,
"which consoled him a little," says Chavigny.

and makes those round him admire the shape of his son, who, from his birth, like his father at a similar moment, gives proofs of the extraordinary appetite [12] which characterizes his race. A short time after, in the very chamber of the Queen, and before the same spectators, the newly-born prince is baptized by the Bishop of Meaux, first almoner. Louis XIII. then sends the Sieur Duperré-Bailleul to Paris, charged with solemnly announcing the happy news [13] to the Corporation. But, borne by the joyous cry of the populace, the news has already traversed with surprising rapidity the distance which separates Saint-Germain from Paris, where it is known at noon. It excites a really sincere enthusiasm there, and the churches, for some months past filled by people who ask of heaven the birth of a Dauphin, at once resound with hymns of thanksgiving.

According to the romance of Soulavie a second son came into the world at eight o'clock in the evening, nine hours after the first, and, conformably to the advice of Richelieu, was hidden, brought up mysteriously, and then placed in confinement. Let us remark, in the first place, that the Cardinal de Richelieu, who is made to play such an important part at Saint-Germain on September 5, 1638, had been absent from that place since the end of July, and was

---

[12] Letters of Louis XIII :—Archives of the Ministry of Foreign Affairs, section France, 5. *Journal d'Héroard. Lettres Missives d'Henri IV.*, vol. v. p. 507.

[13] It is generally believed that the famous vow of Louis XIII., placing his kingdom under the protection of the Virgin, was made on account of Anne of Austria's pregnancy. It was not so. The Queen's condition was manifest in January, 1638, and "the declaration for the protection of the Virgin" is of December, 1637. It was made "on account of gratitude for so many evident favours accorded to the King." —*Lettres et Papiers de Richelieu,* vol. v. p. 908.

then at Saint-Quentin, whence he only returned to Paris on October 2.[14] But do not let us stop at this first error. In cases of twins the presence of the second child is invariably denoted by signs impossible to be mistaken or passed over. Thus, even if the second birth did not at once follow the first, in which case it would have had for witnesses the whole of the persons assembled in the chamber, it would certainly have been anticipated, and an expectation such as this could not have been kept concealed from the crowd.[15]

But how can it be admitted that a fact of such importance was known to so many persons without any of them betraying the secret in a conversation which would have been eagerly seized upon by some contemporary writer, or in one of those memoirs which numerous great personages then delighted in. leaving behind them? And yet they all preserve the most complete silence on this subject. Contemporaries have told us everything about the veritable actions

---

[14] Richelieu left Ruel at the end of July, and went successively to Amiens, Abbeville, Ham, and Saint-Quentin. It was in this last town that he learnt the happy event and went at once to the church with a grand *cortège.* "He heard mass sung there by his chaplain, then the *Te Deum* and the *Domine salvum.*" He then wrote to the King and Queen to congratulate them.—*Gazette de France,* p. 535 ; *Lettres et Papiers de Richelieu,* vol. vi. p. 75, *et seq.* The 2nd October, Richelieu left the army to return to Saint-Germain. "The King arrived on Wednesday at Saint-Germain, whither the Cardinal-duke repaired from our armies the same day and almost the same hour as his Majesty, whom he found in the room of Monseigneur the Dauphin, where the Queen also was. It would be difficult to express with what transports of joy his eminence was seized on seeing between the father and the mother this admirable child, the object of his desires and the limit of his content."—*Gazette de France,* p. 580.

[15] At this part of his work, M. Topin has thought it necessary for his argument to dwell on certain medical details, which, out of delicacy to English readers, I have preferred to suppress.—*Trans.*

as well as the imaginary acts of Anne of Austria. They have penetrated to the recesses of her private life, but nothing in their writings, not even the most indirect allusion, permits one to suspect such an important event.

Supposing, however, that, extraordinarily and contrariwise to what observation proves every day, this second birth took place nine hours after the first, and without having been previously announced by any revealing sign, and that the witnesses were very few in number and remarkably discreet, what interest had Louis XIII. in concealing this birth? Amongst the Romans, in France during the Middle Ages, as in modern times, the twin that first comes into the world has always been the eldest. Far, therefore, from being dismayed, as Soulavie relates,[16] at this second birth, Louis XIII. ought to have rejoiced at it, since it would have strengthened the direct line in his family.

There is nothing to disprove that a double birth may have been prophesied by the two shepherds. Popular imagination, lively excited by the universal desire for a Dauphin, and by the unexpected announcement of the Queen's condition, welcomed a thousand superstitious predictions, that for some months served as food for conversation, and helped to soften the delay. But this is the sole incident which is not evidently false in the relation of Soulavie, which is refuted, for the rest, by the impossibility of hiding a second birth from the innumerable witnesses of the first, and by the absolute silence of contemporaries, as well as by the incontestable inutility of the removal and suppression of this younger brother of Louis XIV.

---

[16] In the account we have reproduced in Chap. I. See p. 15 *ante.*

CHAPTER V.

Motives which hinder one from admitting the Existence, the Arrest and the Imprisonment of a mysterious Son of Anne of Austria—The Period at which he is said to have been handed over to Saint-Mars, according to the Authors of this Theory, cannot be reconciled with any of the Dates at which Prisoners were sent to this Gaoler— Other Considerations which formally oppose even the Probability of the Theory that makes the Man with the Iron Mask a Brother of Louis XIV.

LET us forget the scenes that have just been recalled. Let us cease for an instant to take into account proofs brought forward and considerations advanced, and consent to admit each of the assertions previously combated. This mysterious son of Anne of Austria came into the world either in 1629, having Buckingham for father ; or, in 1631, on account of the danger that the life of Louis XIII. was in ; or else in 1638, some hours after the birth of a brother. He exists. Received by an agent as devoted as discreet, he has been brought up in the country, the resemblance which reveals his high origin has been successfully hidden from every one, and his person placed in security from all investigations. But at what period was he imprisoned, and for what cause ? Of his youth, of his early years, passed in the obscurity of a retreat far from the court, there are no traces, and there is no reason for surprise at this. But as soon as he becomes the famous prisoner whom Saint-Mars brought in 1698 from the Isles Sainte-Marguerite to the Bastille, we have the right to ask, and we must seek when, how, and under what circumstances he was arrested and confided to his gaoler.

It would be to a certain extent probable that, left at liberty as long as his mother was alive, he was imprisoned only after her death. But Anne of Austria dies on January 20, 1666, and Saint-Mars receives no prisoner. Does the arrest date, as Voltaire affirms, from the year 1661, when Mazarin died? But Saint-Mars was then, and was to remain for three years, a brigadier of musketeers; and it is in December, 1664, that D'Artagnan, his captain, points him out to the choice of Louis XIV. as governor of the prison of Pignerol, whither, a month afterwards, Fouquet is taken and confided to his vigilant guardianship. On August 20, 1669, a second prisoner, Eustache d'Auger, arrives; but he is only an obscure spy, and is soon placed with Fouquet to serve him as a domestic. Would one have charged with this care,—would one have placed in the service of Fouquet, who, during the whole of his life had lived near Louis XIV. and Anne of Austria, a prince whose features recalled those of the King? No other prisoner is brought to Saint-Mars until the arrival of the Count de Lauzun in 1671. Since then, and from time to time, others are confided to him, but we know their crimes or their offences, are not ignorant of the causes of their arrest, and see them rather badly treated; and when, in 1681, Saint-Mars passes from the governorship of Pignerol to that of the fortress of Exiles, he only takes with him two prisoners, of whom he speaks contemptuously as "two crows." [1] At Exilès as at Pignerol—at the Isles Sainte-Marguerite, of which Saint-Mars was in 1687 appointed governor, as at Exiles—if fresh culprits are confided to him, we know to what motive to attribute their detention, and nothing in their past, nothing in the treatment of which they are the object, nothing in their actions, allows us to suspect in any one of them a brother of Louis XIV. Certainly, one would hardly expect to find a despatch designating one of Saint-Mars' prisoners by the title of prince, and in order to be convinced we do not exact anything of the kind. But when, examining, one by one, each of the captives sent to the future governor of the Bastille, and amongst whom is necessarily the one that he traversed France with in 1698, we account for the causes of their arrest, and penetrate into their past; when a hundred authentic despatches [2] enable us to affirm that there are no other prisoners besides these, are we not justified in demanding where, then, is the son of Anne of Austria?

This famous despatch, a fragment of which was timidly quoted some years ago in a work from which it has since been omitted, [3]—this despatch, in the existence of which criticism had concluded to disbelieve, [4] and which is of

---

[1] All these facts come from official documents, authentic and transcribed by us. We shall give them further on when we introduce Saint-Mars into the story.

[2] Archives of the Ministry of Marine; Archives of the Ministry of War; Archives of the Ministry of Foreign Affairs; Imperial Archives; Registers of the Secretary's Office of the King's Household.

[3] *Biographie Universelle* of Michaud, article on the " Man with the Iron Mask," by Weiss. The second edition does not give the extract from this despatch, given in the first.

[4] See, amongst others, the opinion of M. Jules Loiseleur, *Revue Contemporaine,* article already cited.

capital importance, actually does exist and is authentic. It was dictated by Barbézieux,[5] and addressed to Saint-Mars, at the moment when the latter had under his guardianship the prisoner whom he was to take with him to the Bastille, and who died there in 1703 :—

" Monsieur—I have received, with your letter of the 10th of this month, the copy of that which Monsieur de Pontchartrain has written to you concerning the prisoners who are at the Isles Sainte-Marguerite, upon orders of the King, signed by him, or of the late Monsieur de Seignelay. You have no other rules of conduct to follow with respect to all those who are confided to your keeping beyond continuing to look to their security, *without explaining yourself to any one whatever about what your old prisoner* HAS DONE." [6]

But what crime could this pretended brother of Louis XIV. have committed, except, indeed, that of coming into the world ? Is it objected that a slight fault committed in prison may be referred to, and that Barbézieux, in this despatch, alludes to a recent occurrence ? But, if he recommends Saint-Mars not to explain himself to any one whatever, it is evident that curiosity had been excited, and that every one on the island trying to satisfy it, the Minister thought it right to recommend, more energetically than ever, an absolute discretion. Would this discretion have been necessary, and would Saint-Mars have been

---

5 Louis François Le Tellier, Marquis de Barbézieux, many of whose despatches are quoted in the course of this work, succeeded his father Louvois as Minister of War, on the death of the latter in 1691.—*Trans.*

6 Archives of the Ministry of Marine ; Archives of the Ministry of War ; Imperial Archives ; Registers of the Secretary's Office of the King's Household.

questioned, if only an insignificant breach of the internal rules of the prison had been in question?

Finally, what is one to think of the attentions, respect, particular care, evidences of an humble deference, all the accessory circumstances that have been invoked in favour of an opinion which nothing certain justifies? Amongst the incidents upon which so much stress has been laid, and which form, in some degree, the romantic *dossier* of the Man with the Iron Mask, some are exact, and will find their natural explanation further on. Others, such as the visit of Louvois to the Isles Sainte-Marguerite, have been invented at pleasure by popular imagination, and too easily welcomed by a complaisant credulity. It has been said, and is repeated every day, that the Minister visited this island, and there spoke to the prisoner " with a degree of consideration which partook of respect,"[7] styling him " monseigneur." Now Louvois was only absent from the court in 1680 for a few weeks in order to go to Baréges. We have, day for day, the names of the towns he passed through.[8] The Isles Sainte-Marguerite, where, by the way, Saint-Mars did not arrive till seven years later, do not figure in the itinerary; and, after this journey, Louvois never returned again to the South of France. As to the dramatic episode of the silver dish thrown out of the window, which exposes the fisherman who finds it at his feet to a great danger, it has its origin in a similar attempt made by a Protestant minister confined, in 1692, at the Isles Sainte-

---

[7] Voltaire, *Siècle de Louis XIV.*, chap. xxv.

[8] Louvois had broken his leg the 3rd August, 1679. To complete the cure, which was slow, the doctors advised the Minister to go to Baréges. (See vol. iii. p. 513 *et seq.* of the excellent *Histoire de Louvois* of M. Camille Rousset).

Marguerite. This minister tried to interest people in his lot, by writing his complaints, not on a silver dish, which he did not have at his disposition, but upon a pewter plate, which determined Saint-Mars to give him only earthenware for the future.[9] The fact has been applied later to the Man with the Iron Mask, to whom, as to all legendary heroes, the adventures of very different personages are ascribed. A careful examination of all the despatches collected will enable one to trace back each of these rumours to its origin, and separate what is purely legendary from what is really historical.

But because the exactitude of many of the acts attributed to the Man with the Iron Mask is disproved by this examination, one would be wrong in concluding that he never existed, or that, at least, there was not a great interest in concealing his existence. It is incontestable that Saint-Mars did, in 1698, escort to Paris a prisoner who died there five years later, who was known at the Bastille only under the name of "the prisoner from Provence," and whose mysterious memory was perpetuated in the redoubtable fortress, to spread rapidly afterwards through the entire world. These are the real data of the problem. Although freed from all the foreign elements that have been mixed up with it, it exists and it remains to be solved. It is true that in the eyes of some, to take away the seductive figure of a brother of Louis XIV. is greatly to diminish the interest. But, addressing ourselves to those for whom truth alone has a sovereign and incomparable charm, we say to

---

[9] Despatches from Seignelay to Saint-Mars; Archives of the Ministry of Marine; Imperial Archives; Registers of the Secretary's Office of the King's Household.

them : The Man with the Iron Mask is not a son of Anne
of Austria, because to the impossibility of fixing the date
of his birth is added the not less evident impossibility of
proving his incarceration. If, in order to show that his
birth is imaginary, we have touched upon many delicate
points, it is because the gravity of the accusations with
which, in our days, the memory of Anne of Austria has been
stigmatized, render such justifications necessary. In addition to which, even should these researches be indiscreet, it
is much less blamable to have made them for the purpose
of defence rather than of accusation, and to have raised
certain veils, in order to let innocence shine forth in place
of calumniating it.

CHAPTER VI.

The Count de Vermandois—His Portrait—Mademoiselle de la Vallière, his Mother — Anecdote from the *Mémoires Secrets pour servir à l'Histoire de Perse*—Father Griffet adopts its Conclusions—Arguments that he advances—Motives which render certain of Mademoiselle de Montpensier's Appreciations suspicious—Improbability of the Story in the *Mémoires de Perse*—Illness of the Count de Vermandois — Reality of his Death attested by the most authentic Despatches—Magnificence of his Obsequies—Pious Endowments at Arras.

THOSE whose minds are naturally inclined to the romantic, but whom even a superficial examination of the question of the Man with the Iron Mask has determined to put the hypothesis which makes him a son of Anne of Austria, on one side,[1] willingly see in him the Count de Vermandois,

---

[1] In the preceding chapters we have made no mention of a *Mémoire de M. de Saint-Mars sur la Naissance de l'Homme au Masque de Fer*, published in vol. iii. of the *Mémoires de Tous* (Levasseur, 1835, 8vo). According to this document, "copied by M. Billiard from the Archives of the Ministry of Foreign Affairs," M. de Saint-Mars had been the governor of the mysterious son of Anne of Austria, whose high origin was carefully hidden from him. But this brother of Louis XIV. having discovered it, was sent to the Isles Sainte-Marguerite, the command of which was then (in 1687) confided to his governor. If we have not spoken of this document, it is because its authenticity has already been completely disproved. It is nothing else than a copy of the apocryphal narrative of Soulavie, which we have transcribed and refuted in the first part of our work (see page 15). The

natural son of Louis XIV. and Mademoiselle de la Vallière. This opinion is a kind of compromise between the impossibility of accepting an imaginary being for hero, and the desire of seeing in the mysterious prisoner a very high personage. After having sacrificed to truth this unfortunate brother of Louis XIV., called to the throne by his origin, and kept away from it by a perpetual detention, they take refuge in an intermediary system, undoubtedly less tempting, but of which the attraction is still very exciting, and which, in a certain degree, reconciles the exigencies of truth with the taste for the romantic.

author of this copy has contented himself with substituting Saint-Mars for the "anonymous governor of the unfortunate prince." He did not think that he thereby added a fresh impossibility to those contained in the narrative of Soulavie. For how could Saint-Mars, before 1687, have been the governor of a brother of Louis XIV., when a hundred despatches establish the fact that, from 1664, he was successively governor of the donjon of Pignerol and of Exiles? As to the presence of this document in the Archives of the Ministry of Foreign Affairs, there is no reason for astonishment. It is explained, like the presence of so many other documents in our archives, by the seizure of the papers of great personages after their deaths, or, more commonly, by having been transmitted by some ambassador inhabiting the country in which these apocryphal writings circulated freely. But the place where they are found gives them no authenticity. At all periods, and to-day even, ambassadors send to the Government copies of anonymous memoirs, pamphlets, and different papers, which remain joined to their despatches, but to which no historical value can be ascribed. It has been the same with this pretended *Mémoire de Saint-Mars*, of which, in addition, a mere perusal demonstrates the untruth to any one acquainted with the usual style of the illiterate governor of the Isles Sainte-Marguerite. One sometimes hears it related—and this fact has been repeated to ourselves—that a great personage of a former Government introduced one of his friends, with much precaution, into the galleries of the Archives of the Ministry of Foreign Affairs, and there showed him a document which contained the secret of the Man with the Iron Mask. It is doubtless the document attributed to Saint-Mars that is referred to in this anecdote.

It is no longer the question of a prince of whose very birth we are ignorant. The present one actually existed, and such interest as he inspires from the moment he comes into the world he owes to her who gave him birth. He is the son of that La Vallière, equally touching in her heroic resistance to the inclination which impels her towards Louis XIV., and in her yielding, whom one esteems even when she succumbs, and whom one admires when she rises again to flee from the peril; who, long virtuous, always upright and disinterested, lives entirely absorbed in her passion, then takes refuge in penitence, and powerful without having desired it; ignorant or careless of her influence, strong in her very weakness, subjugates without art and without study the most imperious of kings; who, after having charmed all her contemporaries by her sweet and simple grace, and passed from the torments of a love unceasingly combated to the voluntary rigours of an expiation courageously submitted to for thirty years, has remained the most pleasing and most interesting character of this great reign, and will seduce even the most remote posterity.

Louis de Bourbon, Count de Vermandois, inherited his mother's grace. He was tall and well made, and, like her, instinctively possessed that gift of pleasing which is never so engaging as when all about it is natural and nothing appears to depend upon art. Good and liberal, he had ways of obliging that were peculiar to himself,[2] and the

---

[2] Letter of Madame la Présidente d'Osembray to Bussy-Rabutin, dated December 22, 1683:—*Lettres de Roger de Rabutin, Comte de Bussy*, vol. vi. p. 135, edition of 1716. Testimony of Lauzun in the *Mémoires de Mademoiselle de Montpensier*, vol. vii. pp. 90, 92.

most sensitive of men could not feel offended at his kindnesses. With such as these, when he wished to aid them,
he made bets which he was certain to lose, or he sent them
money by a hand which remained unknown. He was suspected of acts of generosity, which he never acknowledged
himself the author of, and those whom he obliged had their
necessities relieved without being required to testify their
gratitude. His proud bearing and the air of supreme distinction which he inherited from his royal father, drew attention
towards him still more than his high origin. To these out-
ward charms, to these sentiments of exquisite delicacy and
natural kindliness, which attached to him the soldier as
much as the officer, Vermandois united a ready wit, a well-
proved courage, a lively wish to distinguish himself, and to
merit by splendid achievements the high dignity[3] to which, at
the age of two years, he had been raised by the affection and
pride of Louis XIV. Whilst still very young, and already
in the midst of the army of Flanders, he had concealed a
severe illness in order not to miss the noble rendezvous
of an attack.[4] Like many of those destined to die prematurely, and who appear to foresee it, Vermandois

---

[3] That of High Admiral. See amongst the papers of Colbert,
MSS. of the Imperial Library, a curious memorandum drawn up by
him, "to know what name and title it is necessary to give to M. le
Comte de Vermandois." Vermandois was endowed on November 12,
1669, at the age of twenty-two months, with this office of High
Admiral of France, which, suppressed in 1626 by Richelieu, and
changed by him into the office of "Grand Master, Chief, and General
Superintendent of the Navigation and Commerce of France," had been
held successively by the Cardinal himself; his nephew Armand de
Maillé-Brézé, Duke de Fronsac; Anne of Austria; César, Duke de
Vendôme; and his son François de Vendôme, Duke de Beaufort.

[4] Letter of the Présidente d'Osembray, already cited.

hastened as it were through life, and seemed to strive, in endeavouring to render himself early illustrious, to anticipate the blow that was about to strike him. But sufficient time to attain glory was to fail him, and it was his destiny to leave behind him only the touching souvenir that attaches itself to beautiful hopes suddenly dissipated by death.

An unforeseen *amende* was, nevertheless, reserved for his memory. Sixty years after his sad end an idea suddenly sprang up of adding twenty years of captivity to his short existence, and with the view of rendering his destiny still more lamentable, of representing him as the mysterious victim of the rigours of Louis XIV.

In 1745 there appeared at Amsterdam the *Mémoires Secrets pour servir à l'Histoire de Perse*, [5] which, under supposititious names, contain the anecdotic history of the Court of France. This book, which had a prodigious success, and the editions of which were rapidly multiplied, owed in a great measure its celebrity to the following narration : " Cha-abas (Louis XIV.) had a legitimate son, Sephi-Mirza (Louis, Dauphin of France), and a natural son, Giafer (Louis de Bourbon, Count de Vermandois). Almost of the same age, they were of opposite characters. The latter did not allow any occasion to escape of saying that he pitied the French being destined some day to obey a prince without talent, and so little worthy to rule them. Cha-abas, to whom this conduct was reported, was fully sensible of its danger. But authority yielded to paternal love, and this absolute monarch had not sufficient strength to impose his will upon a son who abused his kindness. Finally,

---

[5] Published by the Compagnie des Libraires Associés (Company of Associated Booksellers) in 12mo.

Giafer so far forgot himself one day as to strike Sephi-Mirza. Cha-abas is at once informed of this. He trembles for the culprit, but, however desirous he may be of feigning to ignore this crime, what he owes to himself and to his crown, combined with the noise this action has made at court, will not allow him to pay regard to his affection. He assembles, not without doing violence to his feelings, his most intimate confidants, allows them to see all his grief, and asks their advice. In view of the magnitude of the crime and conformably to the laws of the State, every one is in favour of inflicting the punishment of death. What a blow for so tender a father! However, one of the Ministers, more sensitive to the affliction of Cha-abas than the rest, tells him that there is a method of punishing Giafer without depriving him of life; that he should be sent to the army, which was then upon the frontiers of Feldran (Flanders); that shortly after his arrival, rumours could be spread that he was attacked by the plague, in order to alarm and keep away from him all those who might wish to see him; that at the end of several days of feigned illness, he should be made to pass for dead, and that, whilst in the presence of the whole army obsequies worthy of his birth were performed for him, he should be transferred by night with great secrecy to the citadel of the island of Ormus (Isle Sainte-Marguerite). This advice was generally approved of, and above all by an afflicted father. Faithful and discreet people were chosen for the management of the affair. Giafer starts for the army with a magnificent train. Everything is carried out as had been projected, and whilst the death of this unfortunate prince is being lamented in the camp, he is conveyed by by-roads to the island of

Ormus, and placed in charge of the governor, who had received in advance the order of Cha-abas not to let his prisoner be seen by any one whatever. A single servant, who was in the secret, was sent with the Prince. But, having died upon the journey, the leaders of the escort disfigured his face with dagger-strokes in order to prevent his being recognized, left him lying upon the road, and after having stripped him as a further precaution, continued their route. Giafer was transferred to the citadel of Ispahan (the Bastille) when Cha-abas bestowed the governorship of it upon the governor of the island of Ormus as a recompence for his fidelity. The precaution was taken at the island of Ormus, as at the citadel of Ispahan, to put a mask over the face of Giafer, when on account of illness, or other causes, it was necessary to let him be seen by any one." [6]

This narration, which for the first time presented to public curiosity the anecdote of the Man with the Iron Mask, at once furnished food for conversation and became the subject of the most lively controversies. Several distinguished critics hastened to adopt the opinion it expressed, while others combated it, and for a long time the *Année Littéraire* of Fréron was the theatre of a debate which had the *savants* and the curious of the whole world for attentive audience. Voltaire himself, in introducing for the first time the hypothesis which makes the Man with the Iron Mask a brother of Louis XIV., did not succeed in stifling an opinion which had secured a clever defender. Father Griffet, a patient disciple of Father Daniel, and the author of an excellent *Histoire de Louis XIII.*, published in 1765,

---

[6] *Mémoires Secrets pour servir à l'Histoire de Perse.*

in his fine *Traité des Différentes Sortes des Preuves qui servent à établir la Vérité dans l'Histoire*, a long dissertation upon the Man with the Iron Mask, and in it pronounced resolutely for the Count de Vermandois. What proofs, or at least what probabilities, did he invoke?

He bases his argument upon the *Mémoires de Mademoiselle de Montpensier*, in which we read that "when Vermandois left for the siege of Courtray, he had not long returned to the court; that the King had been displeased with his conduct and would not see him, on account of his having been mixed up with parties of debauchery; that since that time he had lived in a very retired manner, and only went out to go to the Academy[7] and to mass in the morning; that those whose company he had been keeping were not agreeable to the King, which caused much grief to Mademoiselle de la Vallière, by whom he was well scolded."[8] Father Griffet added that, long before the publication of the *Mémoires Secrets de Perse*, a rumour had spread that the Count de Vermandois had been guilty, before his departure for the army, of some great crime, such as a blow given to the Dauphin. "It had been generally spoken of," says he, "on the strength of one of those traditions which have need, indeed, of being proved, but which are not necessarily false; the remembrance of this one had always been preserved, although there was not much noise made about it in the time of the late King, for fear of displeasing him; of this many people who lived under his reign can bear

---

[7] The academy here mentioned is not the present French Academy, but a kind of gymnasium, where the nobles met to learn riding, fencing, dancing, &c. It is frequently referred to in the memoirs of the time.— *Trans.*

[8] *Mémoires de Mademoiselle de Montpensier*, vol. vii. p. 91.

witness." The learned historian found another argument in the very name under which the prisoner of Saint-Mars was inscribed in the registers of the Church of Saint-Paul, the letters which form this name of Marchiali being those of the two words *hic amiral*, and designating thus by an anagram the high dignity of the son of Mademoiselle de la Vallière. Finally, he published in the *Année Littéraire* a second tradition, according to which "on the very day the body of the Count de Vermandois was to be transported to Arras, there left the camp, by a by-way, a litter in which it was believed there was a prisoner of importance, although the rumour was spread that the military chest was enclosed in it."

Of all these allegations, the only one that deserves to be discussed is that which, reposing upon special evidence, namely, the *Mémoires de Mademoiselle de Montpensier*, shows us the Count de Vermandois, fallen into disgrace with Louis XIV. for having mixed himself up in certain debaucheries, and starting almost at once for Courtray, where he was to meet his death. One certainly finds no allusion to "a great crime" committed by Vermandois upon the person of his legitimate brother, and this very silence would suffice to invalidate the pretended tradition invoked by Father Griffet. But as, from another point of view, these *Mémoires* furnish a kind of basis for his argument, reveal a stain on the memory of Vermandois, and indicate a period at which the offence might have been possible, it is essential the value of this evidence should be weighed.

In his *Traité des Différentes Sortes de Preuves qui servent à établir la Vérité dans l'Histoire*, Father Griffet himself very judiciously remarks that before adopting the opinion of a writer upon an individual whose contemporary he had been, it is desirable to examine whether he had not a powerful interest either to praise or to blame him. Father Griffet displayed more prudent sagacity when he enunciated this excellent precept than when he neglected to apply it to the *Mémoires de Mademoiselle de Montpensier*. He ought to have shown this romantic princess in her true light, endowed with a too lively imagination, whose self-esteem rendered her extremely accessible to the influence of others and incapable of protecting herself against interested suggestions; whom Madame de Montespan and Madame de Maintenon, by incessant attentions and delicate and careful acts of civility, easily gained over to their long-time common cause; and, in a word, whose credulous mind was entrapped by Madame de Maintenon in favour of the children of whom she was governess, and whom Madame de Montespan had had by Louis XIV. To love these, and above all the awkward Duke du Maine, must have led her almost infallibly to repulse the highly-gifted son of Mademoiselle de la Vallière, who had the least intriguing and the most disinterested of the royal favourites for mother, whilst his brother, better seconded, received from those surrounding him advice suitable to gain the heart, and perhaps one day assure him the immense fortune,[9] of the opulent cousin of Louis XIV. To attain this object, to influence her, as was done, in favour of a child deprived of all attractive qualities, they did not hesitate dictating for her the most affectionate letters to the Duke du Maine, pointing out to him the steps

---

[9] We shall see, in the course of this work, that they succeeded in securing at least a portion of this enormous fortune, thanks to the imprisonment of Lauzun, the husband of Mademoiselle de Montpensier.

most likely to please her, and suggesting to him filial sentiments for a Princess whom they ended by inspiring with a veritable maternal love, of which Mademoiselle de Montpensier had all the jealousy, at first provoked but afterwards spontaneous, and which led her to detest the brilliant rival of the very insignificant but attentive Duke du Maine. This sentiment breaks out in several parts of her *Mémoires.* "It seemed to me," she remarks, "that it was in order to disparage M. du Maine people said that no one would ever equal M. de Vermandois." And elsewhere, "I was not vexed at the death of M. de Vermandois, I was well pleased that M. du Maine had nothing to do with his affairs."[10]   How, after this, can we put faith in such suspicious testimony?   There is nothing to prove and nothing to disprove that Vermandois may have been led away by youth into being present at some dissolute pleasure-party unknown to the King, and that he may have incurred the latter's reproaches by this conduct. But his disgrace and the causes to which it is ascribed, his hasty departure, his father refusing to see him and banishing him from his presence, Mademoiselle de la Vallière in distress: all these circumstances, which are only to be found in the *Mémoires* of the adoptive mother of the Duke du Maine— must we accept them when impartial witnesses bestow unqualified praises upon the Count de Vermandois[11] and relate nothing that can tarnish his memory? Must we accept them when, some days after this pretended disgrace,

---

[10] *Mémoires* already cited, vol. vii. p. 92.

[11] Such as Lauzun, who was present at the siege of Courtray, and the Présidente d'Osembray.—See *Lettres de Bussy-Rabutin*, already cited, vol. vi. p. 13.

and at the first news of what was thought to be only a slight indisposition, Louis XIV. writes to the Marquis de Montchevreuil to cause Vermandois to return at once to the court, in order that greater care may be taken of him and that he may more thoroughly recover.[12]

Is there any need to set forth the impossibility of admitting that of two sons of Louis XIV., one, the Grand-Dauphin, the heir to the crown, could have received from the other the gravest of insults, in the midst of the court and at the end of a violent discussion, without any contemporary writer having spoken of an event which would have had an inevitable celebrity? In order to make this circumstance appear less improbable, the *Mémoires de Perse* represent Vermandois as fiery, haughty, and unsubmissive to a brother who would one day be his king, whereas the most unexceptionable testimony [13] establishes the fact that he was mild, affable, full of deference, and only anxious to acquire glory. The author of these *Mémoires*, in order to render a dispute between the two brothers more plausible, asserts, in addition, that they were of the same age, instead of which there were six years between them ; and, at the period when

---

[12] Dated November 4, 1683. The King to the Marquis de Montchevreuil. "Monsieur le Marquis de Montchevreuil—I have received the letter which you wrote to me from the camp of Courtray. I am very well pleased with what you tell me of my son, the Count de Vermandois. But I am not the less uneasy, as the Sieur d'Aquin has told me that the fever has become continuous. You have done well to take him to Lille " (we shall see that they did not have the time to remove him to Lille) ; " he may remain there as long as may be needful for his health ; but as soon as it allows him to travel I shall be pleased at his returning here. Having nothing else to add, except that I am always very well pleased at your conduct, I pray God to take you, Monsieur le Marquis de Montchevreuil, into his holy keeping.—LOUIS."

[13] See *ante*, p. 67.

this passionate act is ascribed to him, Vermandois was barely sixteen, while the Dauphin was already the father of the Duke de Bourgogne.

There remains his premature death. Tacitus has said that when princes or extraordinary men die young, one finds it difficult to believe that they have been carried off by a natural course. This remark applies with justice to all epochs, and in our annals how many crimes are there, imagined by popular passion and credited through the ignorance of the time, of which a healthy criticism, aided by the progress of medical science,[14] has in our days acquitted the pretended authors? Is there, in the last moments of Vermandois and in the transport of his remains to Arras, where he was buried, the smallest circumstance that can allow the most credulous mind to retain a single doubt, and to suppose that he left the camp of Courtray alive to be confided to the guardianship of Saint-Mars?

On November 6, 1683, the Count de Vermandois takes to his bed at Courtray. Ill for several days before, he has concealed his condition in order not to quit the army, and to be able to assist at the attack on the faubourg of Menin, where he displayed the highest courage.

Consumed by fever, he is at length compelled to separate from the first *corps-d'armée*, which is about to form the camp of Harlebeck. Marshal d'Humières had had the intention of causing him to be transported to Lille, and

---

[14] See, amongst others, the excellent work of M. Jules Loiseleur, *Problèmes Historiques ;* the review, *La Philosophie Positive*, of M. Littré ; the fourth volume of the *Histoire de Louvois*, of M. Camille Rousset, already cited ; the very curious appendices given by M. Chéruel at the end of each volume of his fine edition of the *Mémoires de Saint-Simon*, &c.

with this object had already made arrangements with the
Marquis de Montchevreuil.[15]   But a speedy aggravation of
the invalid's condition hinders the execution of this project.
On the 8th bleeding relieves him;[16] but, on the 12th,
Marshal d'Humières writes to Louvois that there are grounds
for considerable uneasiness.[17]   On the 13th Boufflers writes
to the court that, the head of Vermandois commencing to
be affected by the disease, bleeding from the feet has become
necessary.[18]   On the 14th Marshal d'Humières, who had
come to Courtray from the camp of Rousselaer, of which he
is commander, finds Vermandois at the worst, the doctors
very undecided, "and not daring to resort to extreme
remedies."   They determine to try them, however, but,
doubtless, too late; for, after a tolerably favourable day,
during which the fever seemed to diminish and the brain to
become clearer, a violent agitation ensues, abundant per-
spiration exhausts the patient,[19] and, on the 16th, Boufflers
announces that Vermandois has just received the last communion,[20] and that there is no longer any hope except in his
youth.   At the moment that he was writing this letter,
Madame de Maintenon wrote to Madame de Brinon:[21]
" M. de Vermandois is very ill; have our great saint prayed

---

[15] Archives of the Ministry of War; Letter from Marshal d'Humières
to Louvois, " Camp of Courtray, November 7, 1683."

[16] *Ibid.* Marshal d'Humières to Louvois, "Camp of Harlebeck,
November 8, 1683."

[17] *Ibid.*   D'Humières to Louvois, " Camp of Rousselaer, November 12, 1683."

[18] *Ibid.*   Boufflers to Louvois, " Courtray, November 13, 1683."

[19] *Ibid.*   D'Humières to Louvois, " Courtray, November 14, 15,
1683," and Boufflers to Louvois, " Courtray, November 15, 1683."

[20] *Ibid.*   Boufflers to Louvois, " Courtray, November 16, 1683."

[21] Letter from Madame de Maintenon to Madame de Brinon, of
November 15, 1683.

to for him." Vain hope, useless prayers ! On November 18 the son of La Vallière died of a malignant fever, surrounded by Marshal d'Humières, whom he had begged to remain near him, the Marquis de Montchevreuil, and Lieutenant-General Boufflers.[22] In the camp the grief was general, and the troops wept for him, for the good which he had done and the great things he had promised. At the court the impressions were various. The Hôtel de Condé deeply regretted this death, because the Prince was betrothed to Mademoiselle de Bourbon. The Princess de Conti, sister to Vermandois, was inconsolable.[23]

Louis XIV., much more sensitive than tender, and whose grief relieved itself all at once in a flood of tears which was of very short duration, had, moreover, already shown in favour of the children he had had by Madame de Montespan a sentiment of predilection which was to survive their mother's disgrace, and which Madame de Maintenon, their former governess, carefully cherished. As to Mademoiselle de la Vallière, Voltaire has said,[24] and it has been often repeated after him, that she exclaimed on learning the fatal news : " It is not his death that I should lament, but his birth." This exclamation is not true; it is not that of a mother. That the pious Carmelite offered as a sacrifice this new blow that smote her, that she accepted it as an additional expiation for her faults, one may admit. But that her tears only flowed because she had brought Vermandois into the world, that, at the announcement of the most painful of

---

22 Archives of the Ministry of War ; Boufflers to Louvois, " Courtray, November 19, 1683."

23 Letter of Madame d'Osembray, December 22, 1683.

24 *Siècle de Louis XIV.*

afflictions, she was so little crushed by it as to be able to utter such words, is what no mother will believe. How much more acceptable is that testimony which Madame de Sevigné bears in saying "that she perfectly tempered her maternal love with that of the spouse of Jesus Christ." "Mademoiselle de la Vallière is all day at the foot of the crucifix," says the Présidente d'Osembray [25] on December 22. This is the true language of two mothers speaking of another mother who had just lost her son.

Pompous obsequies were performed over the remains of the son of Louis XIV. On November 21, the King sent word to the Chapter of Arras that the body of the Count de Vermandois would be transported to that town and buried in the choir of its cathedral church. [26] On the 24th, the mayors and échevins, bearing wax tapers, proceed to the

---

[25] *Lettres de Bussy-Rabutin*, vol. vi. p. 135.

[26] The letter which we extract is from a learned article of Baron de Hautecloque, ex-mayor of Arras, published in the *Chroniques Artésiennes* of M. P. Roger, member of the Society of Antiquarians of Picardy ; of the Count d'Allonville, Councillor of State, and of M. Dusevel, Inspector of Historical Monuments for the Department of the Somme :—

"Very dear and well-beloved—Having learnt with very sensible sorrow, that our very dear and well-beloved son, the *Duke* de Vermandois,* Admiral of France, has lately died in the town of Courtray in Flanders, and desiring him to be placed in the cathedral church of our town of Arras, we send word to the Sieur Bishop of Arras to receive the body of our said son, when it is brought to the said church, and to have it buried in the choir of the said church with the ceremonies observed at the burial of persons of his birth.

"All of which we have desired to make known to you by this

---

* This title may appear singular, but an old and curious book "*Les Estats de France,*" which contains the genealogies of all the nobles of this period, describes him as "the Count de Vermandois, *duke* and peer of France."—*Trans.*

Méaulens Gate, where are already assembled the governors of the town and citadel, all the officers of the staff, the clergy of the different parishes, and the friars of the mendicant orders. The infantry line the road from the entrance of the town to the cathedral.[27] At noon the roar of cannon and the tolling of bells announces the arrival of the remains, which are contained in a coach hung with black cloth, and escorted by the cavalry of the garrison. The Bishop of Arras, clothed in his pontifical robes, and his chapter, advance in procession and receive the body, which, removed from the coach, is borne by canons, and followed by the officers of the Council of Artois, those of the bailiwick, and all the other dignitaries of the county. Until Saturday the 27th, the day fixed for the solemn service, masses were said without intermission from six o'clock till noon in the Chapel of Saint-Vaast, where the body had been placed, and the canons and chaplains succeeded each other in praying there, the first during the day, the others during the night.[28] They selected, in the middle of the choir of the cathedral, in the place of "the angel," the spot that

---

letter, and to state that our intention is that you should conform to our will in this and assist in a body at this ceremony as is customary, on such occasions ; and assuring ourselves that you will satisfy us in this, we do not make this present letter longer or more express ; do not fail ; for such is our pleasure.

" Given at Versailles, the xix* November, 1683.

Signed, " LOUIS," and lower down, " LE TELLIER."

[27] Register of the Hôtel de Ville of Arras and of the Chapter.

[28] *Ibid.*

---

* We think, with M. de Hautecloque, that this date should be the 21st. In the registers of the chapter it is in Roman figures, and there is reason to suppose that a clumsy copyist has inverted the order of them and put xix for xxi. The comparison of dates and the very expressions of the King's letter indicate it sufficiently.

appeared most distinguished for the inhumation, for, five hundred years before, it had served for the interment of Isabelle de Vermandois, wife of Philip d'Alsace, Count of Flanders, and descendant in the direct line of Henri I., King of France. The last ceremony was worthy, in its pomp and splendour, of the King who had commanded it, and of the Prince in whose honour it was performed. The choir and the nave of the cathedral, entirely hung with black velvet, upon which shone silver escutcheons emblazoned with the arms of Vermandois, the lugubrious harmony of the service, the funereal light of the tapers, the sad and silent troops, the spectators all clothed in mourning, and, still more than these external signs, a sincere grief manifesting itself, especially amongst the gentlemen of the Prince's suite, in tears and sobs; such is the spectacle that the interior of the cathedral church of Arras presents on November 27, 1683.

The evidences of the King's piety, and of the eagerness of the Chapter to satisfy it, did not end here. On January 24, 1684, M. Chauvelin, Intendant of the province, drew up with the Chapter, in the name of Louis XIV., a deed in which it was stipulated " that the prelate, dean, and canons should say every day, each in his turn and during the year following the inhumation, a low requiem mass in the *chapelle ardente*,[29] prepared and hung with mourning for this purpose; that on the 18th November of every year, or in case of hindrance on another day near that date, there

---

[29] [Chapel in which a dead person lies in state.—*Trans.*] The cathedral in which Vermandois was interred no longer exists. Devastated and greatly mutilated during the revolutionary period, it was almost in ruins, and was later completely demolished. The Church of Saint-Nicolas was built upon the site which it occupied in that part

should be celebrated in perpetuity in their church a solemn service, preceded by vigils of nine psalms and nine lessons ; that the Chapter should distribute annually to fifty poor people, who were to be present at these offices, five sols each, and an eight-pounds loaf; that there should also be given every year by the Chapter on the day of the service, to the poor *Clairisses* [30] of the city of Arras, a sum of six livres, in order that their community might pray for the soul of the Count de Vermandois, and that all the bells should be tolled on the day, and on the evening before, as is customary at the obits of the bishops." In order to indemnify the Chapter for the expenditure imposed by him, Louis XIV. bestowed upon it, in addition to magnificent presents, a sum of 10,000 livres, which served to purchase at the village of La Coutaie, near Béthune, a farm, since then, and for that cause, known as the Ferme de Vermandois. Until the year 1789, the stipulations contained in this deed were faithfully executed, and, during more than a century, November 25 witnessed a renewal of the alms of the Chapter, the prayers of the clergy, the assemblage of all the magistrates and municipal officers, and, in this manner, the remembrance of the son of La Vallière.

In supposing that Vermandois could have given way to such a violent and hasty act towards the Dauphin, without the proof of it being handed down to us ; that Louis XIV. was cruel enough to condemn a beloved son to perpetual imprisonment ; and, finally, that it was possible to keep

---

of Arras styled the Cité, formerly completely distinct from the town properly so called. The Chapel of Saint-Vaast, in which the body of Vermandois was first deposited, formed part of the Abbey of Saint-Vaast. This chapel is the present cathedral of Arras.

[30] Nuns of the order of Sainte-Claire.—*Trans.*

his abduction secret in the midst of the troops, how can we possibly admit that ceremonies, which the pious monarch always regarded as sacred, could have been ordered by him to deceive his subjects and take advantage of their credulity? How can we admit that this illness, of which we have traced all the phases, was feigned; that the despatches that have been analysed were false; that Louis XIV. had for the accomplices of his stratagem men such as the Lieutenant-General Boufflers, Marshal d'Humières, and the Marquis de Montchevreuil; that, not content with making them take part in such a singular project, he made a mockery of religion the better to mask it? How can we admit that this bier, round which prayers ascended and tears flowed, was empty,[31] and that the Prince, of whom pompous epitaphs vaunt the qualities, was then in rigorous confinement at Pignerol? Finally, how explain, if not as the testimony of his sincere piety and affection, this solemn service, founded in perpetuity by Louis XIV., and which, in prolonging it, would have aggravated an impious derision, and perpetuated the memory of a profane fraud?

---

[31] In 1786, Louis XVI., moved with the rumour referring to this supposition, ordered the coffin to be opened. A *procès-verbal* drawn up December 16, 1786, in the presence of the Bishop of Arras, the provost of the cathedral, the head of the vestry, and the procureur-général, verified the existence "of an entire and well-shaped body." See the very interesting *Vie de Madame Elizabeth*, of M. de Beauchesne, vol. i. p. 543. To this decisive proof we have felt bound to add others for those who might be tempted to believe that another body than that of Vermandois had been enclosed in the coffin.

CHAPTER VII.

"It has been asserted," says M. de Sévelinges, in an article of the *Biographie Universelle*,[1] that the famous Man with the Iron Mask was no other than the Duke of Monmouth. Of all the conjectures that have been made upon this subject, it is perhaps one of the least unreasonable." M. de Sévelinges says truly that in favour of this candidate for the honour of being the Man with the Iron Mask, if we cannot invoke one of those decisive proofs which enforce conviction, there are at least several indications which seem to unite in designating him, and in forming what the English call cumulative evidence. The greatness of the crime to be punished, the powerful interest there was to effect the disappearance of this leader of revolt, and carry him off for ever from his partisans, the persistent

---

[1] *Biographie Universelle* of Michaud, article "Monmouth."

incredulity of the people respecting his death, his near relationship to James II., which renders the penalty of perpetual imprisonment more probable than that of death, are so many circumstances which, in certain respects, justify the opinion put forth in the last century by Saint-Foix, and explain the obstinacy of this publicist in defending it.

Monmouth is one of those historical personages who have been very variously, and in some degree contradictorily, appreciated. Placed at the head of a party which, from the first days of the reign of James II., sought to overthrow a king who remained a Catholic in the midst of a nation almost entirely Protestant; having attempted in 1685 a revolution which, three years later, was to be accomplished with perfect success by a prince better endowed and much more apt in playing this great part, Monmouth has incurred the blind enmity of the Catholics, and met with excessive praise from their adversaries. Unjustly vilified by the one party, insulted beyond measure by the other, he has been represented on the one side as an adventurer devoid of all qualities, and rashly engaging against his uncle in a mad enterprise fatally condemned to insuccess. Others have seen in him the glorious defender of the interests of the Anglican religion, threatened by the sovereign, the worthy precursor of William of Orange, the champion of the true faith, whose failure is to be ascribed to unforeseen circumstances and the incapacity of his lieutenants. The same contradiction that exists in the judgments passed upon his attempt is to be found in the opinions given by his biographers as to his origin. Whilst some deny that he was the natural son of Charles II., and give us to understand that Lucy Walters was already pregnant with him when she became the mistress of the exiled Stuart, others are inclined to see in Monmouth his legitimate offspring, the issue of a regular marriage contracted during his exile by a king deprived of his crown, very thoughtless, and madly in love. As always is the case, the truth lies between these two extremes of disparagement and favour. Charles II. constantly showed the love of a father for Monmouth; but if a marriage had united him to Lucy Walters, the proofs would not have remained hidden in the famous "black box" in which Monmouth's friends supposed them to be. Brought to light, they would have allowed Charles II., deprived of other legitimate descendants, to indulge his fondness for a son, an accomplished gentleman, and already the object at Whitehall of several distinctions reserved only for royal princes,[2] and to whom only legitimacy was wanting for him to be universally received as the heir-presumptive to the throne. During his father's reign he enjoyed, in fact, a popularity which not even great defects had been able to compromise, and which the hatred inspired by the Duke of York increased. People detected in the latter a future king entirely devoted to the Papists, and loved still more in Monmouth a prince of engaging and courteous manner, distinguished without haughtiness, some-times familiar, but without lowering himself, less effeminate in his manners than his royal father,[3] and whose libertinage,

----

[2] He resided in the King's palace, had pages, and when he travelled was everywhere received like a prince. Charles II. created him successively Earl of Orkney, Knight of the Garter, and Duke of Monmouth.

[3] Grammont says of Monmouth in his *Mémoires:* "His face and the graces of his person were such that Nature has perhaps never formed any more accomplished. His countenance was perfectly charming. It

fiery character, and acts of violence, were pardoned in remembrance of his brilliant military exploits, in consideration of his past, and the hopes that were based upon him. But the position at which he had arrived was far above his merits. His birth and the attractions of his person had raised him to it. As long as his father lived he maintained himself in it, supported by the interested affection of the Whigs, and never having to display any qualities but those he was liberally endowed with. When, at the death of Charles II., it was necessary for him to exhibit not only the gifts which had made him the idol of the people, but the talents requisite to accomplish a revolution, and to seize upon a crown, the mediocrity of his faculties soon became apparent. Intrepid upon the field of battle, he lacked decision in the council, and wavered irresolute between contrary suggestions. His natural kindness, which had won him the love of the people, sometimes degenerated into weakness. Of a very malleable disposition, he yielded too easily to the influence of others, and was often only the executant of their will. His ardour in action, above all, arose from the contact of those surrounding him. He hardly ever derived it from his own powers, and, left to himself, he readily sank into indolence. When he learnt in Holland the accession of James II., which closed England to him, he could form no manly resolution, and forgot[4] in the company

---

was the face of a man; nothing insipid, nothing effeminate about it. Every feature had its attraction and its especial delicacy. A marvellous inclination for all kinds of exercises, an engaging manner, an air of grandeur—in short, all bodily advantages pleaded in his favour; but he had no sentiment except such as was inspired by others."

[4] Letter from Monmouth to James, dated from Ringwode, quoted by Macaulay, *Histoire d'Angleterre depuis l'Avénement de Jacques II.*, translation of M. de Peyronnet, vol. i. p. 398.

of a loved woman [5] that he was the hope of a numerous party, the support of a great cause, the pretender to a throne. This inaction had its source in his carelessness and in his indolence of mind, much more than in a taste for obscurity; for he did not long resist the prayers of his friends when they came to drag him from his retreat and arm him against James II.,[6] and not having had sufficient energy to conceive the enterprise himself, he equally lacked the resolution to object to it. Such was the man whose coming a notable part of the English nation longed for, who was about to shake a throne, but without succeeding in overthrowing it; because he had neither the profound views nor the persevering audacity with which great ambitions ripen and execute their projects.

On June 11, 1685, Monmouth, accompanied by eighty men well armed, landed on the coast of Dorsetshire, near the little port of Lyme. The result of this expedition is a matter of history. There is no need to recount the triumphant march to Taunton, the enthusiasm of the West, the fatal field of Sedgemoor, and the ignominious flight of the leader of the insurgents.[7] Some days afterwards a man in tattered garments, with haggard face and hair prematurely white, is dragged from a ditch, at the bottom of which he was crouching, half hidden by the long grass and nettles, trembling and livid with fear, his pockets filled with peas

---

[5] Lady Henrietta Wentworth.—*Trans.*

[6] Burnet, vol. i. p. 630.

[7] M. Topin's narrative has been here condensed, as it was hardly necessary to repeat to English readers the well-known story of Monmouth's futile enterprise, more especially as it has no kind of bearing on the point as to whether he was or was not the Man with the Iron Mask. —*Trans.*

gathered to satisfy the cravings of ravenous hunger. It was the darling of Charles's court, the hero of Bothwell Brig, "King Monmouth."

Finding himself in the power of a monarch whom he had come to overthrow, whose real faults he had not only pointed out, but whom he had also calumniated by accusations as infamous as unmerited, Monmouth did not understand that he was lost, and that James II., always inexorable, would not feel for his most cruel enemy a pity that was unknown to him. Self-respect and his own dignity should have prohibited the vanquished from appealing to the clemency of his conqueror, even had this clemency been at all probable. But mere reason indicated that to ask mercy of James II. would only be a useless abasement, and that there was nothing left but to prepare for death. Monmouth had neither the courage nor the wisdom to reject the thought of an unavailing humiliation. He wrote to James II. in the most abject terms.[8] His letter was that of a man crushed by the approach of death, and who sacrifices to the desire of living his past, his honour, those whom he had sought to gain over without succeeding, as well as the partisans whom he had conducted to their ruin. This was not all: no longer able to arrest himself in his ignominious descent, he desired to see James II., and the latter was sufficiently inhuman to consent to an interview, which it was his unalterable will should remain sterile. Not to spare such an enemy was justified to a certain extent by the violence of his attacks; but to admit him to his presence without pardoning him was a refinement

---

[8] *Original Letters* of Sir H. Ellis; Newspapers of the period; Despatch of the French Ambassador Barillon, July 13, 1685.

of vengeance and harshness. He enjoyed the barbarous pleasure of seeing his redoubtable adversary confounded, falling at his feet, embracing his knees, shedding bitter tears, vainly trying to hold out his fettered hands to him, acknowledging and cursing his crime, offering to abjure his religion, and become a Catholic,[9] beseeching pardon, pardon at any price. To this eagerness for life, to these supplications James II. only opposed silence, and turning away his head he terminated an interview, in which we hardly know whether to feel most indignant at the cold cruelty of the conqueror or at the degrading terror and cowardly humiliation of the vanquished.

It is at this moment that Saint-Foix, introducing Monmouth into this problem, gives him Louis XIV. for a guardian, Saint-Mars for a gaoler, and the prison of Pignerol for a residence.

---

[9] *Letter of James II. to the Prince of Orange, July 14, 1685; Sir J. Bramston's Memoirs,* related by Macaulay; Burnet, vol. i. p. 644.

CHAPTER VIII.

Bases on which Saint-Foix has founded his Theory—Disputes of
Saint-Foix and Father Griffet—The Recollection of Monmouth
becomes Legendary in England—Ballads announcing his Return
—Indisputable Proofs of Monmouth's Death in 1685—Interview of
Monmouth with his Wife and Children—He is conducted to the
Scaffold—His Firmness—The Last Words which he utters—
Awkwardness of the Executioner.

IN an anonymous libel, published in Holland under the title
of *Amours de Charles II. et de Jacques II., Rois d'Angleterre,*
we read "that in 1688, a few days after the departure from
London of King James II., overthrown by William of Orange,
Earl Danby sent to seek Colonel Skelton, who had formerly
been Lieutenant of the Tower, which post the Prince of
Orange had taken away from him, in order to give it to Lord
Lucas. 'Mr. Skelton,' said Earl Danby to him, 'yesterday,
when supping with Robert Johnston, you told him that the
Duke of Monmouth was alive, and that he was imprisoned
in some castle in England.' 'I have not said that he was
alive, and imprisoned in any castle, since I know nothing
about it,' answered Skelton; 'but I have said that the night
after the Duke of Monmouth's pretended execution, the
King, accompanied by three men, came to remove him

from the Tower; that they covered his head with a kind of hood, and that the King and the three men entered a carriage with him.'"[1]

With the exception of this story, in the exactitude of which Saint-Foix himself has not very great confidence, since he says, "These are books whose authors seek only to amuse those who read them,"[2] he invokes for the establishment of his theory merely vague conversations, confused reports which he has collected, and the testimony of public rumour. "A surgeon," he tells us, "named Nélaton, who was in the habit of going every morning to the Café Procope, related there several times, that when first assistant to a surgeon near the Porte Saint-Antoine, he was sent for one day to bleed a person, and that he was taken to the Bastille, where the governor introduced him into the chamber of a prisoner, who had his head covered with a long napkin, tied behind the neck; that this prisoner complained of bad headaches; that his dressing-gown was yellow and black, with large gold flowers; and that from his accent he recognized him to be English." "Father Tournemine," adds Saint-Foix,[3] "has often repeated to me that, having gone to pay a visit to the Duchess of Portsmouth with Father Sanders, formerly King James's confessor, she had said to them, in a succession of conversations, that she should always reproach that Prince's memory with the execution of the Duke of Monmouth, after Charles II., in the hour of death, and ready to communicate, had made him

---

[1] *Amours de Charles II. et de Jacques II., Rois d'Angleterre.* First part, pp. 74, 75.

[2] *Réponse de M. de Saint-Foix au R.P. Griffet,* Paris. Ventes, Libraire à la Montagne Sainte-Geneviève, 1770, p. 94.

[3] *Ibid.,* p. 95 *et seq.*

promise, in the presence of the host, which Huldeston, a Catholic priest, had secretly brought in, that, whatever rebellion the Duke of Monmouth might attempt, he would never have him punished with death. ' Nor did he do so,' replied Father Sanders, with animation." In order to explain how Monmouth could have been carried off alive, and how the people were deceived by this sham execution, Saint-Foix furnishes a proof not a whit less uncertain than the preceding. " It was reported about London," he says, "that an officer of his army, who closely resembled him, being made prisoner, and certain of being condemned to death, had received the proposal to personate him with as much joy as if he had been accorded life, and that, on this being reported abroad, a great lady, having gained over those who could open his coffin, and having looked at his right arm, exclaimed, ' Ah! this is not Monmouth !' " [4]

Slight as was the basis of this theory, it must be admitted that Father Griffet combated it with very inconclusive arguments, and that Saint-Foix had no great difficulty in refuting him in his turn. To the objection founded upon the uselessness of always leaving in mystery the name of the prisoner who died in 1703, when both James II. and William of Orange had also ceased to live, Saint-Foix replied, very judiciously, that Louis XIV. might have consented to guard Monmouth at Pignerol, both in order to oblige James II., his ally, and to have in his power a Stuart, whom he might one day be able to oppose to the ambition of William of Orange, if James II. continued to remain childless ; but that the unexpected

---

[4] *Réponse de M. de Saint-Foix au R. P. Griffet,* p. 96.

birth of a Prince of Wales [5] having rendered this piece of foresight useless, it was natural that Louis XIV. would not wish it known that he had constituted himself the gaoler of an English prince. " It was very likely indeed," added Saint-Foix, [6] " that the partisans of William of Orange having published that this Prince of Wales was a supposititious child, would not have failed to say that since means had been found to represent on the scaffold and behead one man in place of another, it was much easier to feign a pregnancy and a confinement." Now Louis XIV., who had continued to support the exiled Stuarts with sufficient obstinacy to imprudently recognize this Prince of Wales under the title of James III., [7] was bound to prevent a revelation of a nature to confirm the injurious doubts which had arisen at the period of this Prince's birth. [8]

The necessity for the mystery being thus justified by the pride and self-interest of Louis XIV., Saint-Foix refuted Father Griffet not less cleverly on the point of the substitution of an unknown individual for Monmouth about to die on the scaffold. Reproached with its improbability, he answered that this generosity was very easy to compre-

---

[5] Born, June 21, 1688, of James II. and Marie d'Este; recognized as King by Louis XIV., November, 16 1701, on the death of James II.

[6] *Réponse de Saint-Foix au P. Griffet*, p. 118 *et seq.*

[7] On the death of James II. This ill-timed boldness was one of Louis XIV.'s gravest errors, and stirred up the English nation against him. See our work *L'Europe et les Bourbons sous Louis XIV.*, chap. viii. p. 190.

[8] See Chap. IV. (p. 51 *ante*) of the present work, in which this accusation of criminal fraud brought by William of Orange against his father-in-law, James II., has already been considered.

hend—that such an act of devotion had scarcely any merit in an officer of Monmouth's army, condemned, like the latter, to death, and who was sacrificing to his old general, not his life, but simply his name. Finally, a comparative examination of several circumstances connected with the execution, ingeniously touched upon and grouped together, such as the choice of the bishops attending the condemned, the few words that he uttered, the look of reproach which he gave the executioner, who did not kill him at the first blow of the axe,[9] finished by convincing Saint-Foix.

Moreover, Saint-Foix's error was also that of a portion of the English nation, who, through idolizing Monmouth, came to disbelieve in the fact of his death, just as Saint-Foix did through attachment to his theory. The popular affection survived even the generation who had espoused his cause;[10] and the hero, adorned with all the seductive qualities that had made him the idol of the people, and clothed by time with qualities which he the least[11] pos-

---

[9] According to Saint-Foix, the bishops chosen were not acquainted with Monmouth's appearance, and the *pretended* officer only uttered a few words, while the look given by the victim after the third blow of the axe was intended as a reproach to those who had promised that he should die without pain. But these observations are more ingenious than well-founded. Monmouth was accompanied to the scaffold by the bishops who had visited him in prison, and we shall shortly see that he said a good deal, that the execution took place at ten o'clock in the morning, and that far from complaining even by a look of the executioner's unskilfulness, Monmouth bore his horrible punishment with great resignation.

[10] *Observator*, August 1, 1685; *Gazette de France*, November 2, 1686; Letter of Humphrey Wanley, August 25, 1698, in the Aubrey collection, given by Macaulay in his *History of England*.

[11] "If the Duke of Monmouth had been able to have concealed himself or to have escaped, his last action had given him such a good reputation amongst the English that he would have been able to have

sessed, speedily became a legendary character. In Dorsetshire and the neighbouring counties, many, during the
remainder of their lives, cherished the hope of seeing him
again ; and for very many years, on the occasion of any
important event, the old men used confidently to announce
in whispers that the time was approaching when King
Monmouth would reappear. Several ballads foretold this
return :—[12]

> " Though this is a dismal story
> Of the fall of my design,
> Yet I'll come again in glory,
> If I live till eighty-nine ;
> For I'll have a stronger army,
> And of ammunition store."

Again—

> " Then shall Monmouth in his glories
> Unto his English friends appear,
> And will stifle all such stories
> As are vended everywhere.

> They'll see I was not so degraded,
> To be taken gathering pease,
> Or in a cock of hay up braided.
> What strange stories now are these ! "

In many poor families trifling objects which had belonged
to him have been preserved as precious relics even to our
own days, and two impostors having on different occasions
travelled about the country under the name of Monmouth,

---

drawn many persons towards him every time that he might have shown
himself to the people of England," wrote the French ambassador to
Louis XIV., July 19, 1685:—Archives of the Ministry of Foreign Affairs,
section England, 155.

[12] They are to be found in the Pepsyan Collection, and have been
given by Macaulay in his *History of England.*

found everywhere among the lower orders the most cordial reception, as well as encouragement, assistance, and evidence of the most touching and constant affection.

How much more would this adoration, of which Monmouth had rendered himself unworthy by his flight, have nevertheless embellished his memory, and, without absolving him, have made of him a legendary hero; how much more striking still would it have appeared, if, as Saint-Foix believed, he of whom the poets sang in their ballads, of whom the peasants talked by their firesides in the evening, and whose speedy return the people were awaiting, had been, at that very instant, confined in a prison in the remotest parts of the Alps, his face hidden from the gaze of man, unknown to all save a gaoler as rigorous as he was incorruptible?   When the stage took possession of the subject of the Man with the Iron Mask, it preferred to adopt the version which makes him a brother of Louis XIV., as being the most interesting one.   The supposition that Monmouth was the Man with the Iron Mask would have been much more dramatic, because, while in some points touching upon reality, it would, on the one hand, have allowed of representing a whole nation plunged in grief and filled with expectation, and on the other, the conquered of Sedgemoór following Saint-Mars from prison to prison, and after having almost attained a throne, being obscurely interred in the evening by two turnkeys of the Bastille !

But however thrilling this accumulation of misfortune would have been, history cannot admit its truth.   Whatever Saint-Foix may have thought—whatever the English common people may have believed—Monmouth died on the scaffold, July 15, 1685.   Authentic despatches, signed by

Louis XIV.'s ambassador,[13] furnish proof of it; and this monarch, far from having been an accomplice, as has been said, of an abduction of the Duke, and far from having consented to act as his keeper, received day by day exact news of the early progress of his revolt, and of his defeat, capture, and death. In these despatches, penned by an impartial and perfectly independent witness, and which appeared destined never to be divulged, there is nothing that allows us to suppose that a pardon was granted, but we find in them instead irrefragable proof of James II.'s inflexible severity. Almost to his last moment Monmouth showed himself but little worthy of the regret which he was to leave behind him. He saw his wife, but without emotion, and thought only of again beseeching his life from the Earl of Clarendon, who accompanied her. On the evening of Monday, July 14, he learned that he would be led to death the next morning. At once turning pale, he remained for a long time silent, and the first word that he could utter was a demand for a respite. He repeated this in several letters addressed to James II., as well as to the most considerable persons of the court, and desired to see the King once more, a request which was refused him.[14] When he had lost all hope he became shamefully depressed : to agitation, and to the efforts exerted up to that moment to save his life, succeeded a gloomy silence ; to cowardly fears, the dejection of despair. The next day his children were brought to him ; he blessed them, and bade them adieu, as

---

[13] Archives of the Ministry of Foreign Affairs, section England, 155; Despatches, June 23 and 28, and July 12, 19, 23, 25 and 26, 1685.

[14] Despatch from the French Ambassador, July 26, 1685 : " He asked a second time to speak to him, but it was not allowed."

well as his wife, from whom he parted without sorrow. [15]
For many years his affection had been given to Lady Wentworth, whom he said was his wife before God, whilst he had
espoused Lady Monmouth when too young for the marriage
to be according to the spirit of God, although valid before
the law. During the hours which preceded his death, Lady
Wentworth was the constant object of his preoccupations,
of his regrets, and of his most lively solicitude. Sometimes
he maintained that his long relations with her had always
been innocent, sometimes he gave out that he had always
considered her as his legitimate wife. Without doubt it
was the recollection of this noble and distinguished person,
who loved him tenderly, and who a few months afterwards
was to follow him to the tomb, that caused Monmouth to
regain his feeling of dignity, till then disregarded. He all
at once became more firm; and at ten in the morning
entered the carriage of the Lieutenant of the Tower with
a courage worthy of his race and of the woman who had
inspired it in him.

The open space where the scaffold was erected, all the
streets leading to it, and the roofs of the neighbouring
houses were covered with a multitude, who showed its
disapprobation by a silence broken only by sighs and
sobs. Every eye was fixed on Monmouth, who, having
smilingly saluted the soldiers of the guard, was mounting
with a firm foot the steps of the scaffold. Every one awaits
with anxiety his last words. He pronounces them in a loud
and distinct voice, and with the energy of fanaticism. He
finishes by saying, "That he has satisfied his conscience,
and that he dies in peace with God." The Sheriff having

---

[15] Burnet, i. 645 ; Macaulay.

pressed him to declare before the people whether he died in the faith of the English Church, he answered " Yes," without hesitation ; and on the bishops who accompanied him observing that, according to the principles of that church, he ought to obey his lawful king, he replied, " There is no question of that now ; I have nothing to say about it." Then he added, " that he had God's pardon, and that he had nothing to reproach himself with in reference to Lady Wentworth, for whom he entertained as much esteem as affection." The Sheriff having represented to him the scandal which he had caused in Holland by living publicly with this woman, and having asked him if he had married her, " I am sorry for this scandal," replied Monmouth, " but this is not the time to answer your question." The bishops afterwards conversed with him about the consequences of his revolt, of the blood which he had caused to be shed, and of so many companions led on by him to their ruin. Affected by this language, Monmouth said in a low voice that he agreed with them and that he regretted it. Next the bishops present offered up fervent prayers, which the Prince listened to with attention, and to each of which he answered, " Amen !" Then, addressing the executioner, he gave him six guineas, earnestly begging him to do his work quickly, and not to serve him like Lord Russell, whom he had struck three or four times. After having assured himself that the axe was sufficiently sharp, he refused to have his eyes bandaged, and placed his head upon the block. The bishops continue their prayers. The tears of the crowd flow fast. The executioner, probably troubled by the fears which Monmouth had expressed, strikes the first blow unskilfully. The victim lifts up his head ; then, with-

out uttering a word, replaces it on the block.   Three more
blows are struck by the unsure hand of this man, whom the
yells and imprecations of the crowd cause to tremble.   At
length, at the fifth blow, the head is separated from the
body, and the spectators rush upon the scaffold, some, in
a state of fury, wishing to punish the awkward executioner,
others, with pious haste, desirous of dipping their handker-
chiefs in the blood of one whom they considered a martyr.[16]

---

[16] Official despatches from the French Ambassador in England,
July 15–25 and July 16–26, 1685.

CHAPTER IX.

François de Vendôme, Duke de Beaufort—His Portrait—His Conduct
during the War of the Fronde—Unimportance of this Individual—
Motives cited by Lagrange-Chancel in support of his Theory—
Their Improbability—Reasons which determined the Search for
Proofs that leave no doubt of Beaufort's Death at Candia.

LIKE Monmouth, a royal prince and the issue of an illegitimate connection, François de Vendôme had, like Monmouth,
the rare privilege of being sufficiently beloved by the people
for them, during a long time, to have doubted of his death.
Ten years after the expedition to Candia, where he disappeared, the market-women were still in the habit of
having masses said, not for the repose of his soul, but for
the prompt return of his person;[1] and these persistent
doubts have caused Beaufort to be included, like Monmouth,
among those in whom people have beheld the mysterious
prisoner of the Isles Sainte-Marguerite.

But these are the only points of resemblance between
Charles II.'s natural son and Henri IV.'s grandson.   Their

---

[1] "Several persons here wish to wager," wrote Guy-Patin, September 26, 1669, "that M. de Beaufort is not dead. *O utinam !*" And in
another letter, January 14, 1670: "It is said that M. de Vivonne has,
by commission, the office of Vice-Admiral of France for twenty years ;
but there are still those who insist that M. de Beaufort is not dead, and
that he is only a prisoner."

characters, their adventures, and their persons afford the most complete contrast, and these two idols of the English and French peoples have owed their equal popularity to entirely opposite qualities.

Brought up in the country, in the most absolute ignorance, and having devoted his early years exclusively to the rude exercises of the chase, Beaufort, during the whole of his life, retained from this education of nature a coarse impress which made him the most really original personage of the courts of Anne of Austria and of Louis XIV. When, at the close of Louis XIII.'s reign, he appeared at the Louvre, in that court which was as yet far from being the most polished of Europe, he was not long in shocking even the least squeamish, and in opposing himself to the most legitimate requirements. His athletic strength, of which he willingly made a display, his characteristic and expressive features, the intemperate animation of his gestures, his affected habit of always keeping his hand on his hip, the tone of his voice, everything to his moustaches even, curled up out of bravado, contributed to give him the most provoking appearance. The rusticity of his manners was equalled only by the coarseness of his speech. He had not even received the usual education of the middle classes; and wanting sufficient discernment to compensate by observation for his complete ignorance, he would, when speaking, mix up in the strangest manner possible hunting terms, which were very familiar to him, with court expressions, which he used without hardly understanding them.[2] Cynical by habit,

---

[2] *Mémoires de la Duchesse de Nemours,* vol. xxxiv. ; *Mémoires de Brienne,* and of Conrat, Montglat, and of La Rochefoucauld. "He formed," says the Duchess de Nemours, "a kind of jargon of words so

affected through a desire of imitating others, he had formed for himself a language " which," the Cardinal de Retz says, " would have spoilt even Cato's good sense." [3] This jargon ended by rendering ridiculous one whose appearance alone was already displeasing. But he took his revenge in the army, where these defects were less apparent, and where he had opportunities for displaying his manly qualities. Careless of every danger, and even of a reckless courage, capable of enduring the most excessive fatigue, familiar with all the exercises of the body, he ceased to make people laugh at him, excited their admiration at the sieges of Corbie, Hesdin, and Arras, and when he returned to the court, was preceded by a reputation for bravery which rallied around him a portion of his detractors. People shut their eyes to his eccentricities, and were better disposed to appreciate his manly frankness and probity. Accordingly, when, on the eve of Louis XIII.'s death, Anne of Austria was afraid lest the Duke d'Orléans or the Prince de Condé should have the Dauphin and the Duke d'Anjou carried off, it was to the custody of Beaufort, as " the most honest man in France," [4] that she confided her two sons.

Although at first proud of this flattering mark of distinction, he was not long in forgetting it, and in throwing himself very thoughtlessly into the enterprises of the Fronde, in which he made a sad enough figure. Enticed by the Duchess de Montbazon to join the cabal of the *Importants*,[5]

---

vulgar or so badly arranged, that it rendered him ridiculous to everybody, although these words, which he arranged so badly, would perhaps have appeared very good if he had known how to have arranged them better, being bad only in the places where he put them."

[3] *Mémoires du Cardinal de Retz*, p. 9.

[4] It was thus that she then designated him.

[5] The Queen's party.—*Trans.*

brutal in his behaviour towards Mazarin, next imprisoned at Vincennes,[6] allied with the Prince de Condé after having been the enemy of his sister, the Duchess de Longueville, a furious opponent of the court after having shown himself the guardian of the throne and the protector of the Regent, by turns at the service of the narrow passions and beggarly interests of the Dukes d'Elbœuf and de Bouillon, of the Marshal de la Motte, and of the Cardinal de Retz, without exactly knowing either for what cause he was fighting or what aim he was pursuing, Beaufort withdrew from the Fronde as carelessly as he had joined it, and became reconciled to the court with as little gain to himself as he had obtained from the Frondeurs by his alliance with them. To an incapacity for discerning what path he ought to pursue in the midst of contending parties, Beaufort joined a dangerous ignorance of his political nonentity, and like many persons who are wanting in judgment, he endeavoured to rule by the force of qualities in which he was most deficient. As vain as he was thoughtless, believing himself called upon to play a great part,[7] he imagined that he had an aptitude for public business, because he could talk its cant ; he delighted in giving advice to those who were leading him as they chose ; and, wronging his real qualities by those which he wished to affect, he ended by exercising influence

---

[6] He was imprisoned there in 1645, and escaped in 1649. It was referring to this escape that Condé, incarcerated in his turn at Vincennes, on being recommended the *Imitation of Jesus Christ* in order to beguile his captivity, answered that he preferred the *Imitation of the Duke de Beaufort*.

[7] It is known that he one day asked President Bellièvre if he would not change the face of affairs by giving a box on the ears to the Duke d'Elbœuf? "I do not think," answered the magistrate, in a grave tone, "that would change anything except the face of the Duke d'Elbœuf."

only over the multitude; but with them he succeeded perfectly. If, in order to please one's subjects, it is necessary to speak their language, share their tastes, adopt their manners, to be by turns abrupt and familiar, uncouth and haughty, nobody has deserved more than Beaufort to be the " King of the *halles.*" This title, which history has confirmed, his contemporaries decreed to him unanimously, and the people accepted with enthusiasm. In the streets they followed with love this good prince who had consented to come and live near them in the most populous quarter, whose light hair and martial bearing the women admired, and who did not disdain occasionally to descant to the populace from a post, and sometimes to display his strength in street quarrels.

But when Louis XIV. attained his majority, this king of the populace became the most submissive of his subjects. Lagrange-Chancel, in order to establish the theory which makes the Duke de Beaufort the Man with the Iron Mask, and explain his pretended detention at Pignerol, speaks " of his turbulent spirit, of the *rôle* he had played in all the party movements of the time of the Fronde."[8] He adds that "his office of High Admiral placed him daily in a position to thwart the great designs of Colbert, charged with the department of the Marine." Nothing can be less exact, and in 1663, when Beaufort became High Admiral, the passions, kindled during the Fronde, were extinguished, the ambitious satisfied or quelled. The most turbulent chiefs, such as Rochefoucauld, were plunged in an idleness which was scarcely menacing. Those who had been the

---

[8] *Année Littéraire:* Letter of Lagrange-Chancel to M. Fréron on the subject of the Man with the Iron Mask.

most hostile then made a display of their submission and servility. Whilst the Cardinal de Retz, in retirement at Commercy, was making up for his inaction and want of power by writing his immortal Memoirs, the Prince de Conti was espousing the niece of Mazarin, and Condé was gratefully receiving the order of the Holy Ghost from the King.[9] The most indocile and most arrogant of the nobility, who had disturbed the Regent's authority, constrained the court to leave Paris, sent away Mazarin, and agitated the whole kingdom, now crowded the ante-chambers of Louis XIV. and disputed the signal honour of being present when he retired to bed, and of holding a candlestick on the occasion.

Beaufort was not the least assiduous in giving satisfaction to the absolute monarch. Little formed for command, for which an extreme impetuosity rendered him unsuited, he received very humbly the severe reprimands of Louis XIV. and Colbert, and supported the yoke of the master as docilely as he was harsh and imperious to his own officers.[10] If he was always menacing the latter with ill-treatment and with having them thrown into the sea, he submitted, in his naval expeditions, to the control and almost to the rule of the Intendant placed at his side by Colbert.[11] Nothing in him, then, was dangerous to the court: neither his character, for his subordinates alone experienced its violence; nor his talents, which were almost nugatory; nor his pretensions, which had become very much reduced; nor his popu-

---

⁹ *Art de Vérifier les Dates*, vol. vi. pp. 273 and 277.

¹⁰ *Œuvres de Louis XIV.*, vol. v. p. 388 *et seq.*

¹¹ *Relation de Gigéry, faite au Roi par M. de Gadagne, Lieutenant-Général:*—Imperial Library, Manuscripts.

larity, which scarcely extended beyond the boundaries of his kingdom of the *halles*. More than that, he had, in the eyes of the King, the merit of belonging, through his father,[12] to those illegitimate princes whom Louis XIV. was constantly to favour—at first from political interest, with the view of opposing them to the legitimate heirs of the great families ; then from paternal affection, when his own *,amours* had quickly increased their number—and to whom, from a pride more and more immoderate, he was to accord successively precedence over the peers, then the rank of royal princes, and, lastly, to the shame of the whole kingdom, rights to the throne of France. One cannot understand, then, for what motive Louis XIV. would have sought to have got rid of a prince too unimportant to excite his jealousy, too sub-missive for a revolt to be feared from him, and who, the son of a bastard, was preparing for and justifying by his example the early and more and more scandalous elevation of the illegitimate offspring of the great King.

Previous to the expedition to Candia, whither, according to Lagrange-Chancel, and those who share his opinion,[13] Beaufort was sent in order that he might be carried off and afterwards condemned to perpetual imprisonment, was there any act in the Admiral's naval career, by which he had entered into a state of rebellion against the court? Was there anything of the kind in the expedition of 1664, when, in spite of the opinions of his lieutenants, some of whom wished

---

[12] Cæsar de Vendôme, natural son of Henri IV. and Gabrielle d'Estrées, and of whom the Duke de Beaufort was the second son, born in January, 1616:—*Art de Vérifier les Dates*, vol. xii. p. 521.

[13] Such as Lenglet-Dufresnoy, *Plan de l'Histoire Générale et Particulière de la Monarchie Française*, vol. iii. p. 268 *et seq.* Paris, 1754.

to attack Bona first, others Boujeiah,[14] Beaufort, adhering too strictly to Louis XIV.'s detailed instructions, directed an attack on Gigery, of which he possessed himself prematurely, and compromised the results of the campaign by a scrupulous obedience to orders given at a distance, and which he ought to have been bold enough to have disregarded? Was there anything in 1666, when he was charged to command the escort of the new Queen of Portugal,[15] and when, in spite of his ardour and of a noble desire to hasten to an encounter with the English, he agreed, so as to obey orders, to remain immovable in the waters of the Tagus?

But let us admit that the cause of this imprisonment, sought for in vain, can never be known to us, or rather, that the humble deference displayed by Beaufort towards Louis XIV. had not destroyed in the mind of the latter the remembrance of the violent passion which made the Admiral so ungovernable in his behaviour towards his officers. Let us admit an imaginary crime in order to explain an abduction which there is nothing positive to justify. Then the precautions taken after the abduction would be explained to a certain extent, by the popularity which Beaufort enjoyed at Paris, and Saint-Foix, in refuting Lagrange-Chancel, has been too positive in affirming the contrary.

"The King's authority was consolidated," he says,[16] "and the imprisonment of the great Condé himself, if it had been considered necessary to have had him arrested, would not have caused the least disturbance." Assuredly, but

---

[14] *Mémoire de M. de Gadagne,* already quoted.

[15] Marie de Savoie, Duchess de Nemours, wife of Alphonso VI., King of Portugal.

[16] *Réponse de Saint-Foix et Recueil de tout ce qui a été écrit sur le Prisonnier Masqué,* p. 20, 1770.

would things have been the same for the " King of the *halles*," whom the people still thoroughly idolized?

This only of Lagrange's numerous arguments being admitted, and the necessity of hiding Beaufort from the gaze of all being recognized, would his abduction have been possible at Candia, in the midst of the fleet and in the presence of the army? What were the causes of this expedition, and among them can we detect a desire on the part of the King to send Beaufort with it, in order to get rid of him afterwards? Lastly, was this individual, who all the accounts agree in saying had *disappeared*—was he in reality *killed*, and can we invoke perfectly conclusive proofs of his death? This is what it is essential to examine. Contemporary criticism has, up to the present, refuted the opinion which we are combating, by availing itself only of the correspondence of Louvois with Saint-Mars,[17] and by showing that not a line of these despatches permits us to believe that Beaufort was detained at Pignerol. Let us push the demonstration still further, and as we have attempted with regard to the hypothesis of a brother of Louis XIV., and with regard to Vermandois and Monmouth, do not let us content ourselves with this indirect proof; since, to the silence preserved by Saint-Mars and Louvois with reference to each of these individuals, sceptics could bring forward as objections the suppression of the despatches concerning them or the exclusive employment of verbal messages. This is why, instead of invoking the usual argument founded upon an examination of the despatches between the gaoler and the Minister, we have availed ourselves

---

[17] Amongst others, M. Paul Lacroix (Bibliophile Jacob), *Histoire de l'Homme au Masque de Fer*, 1840, p. 161.

of it merely in a subsidiary-manner, and only after having
previously sought to establish that a mysterious brother of
Louis XIV. never existed, that Vermandois succumbed
before Courtray, and that Monmouth died on the scaffold.
This double demonstration has appeared indispensable to
us in a matter where every one, having held a favourite
opinion for a long time, is little disposed to accept another
tending to upset it: so let us try the method for Beaufort in
his turn.

CHAPTER X.

THE causes of the expedition to Candia have not been entirely indicated. It is said[1] "that public opinion in France, having received the peace of Aix-la-Chapelle badly, the army especially complaining of it, Louis XIV. and Louvois eagerly seized the opportunity of diverting this unquiet zeal, of making this flame burn out, and that they willingly allowed themselves to be persuaded by the Nuncio and the Venetian Ambassador to send assistance to Candia, menaced by the Turks." To this consideration, which certainly was of great weight, it is necessary to add the influence of a court intrigue, and to explain the very particular motives which Louis XIV. had for pleasing the Pope.

---

[1] M. Camille Rousset, *Histoire de Louvois,* already quoted, vol. i. p. 257.

Louvois having succeeded in causing his brother, Le Tellier, to be appointed to the coadjutorship of Rheims, in preference to the Duke d'Albret, nephew of Turenne, and the illustrious Marshal, not having been more successful in getting his relation named coadjutor of the Archbishop of Paris, Louis XIV., to appease his resentment, promised the young abbé a cardinal's hat. Madame de Montespan, related to the d'Albret family, and already all-powerful, exerted herself with all her influence to hasten the fulfilment of this promise. On the other hand, the Prince d'Awersberg, one of the principal ministers of Leopold, had received from Grémonville, the French Ambassador, the assurance of Louis XIV.'s support to obtain from Clement IX. a cardinal's hat, in return for his assiduity in serving near the Emperor the interests of the King in the great affair of the treaty for the partition of the Spanish monarchy, signed secretly in 1668. The Pope knew how to turn this double demand to his own profit.[2] He enlarged greatly upon his extreme desire to satisfy the Most Christian King, but also upon his fears of irritating the other Catholic nations by a preference which would be insulting to them. He alleged the necessity which then existed for him not to render any Power discontented, and for causing them all to be united in repelling the common enemy of Christianity. " Thus, Monseigneur," wrote our envoy at Rome to De Lionne, " your Excellency will very easily perceive that if I had something positive to say as to what his Majesty has resolved to do with reference to the affairs of Candia during next season, I should meet with more facility here

---

[2] Letter from the Abbé Bigorre to De Lionne, December 28, 1668:— Archives of the Ministry of Foreign Affairs, section Rome, 1669.

for the advancement of the promotion."[3] That the piety and religious sentiments of Louis XIV. may have counted for something in his resolution to send troops to Candia to fight against the Turks, is'possible. That he may have been determined by the necessity of offering glorious amends to the army, discontented at the peace of Aix-la-Chapelle, can certainly not be denied. But, nevertheless, one must not overlook the influence which would have been exercised upon Louis XIV.'s decision by the certainty of satisfying the Pope in so tender a point, and by being able at one and the same time to keep his engagements towards the Minister of the Empire, content Turenne, and please Madame de Montespan. In any case it is impossible to reckon among these numerous causes a pretended desire to get rid of Beaufort, and there is no need to invoke so unlikely a motive, while so many positive grounds exist to explain this expedition.

The Duke de Beaufort was naturally chosen to command it.[4] In spite of his violence of character, everything called him to it; his birth, his rank of High Admiral, the commands which he had already held in several naval expeditions, and a certain aptitude which he possessed for the sailor's rude and perilous calling. Under his orders, Rochechouart, Count de Vivonne, had the direction of the

---

[3] Letters from the Abbé Bigorre to De Lionne, December 28, 1668. After the expedition to Candia, M. d'Albret alone received the hat. See despatches from the Abbé Bigorre to De Lionne, July 9, 1669, and from the Abbé de Bourlemont to De Lionne, August 9, 1669:—Archives of the Ministry of Foreign Affairs, section Rome, 1669.

[4] *Instruction que le roi a résolu être envoyée à M. le duc de Beaufort, pair, grand maître, chef et surintendant général de la navigation et commerce du royaume, sur l'emploi de l'armée navale que S. M. met en mer sous son commandement pendant la présente campagne :*—Imperial Library, Manuscripts, Colbert's Papers.

galleys, and the Duke de Navailles was the commander of
the landing forces.   These troops were 7,000[5] in number,
and were officered by the *élite* of the nobility,[6] who made it
a duty of chivalry to serve against the infidel.   It was in
some sort a new crusade, and, if it excited less enthusiasm
than when people undertook to deliver the tomb of Christ,
if the powerful lever of a robust faith, which had formerly
raised up entire nations, had long since become weakened,
French audacity and valour found a certain romantic attraction in a distant expedition, directed against a country and
an adversary equally unknown.

In a few days collections, organized throughout the
kingdom, had met the expenses of fitting out the expedition ;
and June 5, 1669, the fleet left Toulon during the finest
possible weather, which lasted the whole of the voyage, and
rendered it extraordinarily quick.   Composed of twenty-two
vessels of the line and of three *galiotes*,[7] the fleet joined, on

---

[5] Letters from De Lionne to the Cardinal Rospigliosi upon the troops
promised by Louis XIV., January 11 and February 26, 1669:—Archives
of the Ministry of Foreign Affairs, section Rome. *État des armées de
mer et de terre envoyées par le roi très-chrétien en Candie, en la présente
année* 1669:—Archives of the Ministry of Marine. Letter from Louvois
to the Governors, February 20, 1669:—Archives of the Ministry of War.

[6] Among them were the Count de Choiseul, MM. de Castellan and
de Dampierre, Marquis de Saint-Vallier, Duke de Château-Thierry,
Marquises d'O, d'Huxelles, and de Sevigné, &c. &c.:—Letter from
Madame de Sevigné to Bussy-Rabutin, August 18, 1669. At the end
of 1668, Count de Saint-Paul and Count de la Feuillade had gone to
succour Candia at the head of three hundred volunteers. But they
returned after a very murderous sally, having lent the Venetians an
assistance more brilliant than actually efficacious.

[7] [These were small vessels of light draught, without any foremast.—
Trans.] The galleys, to the number of thirteen, commanded by Vivonne,
were delayed several days off the coasts of Italy, and only arrived a
week after Beaufort:—Archives of the Ministry of Marine.

the 17th, fourteen Venetian boats charged with horses, near Cape Sapienza, off the point of the Morea. On the 19th, at five o'clock in the morning, the western extremity of the Isle of Candia was sighted. At the head of the squadron sailed the flag-ship *Le Monarque*, its poop covered with brilliantly-gilt carvings by Puget, and at its mast-head the papal standard, richly embroidered with the arms of the Holy See. At the sight of the land, which was in possession of the Turks, ensigns of a thousand colours were displayed on *Le Monarque*. Every other vessel in its turn immediately joined in this proud salute. The French cannon burst forth, the Turkish batteries replied to it from the port of Canea, and, amidst the uproar of this inoffensive discharge, amidst the resplendent gleams of the rising sun, the fleet passed majestically before the enemy; and, doubling the point of the island, directed its course towards the capital, which it had come to defend.

By degrees, as it approached, the delightful spectacle of fertile meadows bounded afar off by green wooded hills, which but lately had been offered to the sight, became changed to a picture of desolation and mourning. During several years the Turks, commanded by the Grand Vizier Mahomet-Kioprili, had little by little taken possession of the entire island, with the exception of the principal town, which the Venetians were holding by desperate efforts against an enemy that unceasingly recruited its losses, and advanced slowly but with indefatigable tenacity. The French fleet, continuing its course, sees before it a country bearing traces of long and cruel devastation. The mountains shorn of their forests to meet the necessities of war, present their bare and ravaged sides to the view. The soil is untilled and arid. Beside immense quarries rise lofty engines for throwing stones upon the besieged. To the deep silence of these solitudes succeeds the reverberations of artillery, whose detonations, at first confused, soon become quite distinct. At times a flash of reddish flames is suddenly perceived,—it is an advanced work blown up by a mine; at others a shell rapidly traverses the air, and, perhaps, lights upon and destroys a building of the town. At last, just as the soldiers, crowded upon the decks, reach the end of their voyage, their attentive looks discern the camp of the Turks, surmounted by waving banners and protected by breast-works, sandy spots where the cavalry are exercising, vast stores of arms, machinery at work, wounded being carried on litters, a formidable army in a state of commotion, animation, movement, and life; and, in the background, standing out from the horizon, the ramparts of Candia over-looked by its silent steeples, its almost deserted towers, with here and there some domes which glitter in the sun.

The evening following their arrival, Beaufort, Navailles, and the general officers, cautiously left the roadstead where the squadron had cast anchor, and in a little row-boat, with carefully muffled oars, succeeded in eluding the vigilance of the Turks, and in penetrating into the port of the besieged town.[8] Their disappointment on arriving there was extreme; and after having been witnesses, during the day, of the energy and vigour displayed by the besiegers, they convinced themselves, during the evening, of the dejection and impotence of the defenders of Candia. Whilst the Ambas-

---

[8] Letters of Saint-André-Montbrun :—Manuscripts of the Imperial Library. Letters from Navailles to the King :—Archives of the Ministry of Marine.

sador of the Venetian Republic had affirmed at Versailles that their number still amounted to 14,000 men, it was, in reality, reduced to 6,000 combatants, who, discouraged and ill, considered the loss of the town as inevitable, and continued to fight through duty, but without hope.[9] The gunners had nearly all perished in the subterranean galleries, where the Turks had pursued them with the implacability of fanaticism. Of the two principal bastions of the place, one, the Bastion Saint-Andrew, was already in the power of the enemy; and the Venetians were too weak to preserve the other—that of the Sablonnière—much longer. The streets, blocked up with rubbish, scarcely afforded a passage for the troops. Here and there smoking ruins, in the midst of an open space, bore witness to a recent fire. Far apart were houses, their upper stories turned into casemates, and looking like isolated citadels, where the unhappy inhabitants had crowded to take refuge. In the open places were to be seen a few soldiers pacing up and down in silence, or perhaps some wounded being carried from the trenches and accompanied by a priest. Everywhere were the certain signs of utter discouragement and of approaching defeat.

"The universal opinion is that the town can only be succoured by a general engagement," wrote the Intendant Delacroix to France.[10] He expressed the opinion of the Council, which had assembled on the 20th at Candia. This was unanimous; and Saint-André-Montbrun,[11] Beaufort,

---

[9] Letter from Navailles to the King, July 5, 1669.

[10] Letter from Delacroix to Louvois, June 22, 1669 :—Archives of the Ministry of War.

[11] The Marquis de Saint-André-Montbrun, a French nobleman, had been for several years in Candia, and by his courage and talents had finished by becoming, under Morosini, the chief general of the Venetians.

Morosini (the captain-general of the Venetians), as well as Navailles, saw some chances of success only in a vigorous sortie from the side of the Sablonnière. There, in truth, a portion of the Turks were separated from their principal army, and exposed to the cross-fire of the town and fleet, and ran, moreover, the danger of being driven into the sea, which was close at hand.

The definitive plan of attack was determined on in a final Council of War, held on the 24th, at seven o'clock in the evening, and its execution fixed for the middle of the following night. Beaufort assembled on board his ship all the captains of the army; and the disembarkation of troops, which commenced at nine o'clock in large and strong launches, was finished, without impediment, by midnight.[12] As each company disembarked, it proceeded to the esplanade situated by the side of the bastion of the Sablonnière. Surprise being the principal condition of success, the officers gave their orders in a low voice, and the soldiers advanced, with many precautions. The troops of Candia not on duty in the bastions were only informed of the plan of attack at one in the morning by their chiefs, who came to awake them, and lead them to their post. When the clock of the church of Saint-Mark struck two, the foot-soldiers were all assembled on the esplanade.[13]

---

[12] *Rélation de ce qui s'est passé dans la sortie qui s'est faite en Candie par toutes les troupes du roy, tant de terre que de mer, pour l'attaque du camp de la Sablonnière, le 25 du mois de Juin*, 1669 :—Archives of Ministry of Marine, Campagne 3. In my account I have chiefly followed this unpublished manuscript, which has every sign of authenticity.

[13] *Rapport adressé par le sieur Brodart à Colbert, à la radde de Candie, à bord de la Princesse, le 27 Juin*, 1669:—Manuscripts of the Imperial Library, *Papiers Colbert*, 153 *bis*. Unpublished document.

In spite of their number, nothing save the pale reflection of their muskets betrayed their presence. Immovable and silent, they awaited the signal of departure; and on this calm and peaceful night, which was about to be marked by a bloody struggle, one heard as yet only the regular and monotonous footsteps of the sentinels on the ramparts. Soon the dull trot of horses advancing over the sand is joined to it. Two hundred of the King's musketeers and five companies of cavalry have come to reinforce the infantry, and are followed by Beaufort, Navailles, and a numerous staff. After having given the countersign,[14] and confided his young nephew, the Chevalier de Vendôme, to the watchful care of the Marquis de Schomberg and the Baron de Saint-Mark, charged to follow him everywhere in the fight,[15] Beaufort addresses a few brave and energetic words, to those about him,[16] and the command is given to advance in silence. The soldiers placed under De Navailles' orders went towards the right. Beaufort was to occupy the left with a large portion of the marines and with his guards, commanded by Colbert de Maulevrier, the Minister's brother. It was arranged that the two divisions should reunite at a signal to be given by that of Navailles.[17]

Arrived at a point very near to the Turks, Beaufort's troops, in order to wait till the night should be less

---

[14] The countersign was : "Louis and forward !"

[15] *Rélation de ce qui s'est passé dans la sortie,* &c., already quoted. This was the nephew, who became the famous Vendôme. He displayed on June 25, 1669, very great courage, and was rather seriously wounded.

[16] *Le siège de Candie,* manuscript of Philibert de Jarry :—Imperial Library.

[17] Letter from Colbert de Maulevrier to his brother Colbert. "At Candie, this Sunday, the last day of June, at five o'clock in the evening:" —Manuscripts, Imperial Library, *Papiers Colbert,* 153 *bis.*

obscure, and to give Navailles, who had a longer distance
to traverse, time to reach the designated spot, lay down
on their stomachs, admiral, soldiers, and officers—the latter
occupying themselves only with the concealing of the links,
and with recommending, in a low voice, the most minute precautions.   Three-quarters of an hour before daybreak the
drums of the Turks were heard.   Some sailors, at Beaufort's
orders, approached the Turkish camp by crawling; and,
returning in the same manner, brought the intelligence that
it was only the usual *réveillée* which had just been beaten,
and that the enemy were in complete ignorance of the
danger which menaced them.[18]   The troops remained extended on the ground, silent and motionless, and Beaufort
listened attentively to catch the signal indicating that
Navailles' division had commenced the attack.

This general had arrived with the same good luck at the
extreme right.   After having been joined there by his reserve
and his rearguard, he sent the former, commanded by the
Count de Choiseul, a little to the westward of Candia, so
as to prevent any communication between the two Turkish
camps, and kept his rearguard with him, in order to
protect the most threatened points.   Then he led forward
Dampierre's corps, charged to commence the attack, and
creeping towards a little hill, which afforded him a good
view, he awaited the result.

Meanwhile, Beaufort, although sure of the quietude and
inaction of the Turks, was with difficulty restraining his
fiery impatience, when, half an hour before dawn, he heard
at the extreme right a deafening discharge of musketry.
Immediately he arose, and all his troops with him, ordered

---

[18] *Rélation*, &c., already quoted:—Archives of the Ministry of Marine.

a salute to be beaten and the charge sounded, and springing to the head of the first battalion, cleared the entrenchment which defended the Turkish camp. Colbert, followed by the company of Guards, rushed towards the left, with the intention of surrounding the adversary. With equal impetuosity they all traversed a ravine which they encountered in the rear of the entrenchment, and without suffering themselves to be checked in their onslaught by the stony nature of the soil, carried at the first attack the trenches of the enemy, who abandoned them after having fired off their arms. The surprise and fright of the Turks were extreme. They fled in disorder, pell-mell; and many of those who escaped Beaufort threw themselves into the sea, pursued by Dampierre's troops. All at once, towards the right, an immense flash of fire was seen, and a fearful explosion shook the ground. The soldiers and sailors surrounding Beaufort stopped suddenly; but he, without appearing alarmed by this noise, the cause of which he did not know, exclaimed, " Courage, children ! courage ! Since they spring a mine in our front, it is a sign that they are flying." He succeeded for a moment in overcoming the terror of his troops, and even prevailed on them to advance a few paces.[19] But on the detachment commanded by Dampierre the effects of this terrible catastrophe were something very different. Caused by the explosion of a magazine, containing twenty-five tons of powder, which had been set alight through the imprudence of a musketeer, it had destroyed an entire battalion of French Guards, and had produced everywhere an unspeakable terror. The troops

---

[19] *Rélation*, &c., already quoted :—Archives of the Ministry of Marine.

were persuaded that the enemy had undermined the whole of their works, and that the ground they were marching over was about to open under their feet. From point to point did this belief spread, until the terrified soldiers threw away their arms and fled with precipitation. It was in vain that Navailles, Dampierre, and the other general officers endeavoured to restrain them. The panic became universal, and the shameful and dreadful cry of "*Sauve qui peut !*" resounded from all parts. This disorder was increased still more by an error which even the obscurity of the night can scarcely explain. The fugitives, meeting Beaufort's sailors, threw themselves upon them as enemies. The long garments of seven or eight Armenians who were at their head, contributed, it seems, to confirm a fatal mistake.[20] In this horrible *mêlée* no one recognized any one else, and fellow-countrymen killed one another in the belief that they were slaying the infidels. Beaufort, utterly abandoned, endeavoured to correct this disastrous error.[21] On his wounded horse, covered with blood and with his clothes rent, he threw himself into the midst of the agitated groups, exclaiming, "To me, my children ! I am your admiral. Rally around me !"[22] Heroic, but unavailing efforts ! Supreme appeal of a voice till then so dear, but now unrecognized—a voice which had just uttered its last words ! The bewildered soldiers remained insensible to these generous supplications, and it was only when daylight began to

---

[20] *Mémoires de Saint-André-Montbrun*, pp. 362, 363.

[21] *Rélation de ce qui s'est passé en la sortie faite sur le camp des Turcs du côté de la Sablonnière, la nuict du 24ᵉ au 25ᵉ Juin*, 1669, *en Candie :*— Archives of the Ministry of War, 238. "M. l'Amiral remained abandoned by all his marines, and did not have a single one of his guards with him."

[22] *Rélation*, &c., already quoted:—Archives of the Ministry of Marine.

illumine this field of carnage that the confusion ceased with the cause which had produced it. But then the Turks, who had had time to recover their courage, and who proved themselves as prompt in rallying as they had been alert in taking to flight, rushed on, shouting the name of the Prophet, and with irresistible impetuosity became in their turn assailants, and pursued the French to the very gates of Candia.[23]

When, under the shelter of the ramparts, an account was taken of the loss, and after the wounded who had managed to reach the town had been examined, Beaufort's absence was perceived. Those who explain this absence by an abduction which Colbert, his enemy, had ordered, do not fail to note the presence of the Minister's brother, Colbert de Maulevrier, by the side of Beaufort during the battle, and they see in the commandant of the Guards the executioner of the Minister's vengeance. But how can this singular belief be held, when a letter from Maulevrier to his brother, the first which he wrote to him after the battle, far from giving the Minister an account of Beaufort's abduction, contains these words:[24]—" The unhappy fate of M. l'Amiral is the most deplorable thing in the world. ·· As I was obliged to go backwards and forwards during the whole time that the attack lasted, in order to assemble what I could of the troops, there was no one of whom I did not make inquiries respecting him,[25] and not one could ever tell me anything of

----

[23] Navailles, despairing of being able to save Candia, re-embarked his troops at the end of August, and set sail on the 31st; but as we are only occupied here with Beaufort, there is no need to relate the end of an expedition which the disaster of June 25 had caused to miscarry.

[24] Manuscripts of the Imperial Library, *Papiers Colbert*, 153 *bis.*

[25] This was of course during the battle.

him." It is true that these words, if they destroy the supposition of an abduction ordered by Colbert, may still allow it to be supposed that Beaufort was a prisoner of the Turks. But the laconism of this portion of the letter is accounted for when one discovers from the remainder of it that the writer was suffering from his wounds, worn-out with fatigue, and solely preoccupied with his restoration to health. It is true again that Navailles, in his despatch, makes use of the word *perte*,[26] applicable equally to the death of the Admiral and to the hypothesis that he was a prisoner in the hands of the Turks. But how can a single doubt remain when the account addressed to the Minister of Marine states that the Chevalier de Flacourt, having been sent to the Turkish camp with a flag of truce, for the purpose of making inquiries respecting the Admiral, learned that he was not among the prisoners;[27] and when a report addressed to Colbert on the 27th, not by a sick man, deprived of news, but by a witness in a position to know everything, infers that the Admiral was dead?[28] How can one have any further doubts, above all, when the circumstances just related, and the courage displayed by this bold adventurer, render this end so probable? That the age of Beaufort, born in 1616, which would make the mysterious corpse of

---

[26] Archives of the Ministry of War, 238.

[27] *Rélation*, &c., already quoted:—Archives of the Ministry of Marine.

[28] Manuscripts of the Imperial Library, *Papiers Colbert, Rapport adressé par le sieur Brodart à Colbert*, &c., already quoted. [The biographies of the Duke de Beaufort say it was commonly believed at the time that, according to the barbarous custom of the Turks, his dead body was beheaded by them, which would account for its not having been found on the field of battle.—See *Biographie Universelle* of Michaud, &c.—*Trans.*]

1703 a nonagenarian, almost suffices to overthrow the system of Lagrange-Chancel and Langlet-Dufresnoy, is incontestable. But this proof not having appeared sufficiently decisive to these writers, it became essential to seek for every kind of testimony, in order, so far as was just, to restore to this grandson of Henri IV. the glory of having died with arms in his hand on the field of battle, and of having thus crowned a life of adventures by an end worthy of his valour, his race, and his country.

CHAPTER XI.

General Considerations on the Abduction of the Armenian Patriarch Avedick—Despatch of the Marquis de Ferriol to Constantinople as Ambassador—Difficulties peculiar to this Post—Incautious Conduct of some of Ferriol's Predecessors—Quiclet's Adventures—Portrait of Ferriol — His Pretensions at Constantinople — His Eccentricity of Manner—His Behaviour in Religious Matters—The Armènian Church—Short Account of its History—Ardent Desire of the Catholic Missionaries to make Converts—Their Imprudence — Ferriol at first attempts to repair it — Obstinate Resistance of Father Braconnier, a Jesuit—Encroachments and Requirements of the Jesuits.

WE now come to the story of a most audacious violation of the law of nations, conceived by the fanaticism of an ambassador, ventured upon in a friendly country, with a singular boldness and energy, accomplished by stratagem and imposture, and thus kept from the knowledge of an entire people. The high rank of the victim, the character of the means employed, the ardour of the passions then excited, give an especial importance to this act of violence, which was crowned by a *dénoûment* as startling as up to the present it was little known. People were aware that an Armenian Patriarch, who combined with his civil power enormous religious authority, had been carried off from Constantinople towards the end of Louis XIV.'s reign.

But what became of him afterwards, and what adventures terminated the existence of this personage who had been rudely snatched away from his country and precipitated from the pinnacle of honour and the highest dignity? Must we see in him the mysterious prisoner of the Isles Sainte-Marguerite, as Taulès and the grave German historian Hammer have affirmed?[1] Or, as others believe, did he rather end his days in the *bagne* of Marseilles, or in the obscurity of a prison of Messina, or, more likely still, in one of the dungeons of the Inquisition?[2] What were the real causes of this extraordinary crime, which almost made the Sultan link himself with the numerous enemies of Louis XIV., and how did this monarch, vanquished and crushed by a coalition which was already formidable, contrive to appease the resentment of the Ottoman Porte? Such are the points which documents, entirely unpublished and of indisputable authenticity, will enable us to make clear. And this we shall do with the sole desire for truth, and without seeking to exaggerate or to extenuate the responsibility attaching to the authors of the crime. The more profound the mystery with which it has been surrounded, the more necessary it is to entirely penetrate it, and, after so many deeds which justly entitle Louis XIV. to admiration and gratitude, the more necessary also is it not to leave in obscurity, the only

---

1 *L'Homme au Masque de Fer, Mémoire Historique, par le Chevalier de Taulès, Ancien Consul-général en Syrie*, Paris, 1825. Hammer, *Histoire de l'Empire Ottoman depuis son Origine jusqu'à nos Jours*, vol. xiii. p. 187. M. Ubicini, *Lettres sur la Turquie*, Paris, Dumaine, 1854, part ii. p. 256.

2 Aubry de la Motraye, *Voyage en Europe, Asie, et Afrique*, La Haye, 1727, 2 vols. in folio, vol. i. p. 371. Didot's *Biographie Universelle*, article " Avedick."

one perhaps where he has made use of the worst of violences, that which is aided by lying and hypocrisy.

In 1699, Louis XIV. appointed the Marquis de Ferriol his ambassador at Constantinople. This post was beset with difficulties. To represent among Mussulmen a highly Catholic nation; and in a country divided among several dissenting Churches, to be the natural and appointed pro- tector of a very small Latin minority, unceasingly aspiring to increase in number, and encouraged in proselytism by ardent and active missionaries; to restrain the often thought- less zeal of these missionaries, and, moreover, to prevent this Latin minority from ceding to the offers of the German Empire and placing themselves under its protection;[3] to defend the interests of merchants, more and more exact- ing in their demands, often unjust in their complaints,[4] and whose encroachments met with opposition not only from the Turks, but especially from the English, the Genoese, and the Venetians; to act in the name of an extremely haughty monarch near a very touchy Government, and one still too much isolated and too much aloof from the great enterprises of Europe for it to give Louis XIV.

---

[3] Instructions given to M. de Ferriol on his departure for Constan- tinople :—Archives of the Ministry of Foreign Affairs, section Turkey, 33.

[4] And often abusing the ignorance of the Turks. "It is very sad," writes Louis XIV. to Ferriol, February 15, 1707, "that the French bring themselves into discredit by their failures, and that the Turks set them the example of that good faith which they ought to observe in commerce."—Archives of the Ministry of Foreign Affairs, section Turkey, 44. "There are no people in the world so easily deceived and who have been more deceived than the Turks. They are naturally simple and dull, and ready in believing. Thus it is customary for the Christians to impose upon them in a variety of ways and to play them many scandalous tricks."—Chardin, *Voyage en Perse et autres lieux de l'Orient,* vol. i. p. 17, Langlès' edition.

credit for the as yet continued success of his arms and the brilliancy of his reign ; to maintain the misunderstanding between the Germans and the Turks, by inducing the former to send assistance to the rebellious Hungarians, and to keep up the resentment of the Porte against the Venetians, but nevertheless without going to the extremity of causing it to break out in war ; to live in the midst of manners altogether peculiar and in certain respects always barbarous, to imitate Asiatic luxury, and to submit to customs [5] which were sometimes extremely onerous ; to assist at frequent and unexpected *révolutions de palais*, which would in a day upset the policy of the Divan and baffle every project : such was then the delicate task of the French ambassadors at Constantinople.

The constant assistance which Louis XIV. had as yet lent to the enemies of the Turks made the position of his representatives, more difficult still. One day, when one of them recalled to the Grand Vizier, Kiuproli-Ogli, the old alliance of France and Turkey, and evoked the recollections of the time of Francis I., " I do not know," answered Kiuproli, "if the French are our allies ; but it is certain

---

[5] We may quote among these usages, the obligation imposed upon the ambassadors of making a superb present to the Grand Vizier, not only when they first arrived at Constantinople, but at every change of Grand Vizier, which happened very frequently. Some of these presents cost as much as nine thousand livres, a rather large sum at that period. They consisted especially of clocks, watches, and mirrors:— Archives of the Ministry of Foreign Affairs, section Turkey, *Mémoires des Dépenses*. "In one year," writes Ferriol, "I have made four presents to four chief viziers, Daltahan, Ramy, Achmet, and Assat-Pacha, and to the whole of the households. It costs me more than 20,000 livres." Despatch from Ferriol to the Count de Pontchartrain, of December 4, 1703:—Archives of the Ministry of Foreign Affairs, section Turkey.

they are invariably to be found among our enemies. There were six thousand of them at the passage of the Raab. Your Admiral, Beaufort, attacked Gigery, and made a cruel war on the Moors placed under our protection, and you have assisted the Venetians in Candia." Far from having appeased these very legitimate feelings of resentment, Ferriol's predecessors had excited them still more by most imprudent acts. Sometimes, even, they had resorted to violence in order to get rid of a difficult situation, and had had recourse to those arbitrary acts of authority, of which the Sultan, it is true, often set them an example in his seraglio, but which should have been impossible to the representatives of a civilized nation.

It was thus that La Haye, ambassador at Constantinople in 1659, did not scruple to free himself by a crime from an extreme peril in which his very equivocal conduct had placed him.[6] France was succouring Candia, besieged by the Turks. It was an assistance quite natural and assuredly very praiseworthy ; but what was less honourable, the French ambassador carried on with the Venetians a continued secret intercourse, and, in a cypher correspondence, kept them informed of all the designs of the Turks. One day the person charged to carry his mysterious news to the Venetians betrayed him, and, seduced by the bait of a reward, presented himself to the Caïmacan[7] of Constantinople and announced that he wished to embrace the Mahometan faith, and to deliver to the Grand Vizier himself a packet of letters

---

[6] Archives of the Ministry of Foreign Affairs, section Turkey *1*, *Mémoires et Documents.*

[7] The Caïmacan is a lieutenant of the Grand Vizier who remains at Constantinople and fills his place when he follows the Sultan to Adrianople.

of great importance. The Ottoman Minister, who already had suspicions of this intercourse, eagerly received the proofs brought to him, but it was in vain that he tried to decipher them, and neither the interpreters nor the renegades who swarmed at the Sultan's court, could penetrate the secret of the intercepted letters. In the meanwhile there arrived at Constantinople a Frenchman, named Quiclet, an adventurer without resources, who boasted of having acquired by long practice the science of deciphering letters without a key. Badly received by La Haye, to whom he had applied for pecuniary assistance, he had the imprudence to menace him with his vengeance, and his wife said to the people of the embassy, " His Excellency refuses money to my husband, but we know very well how to obtain it from the Grand Vizier." La Haye became alarmed when informed of this speech. He feared lest this wretched intriguer might really be able to decipher the despatches, or failing this, might, by aid of his imagination, render them more compromising still. He grew agitated. He saw his life in danger, and his character as Louis XIV.'s ambassador at stake. He sends for Quiclet to the embassy, giving him hopes of assistance. The latter, as imprudent in his confidence as he had been thoughtless in his threats, hastens to the palace. La Haye leads him, while talking, on to a terrace overlooking the embassy garden; some servants throw themselves upon him, and others, posted at the spot where he falls, kill him and inter him there.[8]

This characteristic deed serves as a fitting prologue to the story of the not less revolting abuse of force which

---

[8] Archives of the Ministry of Foreign Affairs, section Turkey 1, *Mémoires et Documents.*

marked the embassy of Ferriol, who was as unscrupulous as La Haye upon the choice of means, and whose implacable animosity knew how to strike the most eminent personages as well as intriguers of low degree. In truth, every expedient appeared to him suitable to be adopted, provided that it was of a nature to aid him in the accomplishment of his designs; and his adventurous and agitated past already announced the new ambassador's line of conduct.

It was by intrigue rather than by his talents that the obscure gentleman of Dauphiné managed to rise by degrees, and from simple King's musketeer to become ambassador at Constantinople. Compelled to quit France, in consequence of a love-affair, and Poland, where he had taken refuge, because of a violent dispute at a gaming-party,[9] compromising the friends who had given him hospitality, but succeeding, nevertheless, in preserving them as active architects of his fortune, Ferriol went first to Candia to fight against the Turks, and then on their side in Hungary against the Imperialists.[10] Instead of confining himself to his military duties, he interfered in matters of diplomacy, gave an account of them to Louis XIV., gained himself supporters in the Turkish camp, and brought his services under the notice of the Marquis de Torcy by means of Madame de Ferriol, his sister-in-law,[11] who possessed great influence

---

[9] With a rich Pole, named Krazcinski:—Archives of the Ministry of Foreign Affairs, section Turkey, supplement 1.

[10] *Correspondance de Ferriol.—Ibid.*

[11] The ambassador was never married. This Madame de Ferriol, his brother's wife, mixed in the best society of Paris, and enjoyed considerable influence with the high personages of the State. She was the sister of the famous Abbé de Tencin, Cardinal, Minister of State, and Archbishop of Lyons, and also of the celebrated nun, notorious for her

over the Minister. This was not all. Not content with increasing the number of his supporters, he made himself the unjust, passionate, and tenacious adversary of the Abbé de Châteauneuf, ambassador at Constantinople. As eager to injure him as he was industrious to give himself importance, he calumniated the man whose post he coveted, and knew, which appeared difficult, how to interest the piety of Louis XIV. in the recall of an ambassador who was a priest, and whom his enemy accused of an inclination for the Turkish religion.[12] To gain his ends by means of an imputation so utterly improbable and so strange was a proof of extreme cleverness, and was doubtless the reason why he was recompensed by Louis XIV. sending him to replace the Abbé de Châteauneuf at Constantinople.

But Ferriol showed less ability in the performance of his functions than he had displayed in obtaining his post. At a time when the most prudent moderation was indispensable, he exhibited, from the day of his arrival, the signs of the most fervid impetuosity, which was already a kind of disease in him, and which, becoming more and more exuberant and excessive, was to degenerate, ten years later, into a species of insanity. In all countries there are certain distinctions which Princes reserve for themselves, and which, for this reason and out of the commonest politeness, ambassadors take care not to appropriate. In Spain, formerly, the Sovereign alone could drive through Madrid in

---

debauchery, the mistress of Dubois and mother of d'Alembert, by the Chevalier Destouches :—*Mémoires de Saint-Simon*, vol. xi. p. 182. Chéruel's edition. See also *Vézelay*, historical study by M. Aimé Chérest, vol. iii. p. 83.

[12] Archives of the Ministry of Foreign Affairs, section Turkey, *Mémoires et Documents*, I.

a coach drawn by six mules.   At Constantinople, the Sultan
and the Grand Vizier exclusively enjoyed the privilege of
sailing on the waters of the Bosphorus in a boat covered by
an awning lined with purple.[13]   Neither the Mufti, the other
grandees of the Porte, nor any foreign representative would
have dared to have usurped to himself what was considered
in Turkey as a peculiar honour.   Ferriol refused to submit
himself to this custom, up to that time respected by every
one.   But on his first appearance in a caïque similar to the
Grand Seignior's, the Bostanji-Bachi[14] ordered a hundred
blows with the stick to be given to the *caichis* who
had manned the boat of the vain-glorious ambassador, and
caused the latter to be informed that on the occasion of a
second infraction he should fire upon and sink it.   Although
aware that ambassadors ought to present themselves un-
armed before the Sultan, and that, as a matter of favour,
a court-sword[15] was sometimes allowed, Ferriol completely
estranged the Turks by attending the Imperial audience
armed with a long rapier.   He not only had contentions
with the officers of the Divan, but also with the other
ambassadors.   Some French deserters from the German
army had aggravated their offence by going to brave, even
in his palace, Count d'Ortinghem, the representative of
the Empire, who had them arrested, less for their desertion
than to punish their arrogance.   Ferriol immediately ordered

---

[13] Archives of the Ministry of Foreign Affairs, Correspondence from
Turkey, I.

[14] Chief of the Bostanji, the Sultan's Guards.

[15] This at least is what was permitted to De Castagnères, Abbé de
Châteauneuf, who informed Louis XIV. that he had been admitted into
the Seraglio with his sword.   But it was very short, and did not attract
attention.

two officers of the German embassy to be carried off by force. Justly irritated, D'Ortinghem demanded their release. The two sides armed themselves. The subjects of each country were called together. A fight was about to stain with blood the streets of Constantinople, and it was only the energetic interference of the representative of Holland that prevented it.[16]

For this inflexibility of character, this haughtiness of conduct, and eccentricity of manners, the pomp and brilliancy of Ferriol's receptions, and his profound knowledge of the country in which he resided, were not sufficient compensation. Well informed of all the affairs of the Levant, he thoughtlessly compromised a precious experience by his impetuous decisions and utter absence of all propriety and decorum. The boldness of certain means attracted more than their illegality restrained him. Being entirely ignorant of the art of gradually smoothing down a difficulty, and, by using time as an auxiliary, of carefully managing obstacles, he blindly threw himself upon them, believing himself able to overcome them by a prompt and hazardous recourse to violence. There still remained in him much of the adventurous Candia volunteer.

. Nevertheless, in religious matters, Ferriol did not at first show himself so audaciously arbitrary as he was afterwards to become. This man, who subsequently allowed himself to be enticed by the missionaries into the most tyrannical and violent resolutions, endeavoured at the commencement of his embassy to restrain their imprudent and immoderate zeal. Everything, moreover, engaged him to it. Every-

---

[16] Archives of the Ministry of Foreign Affairs, section Turkey, *Mémoires et Documents*, 1.

thing should have determined him to persevere in this policy of circumspection which the instructions received from Louis XIV., the character of the schismatic Armenians, and the blamable excesses of the Jesuits equally made a duty to him. "His Majesty orders you," it had been written to Ferriol, "to accord to the Jesuit fathers a protection conformable to the zeal which they show for religion, to their disinterestedness, and to the regularity of their manners. . . . . . Nevertheless, you must beware of the inconsiderate zeal which the missionaries sometimes carry too far; religion often suffers more prejudice from imprudent undertakings or untimely demands than it acquires real advantages of success."[17]   Wise words, too soon disregarded both by him to whom they were addressed, and by the Prince in whose name they had been written, and which, singularly prophetic, announced seven years in advance the misfortunes which the forgetfulness of this judicious warning was to bring upon the Catholics.

No church deserved more than that of the schismatic Armenians the employment of that moderation and prudence so opportunely recommended by Louis XIV. to his ambassador. Naturally good and peaceable, and of a sociable and kind temper, the Armenians readily became intimate with strangers, and had no quarrels with them, except in instances when their own interests were wronged.[16] Long since driven from their ancient kingdom by conquest, or

---

[17] Instructions given to M. de Ferriol, ambassador:—Archives of the Ministry of Foreign Affairs, section Turkey, 33.

[18] This is the testimony which the Jesuits themselves have borne in several accounts; Father Monnier, *Mémoires des Missionnaires de la Compagnie de Jésus*, vol. iii. pp. 46–52; Father Fleuriau, *État présent de l'Arménie*, Paris, 1694. 12mo.

having voluntarily emigrated through the necessities of their commerce, they were dispersed over a very extensive territory, and were encountered in large numbers, not only in the Turkish Empire and in Persia, but also in Tartary, and even in Poland. Everywhere they had acquired the reputation of being alike industrious and persevering. Eager in pursuit of gain, they excelled in commerce. Although losing more and more the recollection of their old country, they carefully preserved the unity of their church, and remained resolutely attached to their faith. They had adopted the language of the Turks, their costume,[19] everything in short save what concerned the Armenian religion, to which they showed themselves scrupulously faithful, and which they respected in every one of its practices as well as in its doctrines and its spirit. The severities which it imposed upon them did not dishearten them, neither did they consider themselves absolved, even by painful journeys, from long and austere fasts. Their churches were the most decorated and most crowded of all the East.[20] Their traditions seemed to them so much the more deserving of veneration because they were more ancient. Having preserved their nationality by means of their religion, tenacious and fertile of resources, they were interesting from their misfortunes, the firmness with which they endured them, and their industrious activity.

For a century past storms had at distant intervals disturbed their ordinarily peaceable state. These troubles, coming from without, were not due, as one might imagine,

---

19 *Lettres sur la Turquie*, by M. A. Ubicini, part 2, p. 252, Paris, Dumaine.

20 Father Monnier, work already mentioned:

to the persecutions of the conqueror. The Turks, tolerant by nature as well as out of obedience to their religion, looked upon all the Christian churches with equal scorn. If they interfered in the internal divisions of these churches, it was because they were engaged to do so by complaints, or else to profit by the voluntary gifts of one of the parties to the controversy. The punctual payment of the legal tribute sufficed to assure to a conquered people not only the free exercise of their religion, but also a material and efficacious support for their patriarchs and bishops.[21] Far from endeavouring to convert its Christian subjects to Mahometanism, the Divan received with extreme reserve and even discouraged those whom the greed of a reward excited to abandon the religion of Christ. Often rigorously exacting in maintaining their political rights, the Mahometans were disdainfully and absolutely indifferent with respect to the religion of the Christians.[22] Although persuaded of the excellence of Islamism, the Mussulman is altogether devoid of the spirit of propagandism. In his eyes the infidels are

---

[21] Hammer, *Histoire de l'Empire Ottoman.* Ubicini, *Lettres sur la Turquie.* Archives of Ministry of Foreign Affairs, section Turkey, *Mémoires et Documents,* 37.

[22] One day a stranger presented himself before the Grand Vizier, Raghib-Pasha, saying that Mahomet had appeared to him to invite him to turn Mussulman, and that he had come on purpose from Dantzic to be converted. "Here is a strange rascal," said the Grand Vizier. "Mahomet has appeared to an infidel, when for more than seventy years I have been exact in the five prayers, and he has never done me such an honour!" And the stranger did not become a Mussulman. "I have heard it said several times by doctors of Mahometan law that, according to their religion, it was not permitted to them to protect one party against another in the dispute which sprang up between the Catholics and the heretics, because, as they said, they were both equally bad." Manuscript *Mémoire* of 1771 on matters of religion :—Archives of Ministry of Foreign Affairs, section Turkey, 37.

not necessarily rejected; since, according to the Koran, " He who hath said there is only one God, he shall enter into Paradise." Moreover, *the number of the elect is fixed from all eternity*, and to endeavour to increase the number is useless as well as contrary to the commands of the sacred book. So they were ignorant of and could not understand that charity, admirable in principle although often carried to excess, which animated the Catholic missionary, inspiring in him a sublime abnegation, and determining him to leave his country, to cross deserts, to suffer and to die, in order to save a single soul and make it share in the consolations and hopes of his faith.

This ardour of propagandism, so highly beneficial to humanity when it serves to spread the beautiful morality of the Gospel among nations where it has not yet penetrated, was early made use of by the Holy See to cause not only idolaters, but also Christians whom very slight differences in doctrine separated from the Roman communion, to submit to its spiritual authority. In 1587, Sixtus V., desirous of removing these differences, sent the Bishop of Sidon to all the Armenian churches; he failed, however, in his attempt.[23] In 1622, there was founded at Rome, by Gregory XV., the congregation " for the propagation of the faith," to which Urban VIII., his successor, added the College of the Propaganda, where young men from every part of the world were instructed and prepared for their missions. At first they had the wisdom to pursue in the East methods of kindness and of persuasion, and by these means succeeded

---

[23] *Relazione di quanto ha trattato il Vescovo di Sidonia nella sua Missione in Oriente, data alla Santità di N.S. Sisto V., alli* 19 *Aprile,* 1587.

in gaining over a rather large number of dissenters. But success soon rendered the missionaries bolder, and too confident in the exclusive excellence of their own doctrines, they substituted for the clever circumspection they had hitherto shown, and the slow but certain influence of a persuasive impressiveness, a proselytism, ardent, impassioned, and too hasty in arriving at its ends. Instead of assisting dissenters to clear the narrow space which separated them from the Roman Church, by showing them how near they were to it,[24] instead of rendering prominent all the points which united them, they proceeded to attack with ill-timed perseverance the questions of liturgy to which the Armenian Church was especially attached. They forbade the Catholics, under the severest penalties, to enter other churches, and when they ought, by judicious indulgence, to have recognized in the majority of the Armenians brothers separated by their observances, but in a very slight degree by their doctrines, they treated them as enemies and barbarians. Justly irritated by this violent conduct, finding themselves subjected to scorn, and menaced in their dearest and most venerated traditions, the schismatics complained to the Divan, and represented the Jesuits not as envoys of peace, but as fomenters of discord and as conspirators, so much

---

[24] See M. Dulaurier's excellent work : *Histoire, Dogmes, Traditions et Liturgie de l'Église Arménienne Orientale,* Paris, Durand libraire, 1859. This book combats the generally received opinion that the Armenians have embraced monophysism, such as has been taught by Eutyches and his adherents, who recognized only the divine nature in Christ. Not only, in truth, have the Armenians always condemned Eutyches, whom their church excommunicates, but also they profess, like the Greek and Latin churches, the dogma of the two natures, the two wills, and the two operations in Jesus Christ.

more dangerous, because they were in the pay of foreign courts.[25]

Ferriol comprehended the imprudent behaviour of the Jesuits, and attempted to repair it. In 1701 he arranged a reconciliation between the principal dissenters and the chiefs of the Catholics, and succeeded in moderating the demands of the latter, and in appeasing the legitimate resentment of the former. A kind of treaty of union was drawn up, which, approved by the Grand Patriarch of Armenia, and by the Catholic archbishop, was to be submitted afterwards to the ratification of the Court of Rome, and was to regulate the future relations of the two churches. But the happy effects which would have resulted from this transaction were sacrificed by the implacable resistance which Father Braconnier, superior of the Jesuit mission in the East, opposed to it.[26] In vain Ferriol observed to him "that they were threatened with a general persecution of the Catholics throughout the Turkish empire; that the Sultan could issue severe orders, which would give a mortal blow to the religion by reason of the little firmness which the Catholics possessed, and that a persecution ought to be avoided when this could be done without injuring religion and without offending it." To these pressing reasons, inspired by humanity and foresight, Father Braconnier replied, "that the Church had formerly suffered persecutions much more cruel; that the Armenians ought to know how to

---

[25] Borée, *l'Arménie*, p. 54; Serpos, *Compendio storico sulla Nazione Armena*, p. 204, Venice, 1786; M. Ubicini, *Lettres sur la Turquie*, part 2, p. 254.

[26] Unpublished letter from Ferriol to Father Fleuriau, of November 4, 1701:—Archives of the Ministry of Foreign Affairs, section Turkey, 37.

suffer ; that he could not permit the Catholics to have the least communication with their schismatic brethren, and that they ought rather to expose themselves to the harshest treatment." [27]

Unfortunately Ferriol had neither sufficient firmness to make his opinion prevail, nor even perseverance to resolutely maintain it. All at once abandoning his attempt at reconciliation, he desperately threw himself into the party óf action much more suitable to his vehement character, and to his strong liking for contest, and also, we must admit, to the delicate position in which the encroachments of Rome and the requirements of the Jesuits placed him. The ambassador of the King of France at Constantinople was then indeed the representative of the Holy See quite as much as of the court of Versailles, and he submitted to the custom of corresponding regularly either with the Pope or with the principal cardinals. Whilst he rendered account to Louis XIV. of matters of commerce and of the political situation, the great religious interests formed the subject of periodical despatches addressed directly to Rome. Very jealous of his authority, Louis XIV. had pointed out the inconvenience of this correspondence, [28] then he had tolerated it, and, as often happens, the custom had grown into an obligation. On the other hand, the Jesuits had more and more exaggerated the importance of their part, and to the direct influence which the court of Rome exercised upon the French ambassador by its pressing

---

[27] Letter from Ferriol to Father Fleuriau, already referred to, in which Father Braconnier's own words are quoted.

[28] Archives of the Ministry of Foreign Affairs, Correspondence of Ferriol and Louis XIV., section Turkey.

despatches,[29] they added the effects of their constant recriminations, of their feverish and turbulent activity, of their audacious encroachments. Instructing the Holy See according to their own fancy and inspiring its orders; ruling Ferriol through Versailles quite as much as through Rome; ready to calumniate him if he ceased to be their tool, and even powerful enough to overthrow him; present and influential everywhere, they were in reality the masters of the situation, and their responsibility before history is as incontestable as their power.

While submitting to their yoke, Ferriol sometimes could not prevent himself from complaining of it. "All here wish to pass for ministers," he wrote to Torcy. "They believe themselves more enlightened than the ambassadors, and the order of each is reversed. These good fathers, who ought only to go to the convict-prison and the houses of Christians established in the country, do not abstain from visiting persons of power, and from imposing upon everybody in political affairs. When an ambassador wishes to reduce them within the bounds which seem to be prescribed for them, they treat him as a man devoid of religion who sacrifices everything to his ambition." [30] Assuredly this is the language of truth, everything proves it. But

---

[29] But only by its despatches. The court of Rome was very niggard of its money. "I pray your Majesty to have this account paid me," wrote Ferriol to the King, October 17, 1705, "since I receive from the court of Rome only briefs and indulgences."

[30] Unpublished letter of Ferriol to the Marquis de Torcy, Minister of Exterior Relations, April 5, 1704:—Archives of the Ministry of Foreign Affairs, section Turkey, 40. We read in another despatch from Ferriol to the Cardinal de la Trémouille, Louis XIV.'s ambassador at Rome: "Most of the missionaries complain directly they find the least obstacle to their desires. Patience is a great virtue which they rarely

although these complaints were well founded, although the domination of the Jesuits was then real enough, we cannot feel much concern for this voluntary victim of their encroachments. Not only, indeed, did Ferriol refrain from endeavouring to throw off their heavy yoke, although it sometimes weighed on his self-esteem ; but also, forgetting the character with which he was invested, and passing from a brief and honourable independence to a servile devotion, he became the executioner of the vengeance of a few missionaries with so much implacability, that in fighting their adversaries he seemed to be engaging his own personal enemies. His hatred, revived and cleverly kept up by baleful excitements, is about to docilely follow the direction indicated to it, and to strike without pity, to pursue without respite, to cause to disappear and overwhelm, a long time even after his own fall, a great Armenian personage whom it is now time to introduce in his turn into this story, and to make known to our readers.

---

practise, although very necessary for the proper cultivation of the Lord's vineyard :"—Unpublished letter of Ferriol, March 5, 1709, Archives of the Ministry of Foreign Affairs, section Turkey, 46.

CHAPTER XII.

Sprung from the ranks of the people, and belonging to a poor and obscure family of Tokat,[1] Avedick[2] had been early admitted into the number of *vertahieds*, or doctors charged with preserving and teaching the doctrines of the Armenian Church. Quickly· becoming bishop, and then archbishop, he had distinguished himself by his firmness, which Ferriol terms impudence, in supporting the interests of his co-religionists. The commencement of his long struggle with the French ambassador, in which the one

---

1 Archives of the Ministry of Foreign Affairs, section Turkey, *Déclaration Authentique de M. Pétis de la Croix, Secrétaire-Interprète du Roi en Langues Turque, Arabe, et autres Orientales*, which will be quoted hereafter.

2 Avedick or Arwedik, or Aviedik. In the present work Ferriol's orthography has been adopted.

showed a becoming loftiness and the other an extreme violence, and which was to terminate for Avedick by a terrible catastrophe, dates from a period earlier than the arrival of Ferriol as ambassador at Constantinople. The latter being in Hungary in the Turkish camp, and having heard of some disrespectful speeches of Avedick with reference to Louis XIV., had used his influence with the Grand Vizier to get the daring archbishop exiled.[3] But in December, 1701, the excessive rigour of this punishment was made amends for in a striking manner. The Grand Mufti, Feizoulah Effendi, nominally charged with spiritual affairs, but who in reality governed the entire Ottoman empire, by means of his ascendancy over the Sultan Mustapha II.,[4] was formerly, while at Erzeroum, where he had been Cadi, intimately acquainted with Avedick, like himself an inhabitant of this town. Sufficiently powerful to make and overthrow Grand Viziers, this chief dignitary of the Mussulman faith was able to create his friend "Armenian Patriarch of Constantinople and of Jerusalem." In vain did Ferriol demand from the Grand Chancellor of the empire and from the Kiaya of the Grand Vizier the confirmation of Avedick's exile. These two high personages answered the French ambassador[5] that the Mufti's power was supreme, his will in this instance irrevocable, and that it was as useless to wish to offer opposition to his determi-

---

[3] Unpublished despatch of Ferriol to the Cardinal de Janson, April 10, 1702 :—Archives of the Ministry of Foreign Affairs, section Turkey, 37.

[4] *Ibid.* "At this moment the Grand Mufti, so to speak, governs the empire."

[5] Unpublished despatch from Ferriol to Louis XIV., December 31, 1701 :—Archives of the Ministry of Foreign Affairs, section Turkey, 37.

nation, as any endeavour to shake his credit would be dangerous.

There remained to Ferriol nothing but submission. But he, as well as his ardent inspirers, conceived against the Armenian Patriarch, from that period, an implacable resentment, of which we find the proofs in every one of his despatches. Time increased this animosity, the effects of which were not slow in exhibiting themselves. Still at first nothing in the conduct of the chief of the Armenians justified this enmity. No doubt he showed himself less docile with regard to their pretensions than the Jesuits would have wished. No doubt he deceived the hope which they had conceived of buying him over to their side. But in spite of the obstacles raised by Avedick's co-religionists against the treaty of union which Ferriol had proposed, Avedick exhorted them to peace,[6] and for several years the two Churches maintained the most perfect concord. "The liberty allowed the Catholics is so great," writes Ferriol, May 1, 1703, "that every one admits that they could not enjoy more in a Christian country. The reverend Jesuit Fathers at Easter made the procession of Sainte-Anne, in the middle of Galata, carrying the cross, the banners, and the relics, with an infinite number of lighted candles and a prodigious assemblage of people. Formerly this ceremony was only performed within the walls of the church."[7] Instead of giving Avedick credit for this prosperous condition of affairs, Ferriol availed himself of the first pretext

----

[6] Unpublished letters of Ferriol to Count de Pontchartrain, May 11 and June 8, 1702, and to Louis XIV., October 2, 1702 :—Archives of the Ministry of Foreign Affairs, section Turkey, 39.

[7] Unpublished letter of Ferriol to Louis XIV., May 1, 1703 :—*Ibid.*

to attempt his overthrow. But it was in vain that he denounced him to the Kiaya of the Grand Vizier as having corrupted a courier and intercepted Louis XIV.'s despatches.[8] . This offence, then very common in Turkey, and for which, moreover, the exile demanded by Ferriol would have been a great deal too severe a penalty, remained unpunished, and the high protection of the Mufti continued to screen the Patriarch.

But on this stage of sudden revolutions and unforeseen overthrows, supreme power was then nearly always followed by a profound fall, brought about most frequently by a laconic order from the seraglio, though at times the clamour of the irritated populace was sufficient to precipitate the favourites of a day from the pinnacle of power, and in these frequent catastrophes the axe of the executioner was never inactive. At the moment when Avedick appeared likely to enjoy for a long time the powerful support of the Mufti, a formidable revolution broke out at Constantinople. Two hundred thousand men in arms demanded the presence of the Grand Seignior, insisting upon the observance of the law according to which he was not permitted in times of peace to absent himself from the capital; all the troops uniting with the people and the men of law, the troops to complain of not having been paid, the people to attribute their misery to the residence of the Sultan at Adrianople, the men of law to protest against the cupidity of the Mufti.[9] The latter had his throat cut, the Sultan, Mustapha II., was

---

[8] Unpublished letter from Ferriol to the Kiaya of the Grand Vizier, May 14, 1703 :—*Ibid.*

[9] Unpublished despatch from Ferriol to Louis XIV., July 23, 1703:—*Ibid.* The revolt commenced July 17.

deposed, and his brother, Achmet III., was drawn from the recesses of the seraglio and placed on the throne : such was the rapid revolution which all at once deprived Avedick of his protector and delivered him up to Ferriol's resentment. Indeed, less than two months afterwards, the Armenian Patriarch was deposed and imprisoned in the fortress of the Seven Towers,[10] and then, on the repeated entreaties of the ambassador, exiled to Abratadas in Syria. The Armenians refused to obey the new Patriarch, Kaisac, and demanded in vain their beloved chief.[11] Ferriol's influence was sufficiently great to allow him to indulge in the most minute and cruel precautions. Cast on a barren rock, far from Constantinople, the ex-Patriarch still seemed redoubtable. Ferriol, therefore, rendered his imprisonment as painful as possible, and with a barbarity the proofs of which one would hesitate to admit, if they did not èmanate from him who was guilty of it, he considered it necessary to have his victim shut up " in a dungeon full of water, and from which one could not see the daylight."[12] Ferriol mentions this refinement of cruelty in his despatches, without in the least appearing to regret it, and in his account, as well as in the replies of the King and the Ministers to whom he addresses himself, one seeks in vain, on the one hand, for an attempt at a justification, and, on the other, for a disavowal, or at least for an expression of surprise. In

---

[10] Unpublished despatch from Ferriol to Pontchartrain, September 18, 1703. The fortress of the Seven Towers was at that time the principal State prison of Constantinople.

[11] Unpublished despatches from Ferriol to Louis XIV., November 9, 1703, and from Ferriol to Pontchartrain, November 11, 1703 :— Archives of the Ministry of Foreign Affairs, section Turkey, 39.

[12] Despatch from Ferriol to Pontchartrain, June 12, 1704.

consequence of this silence the Government of Louis XIV. bears its share of responsibility for the barbarous conduct of its ambassador.

But the affection of the Armenians proved more powerful than Ferriol's hatred. The enormous sum of four hundred purses[13] was collected by the schismatics, and tempted the cupidity of the Grand Vizier and his principal officers. The promises made Ferriol were forgotten, and, a year after having been deposed, Avedick re-ascended the patriarchal throne.[14] "He has united himself with the Greeks," wrote Ferriol to Pontchartrain, "and I foresee terrible persecutions against the Catholics."[15] And, before assuring himself that there was any foundation for these fears, the ambassador, whose mind is fruitful in vigorous measures, immediately proposes a means, not of preventing persecution, but of avenging himself for it in advance, and continuing to set his enemies an example of violence. He requests the Pope

---

[13] Or in money of to-day, 880,000 francs (35,200*l.*) There used to be purses of silver and purses of gold, the latter much the less common and worth 6,750*l.* sterling, or 148,500 livres (francs). There can be no question that purses of gold are not referred to, since four hundred of these would amount to an exorbitant sum, beyond the resources of the richest Armenians. Moreover, when the word *purse* is used alone, it is to be understood in the sense of purse of silver:—*Encyclopédie des Sciences, des Arts, et des Métiers*, vol. x. p. 655 ; Edition of 1765. According to the *Notices et Extraits des Manuscrits de la Bibliothèque du Roi*, vol. i. p. 191, note S, the purse was worth 500 piastres. This piastre not being an imitation of the Spanish piastre, but a piece of money peculiar to Turkey, which in 1753 was worth 4 fr. 40 c. ; we thus get for the 400 purses, the sum collected by the Armenians, and mentioned in the despatch, the figure of 880,000 francs.

[14] Unpublished despatch from Ferriol to Pontchartrain, December 16, 1704 :—Archives of Ministry of Foreign Affairs, section Turkey, 41.

[15] *Ibid.*

and the Grand Master of Malta to arrest the Greeks and Armenians who navigate the waters of the Archipelago, or who may be found in the islands, and to take possession of their effects and guard their persons. As they had a very large number of vessels, and the isles were open and without defence against a sudden attack, the ambassador foresaw that the repression would necessarily be formidable.[16]

Which is the persecutor? This man so industrious in contriving these rigorous measures, so prompt in taking advantage of his enemies, or the Armenians, faithful to the religion of their fathers and withstanding an impassioned and ardent proselytism? Which are the persecuted? That since his exile to Abratadas, Avedick had conceived a violent hatred against the Catholics must be admitted, and one cannot be astonished at his having done so. But it is undeniable that, having quitted his prison and resumed his position as head of the Armenians, he dissimulated his resentment and lived in peace with the Catholic population. "He makes no move," wrote Ferriol on January 20, 1705, and on March 11: "He behaves with great respect, and religious affairs are very tranquil here." "Avedick causes no annoyance to the Catholics," we read in a despatch of August 13. But the ambassador immediately adds, "I hope that he will burst forth, and I shall not lose the occasion of destroying him."[17] "I shall not give him," writes he to the Cardinal de Janson, "a moment of rest; knowing him to be a very wicked man and capable of great dissimulation."[18]

---

[16] Unpublished despatch from Ferriol to Pontchartrain, of December 16, 1704 :—*Ibid.*

[17] Letters from Ferriol to Louis XIV. and to Cardinal de Janson.

[18] Archives of the Ministry of Foreign Affairs, section Turkey, 41.

With the view of consolidating a peace which he believed
might be made definitive, Avedick proceeded, on December 26, 1705, to the French embassy.[19]   He presented himself there neither as a suppliant nor out of bravado.   Accompanied by three hundred Armenians of good standing, he
came to propose to the representative of the Protector of
the Catholic religion in the Levant to forbid in his churches
the anathemas launched against certain heretics, and he
asked that the Jesuits, who had long since received permission to preach in the Turkish language in the Armenian
places of worship, should do so without passion and with
moderation.   Far from being disarmed by this proud but
by no means provocatory proceeding, Ferriol characterized
it as impudent,[20] and avowed that if he had not previously
given him a safe conduct, he should certainly have had the
Patriarch arrested.   His aversion suffered neither truce nor
repose.   Not feeling himself sufficiently powerful to arrive
single-handed at his ends, he stirred up among the Armenians themselves adversaries to his enemy.   He encouraged
the ambitious patriarch of Sissem, who aspired to replace
Avedick as Grand Patriarch, receiving him in the palace of
the embassy,[21] supporting him with his influence and aiding
him with his counsels.   At length, after a year of constant
efforts, of corruption practised among the officers of the
Divan, of threats, intrigues, and underhand manœuvres of
every kind, Ferriol had the satisfaction of being able to
announce to Louis XIV.[22] that Avedick had been deposed

---

[19] Letter from Ferriol to Pontchartrain, December 17, 1705.

[20] Archives of the Ministry of Foreign Affairs, section Turkey, 41.

[21] Unpublished despatch from Ferriol to Cardinal de Janson, September 16, 1705.

[22] Despatch of February 25, 1706.

for the second time, and for the third time sent into exile.

It was, then, with the view of rendering this fall final, and in order to disembarrass himself for ever of his enemy, that Ferriol imagined, in the middle of the eighteenth century, one of the most violent and strangest acts that a representative of a civilized nation could ever have dared to commit. It was he who had the sad honour of having conceived the plan. But a despatch,[23] which tells overwhelmingly against the Catholic missionaries, proves clearly that their incitement induced Ferriol to regard this act as indispensable, and that, by never ceasing to recall to the ambassador the pretended dangers which the Patriarch, exiled and powerless, still offered, they determined him in his resolution to have recourse to an abduction.

Avedick was deposed on February 25, 1706. Two months afterwards he was carried into exile. On April 20, he left Constantinople, which he was never to see again, and his beloved Armenians, from whom he was this time being separated for ever, and for whom, during the whole of their lives, he was about to become the object of anxious care, of constant regret, and of incessant but fruitless researches. Ferriol had bought over the *Chiaoux* in charge of the ex-Patriarch, and had forwarded instructions to the Sieur Bonnal, vice-consul at Chio, on his passage through

---

[23] Unpublished letter from Ferriol to Pontchartrain, February 2, 1708. "I have examined myself attentively, and if any one has urged me to a violent resolution against Avedick, I should say that it was Father Hyacinthe alone, who every day exaggerated to me his wickedness and crimes: "—Archives of the Ministry of Foreign Affairs, section Turkey, 45.

which Avedick had to stop for a few hours.[24]　It was here that a most audacious crime against the law of nations was committed.　Bonnal, assisted by Father Tarillon, a Jesuit,[25] had, according to Ferriol's injunctions, chartered a small merchant-vessel, commanded by a Frenchman, who received orders to proceed to Marseilles.　On his arrival at Chio, the bribed *Chiaoux* delivered up the great personage committed to his charge, and the representative of Louis XIV., accompanied by the Jesuit Tarillon, took possession of the Sultan's subject and imprisoned him on board the French ship.　There was no obstacle to the abduction, and the protestations of the old man against this abuse of force were vain, and remained without response.　During the voyage no pirates were encountered as Ferriol feared there might be,[26] and as, doubtless, the prisoner hoped for, since to fall into their hands would have been a hundred times preferable to the treatment which was reserved for him in France.　Nevertheless it was given to him to indulge in some hope.　Contrary winds drove the vessel to Genoa.[27]　There Avedick, watched over as he is by his gaoler, eludes his vigilance and confides to a Greek, named Spartaly, two letters, one addressed to Maurocordato, first interpreter of the Porte, the other to the Armenian

---

[24] Despatches from Ferriol to Louis XIV., May 6 and June 1, 1706, already given by the Chevalier de Taulès, with six others which we shall indicate when we have to make use of them.

[25] Memorandum of the Marquis de Bonnac, French ambassador to Turkey in 1724 :—Archives of the Ministry of Foreign Affairs.

[26] Letters from Ferriol to Pontchartrain, May 6, and to Louis XIV., June 1, 1706.

[27] Unpublished letter from Ferriol to Ponchartrain, February 19, 1707 :—Archives of the Ministry of Foreign Affairs, section Turkey, 45.

Theodat, in which he names the persons concerned in his abduction and demands vengeance. But misfortune seems to have been inexorable to the ex-Patriarch. Spartaly sailed to Smyrna on board an English ship, and was about to proceed to Constantinople with the revelatory letters, when he meets and imparts his secret to Justimany, another Greek of Chio, who forthwith sells his compatriot's secret to the French consul.[28] The latter, perfectly understanding the importance of the revelation, sends for Spartaly, buys him over in his turn, and detains him at Smyrna. Whilst he is sending to Ferriol the intercepted letters, which, instead of saving the prisoner, are about to draw down upon him greater rigour, Avedick, indulging in the belief that he can count upon their happy effect, and anticipating an early release, arrives at Marseilles, is delivered into the hands of M. de Montmor, intendant of the galleys, and thrown into the dungeons of the Arsenal.[29]

---

[28] Royer by name. All these details are taken from the unpublished despatch already quoted. Royer placed Justimany under the protection of France with the view of preventing him from being molested in the event of his treason being discovered.

[29] Letter from Ferriol to Louis XIV., June 1, 1706. Letter from Louis XIV., November 10, 1706. *Correspondance Administrative du Règne de Louis XIV.*, vol. iv. p. 255, collected by M. Depping and finished with much care by his son, M. Guillaume Depping, of the Bibliothèque Impériale. In this work several despatches relating to Avedick are given, of which we shall continue to indicate the source as we make use of them. It is by means of these despatches, and of the unpublished ones from the Ministry of Foreign Affairs, that we are enabled to relate the Patriarch's end, even to the smallest details.

CHAPTER XIII.

The Chevalier de Taulès—How he was led to believe that Avedick was the Man with the Iron Mask—A clear Proof furnished him of the impossibility of his Theory—Taulès persists and accuses the Jesuit Fathers of Forgery—Examination of Dujonca's Journal—Its complete Authenticity and the unaffected Sincerity of the Writer cannot be doubted—New Proofs of this Authenticity and of Dujonca's Exactitude.

" I HAVE discovered the Man with the Iron Mask, and it is my duty to render an account to Europe and to posterity of my discovery," exclaims the Chevalier de Taulès,[1] with a conviction which posterity does not share, and a solemnity of manner so little justified by results, that an extreme reserve is imposed on those who venture after him to engage in a pursuit so fruitful in checks.

The intelligence of this discovery was at first received with a confidence which was explained by the position of the individual who claimed to have made it. Sprung from one of the oldest and most respectable families of Bearn ; admitted, in 1754, into the gendarmes of the King's Guard ; starting, ten years afterwards, in the career of diplomacy, which he pursued always with honour, sometimes with success ; sent successively to Switzerland, Poland, and later

---

[1] *L'Homme au Masque de Fer : Mémoire Historique par le Chevalier de Taulès, ancien consul-général en Syrie*, p. 1.

to Syria, as consul-general ; corresponding on terms of friendship with Voltaire, who showed some deference for his opinions ;[2] M. de Taulès enjoyed among his contemporaries an authority due as much to the qualities of his mind as to his honourable character. He had lived through the first Empire without desiring to re-enter the service of the State, and had devoted to historical studies the leisure which his independent spirit had created. It was the perusal of an unpublished manuscript memorandum of the Marquis de Bonnac, ambassador at Constantinople, that revealed to Taulès the existence of the Grand Patriarch, Avedick, and his abduction by Ferriol. The writer of this memorandum added that Avedick had been afterwards sent to the Isles Sainte-Marguerite, and then transferred to the Bastille, where he had died. "On reading this passage," says Taulès, "the thought suddenly struck me that this individual might very well be the Iron Mask. Becoming subsequently more and more confirmed in this conjecture by a number of facts which the perusal of the memorandum had confusedly recalled to me, I said to myself, with fresh assurance, 'Yes, it is himself: this is the Iron Mask!'"[3]

In truth, this very natural thought must arise in the mind of every one who reads this memorandum; and if Taulès believed that he at length possessed the solution of the problem, there were many others who would have felt equally self-persuaded. His only fault—but it was a great

---

[2] From 1752 to 1768, Taulès and Voltaire had a long and interesting correspondence, published by Gaultier-Laguionie (Paris, 1825), at the end of various memoirs of Taulès.

[3] *L'Homme au Masque de Fer: Mémoire Historique,* p. 21.

one—was that of obstinately holding to this opinion when a more complete study of the question would have shown him his error; and of endeavouring to support his theory when it was being shattered, by an accusation of forgery as grave as it was unjust.

Assuredly, the interest which Louis XIV. had in hiding the existence of such a prisoner as Avedick, the indispensability there was of shrouding from every eye the victim of so enormous a crime against the law of nations, the necessity, too, of removing from the ex-Patriarch every means of informing the Ottoman Porte of the country where he was detained, the clamour which his disappearance had caused throughout the entire East, the precarious situation in which the King of France then found himself, constrained as he was to treat Turkey with consideration, were all so many arguments that crowded upon the mind in favour of Taulès' opinion. This theory presented, moreover, the advantage of explaining several circumstances, true or supposed, in the life of Saint-Mars' mysterious prisoner. For instance, the silence almost constantly observed by him, which caused it to be continually said that he was condemned to it under pain of death, was accounted for by the Armenian Patriarch's ignorance of our language. Again, that strange accent noticed by the surgeon Nélaton, in a visit made by him to the Bastille,[4] and which struck him in the few syllables articulated by the prisoner, finds its natural explanation in Avedick. The famous reply of Louis XV. to his valet-de-chambre, Laborde, who questioned him about the Man with the Iron Mask, " The imprisonment of this

---

[4] This has already been referred to in Chapter VIII. of this work. See page 93 *ante.*

unfortunate individual has wronged nobody but himself," applied sufficiently exactly to the Patriarch. Lastly, in default of those official despatches, which, to-day, a sovereign and indispensable proof, alone allow one to erect a theory upon a firm basis, the suggestion of Taulès united in its favour several strong presumptions, and did not at the outset meet with any fundamental objection.

But the originator was not to experience for long an unmixed joy. His conviction was most firmly rooted. " Perhaps nothing," he says, " has ever appeared to me so very plainly. *I do not more clearly feel my existence than I recognize the Patriarch in all the features of the Iron Mask."* [5] All at once, the Minister of Foreign Affairs,[6] who had ordered researches to be made among his archives, caused the Chevalier de Taulès to be informed that an important Armenian personage had really been abducted from Constantinople and taken to France, but that as indisputable despatches established the fact that he was still in Turkey during the early part of 1706, he could not be the prisoner brought by Saint-Mars from the Isles Sainte-Marguerite to the Bastille on September 18, 1698, and who died in that fortress on November 19, 1703. Taulès at first accepted with resignation this truly startling revelation. His theory was completely overthrown, his reasoning destroyed, his discovery annihilated. He acknowledged it. He regretted not having sooner recalled that maxim which he had often heard repeated by D'Alembert himself, " In this world one must neither deny nor affirm anything." He avowed his mistake, and the man of sense gracefully repaired the very excusable error committed

---

[5] *L'Homme au Masque de Fer*, p. 61.   [6] M. de Vergennes.

by the historian.   But his theory had become so profoundly
and tenaciously impressed upon his brain, that he could not
entirely rid himself of it.   A germ remained which developed
by degrees, and in a fashion which of itself deserves attention, independently of the interest which is inspired by
everything that relates to the Man with the Iron Mask.

"Is it possible," Taulès asks himself, "that a proof so
powerful can yet leave me any resources?   To argue in the
train of a *fact so destructive to my opinion*, and the truth of
which I am obliged to admit, would it not be endeavouring
in a deliberate manner to push prejudice to its utmost
length?"[7]   We see that at first Taulès did not contest the
accuracy of the two dates, and the impossibility of reconcil-
ing them with his theory; but by degrees he modifies the
terms of the problem to be resolved.   He no longer makes
it his business to discover who was the Man with the Iron
Mask, but to prove, in spite of a capital objection, that the
Man with the Iron Mask was Avedick.   This fact is worthy
of remark, and the chain of Taulès' successive ideas is here
very significant.   He does not commence by seeking if a
forgery has been committed by the Jesuits, in order to
establish afterwards that Avedick is the Man with the
Iron Mask.   No.   It is the necessity in which he believes
himself placed, of establishing this identity, that first gives
him the idea of a forgery, then we have his inquiry, and
then the certainty that this forgery has been committed.
"However bold my observation may appear, I shall dare to
make it, *I feel hope revive in my soul*, and in spite of all I
have just avowed against myself, I do not renounce my
discovery . . . . .   If I am deceiving myself, I shall deserve

---

[7] *L'Homme au Masque de Fer*, p. 62.

to be doubly confounded.   But if, as everything assures me
I shall do, I come victorious out of this struggle, confusion
will altogether be the portion of those who have wished to
deprive me of the honour of this discovery."[8]   From this
time all Taulès' efforts tended to destroy the positive information till then accepted by him.   Not being able to deny
the authenticity of the despatches of the Ministry of Foreign
Affairs establishing that Avedick was still at Constantinople
in 1706, and this obstacle being insurmountable, Taulès
directed his attention towards Dujonca's journal.   Father
Griffet was the first who quoted[9] the two pages of this
journal relating to the mysterious prisoner and bearing the
dates of September 19, 1698, the day of his arrival at the
Bastille, and of November 18, 1703, the day of his death.
But Father Griffet was a Jesuit.   On this score, and in the
interest, in his eyes superior to all other, of the order to which
he belonged, might he not have been able to alter, to falsify
this document, in such a manner that it might be opposed to
those who should one day, perhaps, arise to accuse the
Jesuits of the abduction of Avedick, and perhaps see in
this individual the Man with the Iron Mask?   This suspicion
had scarcely entered the mind of Taulès before it took
possession of it and ruled it, when everything immediately
became for him an irresistible argument for, and formal
proof of a falsification.

This journal is divided into two parts, each forming a
volume.   The first has for title : " List of prisoners who are
sent by the King's order to the Bastille, to commence from

---

8 *L'Homme au Masque de Fer*, p. 63.

9 In his *Traité des Différentes Sortes de Preuves qui servent à établir
la Vérité dans l'Histoire.*

Wednesday the eleventh of the month of October, when I am entered into the office of Lieutenant of the King, in the year 1690," and at the back of folio 37 we have word for word what follows :—

"On thursday 18th september 1698, at 3 o'clock of the afternoon, Monsieur de St.-Mars governor of the château of the bastille has arrived to enter upon his functions coming from his government of the isles St.-Marguerite honorat having brought with him in his litter an old prisoner whom he had at pignerol whom he always kept masked [and] whose name was not mentioned and having had him placed on leaving the litter in the first chamber of the tower of the bassinnière until the night in order to place him and conduct him myself at 9 o'clock of the evening with M. de rosarges one of the sergeants whom monsieur the governor had brought into the third chamber south of the tower of the Bretaudière [10] which I had had furnished with everything some days before his arrival having received Monsieur de St.-Mars' order for it which prisoner will be subject to and served by Mr. de rosarge and provisioned by monsieur the Governor."

The second part, of which the title is, "List of prisoners who left the Bastille, to commence from the eleventh of the month of October, when I am entered into possession in the year 1690," contains, at the back of folio 80, what follows :—

"On the same day monday 19th november 1703 —— the unknown prisoner always masked with a mask of black velvet whom Monsieur de St.-Mars governor had brought

---

[10] This and the tower mentioned just above are supposed to have been named after their builders.—*Trans.*

with him on coming from the isles St.-Marguerite whom he had guarded since a long time [and] who having found himself yesterday rather ill on leaving mass died to-day at ten o'clock at night without having had any great illness he could not have had less. M. Giraut our chaplain confessed him yesterday [but] surprised by his death he has not received the sacraments and our chaplain exhorted him a moment before dying and this unknown prisoner so long detained was interred on tuesday 20th november at four o'clock of the afternoon in the cemetery of St-Paul our parish on the register of deaths ǂ was also given a name unknown to monsieur de rosarges major and Mr. Reil surgeon who have signed the register.'

" ǂ I have since learnt that he was named on the register M. de Marchiel [and] that 40 l. were paid for his burial." [11]

For every unprejudiced and impartial reader, these unaffected pages are conclusive, and do not inspire any doubt. But it is not the same for Taulès. According to him, Father Griffet himself, and not Dujonca, is the author of this document, in which, with infinite art, he has introduced several points of obscurity, and succeeded in misleading for ever all those who should be tempted to raise the veil. He has commenced by imagining the two dates of 1698 and 1703, so that it would be impossible to apply them to Avedick, who was still at Constantinople in 1706. It is designedly that, with an infinity of precautions, he has drawn attention to this fact which he had invented at will: "Saint-Mars had this prisoner at Pignerol," a point on

---

[11] Archives of the Library of the Arsenal, Manuscript Journal of Dujonca.

which he insists by saying further on : " This prisoner whom he had guarded since a long time." To make Dujonca twice affirm that the Man with the Iron Mask was first detained at Pignerol of course absolutely sets Avedick aside. The affectation of speaking several times of the Abbé Giraut, chaplain of the Bastille, is equally significant to Taulès, in so much that it reveals the cunning intention of carefully avoiding having to name the Jesuits, even when it concerns the Bastille, to which one of them was constantly attached. It is true that the registers of the Church of Saint-Paul confirm Dujonca's journal, since the interment of the prisoner is related in them under the date of November 20, 1703.[12] But this objection does not embarrass Taulès. Without going so far as to suppose that these registers have also been falsified, he is very willing to accept them as authentic. " But," says he, " this prisoner interred November 20, 1703, is not the one brought by Saint-Mars to the Bastille. It is some obscure stranger, and Father Griffet finding on the registers of this church the proof of his death in 1703, has used it as a basis on which to erect his falsehoods, and by attracting to him the exclusive attention of posterity, has turned it aside from Avedick, and has necessarily rendered ulterior investigations fruitless."

But it is nothing of the kind. In this painful episode of Louis XIV.'s reign, the Jesuits have their share of responsibility, owing to the pressure which they put upon Ferriol, but they are completely innocent of the forgeries of which they have been accused.

---

[12] Archives of the Hôtel de Ville, *Registres des Baptêmes, Mariages et Sépultures de la Paroisse de Saint-Paul:* Saint-Paul 5, 1703–1705, vol. ii. No. 166.

The perfect authenticity of Dujonca's journal is shown by many proofs. It suffices to have read it and assured oneself that it is not composed of detached leaves afterwards bound together, but has been written all entire by the same incorrect and simple pen, in order to be convinced of the impossibility of the least alteration. Either it is a forgery from beginning to end, or the pages relating to the Iron Mask have for their author that kind of general superintendent of the Bastille, sometimes too pompously styled Lieutenant of the King, sometimes fulfilling the humble functions of turnkey, devoted to his multifarious duties,[13]

---

[13] I have found among the Archives of the Arsenal another document also emanating from the pen of Dujonca, whose journal up to the present time was alone known. These are notes in which he enumerates the heavy occupations that weighed him down. This document throws a certain light upon the interior arrangements of the Bastille. It is the same large writing as that of the Journal, with the same faults of language, the same simple-mindedness. It is too long to be quoted here. I merely extract the statement of everything that Dujonca had to do.

" For more than a year since I have entered the Bastille I have been obliged to perform the service which follows :—

"To rise every morning the first and to go to bed the last—To place the guard very often instead of the officers of Monsieur de Besemaux; to make the round and the visit every evening in the uncertainty as to whether these gentlemen will do it; to close the doors very often, not being able to rely upon any one—To take every care of the guard of the château, being unable either to trust or rely upon the governor's two officers, who do only what pleases them, and render account of what passes only to Monsieur de Besemaux—When Monsieur de la Venice or other commissaries come to interrogate prisoners, it is necessary to go and take them from their chamber and to lead them into Monsieur de Besemaux's room, traversing all the courts, and it is necessary to wait outside the door very often for eight hours at a time, in order to retake possession of the prisoner, and conduct him back to the place whence he had been taken—The prisoners to whom it is permitted to see visitors it is also necessary to go and take from their chambers, to lead them through all the courts into the common room,

who ought to be believed for his ignorance of certain things as much as for his complete knowledge of others, for the unfeigned simplicity of his language, and the tone of sincere assurance that runs uniformly throughout the entire journal. Moreover, not only is all that concerns the other prisoners corroborated by indisputable despatches deposited in other

---

where the relations or friends await them, and it is very often necessary to remain with them quite as long as they wish, being obliged to keep them in sight, and afterwards to take them back again—It is necessary to have the same care and application for certain people of the reformed religion, who are seen and talked to by Father Bordes, M. Latour Dalier and Madame Chardon, in order to convert them—To follow and guard the prisoners who have permission to go and walk in the garden and on the terrace from time to time. All the sick prisoners it is necessary to go and visit often, and to take care of them—Those who have need of the doctor and apothecary, it is necessary to conduct where the sick go ; and in order to be more assured of what passes and of the remedies which they are ordered to take, it is necessary to be present when they are brought to them—For the prisoner who is very ill and in danger of death, it is necessary to redouble all these cares in order to make him confess and receive all the sacraments, and when he is dead it is necessary to fulfil all the duties of a good Christian—On the arrival of a prisoner who is to be confined it is necessary to commence by examining and searching him all over, as well as the whole of his clothing, and to conduct him to the chamber assigned to him. Moreover, it is necessary to take care to have given and brought to him all that is essential for the furnishing of his chamber, paying very dearly for it to Monsieur de Besemaux's upholsterer, or else the *maîtresse d'autel*—It is necessary, also, to search all the confined prisoners who obtain their entire liberty, and to examine their clothes before they leave in consequence of the great communication which exists between the prisoners. It is necessary also to take the same care in searching the prisoners who are confined in order to place them in the liberty of the court, which happens sufficiently often—To visit all the chambers and to search everywhere, even all the prisoners and their clothing—It is also necessary to examine everything which comes from without for the prisoners confined here, and their clothing that goes out, in order to be mended or washed—Amongst the number of prisoners there are some who daily find themselves in necessity or need of something, or else of some complaint of

archives,[14] but the most reliable documents absolutely confirm the dates, and even some of the points indicated in the two accounts we have just quoted. Dujonca says in the first : "I had had his chamber furnished with everything some days before his arrival, *having received M. de Saint-Mars' order for it.*" Now a despatch as yet unpublished and of especial importance contains what follows : "Barbézieux to Saint-Mars. — Marly, July 19, 1698—I have received the letter which you have taken the trouble to write to me the 9th of this month. The King

---

their food, or of the bad usage of the turnkeys who attend upon them, which prisoners in their distress are compelled to beat their doors so as to give notice of their wants ; these are occasions which often happen and cause a great noise, so that it is necessary to go and make frequent visits—It is necessary to pay attention to the food given the prisoners, being very often bad, with bad wine and dirty table-linen—To frequently examine all the plate usually used for the prisoners confined here, *who very often write on the dishes and plates in order to give news of themselves to one another*—To keep guard over and carefully observe all the persons who enter the Bastille, especially the women and girls who come to see the prisoners who are in the liberty of the court—On the principal festivals of the year it is necessary to take every care to make those prisoners who are allowed by orders to do so, confess, hear mass, and communicate—To go several times during the day and the evening on to the platforms outside the château, in order to prevent the prisoners in one tower talking to those in another, and to send soldiers in the neighbourhood of the Bastille in order to arrest the persons who make signs to the prisoners whom they know, and very often these are prisoners who have received their liberty wishing to render service to those who remain, there being communication everywhere, and the cause of all these disorders."

[14] A single example will suffice. The person confined in the Bastille a few days before the Iron Mask is, according to Dujonca, the famous Madame Guyon, and a letter from Count de Pontchartrain to Saint-Mars, of November 3, 1698, says : "As for Madame Guyon, it is not necessary to do anything with reference to her except by the advice of the Archbishop : "—Imperial Archives, Registers of the Secretary's office of the King's Household.

finds it good that you should leave the Isles Sainte-Marguerite to go to the Bastille with your old prisoner, taking your precautions to prevent his being either seen or known by any one. *You can write in advance to His Majesty's Lieutenant of this château to have a chamber ready so as to be able to place your prisoner in it on your arrival.*"

This despatch cannot be questioned. It exists in the archives of the Ministry of War. It was written by the Minister, Barbézieux, a short time previous to Saint-Mars' departure for the Bastille, and like many others which we shall quote hereafter, it establishes in a formal manner that in 1698, and not later, the Man with the Iron Mask entered the Bastille, and that no alteration has consequently been made in Dujonca's journal.

But to these definitive proofs let us add others drawn from Avedick's very singular end. Let us return to this individual at the moment when he treads the French soil for the first time, and let us follow him to his death, less in order to complete our demonstration that he is not the Man with the Iron Mask—which would be superfluous—than to throw every light upon this little-known individual, and pursue to its *dénoûment* the story of this extraordinary crime.

CHAPTER XIV.

Avedick is at first confined in the Prisons of the Arsenal—From Marseilles he is conducted to Mount Saint-Michel—Description of Mount Saint-Michel—Treatment to which Avedick is exposed —His useless Protestations against this Abuse of Force—Universal Emotion excited throughout the East—Complaints of the Divan — Ferriol's Impudence — Terrible Reprisals practised on the Catholics—False Avedicks—Expedients to which Ferriol is reduced—Inquietude of the Roman Court—Duplicity of Louis XIV.'s Government—Avedick is transferred to the Bastille—Suggestions of which he is the Object—He abjures and is set at Liberty—He dies at Paris in the Rue Férou—Delusive Document drawn up with Reference to this Death—Share of Responsibility which attaches to each of the Authors of the Abduction.

IT was not at Marseilles that Avedick was detained, neither was he sent, as has been said, to Messina, or to the Isles Sainte-Marguerite to be imprisoned. Louis XIV. was too prudent and too circumspect to leave in a port of the Mediterranean an individual whom his co-religionists, supported by the Ottoman Porte, were energetically demanding and seeking with anxious solicitude. Directly the Government of Louis XIV. was advised of the outcry which the disappearance of the Grand Patriarch had excited in the East, an Exempt was sent to Marseilles, to M. de Montmor, intendant of the galleys, in order to withdraw Avedick from the prisons of the Arsenal, and conduct him, "under good and sure guard," to the other extremity of France. At the same time it was enjoined "to all governors, mayors, syndics, and other officials, to give the Exempt every protection, aid, and assistance in case of need,"[1] rather an unnecessary precaution in the case of this weak and inoffensive old man.

Near the ancient boundary of Brittany and Normandy,[2] rises a narrow rock surrounded on all sides by the waves, or by quicksands left uncovered by the sea when it falls at every tide. These sands, which extend to the firm land over a distance of nearly a couple of miles, are rendered very dangerous to cross by the mouths of several small streams.[3] On this rock, impressed with a savage grandeur, some monks had, in the eighth century,[4] constructed a monastery, where they lived isolated from the rest of the world, from which they were sometimes separated by vast plains of sand, and sometimes by the waters of the sea at regular but not far distant intervals. It was to this Abbey of Mount Saint-Michel, occupied by Benedictines, alternately devoting themselves to work and prayer, that the Grand Patriarch of the Armenians was conducted. The Prior of the abbey received orders to strictly guard the prisoner brought to him, "without allowing him to hold communication with any one, either by word of mouth or by writing,"[5] a

---

[1] Order of Louis XIV., dated from Versailles, November 10, 1706:—*Correspondance Administrative du Règne de Louis XIV.*, vol. iv. p. 255.

[2] *Gallia Christiana*, vol. xi. p. 310 : "In confinio Britonum ac Normannorum, medio in mari."

[3] Such as the Sée, Célune, and Coësnon.

[4] XVII. calend. Novembris, 709:—*Gallia Christiana*, vol. xi. p. 511.

[5] Letter from Louis XIV. to the Prior of Mount Saint-Michel, November 10, 1706 :—*Correspondance Administrative du Règne de Louis XIV.*, vol. iv. pp. 204 and 205.

very superfluous precaution in the case of an Armenian whose language nobody knew, who was ignorant of French, and who found himself in the midst of monks who from his arrival were taught to curse him. He was represented to them, indeed, as a detestable persecutor of Catholics[6]— this man who had been three times exiled and twice deposed by them, snatched violently from his country, at one time cast upon the coast of Syria and confined in a dungeon into which the water penetrated, at another carried into a strange land, thousands of miles from his native land, where for five years he was to drag out a miserable existence and then die. An object of horror to the monks, doubly exiled in this place of exile, like them separated from the world by obstacles almost as insuperable as those which parted them, separated from them also by the repulsion which he inspired, more unhappy still than in his first prison, where at least he breathed the air of his native land, Avedick could not even preserve the hope of being delivered. That consolatory prospect which his meeting with Spartaly at Genoa had permitted him to entertain, he was now obliged to renounce; since, even supposing that his letters had reached the Ottoman Porte,[7] no one would dream of coming to seek him on so distant and desert a coast. As far as his gaze extended he could expect to see no vessel of deliverance appear. Whether the sea covered the

---

[6] "He has been depicted to the King as a very great scoundrel and as a persecutor of Catholics." See letters from the Count de Pontchartrain to the Prior of Mount Saint-Michel of July 13, 1707, and August 22, 1708 :—*Correspondance Administrative du Règne de Louis XIV.*, vol. iv. pp. 264 and 265.

[7] We have already seen (Chapter XII. p. 157 *ante*) that they were intercepted and sent to Ferriol.

sands or whether it ebbed and left them dry, there was the same frightful solitude, the same mournful silence, broken at times by the roar of the waves beating against the rock, or by the peaceful and monotonous chants of the monks.

For ten months he listened to their prayers without being allowed to take part in them, and he lived in the most absolute isolation. But on July 13, 1707, Pontchartrain wrote to the Prior of Mount Saint-Michel that he might allow the prisoner to hear mass, and even admit him to confession. "The King," he added, "does not pretend to deprive him of the succour which he might find in this sacrament; and his Majesty has merely thought that, before admitting him to it, you ought to have him examined with especial care, as it is to be feared, from what has already happened, that his devotion is only feigned and illusory, in order to deceive and induce you to guard him with less care.[8] Singular fear of a flight, impracticable in itself, and impossible to be prolonged for any length of time in a country where all was strange and hostile to him! Pontchartrain requested the General of the Benedictines at Rome to send to Mount Saint-Michel a monk learned in Oriental languages, to whom the most absolute discretion was prescribed with respect to the disclosures which Avedick might make to him otherwise than under the seal of confession,[9] but which were not to be kept secret from the Prior, who was charged to transmit them to the Minister. Thus it was that they did not content themselves with detaining the person of

---

[8] Letter from Pontchartrain to the Prior of Mount Saint-Michel, July 13, 1707.
[9] *Ibid.*

the Patriarch : they endeavoured to penetrate to the recesses of his soul, with the view of enlightening themselves upon the true sentiments,[10] and possibly upon the projects of the prisoner. The first word that he utters, and which can be understood, is a protest of right against might. "Let them judge me," he says,[11] "and condemn me to the punishment that I deserve ; or, if I am innocent, let it be proclaimed, and let them set me at liberty !"

He was neither judged nor set at liberty; and his protest, forwarded by the Prior to Versailles, was suppressed in Pontchartrain's cabinet. It is true that at the same time the most alarming intelligence reached the Minister from Constantinople, coupled with the most pressing entreaties from the court of the Vatican, and from the French embassy at the Porte, to isolate and guard the prisoner more strictly still.

On receiving the news of Avedick's disappearance, the officers of the Divan and the Grand Vizier himself, justly excited, had demanded of Ferriol what had become of him. The French ambassador answered with assurance that the individual in question had not been given in charge to him, and that no doubt the vessel on board which he had been carried into exile was one of those English or Dutch corsairs which the Grand Seignior tolerated, even in the Dardanelles, to the prejudice of his custom-house officers and of the interests of his sovereignty.[12] This attempted diversion did

---

[10] "One can change at any moment," writes Pontchartrain, who was already hoping for a conversion.

[11] Letter from the Count de Pontchartrain to the Prior of Mount Saint-Michel, August 22, 1708.

[12] Unpublished despatch from Ferriol to Pontchartrain, June 1, 1706 :—Archives of the Ministry of Foreign Affairs, section Turkey, 45.

not succeed for any length of time. English and Dutch, questioned in their turn, having no satisfactory reply to give, the Grand Vizier ordered torture to be applied to the *Chiaoux* who had conducted Avedick to Chio; and in the midst of his torments the wretch avowed the whole truth.[18] The Vizier at once solemnly sent the *Chiaoux-Bachi* to the French embassy in order to claim Avedick as a subject of the Grand Seignior. Maurocordato, the first interpreter of the Divan, presented himself a few minutes afterwards to join his demands to those of the *Chiaoux-Bachi*, and to insist that the abducted person should be immediately sent back to Constantinople. The preciseness and energy of the demand did not trouble Ferriol, and with great presence of mind he replied, "I am ignorant of all that has happened; and truly I cannot have any confidence in the depositions of the *Chiaoux* charged to conduct Avedick. He declared, on returning to Constantinople, that he had been taken prisoner by a corsair. Who will say that the second deposition, made during the torments of the torture, is more accurate than the first? Moreover, if the French captain has carried off Avedick by force to Italy or France, he will be punished. But may it not be the case that the ex-Patriarch, fearing death in his third exile, has employed the captain to take him to a place of safety?" Little satisfied with this reply, Maurocordato threatened Ferriol, in the Sultan's name, with general persecutions against the Armenian Catholics. "If Avedick is in France," answered Ferriol, "I shall write with the view of his being compelled to return. But the Grand Seignior is

---

[18] Unpublished despatch from Ferriol to Pontchartrain, July 3, 1706:—Archives of the Ministry of Foreign Affairs, section Turkey, 45.

master of his own subjects. He can have all the
Armenians put to death indifferently, without any such
threat being able to make me acknowledge that of which
I am ignorant.[14]

The threat was put into execution, and the Catholics,
in whose pretended interest Avedick was abducted, were
the objects of a frightful vengeance. A *hatti-cherif* ordered
the arrest of the principal Armenians of the Latin rite,[15] nine
of whom escaped death by apostasy, and three intrepidly
confessing their faith, died martyrs near the Pama-Capou
Gate ;[16] several Armenians were put to the torture and
questioned during their torments as to the fate of
Avedick ;[17] all proselytizing was interdicted to the Jesuits,
and the printing establishment which they had founded was
destroyed ; the two Armenian patriarchs, who had authorised
the Catholic missionaries to preach in their churches, were
arrested and thrown into prison; a *barat* of the Sultan
recalled Avedick to the post of Grand Patriarch ; his *vekil*
or vicar, Joanes, was appointed to fulfil his duties *ad
interim*,[18] the measures of rigour and the proscriptions[19]
being increased from the moment of his elevation to power ;

---

[14] Unpublished despatch from Ferriol to Pontchartrain, July 6,
1706.

[15] La Motraye, work already quoted, p. 381.

[16] Unpublished despatch from Ferriol to Louis XIV., July 10, 1706 :
—Archives of the Ministry of Foreign Affairs, section Turkey, 43.

[17] Unpublished despatch from Ferriol to Pontchartrain, July 10,
1706.

[18] Unpublished despatch from Ferriol to Pontchartrain, July 3, 1706 :
—Archives of the Ministry of Foreign Affairs, section Turkey, 45.

[19] Unpublished letters from Ferriol to the Pope, November 30,
1707 ; to the Cardinal de la Trémouille, November 4, 1707 ; and to
the Marquis de Torcy, December 5, 1707.

all the Catholics were obliged to fly or hide themselves; against them universal fury was directed, amongst them were desolation and ruin; such, at Constantinople and throughout the whole Turkish empire, were the immediate and terrible consequences of Avedick's abduction. So true is it that violence invariably leads to violence, and that an abuse of force is sooner or later followed by reprisals which, although they are to be deplored, cannot be altogether condemned, since, if they are without excuse, they, at least, have their explanation in an immutable law common to all nations and all epochs !

This exasperation against the Catholics was equalled only by the affection which their unfortunate victim inspired. In all the churches prayers were said every evening for his prompt return. For a moment it was believed that they were answered.[20] The news spread through Constantinople that Avedick was at Rodosto, a town thirty leagues off. Some Armenians immediately set off to meet him, with the view of bringing him back in triumph. But they only found an impostor who had succeeded in deceiving a large number of schismatics, and in collecting a considerable sum in alms, by taking advantage of the enthusiasm excited everywhere by the mere name of the Patriarch.[21]

All that concerned the fate of this beloved chief was sought after with avidity, and accepted with a credulous but touching confidence. One day an Armenian affirmed that he had seen him in Holland, and received a magnificent

---

[20] Unpublished letter from Ferriol to Pontchartrain, July 6, 1706 :— Archives of the Ministry of Foreign Affairs, section Turkey, 45.

[21] This pseudo-Avedick was arrested and imprisoned in Constantinople, but he managed to escape by applying the money he had collected to corrupt his gaolers.

present for this happy piece of news; he disappeared, however, before it was discovered to be false.[22] Later, two Turkish slaves from Malta affirmed that Avedick was detained there a prisoner. They contrived by this artifice to get their ransoms paid, and the false information brought by them not being devoid of probability, two rich Armenians determined to charter a vessel and proceed to Malta to claim the prisoner. Ferriol, called upon to furnish them with a letter of recommendation both for Malta and for Rome, where they were to continue their researches, ostensibly did so. But he secretly forwarded by another channel to the Cardinal de la Trémouille, French ambassador to the Holy See, a private despatch,[23] in which he recommended the greatest circumspection and the exercise of an incessant surveillance over the two Armenians.

---

[22] Unpublished letter from Ferriol to Pontchartrain, May 15, 1707 :—Archives of Ministry of Foreign Affairs, section Turkey, 45.

[23] Here are the two despatches, dated the same day and sent by different channels :—" Pera, November 16, 1707.—Monseigneur—The Grand Vizier, desiring that Avedick, the Patriarch of the schismatic Armenians, who is said to have gone into Christian lands, should return to Constantinople, sends two Armenians to Malta, named Hazadour, son of Margos, and Donabit, son of Yartan, in order to search for the said Patriarch Avedick, and to bring him back to Constantinople, two Turks, formerly at Malta, having assured the Grand Vizier that they had seen him there two months and a half ago. As I have nothing so much at heart as to please the Grand Vizier, I have given passports to the Armenians and a letter of recommendation for M. le Bailli de Tincourt, to the end that they may have every sort of liberty to seek and bring here the said Patriarch Avedick, and return to Constantinople when it shall seem good to them, without suffering any difficulty or impediment ; but that on the contrary every kind of assistance should be given to them. As, however, the Turks, who were slaves at Malta, asserted that the said Patriarch Avedick was going on to Rome, I beg your Eminence very humbly to render every kind of assistance to the Armenians, to facilitate their search for the Patriarch

With reference to the Divan, whose demands continued to be both precise and firm, Ferriol, reduced to shifts, was always contriving fresh artifices in order to appease the Grand Vizier's resentment.[24]　At times he promised to send one of the officers of the embassy in search of Avedick. Then the report having spread abroad that the Grand Patriarch was confined at Messina, Ferriol engaged to beg the King of France to demand of his grandson, Philip V., King of Spain, that he should be set at liberty and sent back.[25]　But he always affirmed that he was a stranger to the abduction, and that he was entirely ignorant of where Avedick was.　On this last point, and on that only, he was sincere.　The government of Louis XIV. had concealed even from its representative at Constantinople the transfer of the prisoner to Mount Saint-Michel, and Ferriol, very well informed of every detail of Avedick's transport to Marseilles, had been prudently kept in the most complete ignorance of ulterior decisions.　But if he was unacquainted

---

Avedick, and give them the means of bringing him back to Constantinople in all security."

Here is now the secret despatch :—" Pera, November 16, 1707.—Monseigneur—As the two Turks have said that Avedick was going to Rome, I have, at the request of the Grand Vizier, given the Armenians a letter of recommendation to your Eminence. You can judge of the character of these persons. It is, however, important that they should not be ill-treated, and, after having sought Avedick, that they should be permitted to return to Constantinople. But all their proceedings ought to be watched in such a way that they can neither complain of this course nor enter on their return into new plots."—Archives of the Ministry of Foreign Affairs, section Turkey, 45.

[24] Unpublished letters from Ferriol to Pontchartrain, September 1, 1706, and February 19, 1707 :—Archives of the Ministry of Foreign Affairs, section Turkey, 45.

[25] Unpublished letters from Ferriol to Pontchartrain, July 18, and September 16, 1706.

with them, he at least inspired them by his spiteful insist-ance, by his implacability in pursuing his enemy even in his most profound and most irretrievable fall. "He does not care to demand the death of the sinner," he says, "but he must do penance, and must never be set at liberty." "If Avedick is in the prisons of the Holy Office," we read in another despatch, "he will never leave them; if he is in France, I beg of you to order him to be placed in a dark chamber, from which he can never behold the day." "Whatever penance," says he, elsewhere, "he may perform for his crimes and for his persecution of the Latins, will never be sufficiently great." [26]

From Rome also the most earnest entreaties and the most pressing recommendations "to confine the prisoner still more closely" [27] reached Louis XIV. Twice did the Minister of Exterior Relations, the Marquis de Torcy, charge the Cardinal de la Trémouille to remove the inquietudes of the congregation of the Holy Office. "The orders to redouble attention and watchfulness," wrote Torcy, "have been renewed. He is seen only by the person who gives him his food. They converse only by signs, and, when he hears mass on fête-days and Sundays, he is put in

---

[26] Unpublished letters from Ferriol to Pontchartrain, June 1, and September 10, 1706, and February 19, 1707. It should be remarked that it is especially after the abduction that Ferriol so vehemently accuses Avedick of terrible persecutions. Extracts from his despatches, written previous to the abduction, and which we have given in Chapter XII. (pp. 149 and 153 *ante*), show that this accusation had much less foundation than the French ambassador wished to make believe, with the evident intention of justifying the abduction of the Patriarch.

[27] Unpublished despatch from the Cardinal de la Trémouille to Torcy, July 21, 1708:—Archives of Ministry of Foreign Affairs, section Rome, 491.

a place apart from all others." At the same time,[28] the Minister informed the Cardinal that the Armenians, who had come to Marseilles, had departed again without being able to find any traces of Avedick. "We know," he added,[29] "that the valet of the Patriarch is about to come from Leghorn to France, likewise with the view of discovering what has become of his master. But on his arrival he will be arrested and closely imprisoned." These despatches were, we see, of a nature to entirely reassure the Holy Office,[30] and Louis XIV. showed himself as vigilant a guardian of Avedick's person as he had been, through his ambassador, the principal author, and, in his despatches, the unreserved approver of the abduction.

He went further still, and entering in his turn on that path of duplicity in which Ferriol had long since outstripped him, Louis XIV. wrote to his representative near the Porte: "It is impossible for us to satisfy the Grand Vizier's demands with reference to Avedick. He is no longer in a state to be sent living to Constantinople."[31] Louis XIV. added "that the news of his death had been given him, at the very moment when, in order to be agreeable to the

---

[28] Unpublished letters from Torcy to La Trémouille, August 17, and September 6, 1708 :—Archives of the Ministry of Foreign Affairs, section Rome, 484 and 492.

[29] Archives of the Ministry of Foreign Affairs, section Rome, 492.

[30] Only a very few persons at Rome knew that Avedick was in France, and even they were ignorant of the precise place where he was detained. The other Cardinals had, with reference to this matter, only vague and inexact information, as is proved by a letter written from Rome, July 27, 1706, in which it is stated that Avedick was a prisoner at Messina.—Archives of the Empire, *Monuments Historiques*, xi. : *Négociations*, K 1315-1326.

[31] Letter, February 14, 1707 :—Archives of the Ministry of Foreign Affairs, section Turkey, 44.

Grand Vizier, he was having the Patriarch sought for in Spain and Italy with the view of delivering him up to his legitimate sovereign."

. This prisoner, still sufficiently menacing and formidable at the bottom of his dungeon for Rome as well as Versailles to be thus concerned about his fate, this old man, the object of so many preoccupations, and, throughout the whole of the Levant, of regrets which ·he did not even have the consolation of knowing, was not thought to be sufficiently surely isolated by the sands and the sea that surround Mount Saint-Michel. The moats, the massive doors, and the towers of the Bastille were considered necessary. " On December 18, 1709," says Dujonca in his journal, " there has entered a very important prisoner, whose name was not mentioned." [32] This was Avedick, whose death, announced by Louis XIV., the majority of the Armenians had long since been mourning. The same recommendations which the Prior of Mount Saint-Michel had received were given to M. de Bernaville, governor of the State prison, and he was forbidden " to allow the slightest communication between his new prisoner and any other person." [33] However, Louis XIV. was not slow in authorising an exception to this rule. A project, long since favoured by the King's government, and the execution of which would render it for ever impossible for Avedick to return to Constantinople,

---

[32] Manuscripts of the Arsenal Library, Dujonca's Journal, *Registres des Entrées.* This new extract from this journal proves once more its perfect authenticity, since the date is corroborated by the letter to the governor which we are about to quote.

[33] Letter from Louis XIV. to M. de Bernaville, at " Marly, December 18, 1709 : "—*Correspondance Administrative du Règne de Louis XIV.,* vol. iv. p. 285.

was about to be realized. This was to instruct him in the Catholic religion, to determine him to submit to the authority of the Holy See, and thus to lead him to discredit himself with those of his co-religionists who still doubted of his death. Such was the end, for the accomplishment of which a monk had been placed near the Patriarch during the two years of his stay at Mount Saint-Michel. At the Bastille the suggestions became more pressing, and Armenian books were given to him,[34] in which he might learn the Catholic doctrines, and convince himself how narrow were the grounds of difference which separated the Latin Armenians from the schismatics. These he traversed, and, on September 22, 1710, he abjured between the hands of the Cardinal de Noailles, Archbishop of Paris, by an instrument written in the Armenian language, three translations of which in Latin were delivered, one to the Cardinal, another to the Minister of Exterior Relations, and the third to Avedick himself.[35] A few days afterwards he was ordained priest in the church of Notre-Dame. This abjuration was the only means Avedick had of recovering his liberty; and, depressed by so many storms, he ceded, after five years of close captivity, to the natural desire of breathing a free air during the few remaining years that he had to live.

In the early part of 1711, an old man, bowed by adversity still more than by weight of years, his countenance

---

[34] *Déclaration authentique de M. Pétis de la Croix, Secrétaire-interprète du Roi en langues Arabe, Turque, et autres Orientales,* Aug. 24, 1711 :—Archives of the Ministry of Foreign Affairs.

[35] *Profession de foy et réunion d'Avedick, Patriarche Arménien, à la Sainte Église Romaine,* Monday, September 22, 1710 :—Archives of the Ministry of Foreign Affairs.

furrowed by deep wrinkles, his eyesight nearly gone, might be seen every morning to leave a little house in the Rue Férou, where he dwelt with his interpreter.[36]   Having preserved in his attire some remnant of the Armenian costume, being a foreigner in language and manners, and sustaining by the aid of a stick his enfeebled body, he attracted' attention, and people followed him with their glances to the church of Saint-Sulpice, to which he was attached as priest, and where he every day said mass.[37]   This was the religious chief and civil protector of several millions of Armenians, the enemy of Ferriol and of the Jesuits, and the vanquished in the long struggle sustained against them. He did not long enjoy his liberty, but died on July 21, 1711, ten months after having quitted the Bastille, without relations or friends, having demanded and received the consolations and the sacraments of that Roman Church [38] whose ardent missionaries had been the cause of all his misfortunes.   Thus terminated this life, commenced in obscurity and misery, continued on the patriarchal throne, crossed with unhoped-for elevations and sudden falls, and completed mournfully in exile.

Louis XIV., exhausting precautions, and pushing imposture and mockery to their extreme limits, had an instrument drawn up by the Lieutenant of Police d'Argenson, in which were attested the King's sorrow on hearing of this death, and *the promptitude which the monarch had shown*

---

[36] Pétis de la Croix, *Déclaration authentique, &c.*, already quoted.

[37] Extract from the *Registres des Convoys et Enterrements à l'Église paroissiale à Saint-Sulpice, à Paris*, delivered by the S. Joachim de la Chétardye, curé of Saint-Sulpice, August 14, 1711.

[38] *Ibid.*   Avedick was interred in the cemetery of the Church of Saint-Sulpice.

in giving liberty to the prisoner directly the foreigner had been able to make . it understood what his quality was. By a singular euphemism, Avedick was termed a *disgracié*, and Louis XIV. declared that *he had never approved the violence, and still less the crimes, which, unknown to his Majesty, had been committed in Turkey on the person of the deceased.*[39] This lying document was to have been sent to Constantinople in case the Porte should reclaim Avedick in too menacing a manner. But it was unnecessary. Several changes of Grand Viziers contributed to abate the demands, and to render them less pressing. At long intervals the name of the ex-Patriarch recurred in the conversations between the Ottoman prime minister and the French ambassador ;[40] then, by degrees, the Divan no longer occupied itself with it. The remembrance of Avedick was less profoundly engrafted there than in the grateful hearts of the Armenians.

But this is not the complete *dénoûment* of the drama. At the very time when Ferriol's victim was dying, he himself was returning from Constantinople insane, having been, two years since, replaced in his post, which, with an extravagant pretension,[41] he had, however, up to that time refused to quit.

---

[39] Despatches from the Count de Pontchartrain to the Lieutenant of Police d'Argenson, July 22 and 30, 1711 :—*Correspondance Administrative du Règne de Louis XIV.*, vol. iv. pp. 292 and 293. *Procès-verbal de M. d'Argenson, contenant enqueste sur la vie et la mort de Monseigneur Avedick, patriarche des Arméniens à Constantinople,* September 15, 1711 :—Manuscripts of the Arsenal Library, *Papiers d'Argenson.*

[40] Letters from Count Desalleurs, ambassador of France at Constantinople, to the Marquis de Torcy, June 16, 1710, and Aug. 1, 1713.

[41] I have a number of most interesting despatches relating to this end, and to some very curious scenes which occurred during the last years passed by Ferriol at Constantinople. Perhaps I shall utilize them some

It was, in some measure, necessary to use force to compel him to embark.[42] For a long time he had recognized the enormous fault he had committed, and on January 6, 1709, had written to Torcy, " I know only of one thing for which people can reproach me—it is the abduction of Avedick."[43] But this was not the cause of his recall, which was evidently entirely due to the too certain signs of his insanity.[44] It cannot be denied that Louis XIV.[45] approved the violation

---

day. But the laws of proportion prevent me from doing so here and oblige me not to prolong this story beyond the death of the principal personage. After his return to France, whither he had brought that beautiful Circassian slave, who became celebrated under the name of Mademoiselle Aïssé, Ferriol lived in obscurity, much, however, against his will, since he did not cease soliciting being sent back to Constantinople as ambassador, and to deny his madness with a vehemence and an excess of language which made his statement seem very improbable.

[42] Unpublished despatches from the King to the Count Desalleurs, ambassador at Constantinople after Ferriol, September 25, 1710, and from the Marquis de Torcy to the same, of the same day :—Archives of the Ministry of Foreign Affairs, section Turkey, 48.

[43] Archives of the Ministry of Foreign Affairs, section Turkey, 48.

[44] Unpublished despatches from the King to M. de Fontenu, Consul at Smyrna, September 19, 1709 ; from Torcy to Ferriol, November 5, 1709 ; from the King to Ferriol, March 27, 1710:—Archives of the Ministry of Foreign Affairs, section Turkey, 48 ; and from Ferriol to Torcy, May 23, 1711 (*ibid.* Turkey, 49).

[45] We think it unnecessary to demonstrate this after the circumstantial account we have given. It suffices to add :—1st. That Louis XIV. paid the expenses occasioned by the abduction, which for one consul alone amounted to 105 ounces of gold (unpublished despatches from Ferriol to Pontchartrain, June 25, 1706, and Nov. 8, 1707, Archives of the Ministry of Foreign Affairs, section Turkey, 45). 2nd. That the first despatch addressed by the King to Ferriol, on October 17, 1706, after the news of the abduction had arrived at Versailles, far from conveying a reprimand, contains the following :—" Versailles, October 17, 1706.—I approve your attention in procuring for the Christian slaves in the Crimea the spiritual succours of which up to the present time they have been deprived, and as you know

of the law of nations, of which Avedick was the victim; and if the Catholic missionaries are responsible for having suggested this crime, as Ferriol is for the orders transmitted to Chio, the government of Louis XIV. is not the less so for having prolonged and aggravated its consequences by the treatment to which the prisoner was subjected.

---

my sentiments concerning the protection which I wish on all occasions to accord to the Catholic religion throughout the Ottoman empire, you can render me no more agreeable service than to continue to make the effects of it manifest, either publicly or *by secret ways*, to all those who profess it and who find themselves oppressed by the officers of the Grand Seignior, *whether they are his subjects, or of whatever nation they may be*, and the more violent you remark the persecution against them on the part of the Vizier to be, the more attentive you ought to show yourself to procure them, with suitable caution, the assistance which they have a right to expect from you."—(*Ibid.* Turkey, 43.) 3rd. That in the instructions sent to Count Desalleurs, Ferriol's successor at Constantinople, Ferriol's conduct is approved.—(*Ibid.* Turkey, 47). 4th. That Ferriol's recall took place three years after the abduction, and was due solely to the proofs of insanity he had exhibited, and of which Louis XIV. had been informed by the chief officers of the embassy.

CHAPTER XV.

Description of Pignerol—Its Past, its Situation—Portrait of Saint-Mars — His Scruples and his Integrity — Fouquet's Arrival at Pignerol—Brief Account of the Surintendant's Career—His Error with regard to Louis XIV., whom he betrays—Causes of Fouquet's Fall—His Arrest—His Trial—His Condemnation—No kind of Obscurity in this Affair.

OF the principal personages in whom people have seen the Man with the Iron Mask, we have first got rid of those imaginary beings, those pretended brothers of Louis XIV., whom it was necessary to banish to the domain of fiction. Afterwards entering into that of reality, we have studied the lives of several princes whom people have also covered with the mysterious mask,[1] but whom we have

---

[1] It is needless to say that I have put on one side the numerous opinions which are not worthy of being discussed, simply because they do not rest upon a pretext even. There was a period (that of the public disputes between Fréron, Saint-Foix, Lagrange-Chancel, Father Griffet, and Voltaire) when to imagine a solution of this problem was in fashion, and people suggested a name without troubling themselves with the proofs, or at least with the motives which might render this name probable. It is in this manner that two-and-twenty so-styled solutions have been put forward. I have discussed those which concern the brothers of Louis XIV. (son of Buckingham and Anne of Austria, son of Anne of Austria and an unknown person, son of Anne of Austria and Lous XIII., born some hours after Louis XIV.) I have

shown as dying elsewhere than at the Bastille; as Vermandois before Courtray, Monmouth on the scaffold, and Beaufort at the siege of Candia.   These accounts have been

---

subsequently refuted the Vermandois solution, and the Monmouth, Beaufort, and Avedick.   I shall content myself with simply mentioning the opinions which make the Man with the Iron Mask a natural and adulterine son of Marie-Louise d'Orléans, wife of Charles II., King of Spain; a natural and adulterine son of Marie-Anne de Neubourg, second wife of Charles II., King of Spain, who would have been put out of the way by Louis XIV.; a natural son of the Duchess Henriette d'Orléans and Louis XIV.; a natural son of the same Princess and the Count de Guiche; a natural son of Marie-Thèrese, wife of Louis XIV. and of the negro servant whom she had brought with her from Spain; a son of Christine of Sweden and of her Grand Equerry Monaldeschi; a son of Cromwell; a lover of Louise d'Orléans, imprisoned when she became Queen of Spain; a woman; a pupil of the Jesuits incarcerated for an abusive distich, and sent to the Isles Sainte-Marguerite.   All these opinions have, as may be seen, very little weight.

Lastly, it is proper to name the Chevalier Louis de Rohan, Master of the Hounds, condemned to death in 1674, as a conspirator, and who, according to one theory, had his life spared.   M. Pierre Clément, in the work which he has devoted to this individual (*Enguerrand de Marigny, Beaune de Semblançay, le Chevalier de Rohan, épisodes de l'Histoire de France*), and in chapter vi. of his curious volume, *La Police sous Louis XIV.*, has clearly established that the Chevalier de Rohan was beheaded.   He was executed with his accomplices in front of the Bastille, November 27, 1674.   The execution was public, and it was impossible to have substituted any one else.   It was not because no effort was made to move the heart of Louis XIV.; but Louvois was always on the watch, and in this instance thought it desirable to renew the severities of Richelieu.   Even supposing it were possible to prove that Louis XIV. had spared the life of this conspirator, it would also be necessary to prove that he was the Man with the Iron Mask, and not merely by showing the probabilities and indicating the possibilities. Such a process, indeed, sufficed in the last century to build up a theory; but historical criticism in our own times is rightly more exacting.   It is essential now-a-days to establish the perfect conformity between the Chevalier de Rohan and the Man with the Iron Mask, by following the former from prison to prison, from the time that his life is said to have

followed by the story of a great State prisoner under Louis XIV., in whose favour very strong presumptions have been advanced, but who was incarcerated neither at Pignerol nor at the Isles Sainte-Marguerite, and who ended his days in liberty. Let us now penetrate with Saint-Mars into Pignerol, and among the individuals confided to his care, let us seek which of them, confined for a long time in this fortress, next at the Isles Sainte-Marguerite, and lastly conducted to the Bastille, where he died on November 19, 1703, is really the Man with the Iron Mask.

At the entrance to the valleys of the Chisone and the Lemina, on the slope of one of those hills in which by insensible gradations the great chain of the Alps terminates on the side of Piedmont, there arose in the form of an amphitheatre a little town which, from the twelfth century, the

---

been spared until his death in 1703. But this is utterly impossible. One prisoner only was brought to Saint-Mars in 1674, but on *April* 18, long before the Chevalier's trial : this prisoner was an insignificant and obscure monk. Now we are acquainted with all the prisoners confided to Saint-Mars since that time, we know the causes of their imprisonment, and there is no doubt, moreover, that he had no others. Numerous despatches attest this fact, and it has been established and recognized since a long time. The only doubtful point is which of Saint-Mars' prisoners was the Man with the Iron Mask. But not one of them has, in his existence, his age, the manner in which he was treated, the time at which he was incarcerated, any feature which resembles the Chevalier de Rohan even in conjecture. See, besides the two volumes mentioned : Imperial Archives, Manuscript Registers of the Secretary's office of the King's Household, year 1674, pp. 133, 165, 184. Archives of the Ministry of War, letter from Louvois to the King, October 6, 1674. *Mémoires Militaires de Louis XIV.*, vol. iii. p. 522 ; Basnage, chap. civ. p. 549 ; La Hode, book xxxv. p. 514 ; Limiers, book vi. p. 274 ; Lafare, chap. vii. p. 211 ; Sismondi, *Histoire des Français*, vol. xxv. pp. 280 and 282 ; Camille Rousset, *Histoire de Louvois*, vol. ii. p. 120.

Princes of Savoy had caused to be fortified for the safety of
their States, the approach to which it defended.   At the
summit of the hill, formerly covered with a forest of pines,
whence the town received its name, a citadel, surrounded
by fortifications, had been constructed, which was commanded on the north alone by the mountain of Sainte-
Brigitte, soon to be itself covered with redoubts and
entrenchments.   Having thus become a military position of
the greatest importance, and, as the key of Italy, able in
turns to check or favour foreign invasions, the position of
Pignerol, coveted by the Kings of France, and so precious
to the Dukes of Piedmont, was long disputed by arms, or
claimed by diplomacy.   Captured in 1532 by Francis I.
from the too feeble Duke Charles III., restored by
Henry III. in 1574 to Philibert-Emmanuel,[2] attacked
unsuccessfully in 1595 by the Duke de Lesdiguières, it
ended in 1630 by falling into the power of Cardinal de
Richelieu, who took possession of it at the head of 40,000
men, and placed it under the rule of the King of France, to
whom it was destined to belong until the disasters of the
latter years of Louis XIV.   Richelieu, Mazarin, and
Louvois contributed to render its fortifications formidable.
To-day there remain only a few ruins of them, near to the
cathedral of Saint-Maurice, whence there is a charming
view.[3]   Very different, however, was the appearance of
Pignerol in 1664, the period at which Saint-Mars proceeded

---

[2] *Cessione di Pinerolo, fatta da Enrico III. ad Emanuele Filiberto
il Grande Duca di Savoia,* Pinèrolo, 1858.

[3] *Pinerolo antico e moderno e suoi dintorni,* del Canonico G. Groset-
Monchet ; *Veduta di S. Maurizio,* dell' Abate Car. Jacopo Bernardi,
Pinerolo, 1858.

thither to take possession of the donjon of the citadel, converted into a State prison.[4]   On the side of the hill were to be seen the houses of the town with their low red-tiled roofs, their slight-looking companiles, and their chimneys in the form of turrets; here and there on certain houses, battlements and loop-holes might be detected, the remains of some old defence or a useful precaution against future attack. As one raised the eyes life and action were seen to gradually disappear, giving place to the dull monotonous service of a fortified post. On the summit wide ditches isolated the citadel from the town, whilst beyond, a double line of thick walls formed a vast parallelogram flanked by four lofty towers; along the breastworks, near the drawbridges and on the bastions, soldiers were on guard, and in the courtyards others were lounging about; lastly, in the centre of all these fortifications, was a large square donjon, silent yet appearing as though inhabited, and having its windows covered with iron bars. Sombre and sinister in aspect this black-looking mass towered to the skies. Such may we picture to ourselves, after the lapse of a couple of centuries, was the dwelling of those prisoners, some celebrated like Fouquet, others mysterious like the Iron Mask, who have rendered Pignerol for ever famous in history and legend.

Between the severe aspect of this donjon and the character of its new commandant, there was a perfect similarity, and no one united in himself more completely than Saint-Mars the necessary qualities for fulfilling the duties confided to him. Bénigne d'Auvergne, Seigneur de Saint-Mars, was a petty gentleman of Champagne, from the neighbourhood of Montfort-l'Amaury, when he entered the

---

[4] *Corografia fisica dell' Italia*, di Attilio Zuccagni-Orlandini.

first company of the King's Musketeers.[5]   At thirty-four
years of age, he had just attained the rank of quartermaster,[6]
when Fouquet was arrested at Nantes in 1661.   In this
affair he shared the royal confidence with his lieutenant,
D'Artagnan, and whilst the latter was charged with the arrest
of the Surintendant, Saint-Mars had confided to·· him the
mission of arresting Pellisson and conducting him to Angers.[7]
Selected by Louis XIV., in 1664, as being capable of securely
guarding Fouquet at Pignerol, he was named Commandant
of the donjon of this place, and Captain of a free company.[8]
He immediately proceeded to Pignerol, and from that time
devoted himself to those weighty duties of gaoler with which
he was to be occupied in various prisons, and last of all at the
Bastille, until his death, always with the same overpowering
sense of his responsibility which made him in reality the

<hr>

[5] *Mémoires de D'Artagnan*, by Sandraz de Courtilz, Cologne, 1701,
vol. iii. pp. 222 and 385 ; *Annales de la Cour et de Paris*, for the years
1697 and 1698, vol. ii. p. 380.

[6] Order of Le Tellier to d'Artagnan, December 3, 1661 :—Archives of
the Ministry of War.

[7] *Ibid.*

[8] Despatches from Louvois to Saint-Mars, January 17, 23, and 29,
1665.   Saint-Mars espoused the sister of Louvois' mistress, whose
acquaintance he made, not in one of his journeys to Paris (for these
were extremly rare), but at Pignerol itself.   The Sieur Damorezan (and
not De Morésant, as MM. Paul Lacroix and Jules Loiseleur have written
it), muster-master at Pignerol, had two sisters, one of whom, Madame
Dufresnoy, became mistress of Louvois, and through his influence,
lady of the bed-chamber to the Queen, while the other married Saint-
Mars.   The latter had 6,000 livres (240*l.*) salary, *plus* gratuities,
which were often very considerable.   He alone commanded in the
donjon, and his authority was independent of that of the Marquis
d'Herleville, governor of the town of Pignerol, and of M. Lamothe de
Rissan, Lieutenant of the King in the citadel.   There were, however,
between the latter and Saint-Mars occasional jealousies which Louvois
sought to remove, but not always with success.

chief of Louis XIV.'s State prisoners. He possessed the gaoler's two principal qualifications: a discretion which was proof against everything, combined with a distrust such as the suspicious Louvois himself had occasionally to restrain while he had but rarely to put him on the alert. He was not, like D'Artagnan, an intelligent, generous, and frank executer of the royal will. With a somewhat narrow and extremely timid disposition, alike taciturn and restless, one thought alone possessed and ruled him,—the servile accomplishment of the King's orders. To discuss them would have seemed a crime to him; to seek to interpret them appeared superfluous. He answered for the prisoners confided to his care. The height of the walls, the depth and width of the moats, the vigilance of the sentinels, the carefulness of the watchmen, the strength of the iron gratings, did not suffice to calm the inquietude of his suspicious mind. In endeavouring to dissipate it, he did not content himself with informing Louvois of the most minute details, the most puerile circumstances; his scruples and uneasiness were everlastingly reviving. Everything was in his eyes a matter for suspicion, and his troubled imagination never ceased to foresee pretended plans of flight. A stranger visiting Pignerol, and regarding the citadel with a little attention, immediately became an object of suspicion to him and was arrested, subjected to a long examination, and imprisoned for a length of time.[9] Every month he had a list drawn up of strangers arriving in the town,[10] with the view of noticing the names which appeared in it too

---

[9] Unpublished letter from Saint-Mars to Louvois, May 6, 1673: —Archives of the Ministry of War, vol. cccliv. fo. 214.

[10] Unpublished letter from Saint-Mars to Louvois, March 17, 1673: —*Ibid.*, vol. cccliv. fo. 230.

frequently. The linen of his prisoners before leaving the donjon was carefully plunged into a tub of water, and then dried at a fire in the presence of officers charged in rotation to assure themselves of the absence of all writing upon it.[11] The least change observed in the habits of the prisoners was a source of painful worry to Saint-Mars, appearing to him in the light of a mysterious signal designed to expedite a criminal attempt; and one day, after his usual visit and long search in the rooms of Fouquet and De Lauzun, not having been able to discover the slightest sign of anything abnormal,[12] he was at first surprised and then very much alarmed. This absence of signals doubtless seemed to him a signal of itself. For the rest, an honest man,[13] greedy of gain,[14] but seeking it only by legitimate means, insensible to the reproaches of his prisoners, finding in the sentiment of having done his duty sufficient strength to be able to disdain their abuse, and acting humanely on the very rare occasions

---

[11] Unpublished letter from Saint-Mars to Louvois, February 20, 1672 :—*Ibid.*, vol. ccxcix. fo. 67.

[12] Unpublished letter from Saint-Mars to Louvois, April 22, 1673 :—*Ibid.*, vol. cccliv. fo. 193.

[13] This is the testimony which Madame de Sévigné gives about him in a letter dated January 25, 1675 : " He was a discreet man and very exact in duty," say the *Mémoires de D'Artagnan.*

[14] An unpublished letter, written June 4, 1689, by Seignelay to Saint-Mars, who was then at the Isles Saint-Marguerite, furnishes a proof of this eagerness for gain :—Archives of Ministry of Marine, *Lettres des Secrétaires d'État,* 1689. Saint-Mars, like all the governors of the Bastille, left a large fortune. The profits realized in this position were, however, in no degree prejudicial to the prisoners' nourishment, the expenses being defrayed on a very liberal footing, as M. Ravaisson has perfectly established in his learned introduction to the *Archives de la Bastille,* p. xxviii. *et seq.* He received presents from Louis XIV., one of which one day amounted to 10,000 crowns (1,250*l.*) :—Letter from Louvois to Saint-Mars, January 11, 1677.

when their safety did not seem to be compromised. After having perused his frank and unaffected correspondence, in which one has a complete portrait of him, one is almost tempted to pity Saint-Mars as much as his prisoners, because, while enjoying as little liberty as they did, he was to some extent their victim, being secretly preyed upon by the incessant and painful fear of their escape. The continual inquietude by which he was agitated rendered him a prematurely old man, and contemporaries represent him as bent in figure, very thin, his head, hands, and entire body[15] trembling; in a word, overwhelmed by the heavy burden of the responsibility which weighed him down.

It was under the care of this man that Fouquet was to pass the last sixteen years of his life. It was with him that the imprisonment of the Surintendant was in reality about to commence. From the day of his arrest, indeed, until his arrival at Pignerol, a thousand intrigues had been brewing around him. The threats of his enemies, the pressing exertions of his friends, by turns the danger of capital punishment and the hope of being saved, with constant changes of prison[16] and the preoccupations of the trial, had absorbed his existence and abridged the length of the four years which had elapsed. But when he found himself at Pignerol in a chamber into which the light penetrated only through osier-screens fixed on enormous bars of iron, waited upon by unknown individuals who were removed so soon as he endeavoured to interest them in his misfortunes, and who were continued in his service if they consented to act as

---

[15] *Histoire de la Bastille* of Constantin de Renneville, vol. i. p. 32.

[16] Nantes, Angers, Amboise, Vincennes, Moret, Fontainebleau, the Bastille.

spies over him; when the only visits he received were those of his gaoler coming every day to carefully examine his furniture, rummage over his effects, consult his countenance, and surprise his thoughts; when all correspondence was forbidden him, and when he might believe himself for ever separated from those who were dearest to him; then, and then alone, there appeared to him in all its reality the horror of his lot, rendered still more bitter by the recollection of past splendours. How often in his isolation did he invoke the dazzling picture of his unprecedented fortune! How many times did he recount to himself the great part he had played during the Fronde, the legitimate influence acquired over Anne of Austria and Mazarin, whose devoted auxiliary he had been, so many and such high functions united in his own person, a great part of the court at his feet, friends like Corneille and Molière, Madame de Sévigné, Pellisson, and La Fontaine, dwellings much more splendid than the King's,[17] a formidable fortified place for refuge,[18] an island in America for an asylum,[19] the right of sovereignty over many towns,[20] joined to immense riches, the most ardent passions satiated, and the most unbridled ambition satisfied: then a thunderbolt overwhelming in an instant all this greatness and precipitating the daring man into the abyss! "There is no greater sorrow," says Dante, "than to recall when in misery our

---

[17] Versailles was not yet built.

[18] Belle-Isle. [Off Quiberon on the Breton coast.—*Trans.*]

[19] The island of Santa Lucia, then called Sainte-Alouzie. [One of the Caribbee Islands.—*Trans.*]

[20] By himself or his friends, Fouquet ruled over Havre, Calais, Amiens, Hesdin, Conearneau, Guingamp, Guérande, Mount Saint-Michel, and Croisic.

time of happiness."[21] But how much greater still, when the eyes, at length seeing distinctly, can perceive the imprudences and the faults committed ! Rendered more clear-sighted by adversity, Fouquet might remember with bitterness Louis XIV.'s generous conduct towards him on his taking possession of power after the death of Mazarin. "I knew," says the King in his *Mémoires*,[22] "that he possessed intelligence, and had a great knowledge of the home affairs of the State, which made me imagine that, provided he would avow his past faults and promise amendment, he might render me good service." Louis XIV. sincerely desired to continue to employ Fouquet. He conferred with him a long time, begged that he might be informed of everything, and that nothing of the true state of the finances might be concealed from him. On these conditions he consented to forget the past, and in future to consider only the services rendered by the Surintendant entering on a legal and regular course of proceeding and foregoing further peculations.[23]

But, like many others at the court, Fouquet had deceived himself as to the character of the young King. The latter had announced his resolution to govern by himself, to preside in person over the Council, to sign everything after having seen everything, and to gradually enlighten himself upon the administration of his kingdom, with the view of always being able to direct it properly.[24] Very few had believed in the

---

[21]   " Nessun maggior dolore,
Che ricordarsi del tempo felice
Nella miseria."—*Inferno*, v. 41.

[22] *Mémoires de Louis XIV.* Dreyss's edition, vol. ii. p. 388.

[23] *Mémoires de Choisy.* Michaud and Poujoulat's edition, p. 581.

[24] *Mémoires de Louis Henri de Loménie, Comte de Brienne*, vol. ii. pp. 155 and 157 ; *Mémoires de Choisy*, p. 582.

permanence of this resolution of a young King of two-and-twenty, to which, however, he was faithful till his death, and even Anne of Austria herself had derided it.[25]   Conceiving himself master of the King's mind through those who surrounded him, and imagining that, thanks to his numerous spies, he was acquainted with every one of his plans ; convinced, moreover, that his master, occupied with his pleasures, would be quickly repelled by irksome labour, Fouquet had persisted in his criminal conduct, and had remained deaf to the warnings of his friends.[26]   But whilst he daily presented Louis XIV. with falsified accounts, in which the expenses were increased and the receipts diminished, Colbert, to whom they were sent every evening, examined them carefully, indicated the embezzlements, and enlightened the King upon the persevering audacity of his Minister.   At the same time Fouquet continued to fortify his towns, to extend his influence, to fabricate loans to the King, to secure for himself under other names the farming of several taxes, and to appoint his creatures to the most important offices, which he secretly bought for them in the hope of soon rendering himself the sovereign ruler of the State.[27]   This was not all.   This individual, who aspired to replace Mazarin, to whom he was so inferior, because, unlike him, he was not prompted by true national interests, possessed moreover only the lofty aims of the ambitious, but neither tact nor clear-sightedness.   With a keen mind and quick understanding, he very rapidly discerned the surface of things, but was wanting in the Cardinal's penetrating sagacity and

---

[25] *Mémoires de Louis XIV.*, vol. i. p. 37 ; *Mémoires de Choisy*, p. 582.

[26] *Mémoires de Choisy*, p. 581.

[27] *Mémoires de Louis XIV.*, vol. ii. p. 525.

depth of vision, and whilst the latter, with a less vulgar ambition, occupied himself much more with the reality than with the semblance of power, Fouquet, vain and frivolous, could not resist the puèrile satisfaction of making a parade of his authority and wealth. We are acquainted with the scandalous pomp of the fête given in the Château of Vaux, " that anticipated Versailles,"[28] with its magnificent galleries, its splendid gardens, and its shameless luxury. We have this example, the most striking perhaps which history affords, of a man possessed with that folly which precedes great falls, and accelerating by his insolence a catastrophe already rendered inevitable by so many other faults.[29]

There is, indeed, nothing obscure in the causes of this

---

[28] M. Sainte-Beuve, *Causeries du Lundi*, vol. v.

[29] Fouquet, who had purchased the Vicomté of Melun, replaced the old château by a magnificent edifice, which has become celebrated from the fête given there to Louis XIV. It is the *chef-d'œuvre* of the architect Le Vau, and astounds one by its grand and noble proportions. The exterior is profusely covered with sculpture, and the splendour of the interior is fully in keeping with that of the outside, the decorations of the principal apartments having been entrusted to the most celebrated painters of the age. The pleasure-grounds, which cover several hundred acres, were planted by Le Nôtre, and are laid out in straight lines, after the usual custom of the seventeenth century.

The *mémoires* of the time are filled with accounts of Fouquet's fête to Louis XIV., August 17, 1661; and La Fontaine has described it both in prose and verse. Fouquet's fall had long since been prepared by Le Tellier and Colbert, and was already resolved upon when Louis XIV. went to seat himself at his table; but the luxury of this abode and the splendour of the reception singularly increased the irritation of the monarch, who was well aware that it was paid for out of money of which the State had been defrauded. Fouquet was arrested on September 5, only eighteen days after this fête.

The château of Vaux, which, save the ravages of time, is still in much the same state as Fouquet left it, is situated about four miles to the north-east of Melun, on the road from Paris to Meaux.—*Trans.*

catastrophe, whatever may have been said respecting it. How it came to pass, the circumstances which accompanied it, every one of the incidents of a trial which lasted three years, the accusations of the prosecution, as well as the arguments of the defence, have all been brought to light,[30] and it is impossible not to feel convinced that Saint-Mars' first prisoner was justly punished for acknowledged and indisputable faults, and not for the possession of a State secret,[31] or for I know not what hidden crime which he would have mysteriously expiated by wearing, until his death, a velvet mask. It has been pretended, without any authentic proof being furnished, that Louis XIV. not only discovered in him a powerful and wealthy rival, but that the arrest of the Surintendant was simply a piece of revenge on the part of the royal lover of La Vallière.[32] Owing to

---

[30] See *Histoire de Colbert*, by M. Pierre Clément, vol. i. ; *Mémoires sur Nicolas Fouquet*, by M. Chéruel ; *La Police sous Louis XIV.*, by M. P. Clément, pp. 1–61, and the Appendices to vols. viii. and ix. of M. Chéruel's edition of the *Mémoires de Saint-Simon*, vol. viii. p. 447, and vol. ix. p. 414.

[31] We shall prove this hereafter.

[32] As M. Chéruel has remarked (*Mémoires sur Nicolas Fouquet*, vol. ii. p. 173, note 3) the letter which is relied on in order to support this allegation is far from authentic. It has been transcribed in the *Manuscrits Conrart* (vol. xi. folio, p. 152), with many other letters "which are said to have been found in Fouquet's casket." But we know what took place with reference to this famous casket. Greedy of scandal, and not finding sufficient in the real letters which were published at that time, the courtiers invented a very great number, attributing them to ladies of the court, whose names they gave. They were collected with care, in the papers of Conrart and Vallant, and have thus been handed down to us : (Manuscripts of the Arsenal for the *Papiers de Conrart* and of the Imperial Library for those of Vallant). Such was the publicity given to these letters, that at the commencement of the trial the Chancellor Séguier thought it his duty to declare to the court that they were forgeries : See M. Chéruel's work already

the steadfast friendship of La Fontaine, and Madame de Sévigné, to their persistence in their illusions and to the eloquent sincerity of their complaints, Fouquet must always have many partisans. Even among his contemporaries, the touching devotion of his friends, the passionate attacks of some of his adversaries, and the length of his trial, induced a reaction ; and while at first the indignant populace showed their exasperation against him by imprecations and threats,[33] by degrees, as often happens, public opinion changed into sympathy for the victim,[34] and to regarding his judges as persecutors. Lastly, that mysterious legend of the Man with the Iron Mask, which some persons wish to make the climax of Fouquet's career, commences, according to them, from his arrest, and the minute precautions then taken by the King at once indicate and explain all those of which the famous masked prisoner was later to be the object.

Louis XIV. was naturally inclined to dissimulation. Mazarin not only set him the example of " this cunning and necessary virtue," [35] but advised him to practise it,[36] and never, it must be remembered, was this counsel more

---

referred to, vol. ii. p. 289, *et seq.*, and M. Feuillet de Conches' *Causeries d'un Curieux*, vol. ii. p. 518, *et seq.*

[33] " Do not fear that he will escape," said they at Angers to D'Artagnan : " we will strangle him first : "—*Journal d'Olivier d'Ormesson*, published by M. Chéruel in the *Collection des Documents Inédits sur l'Histoire de France*, vol. ii. p. 99. The same hatred manifested itself at Tours, whence it was necessary to set out with Fouquet at three o'clock in the morning to escape the threats of the people. At Saint-Mandé and Vincennes it was the same : *Récit Officiel de l'Arrestation de Fouquet*, by the Registrar Joseph Foucault :—Imperial Library, Manuscripts, No. 235–245 of the 500 of Colbert.

[34] *Mémoires sur Nicolas Fouquet*, vol. ii. p. 386.

[35] So Madame de Motteville terms it in her *Mémoires*.

[36] *Mémoires de Choisy*, p. 189.

strictly followed than during the few months which preceded
Fouquet's fall. From the time it was resolved upon,
Louis XIV., aided by Colbert and Le Tellier, prepared
in detail and in secret everything that could assure the
punctual execution of his orders and anticipate the slightest
difficulty. It cannot be denied that he lulled the Surintendant into security, and cradled him with deceptive hopes,
and that with infinite art he never treated him more graciously
than after he had decided upon his ruin. Fouquet, as Procureur-général to the Parliament, could only be judged by
that body. His acquittal would thus have been nearly
certain, since he had a great number of partisans in it. It
was therefore essential that he should resign this position [37] in
order that he might be brought before a chamber of justice.
It was Colbert, his ardent enemy, who ventured to give
him this pernicious advice, and who, with a skill inspired
by hatred, prevailed on the Surintendant without exciting
his mistrust. Louis XIV. facilitated Colbert's task by
hinting to the vain-glorious Fouquet that the collar of the
order and the dignity of Prime Minister would be irrecon-
cilable with the functions of Procureur-général.[38]   At the
same time he exhibited towards him an unusual confidence,
often called him into his presence, followed his advice, and
overwhelmed his brother, the Bishop of Agde, with favours.
The grand blow of the arrest was to be struck in Brittany,
as it was thought that the presence of the King there would
render resistance on the part of the fortified places in the

---

[37] The office was sold in 1661 to M. de Harlay. See on the subject of the reports of this sale, *Lettres de Guy-Patin*, July 12 and 15,
1661.

[38] *Mémoires de Brienne*, vol. ii. p. 178.

Surintendant's power more difficult, and the idea of advising this journey was suggested to him. The minute precautions taken at the time of the arrest;[39] those musketeers assembled under the pretext of a royal hunt and placed at the disposal of D'Artagnan; the troops occupying the roads and allowing no one but the royal couriers to pass; those long private interviews of Louis XIV., first with Le Tellier and then with D'Artagnan;[40] the most improbable obstacles foreseen and the care taken to leave nothing to chance: all this offers, it is true, the singular spectacle of an absolute monarch conspiring the fall of one of his subjects. But how can one be astonished at it when this subject is Fouquet, alone able to dispose of immense wealth in the midst of general distress, and counting devoted pensioners even amongst the officers surrounding the King? How can one be astonished, moreover, when Louis XIV. could not even place confidence in the captain of his guards?[41] when we know that Fouquet could do as he pleased with the Mediterranean fleets through the Marquis de Créqui, general of the galleys,[42] and with those of the Ocean through the Admiral de Neuchèse,[43] when Brittany had in some degree become his kingdom,[44] and most of the places in the North had his

---

[39] Order of arrest given to D'Artagnan, with the memorandum published by Ravaisson in his *Archives de la Bastille*, vol. i. p. 347–351 : Letters of the Marquis de Coislin to the Chancellor Séguier, September 5, 1661 :—*Ibid.* p. 351–355.

[40] *Procès-verbal* of the Registrar Foucault, already referred to ; *Mémoires de Brienne ; Mémoires de l'Abbé de Choisy.*

[41] The Marquis de Gesvres, whom Louis XIV. did not dare to entrust with the mission of arresting Fouquet.

[42] *Défenses de Fouquet*, vol. iii. p. 357. Edition of 1665.

[43] *Mémoires sur Nicolas Fouquet*, vol. i. p. 398.

[44] This is the title which Fouquet's friends gave to this province.

creatures for commandants ?   How can one be astonished,
above all things, after having read the famous plan of resistance found among the Saint-Mandé papers,[45] a veritable
plan of a civil war long meditated, written entirely by
Fouquet, and one in which he braves and defies the
authority of his sovereign ?   The parts to be played in the
revolt are distributed among his friends ; the chiefs are
designated; the places of refuge indicated.   Fouquet makes
known what arms are to be employed, what hostages it will
be necessary to secure; all the means of agitation are
advised.   Through his two brothers, the coadjutor of
Narbonne and the bishop of Agde, the clergy are to be
stirred up.   By means of certain members of the Parliament,
disturbances are to be excited in Paris, and the war of
pamphlets kindled anew.   By means of the Governors, the
public treasures are to be seized, and the garrisons are to be
sent forth on to the highways.   Lastly, supreme treason,
foreign help is not to be lost sight of, and Lorraine, as well
as Spain, is to be summoned to enter France.[46]

So much audacity and such an exaggerated pride sufficiently explain the dissimulation and the minute solicitude
of Louis XIV., without one's seeking the cause elsewhere.
But if he matured this *coup-d'état* in secret, and accom-

---

[45] Manuscripts of the Imperial Library (500 *de Colbert*, No. 235,
fo. 86 *et seq.*) This plan has been published by M. P. Clément
almost entire in vol. i. p. 41, *et seq.*, of his *Histoire de Colbert*,
and entire by him in the introduction of vol. ii. of the *Lettres de Colbert*,
and in his *Police sous Louis XIV.*, p. 33, *et seq.* M. Chéruel has also
reproduced it entire in Appendix No. vi. of vol. i. of his *Mémoires sur
Nicolas Fouquet*, pp. 488–501. This plan is incontestably authentic,
and Fouquet has never denied having written it.

[46] All these facts are in great part proved by the plan, and by other
papers found at Saint-Mandé, which are now in the Imperial Library.

plished it with a prudence, without which he would have certainly failed, none of the crimes which rendered it necessary were hidden from contemporaries. The preparations for the arrest were alone mysterious. During the three following years, every one of the documents relating to the trial was presented to the judges, communicated to Fouquet,[47] and was the subject of long discussions. From this there resulted the proof of his skill in argument, but not at all of his innocence. On account of his extortions and of his plan of revolt, he had, according to the laws and customs of the time, deserved death. The majority of his judges condemned him to banishment, a punishment rightly considered too lenient by Louis XIV., who changed it into perpetual imprisonment. But long before his condemnation the numerous *mémoires* which the accused composed in order to defend himself had been secretly printed by his friends,[48] and circulated among the people. There had thus been nothing ignored or left in obscurity. There is nothing imaginary or hypothetical in the account of what preceded and brought about Fouquet's imprisonment. It is essential to establish this first of all. Let us now see if, during his stay at Pignerol, any event occurred which, sixteen years after his condemnation, could all at once have determined Louis XIV. to simulate Fouquet's death, and to make of a captive, long since inoffensive and forgotten, that mysterious and nameless prisoner who is to come from the Isles Sainte-Marguerite to die obscurely in the Bastille.

---

[47] *Mémoires sur Nicolas Fouquet*, pp. 367 to 386.
[48] *Histoires de la Détention des Philosophes et des Gens de Lettres*, by Delort, vol. i. p. 21.

CHAPTER XVI.

Remark of Fouquet's Mother—The Prisoner's Piety—Danger which he escapes at Pignerol—Incessant Supervision over him at La Pérouse, near Pignerol—Excessive Scruples of Saint-Mars—Precautions prescribed by Louvois—Espionage exercised over Fouquet by his Servants and his Confessor—Illnesses of the Prisoner—He devotes himself entirely to Study and to religious Meditations—Works to which he gives himself up—His new Motto—Interest which he continues to take in all his Relations and in Louis XIV.—Saint-Mars' laconic Answers.

THE fortitude with which Fouquet supported adversity has almost caused his contemporaries to forget how he had allowed himself to be blinded and led astray by prosperity. Without exhibiting this excessive indulgence, without going so far as to take the part of the victim against his judges, or to forget his errors and his faults, one cannot prevent oneself from owning that at Pignerol he nobly expiated them by his unceasing resignation, by his firmness and by the elevation of his sentiments.

When Fouquet's mother heard of his arrest, she threw herself upon her knees, exclaiming: "It is now, O God, that I have hopes of my son's salvation!"[1] This prayer of a pious woman whom the grandeur of the Surintendant

---

[1] *Mémoires de Choisy*, p. 590.

had never dazzled, and whom his dissipation had caused to mourn, was fully answered. If so unhappy as to survive her son and to be ignorant of none of his sufferings, her sorrow may at least have been softened by the thought that the prisoner of Pignerol sought consolation in religion and study. During the early period of his imprisonment at Angers, depressed by misfortune, but sustained by the remembrance of the counsels and the virtues of his mother, he had, in a touching letter imbued with the most pious[2] sentiments, requested a confessor. A terrible danger encountered by him at Pignerol six months after his arrival, and which he escaped as if by a miracle, went to confirm him more completely in these sentiments. In the middle of the month of June, 1665, a thunderbolt fell upon the donjon of the citadel and set fire to the powder-magazine. A portion of the donjon was blown down, and a large number of soldiers were entombed beneath the ruins. Fouquet's chamber was reached by the explosion. Some of the walls fell and the furniture was shattered to pieces. Saint-Mars thought that his prisoner was killed. But he was found in the embrasure of a projecting window, and had not even received a bruise.[3] As the repairs in the

---

[2] M. Feuillet de Conches, *Causeries d'un Curieux*, vol. ii. p. 529. "M. d'Artagnan told me," says Olivier d'Ormesson in his *Journal*, "that M. Fouquet, during the first three weeks, was very unquiet and amazed, but that his mind grew calmer, and that he became very self-possessed afterwards, giving himself up largely to devotion ; that he fasted every week on Wednesday and Friday, and besides this, lived on Saturday on bread and water ; that he rose before seven o'clock, said his prayers, and after that worked till nine o'clock ; that he subsequently heard mass."—*Journal d'Olivier d'Ormesson*, vol. ii. p. 52.

[3] Letters from Louvois to Saint-Mars, June 29, 1665, and from Colbert to the same, on the same day. People at Paris as well as at

donjon necessitated by this disaster could not be completed in less than a year, Fouquet, by orders of Louis XIV. and Louvois,[4] was transferred for a time to the neighbouring château of La Pérouse.

Here commenced the attempts made by the prisoner, not so much to escape—he could not be mistaken as to the impossibility of succeeding in this—as to write to his mother and his wife, and to obtain from them letters expected in vain since his departure from Paris. "I have received the letters written by M. Fouquet," Louvois informs Saint-Mars, July 26. "The King has seen the whole, and was not surprised that he should do his utmost to obtain news, and that you exert all your efforts to prevent his receiving it."[5] "To give and receive news:" such, indeed, was Fouquet's most lively and very natural desire. In order to satisfy it, he made the most industrious efforts and showed the most ingenious patience. With soot mixed with a few drops of water he made ink, a fowl's bone served him for a pen, and he wrote upon a handkerchief, which he afterwards concealed in the back of his chair.[6] He managed even to compound an ink, which he employed to cover the margin

---

Pignerol did not fail to say that heaven had judged him innocent whom men had condemned. See *Lettres de Madame de Sévigné et de Guy Patin*; *Journal d'Olivier d'Ormesson*, vol. ii. p. 372; *Œuvres de Fouquet*, vol. xvi.

[4] Order of Louis XIV., countersigned by Le Tellier, and dated from Saint-Germain, June 29, 1665. It was Saint-Mars who, with his free company as escort, took Fouquet to La Pérouse, and continued to guard him there till the month of August, 1666, at which period he brought him back to Pignerol.

[5] Delort, *Histoire de la Détention des Philosophes*, vol. i. p. 103.

[6] Letters from Louvois to Saint-Mars, July 26 and December 18, 1665.

of a book with some lines of writing that became visible only after being warmed.[7] But Saint-Mars'[8] vigilance frustrated these attempts. He soon discovered the hidden handkerchief, and not content with sending this alone to the King, also forwarded the clumsy implements fabricated and

---

[7] Louvois inquired in vain as to the manner in which Fouquet had been able to compound this sympathetic ink. "It is necessary," he wrote to Saint-Mars on July 26, 1665, "that you should endeavour to find out from Monsieur de Fouquet's servant how [his master] has written the four lines which appeared upon the book on warming it, and of what he has composed this writing."

[8] The following is one of the first letters written from Pignerol by Saint-Mars. It is one of the rare letters addressed to Colbert. Saint-Mars made some progress in orthography after this, and the later despatches which we have of his show a rather less imperfect knowledge of the French language :—

"At Pignerol, this 13 February, 1665.

"Monseigneur—I have nothing fresh to tell you ; everything is going on all right, in my humble opinion. I had been assured that there was a man of M. Fouquet's here in the town. I had him sought for by the major, he has not been found ; he has not shown himself before the prisoner's windows, and I have taken care to say everywhere that I would not advise him to appear before the donjon, and that [if he did] it would not be a case of live and let live. I believe that this has frightened him. I thank you very humbly, Monseigneur, for the care and kindness that you have for me. I have received, by the last post, an account for the subsistence here for the present month which I am about to draw. My company arrived here on the 9th, and has already mounted guard. There is so much work to do here for the safety of a prisoner that I shall not be altogether settled for three weeks. M. Fouquet wishes to confess every month. I have given him a confessor who is of the household of one M. d'Amorclan, a man altogether devoted to Mgr. le Têlier. For myself, I should approve of him ; but as I have received orders to change him continually, I shall not allow him to confess until I receive your commands. I shall always await them with impatience, having no stronger desire than to please you, and to call myself all my life, Monseigneur, your very humble," &c.—Manuscripts of the Imperial Library, Volumes in Green, C.

used by his prisoner.[9]   The latter having afterwards written upon ribbons, black ones only were in future given him, and his garments were, moreover, lined with stuff of the same colour.   From this period he became the object of a still closer surveillance, the proof of which we find in the numerous letters exchanged between Louvois and Saint-Mars.   Like all timorous people, Saint-Mars was absolutely wanting in the spirit of initiation, and took delight in having recourse to his chief.   He possessed no ambitious desire of exhibiting his zeal, but only an imperious need of dissipating his alarms and of relieving himself from responsibility.   It did not suffice this timid gaoler to adopt the most minute precautions with respect to his prisoner.   He recounted them in his correspondence with the Minister, with the view of obtaining fresh orders, or of receiving an approval which might calm his uneasiness. It was in this spirit that he begged Louvois to authorise him to have a salt-cellar made for Fouquet out of his two broken candlesticks.[10]   It was in this spirit also that after having prevented his prisoner's servant from giving an alms, considering it suspicious, he consulted the Minister on the subject, and solicited his advice.[11]

These excessive scruples sometimes caused him to be wanting in humanity.   He one day considered it necessary to ask Louvois for an authorisation to have a sick prisoner bled, and the Minister, on according it twenty days afterwards, added : "Whenever such circumstances occur, you can have [the prisoner] treated and doctored as may

---

[9] Letter from Louvois to Saint-Mars, August 24, 1665.
[10] *Ibid.*, August 2, 1665.
[11] *Ibid.*, March 26, 1669.

be needful without awaiting orders for it."[12]   The puerile questions and the demands for fresh instructions became so frequent, that the Minister was compelled to write to Saint-Mars : " I have received your two last letters.   They oblige me to tell you that, as the King has charged you with the care of Mons. Fouquet, his Majesty has no new orders to give you to prevent his escape, or his sending or receiving letters."[13]   This outburst is so much the more significant as Louvois, very prone and qualified to enter into the slightest details, and an imperious and most exacting chief, accustomed all his subordinates to extreme deference, and to having incessant recourse to his authority.   But in this case the Minister's prejudices were outstripped, and Saint-Mars alone perhaps had the power to wear out by his pertinacity him who on ordinary occasions was most desirous of being consulted.   Moreover, we must admit, it was the only instance in which the Minister manifested his displeasure.   He habitually replied with care to every detail comprised in the letters from the commandant of Pignerol, and he sometimes even rivalled him in his want of confidence. Thus it was that in December, 1670, Fouquet, who was ill, having obtained authority to have a prescription drawn up by Pecquet, his former medical attendant, Louvois sent it to Saint-Mars with these words : " As soon as you have received it, you will make a very exact copy.   You will show the original to M. Fouquet, and you and he will compare it with the copy which you will leave with him.   You will then burn the original.   By this means the said Sieur Fouquet having seen it will have no doubt,

---

[12] Letter from Louvois to Saint-Mars, September 25, 1669.
[13] *Ibid.*, December 25, 1665.

and you having burnt it will have no anxiety about it." [14] On another occasion, when sending a chest of tea for Fouquet, Louvois prescribed to Saint-Mars: "To empty it into another receptacle, and to take away the chest, and the paper which may be within the chest, so as to leave to M. Fouquet the said tea only." [15] Never were orders more agreeable or more faithfully executed. These precautions of Louvois encouraged Saint-Mars' distrust, who thus found himself supported in his conduct by that authority, most persuasive when it emanates·from one above us in station, namely, example.

Thus stimulated in suspicions to which he naturally inclined, Saint-Mars was not slow to conceive that his means of surveillance were insufficient. To see one's prisoner often, to assure oneself with one's own eyes that he communicates with nobody, to examine with care his furniture and effects, to multiply the difficulties of an escape, seem to constitute all the duties of a conscientious and vigilant gaoler. But the suspicious Saint-Mars was in no-wise satisfied with these precautions. Forgetting that the prisoner's body alone was under his care, he wished to extend his surveillance even to Fouquet's thoughts. To attain this end he had recourse both to his confessor and to the servant who waited upon him. Having, however, soon discerned the interest which the unfortunate prisoner inspired in his servant, Saint-Mars felt that he could not rely upon the sincerity of his reports, and he attached to the person of Fouquet a second valet, who was instructed to watch the first, and was himself the object of a secret

---

[14] Letter from Louvois to Saint-Mars, December 13, 1670.
[15] *Ibid.*, November 27, 1677.

surveillance on the part of the latter.[16] As for the confessor, to control him was impossible, and in fact would have been unnecessary. We read in the correspondence of Louvois and Saint-Mars that "he was a good man,"[17] which is another proof how differently the conduct of men may be appreciated. In the eyes of Louvois and of Saint-Mars Fouquet's confessor was a *good man*, because he consented to act as a spy; because, as Fouquet wrote later to his wife, "instead of having God in view, he acted the cowardly part of making his fortune at the expense of one in trouble." He succeeded; for Saint-Mars obtained a promise from Louvois "that he should receive a living when he should cease to fulfil his office."[18] The first instructions given to Saint-Mars authorised him to change the priest each time that Fouquet desired to confess. But when they had discovered this "good man," they abandoned henceforth this useless precaution, and Fouquet in vain requested to be allowed to make a general confession to the Superior of the Jesuits, then to the Superiors of the Récollets and Capucines of Pignerol.[19]

These proceedings, and the non-success of an attempt made in 1669 by an old servant of Fouquet's,[20] who

---

[16] Letter from Louvois to Saint-Mars, February 14, 1667.

[17] *Ibid.*, February 24, 1665. See also letters of February 20 and April 24, 1665.

[18] Letter of April 17, 1670. Moreover, the King from time to time granted him gratuities. See among others, in Delort, a letter of June 4, 1666.

[19] Letter from Louvois to Saint-Mars, October 1, 1668.

[20] Named Laforest. Five soldiers received money and were severely punished. Laforest was arrested, condemned to death, and executed on the spot. Despatches from Louvois to Saint-Mars, December 17, 1669, and January 1, 1670.

endeavoured, by corrupting some soldiers, to place himself in communication with his master, induced the latter to give himself up entirely to study and religious meditations. He renounced the project of communicating with his relations and friends. The salvation of his soul and the care of his body alone occupied his thoughts. Deprived long since of all physical exercise, and having suddenly exchanged an existence, excited by travel, and adorned by everything that could make life attractive and sweet, for the solitude and inactivity of a prison, Fouquet had seen his health rapidly decay, and innumerable disorders seize on him.[21] "There is not a disease to which the body is liable," he wrote to his wife, "of which mine has not experienced some symptom. I am no sooner quit of one than it is succeeded by another, and I can but suppose that these will only cease with my life. I should require a large volume to describe my sufferings in detail, but the principal one is that my stomach does not act in concert with my liver; what suits one is injurious to the other, and, what is more, my legs are always swollen." . . . . "The best thing to be done," he says afterwards, "is to give up all care of the body, and to think of one's soul. This is important to us, and yet we show more concern for the body." In truth, he gave as much attention to one as to the other. Distrustful of the surgeon of the citadel, he compounded himself the remedies which suited him best; and in order, no doubt, that he might avail himself of his servant as an auxiliary, he instructed him in the art of dispensing.[22]

---

[21] Letters of Louvois to Saint-Mars, November 21, 1667, October 9, 1668, January 2, 1670, April 15, 1675, and July 3, 1677.

[22] Delort, *Histoire de la Détention des Philosophes*, vol. i. p. 33.

The first books which Saint-Mars consented to give him after having received authority to do so, were the Bible and a history of France. Later, the works of Clavius and St. Bonaventura were added; and then, by desire of the prisoner, a dictionary of rhymes.[23] Poetry to him was nothing more than a relaxation, and he devoted himself above all to reading religious works and to the production of several lengthy treatises on morals. The remembrance of his former grandeur clashed in them with the impressions of his profound fall. The Christian preoccupied with his salvation, the philosopher enlightened by adversity, the recluse giving himself up to the contemplation of divine things, hold in their turn a language of sublime and unchangeable serenity. One finds in almost every page proof of this resignation in disgrace, and of this contentment in affliction which Christianity can alone inspire. He whose haughty motto, for a long time justified by events, had been *Quo non ascendam*, now humbly submissive to his lot, adopted the touching emblem of the silkworm in his cocoon with these words: *Inclusum labor illustrat !*

However, Fouquet was not so detached from things terrestrial as not to interest himself in them at all. His mother, wife and several children, being still alive, his thoughts often turned towards these dearly beloved beings, and also, but without bitterness, towards Louis XIV. and his conquests, towards the Court and the Ministers. He often questioned Saint-Mars. The latter's replies were brief, and so unprecise that he considered himself obliged to write

---

[23] Despatches from Louvois to Saint-Mars, March 3, September 12, 1665, October 23, 1666, and April 8, 1678.

to Louvois and inquire in what sense he ought to answer.[24]
Entirely master of his prisoner, sure of those who surrounded
him, he believed that the barrier which he had erected
around him was insuperable, and thought that he would be
able to keep him apprised of contemporary events as he
pleased, or else leave him in the most complete ignorance.
Useless efforts and vain confidence in his power! The
enterprising audacity and industrious perseverance of a
prisoner recently brought to Pignerol, triumphed over even
the innumerable precautions of the most suspicious of
gaolers.

---

[24] Letter from Louvois to Saint-Mars, November 22, 1667 and
March 1, 1673. "There is no great inconvenience," writes Louvois to
Saint-Mars, "in M. Fouquet's knowing that the King has made war
on the Dutch. So do not persuade yourself that you have been deficient in any way in giving him a book which has apprised him of
this."—Letter from Louvois to Saint-Mars, July 2, 1673. "I have
received your letter of the 16th of this month, which requires no answer
except to say that the King approves your informing M. Fouquet
of the current news, according as his Majesty has already permitted
you."—Letter of April 25, 1678.

CHAPTER XVII.

Sudden and singular Arrival of Lauzun in Fouquet's Room—The latter had known him formerly under the Name of the Marquis de Puyguilhem—Lauzun enumerates his Dignities and calls himself the King's Cousin—Fouquet believes his Visitor mad—Portrait of Lauzun—His Adventures—His Arrival at Pignerol—He continues his Visits to Fouquet—The Stories he tells him—Noble Conduct of Louis XIV. towards Lauzun—Audacious Method employed by the latter to overhear a Conversation between Louis XIV. and Madame de Montespan—Difference between the Conduct of Lauzun and that of Fouquet—Lauzun's Outbursts against Saint-Mars—Perplexity of the latter—Singular Mode of Surveillance to which he has recourse—Progressive amelioration of the Lot of the two Prisoners—They receive Permission to see each other—Arrival of Fouquet's Daughter at Pignerol—Misunderstanding between Fouquet and Lauzun—Cause of this Misunderstanding.

One day in the early part of the year 1672, Fouquet hears one of the articles of furniture in his room suddenly thrown down, and perceives a man of short stature and slender figure creep through a narrow opening and advance smiling towards him. He is dressed in the full uniform of Captain of the King's Guard—blue, with red facings. Nothing except the sword is wanting in this costume, the rich embroideries and brilliant insignia of which offer a singular contrast to the place where it is worn. The attitude of the new comer is haughty, and his air almost patronizing. Fouquet hesitates to recognize in him a poor

Gascon cadet, the Marquis of Puyguilhem, without fortune
or position, who had sometimes come to him in the days of
his power to borrow a little money,[1] and who, extremely
fortunate in having been received into the house of the
Marshal de Grammont, his relative, had cut a very sad
figure at court at the time of Fouquet's arrest.   What, therefore, was the astonishment of the latter when his strange
visitor, questioned as to the causes of his detention at
Pignerol, replies that they have been set forth by the King
in a letter addressed to all the French ambassadors abroad.[2]
Fouquet's stupefaction is redoubled when he learns that this
costume is not a masquerade, and that the man whom he
had left in the lowest rank at Versailles is really Captain of
the Guard, and in addition Governor of Berri and Colonel
General of Dragoons, and that a brevet rank of General has
been conferred upon him.   But when his visitor, continuing
his confidences,[3] enumerates his titles, and proclaims himself Count de Lauzun, Duke de Montpensier, Dauphin of
Auvergne, Sovereign of Dombes, Count d'Eu and de Mor-
taing, and, finally, husband of the Grande Mademoiselle and
cousin-german of Louis XIV., Fouquet ceases to feel surprised.   Everything is explained ; the speaker is mad ; the
tortures of a prolonged confinement have unsettled his mind,

---

[1] *Mémoires de Brienne*, vol. ii. pp. 195-197.   *Mémoires sur Nicolas
Fouquet*, vol. ii. p. 237.

[2] In this letter Louis XIV. thought it right to explain why, after
having authorised the marriage of Lauzun with Mademoiselle, he had
withdrawn his word.   The letter is dated December 19, 1670.   It is
amongst the Archives of the Ministry of Foreign Affairs, section France,
vol. cxcii. p. 150.—See *Madame de Montespan et Louis XIV.*, by
M. P. Clément, p. 32.

[3] *Mémoires de Saint-Simon*, vol. xiii. p. 73.

and led him to take all these fancies for real. Every one would have thought as Fouquet did, and this supposition was certainly the most probable one.

Indeed, Lauzun, of whom La Bruyère has said, "that it is not permitted to dream as he lived,"[4] encountered, in his existence of ninety-one years, such diversities of fortune, such striking contrasts, such unheard-of revolutions, that there are few heroes of the imagination to whom one would have dared to ascribe similar adventures. Nothing is more singular than the destiny of this Gascon cadet, reduced at first to beg from the Surintendant, and then raised by Louis XIV. to the highest dignities; suddenly shut up in the Bastille and succeeding in issuing from it and marrying the legitimate granddaughter of Henri IV.; afterwards commanding an army, and next a prisoner for ten years at Pignerol; receiving his pardon, but refusing it; imprisoned for the third time, then exiled, banished apparently for ever from the presence of the King, whom he had coarsely insulted, and nevertheless succeeding "in finding his way back to Versailles, by passing through London,"[5] and there making a friend of James II.; fortune's favourite and victim by turns, without ever being enlightened by its rebuffs, or satisfied by its favours! To obtain these he did not hesitate at any baseness,[6] and the extreme audacity which he sometimes gave proof of was all calculated. He had a certain boldness of mind, but not of heart, for he was naturally

---

[4] La Bruyère's *Caractères*, chapter *De la Cour*. Lauzun is designated in it by the name of Straton.

[5] Madame de Sévigné.

[6] M. P. Clément has given with respect to this a very characteristic letter from Lauzun to Colbert. See *Madame de Montespan et Louis XIV.*, p. 30, note I.

mean. Nothing, unless it be the servile humility of his beginning, equalled the insolence with which he avenged himself for his early abasement. Addicted to cruel raillery, prompt in witticisms,[7] he excelled in laying bare and flagellating the absurdities to which he piqued himself on being superior. "He is the most insolent little man," says La Fare, "that has been seen for a century."[8] Devoid of dignity and endowed with prodigious pliability, he did not hesitate to stoop to the lowest parts, and succeeded in affecting the qualities in which he was most deficient. But when, having gained his end, he threw aside the mask, and became simply himself again, he inspired contempt. Of all the women seduced by his jargon of gallantry and very deceitful appearances, he did not attach himself to one, and the cousin of Louis XIV., over whom he at first exercised so great a sway, died filled with hatred towards him, and ashamed of such an unworthy husband.[9]

But, whilst Lauzun was at Pignerol, the illusions of this princess had not yet been dissipated, and her love, increased

---

[7] He had given some very witty answers—that, amongst others, made to the Regent, whom he had asked for an abbey for his nephew, the famous De Belsunce, bishop of Marseilles. It was some time after the plague, during which the prelate had behaved like a hero. Despite the promise made to Lauzun, the Regent forgot to include his relation in the distribution of benefices, and when Lauzun questioned him on the subject, remained silent and confused. Lauzun, with a great appearance of respect, said, "Monsieur, he will do better another time."

[8] Saint-Simon, whose brother-in-law Lauzun had the good fortune to become towards the end of his life, by marrying at sixty-two years of age the daughter, aged sixteen, of the Marshal de Lorges, is more indulgent for his relation, whose meanness, however, he does not try to hide.

[9] Letter of Bussy-Rabutin, vol. viii. p. 265. of Monmerqué's edition of the *Lettres de Madame de Sévigné; Mémoires de Saint-Simon,* vol. xiii. p. 83.

by separation, manifested itself in loud complaints, in violent scenes, and in attempts to deliver him. Several times she sent agents to Pignerol, who were to try to enter into communication with Lauzun. But they failed in their enterprise, and were driven from the town and forbidden to re-enter it again.[10] On his side, Lauzun, always and everywhere destined to adventures, did not remain inactive. He thought he might be able to escape amidst the disorder and trouble of a fire, and with this intention set light to the flooring of his room. The fire, soon perceived, was, however, at once extinguished. Incapable of resigning himself to his lot, and of seeking some consolation in study, Lauzun, breaking his furniture, gave way to all kinds of outbursts and violence, but without succeeding in moving Saint-Mars. Coldly impassible, the latter was equally insensible to the threats of vengeance and to the insults of his prisoner. It was then that, impelled by curiosity, the latter began, this time with patience and without attracting the attention of his gaoler, to make in the wall [11] a hole which should put him into communication with the room situated above his own. We have seen that he succeeded in this, and how he was received by Fouquet.

By the same route, and thanks to some precautions, the visits of Lauzun were repeated. But, in continuing his confidences, he only confirmed the idea of his madness.

It is thus that Fouquet, without putting faith in him, heard him relate how to all the high offices he had obtained

---

[10] *Mémoires de Saint-Simon*, vol. xiii. p. 74.—Letters from Louvois to Saint-Mars, October 14, November 15 and 22, 1672, March 16, and November 23, 1676.

[11] Saint-Mars only discovered the hole in the wall after the death of Fouquet:—Letter from Louvois to Saint-Mars, April 8, 1680.

he had almost added one still more elevated, that of Grand Master of the Artillery, and in what manner he had avenged his insuccess. The King had promised him the appointment, and, vain as thoughtless, Lauzun had hastened to announce it, despite the secrecy agreed upon between them. Louvois, soon informed of the projects of Louis XIV., succeeded in diverting him from them by representing to him the disadvantages of such a choice. After several days of vain expectation, the favourite, accustomed to please, and hoping to be able to intimidate, watched for and seized upon a *tête-à-tête* with the King. He dared to call upon him to keep his promise, and Louis XIV. having replied that he was released from it by the indiscretion Lauzun had committed, the latter drew his sword, snapt it in pieces, and exclaimed that he would no longer serve a prince thus capable of breaking his promises. Pale with anger the King raised his cane, but, suddenly mastering himself, he threw it out of the window, saying, " that he should be very sorry to have struck a gentleman." [12]   The next day Lauzun was taken to the Bastille.

Fouquet learned from him, without believing it any the more, a still more audacious adventure. Lauzun had soon left the Bastille, and had recovered the King's favour. Beloved by Mademoiselle, he obtained permission to marry her; but vanity again ruined him. Instead of hastening such an unhoped-for union, he wishes to wait, in order that sumptuous liveries may be made and that the marriage may be solemnly celebrated in the royal chapel, in presence of the whole court, "and as between crowned heads." [13]   He

---

[12] *Mémoires de Saint-Simon*, vol. xiii. p. 70.
[13] *Souvenirs de Madame de Caylus.*

thus leaves the princes and Madame de Montespan time
to act, and Louis XIV., yielding to their representations,
withdraws the consent at first accorded.   Lauzun, who
with reason distrusted Madame de Montespan, despite the
assurances of friendship she did not cease to give him,
dared, in order to ascertain the truth, to conceive a most
dangerous project.[14] Taking for his accomplice the waiting-
woman of the powerful favourite, he slipped under the bed
a little before the King's arrival, and, a witness of their interview, he was able to convince himself that Madame de
Montespan was the inveterate enemy to whose advice
Louis XIV. had yielded. "A cough," says Saint Simon,
"the least sound, the slightest accident, might have discovered this rash being, and then what would have become
of him? These are things the relation of which stifles and
terrifies one at the same time."[15] Fortunately, Lauzun was
able to remain motionless. Meeting Madame de Montespan
at the ballet, an hour after the interview, he asked her in an
agreeable manner whether she had deigned to serve his cause
with the King. She replied that, far from having failed to do
so, she had taken pleasure, as ever, in extolling his services.
Lauzun let her speak at length ; then, suddenly, placing
his mouth to her ear, he repeated to her, word for word, the
conversation which she had just had with the King, and
wound up by calling her "liar, hussy, and jade." Madame
de Montespan succeeded in mastering her confusion, but
she never forgot this scene, and a year after, uniting with

---

[14] Racine, *Fragments Historiques.   Mémoires de Saint-Simon,*
vol. xiii. p. 69.

[15] *Mémoires de Saint-Simon, Ibid.*

Louvois,[16] she had brought about the fall of the favourite and his despatch to Pignerol.

Fouquet listened to the narrative of these adventures, which were only too real, as one reads an improbable romance. It was only much later that he was convinced by his relations and friends of the veracity of his companion in captivity. But during several years, not doubting his madness, he resigned himself to listen to him out of courtesy, not seeking occasions to see him, but carefully avoiding to contradict him; behaving, in short, toward him as one does towards an unfortunate being afflicted with a mild and harmless but obstinate mania.[17]

These two victims of fortune, reunited at Pignerol through such opposite causes, and of whom one was not to leave the place alive, whilst the other was to quit his prison to be again the hero of singular adventures, supported their captivity in a very different manner. "M. Fouquet only thinks of praying to God," writes Saint-Mars, on June 20, 1672; "he is as patient and moderate as my other prisoner is furious."[18] The outbursts of Lauzun had for their cause not only the failure of his attempts at escape,[19] but also the very arbitrary conduct of Louis XIV., inspired by Louvois. The ex-favourite cruelly expiated the favours of which he had been the object. Not satisfied with depriving him of his liberty, they tried in addition to wrest

---

[16] *Mémoires de Saint-Simon,* vol. xiii. p. 72. Segrais, a contemporary, adds Madame de Maintenon to these two undoubted authors of the second disgrace of Lauzun. (Segrais, *Mémoires et Anecdotes.*)

[17] *Mémoires sur Nicolas Fouquet,* vol. ii. p. 450.

[18] Unpublished letter from Saint-Mars to Louvois, June 20, 1672 :— Archives of Ministry of War, vol. ccxcix. fol. 48.

[19] Letter from Louvois to Saint-Mars, June 16, 1676.

from him the offices and the immense possessions that an excessive generosity had heaped upon his head, but of which he ought not to have been despoiled by means of the pressure easily put upon a captive. Captain of the Body-guard, he received from Seignelay the invitation to resign this post. [20] Endowed by Mademoiselle with the county of Eu, the duchy of Aumale, the principality of Dombes, and the estate of Thiers, he only recovered his liberty on condition of renouncing all his possessions in favour of the Duke de Maine, natural son of Louis XIV. and Madame de Montespan. At first he angrily repulsed the proposition of Seignelay, and loaded with insults Louvois, whose influence he recognized, and Saint-Mars, the interpreter of Seignelay's orders. [21] Little by little, however, calmness returned to this spirit, till then so agitated and unquiet. Lauzun understood with reason that everything ought to be sacrificed for liberty, and he hoped one day to be able to return to that culminating point of fortune from which his inconsiderate conduct had precipitated him, and which he was in fact again to attain by a supreme effort of audacity. "At court one must always take one thing with another; everything comes in turn," said Madame de Montespan to the Grande Mademoiselle. [22] Lauzun ended by following this maxim, and, by resigning himself to his lot, at length permitted Saint-Mars to taste some repose.

The unhappy gaoler had seen himself reduced, by his excessive scruples and by the conduct of Lauzun, to the

---

[20] Letter from Seignelay to Lauzun, November 9, 1672.

[21] Letters from Louvois to Saint-Mars, November 27, and December 5, 1672.

[22] *Mémoires de Mademoiselle de Montpensier*, vol. iv. p. 456.

most singular extremities.   Scarcely had Fouquet renounced
the hope of escape and given himself. up to study and
prayer, than Lauzun had come to renew and increase the
inquietude of Saint-Mars.   The ill-temper and despair of
the new captive were such that he behaved with the
utmost violence [23] towards his gaoler.   For a long time insensible to his insults, Saint-Mars had at first submitted to
them with indifference ; but this was soon no longer possible,
and he had to discontinue his visits.   How then was he to
execute the orders received and exercise his surveillance ?
The unfortunate gaoler, too much ill-treated to be able to
revisit Lauzun, and too scrupulous to leave off watching
him, was in a state of extreme perplexity.   His alarm was
increased by the impossibility of making his usual perqui-
sitions, and he was constantly representing to himself his
captive imagining and realizing a project of escape.   He at
length released himself from this intolerable situation, but
at what a price !   For a long time the subordinate officials
of Pignerol perceived their chief gliding stealthily amongst
some trees that surrounded the donjon.   Then choosing the
highest and thickest in leaf,[24] overcoming the infirmities of
age, and recovering for an instant the vigour of youth, he
clasped the gnarled trunk, climbed by degrees to the highest
branches, and there, hidden by the foliage, kept his eyes
eagerly fixed upon Lauzun's room, from which coarse insults had banished him.   From this elevated point he
observed the prisoner's conduct without being seen by

---

[23] Letters from Louvois to Saint-Mars, November 27, 1672, and
January 16, 1674.   Delort, *Histoire de la Détention des Philosophes*, p. 43.
[24] Letter from Louvois to Saint-Mars, November 10, 1675.   Delort,
Histoire de la Détention des Philosophes, p. 43.

him,[25] and thus reconciled the duties of his office with the exigencies of his dignity. Surely never did a servant better merit the confidence of his master; and Saint-Mars will remain without a rival amongst the gaolers of all times.

This post of observation ceased to be impenetrable, as Louvois had foreseen: " As the leaves have now fallen," he wrote to Saint-Mars, November 10, 1675, " you will no longer be able to see what M. de Lauzun does in his room." [26]   But this fatiguing surveillance was then rendered less necessary by the resignation and calmness of the so long indocile captive. His submission to the orders of Louis XIV., the proofs of a piety, more or less sincere;[27] the entreaties of Madame de Nogent, his sister, and of several friends, obtained for Lauzun the same favours that, for several years past, Fouquet had owed to the accession to power of his friend Arnauld de Pomponne, and doubtless also to the increasing influence of Madame de Maintenon.[28]

Since 1672 Fouquet had had permission to receive a letter from his wife.[29] Less than two years afterwards he had been allowed to write twice a year to his family.[30]   Finally,

---

[25] It was then that he discovered Lauzun often had a telescope in his hand, and it was taken from him.

[26] Delort, *Histoire de la Détention des Philosophes*, p. 241.

[27] Saint-Simon relates that for fear he should be imposed upon with a false priest, to act as a spy upon him, Lauzun had asked for a capucin, and that as soon as he saw him he seized him by the beard and pulled it very hard, in order to assure himself that it was not false. Saint-Simon says he had this from Lauzun himself. *Mémoires*, vol. xiii. p. 73.

[28] *Mémoires sur Nicolas Fouquet*, vol. ii. p. 450.

[29] Letter from Louvois to Saint-Mars, October 18, 1672.

[30] *Ibid.*, April 10, 1674.

from January 20, 1679, the favours were multiplied, and the two illustrious captives obtained all that could soften their situation.   Louis XIV. authorised them to have full liberty to meet, to take their meals, and to walk together, to converse with the officers of the donjon, and to read all kinds of books and gazettes.[31]   Whilst Madame de Nogent and the Chevalier de Lauzun received permission to come and visit their brother ; Fouquet had at length the happiness of seeing his wife, his daughter, the Count de Vaux, his son, and the Bishop of Agde and M. de Mézières, his brothers.[32] Alone and isolated for fifteen years, the Surintendant had at last this supreme consolation, which, alas ! he was not long to enjoy.   These different members of his family made a rather lengthened stay at the citadel.   But the prisoner's daughter installed herself there in a definite manner, and took up her quarters in rooms directly over those of her father.[33] Almost immediately after her arrival, Lauzun and Fouquet ceased to visit one another.[34]   The cause of this sudden misunderstanding is to be found in the gallant disposition and enterprising audacity of Lauzun.   The insolent favourite could not recognize the devotion of Fouquet's daughter, a voluntary prisoner, and the touching victim of her filial affection.   What passed between these three personages can only be surmised, for no documents exist respecting it. It is only known that, long afterwards, Lauzun paid such

---

[31] Letter of Madame de Sévigné, February 27, 1697.   "Memorandum of the manner in which the King desires Monsieur de Saint-Mars to guard for the future the prisoners in his custody," Jan. 20, 1679 :—Archives of the Ministry of War.

[32] Letters from Louvois to Saint-Mars, May 10 and 28, 1679.

[33] Letter from the same to the same, December 18, 1679.

[34] Letter from the same to the same, January 24, 1680.

frequent visits to Mademoiselle Fouquet in Paris, during which he showed himself so familiar, that the jealousy of Louis XIV.'s cousin was very strongly aroused.[35] It was the destiny of the Surintendant to undergo every misfortune, and, at the moment when he seemed about to receive some alleviation, to find suddenly in his daughter's presence a new source of grief and bitterness.

Was this grief at least the final one? did he die on March 22, 1680, as has been said, or, to this expiation of his faults courageously undergone during sixteen years at Pignerol must a still longer one be added? Did Fouquet continue to drag on his miserable existence for another twenty-three years, and was it to the Bastille that he went to finish it obscurely, dead to all, his face hidden from the world, and, as it were, surviving even himself?

[35] *Mémoires de Mademoiselle de Montpensier*, vol. iv. pp. 401 and 473 ; Delort, *Histoire de la Détention des Philosophes*, p. 52.

CHAPTER XVIII.

Theory which makes Fouquet the Man with the Iron Mask—Arguments advanced by M. Lacroix—Some to be absolutely rejected and some discussed—Fouquet not in possession of a dangerous State Secret—Madame de Maintenon—Her Character—Her Youth — Her Relations with Monsieur and Madame Fouquet — Her honourable Reserve—The Affair of the Poisons—How Fouquet's Name became mixed up in it—Probability of his Death being caused by an attack of Apoplexy—Weakness of the other Arguments advanced by M. Lacroix—Oblivion into which the Surintendant had fallen—Two mysterious Arrests.

A WRITER of much knowledge and much imagination, M. Paul Lacroix, has collected, in a very ingenious and cleverly written work,[1] all the arguments that can be advanced in favour of the theory which makes Fouquet the Man with the Iron Mask.   He begins by reminding us of the discovery, announced on August 13, 1789,[2] of a card found amongst the papers of the Bastille, bearing these words : "Fouquet, arriving from the Isles Sainte-Marguerite with an Iron Mask," and signed with three X's and the

---

[1] *Histoire de l'Homme au Masque de Fer*, by M. Paul Lacroix (Bibliophile Jacob).   Paris, 1840.

[2] *Loisirs d'un Patriote Français*, number of August 13, 1789.   This card found amongst the papers of the Bastille, and which the journalist attests having seen, also bore the number 64,389,000.

name of Kersadion. Nevertheless, M. Lacroix very properly abstains from counting amongst his proofs a paper, the existence of which is not certified by any official document, and which the wording, the strange manner in which it is said to have been found, and the improbability of any note of this character having been made, must equally cause to be rejected. The following are the more solid bases of M. Lacroix's argument :—

"The precautions employed in guarding Fouquet at Pignerol resemble in every point,"[3] says he, "those adopted later for the Man with the Iron Mask at the Bastille and at the Isles Sainte-Marguerite.

"The greater number of the traditions relating to the masked prisoner appear to apply to Fouquet.

"The appearance of the Man with the Iron Mask followed almost immediately upon the pretended death of Fouquet in 1680.

"This death of Fouquet in 1680 is far from being certain.

"Finally, political and private reasons may have determined Louis XIV. to cause him to pass for dead, in preference to getting rid of him by poison or in any other manner."

These two last arguments are the only ones which need be discussed ; for the circumstantial care, excessive vigilance, and incessant precautions of which Fouquet was the object at Pignerol were not peculiar to this prisoner. Lauzun was treated in absolutely the same manner. The instructions given to Saint-Mars every time a new prisoner, even the most obscure, was confided to his

---

[3] *Histoire de l'Homme au Masque de Fer,* p. 175.

care were identical. On July 19, 1669, when announcing
the approaching arrival of that Eustache d'Auger, who
was to become Fouquet's lackey, Louvois wrote to Saint-
Mars as if the fortune of the State was bound up with
this man.[4]   When, later, some Protestant ministers, as
unknown as they were harmless, are sent to him at the
Isles Sainte-Marguerite, there are the same detailed and
complete precautions set forth at length, and equally dear
to the circumstantial Minister [5] who enjoined them, and
the scrupulous gaoler charged with their execution.

As to the " traditions relating to the masked prisoner,"
which appear to M. Lacroix "to apply to Fouquet," we
have seen [6] that the greater number of them are legendary,
and that the others, such as the episode of the silver dish

---

[4] " The King having ordered me to have one Eustache d'Auger
taken to Pignerol, it is of the utmost importance that on his arrival he
should be guarded with great security, and not allowed to give information of his whereabouts in any manner whatever. I give you notice of
this in advance in order that you may prepare a cell in which you will
confine him securely, taking care to arrange that the openings for light
of the place, in which he will be, may not look upon places where
any one may come, and that there be enough closed doors so that our
sentinels may not be able to hear anything : "—Letter from Louvois
to Saint-Mars, July 19, 1669.

These infinite precautions were indeed a form of style. They are
to be found in the orders given to Marshal d'Estrades, in those
which are contained in the Registers of the Secretary's Office of the
King's Household, and in those which are found in the *Correspondance
Administrative sous Louis XIV.* See this correspondence published
by Depping in the collection of the *Documents inédits pour l'Histoire de
France.* See also, Imperial Library, manuscripts, *Papiers d'Estrades,*
vol. xii., and Registers of the Secretary's Office, 6653.

[5] M. Camille Rousset gives a number of proofs of the extreme
pleasure that Louvois found in a combination and excess of precautions.
(See notably vol. iii. p. 38, *et seq.* of his *Histoire de Louvois.*)

[6] Chapter V. of the present work. See pp. 62, 63, *ante.*

thrown from a window, concern several Protestant ministers, confined at the Isles Sainte-Marguerite at almost the same date as the Man with the Iron Mask.

Finally,—and we will establish this further on,—nothing whatever proves that the appearance of the Man with the Iron Mask dates from the year 1680.

But if Fouquet did not die in March, 1680,—if, above all, Louis XIV. "had political and private motives for compassing the disappearance of the Surintendant by a supposititious death," it is incontestable that the theory of M. Lacroix would have a strong chance of being accepted, since it would show what had become of this personage while it explained in a very probable manner the mystery, exaggerated by tradition, but nevertheless true, by which the famous masked prisoner was surrounded. This has been perfectly understood by M. Lacroix, who has first applied himself to contest the death of Fouquet in 1680, and then to seek out the different causes that may have determined Louis XIV. to suddenly separate the Surintendant from the rest of the world, and to make the prolongation of his life a mystery impenetrable to all except Saint-Mars.

Of these causes, those which date beyond 1680 must be peremptorily rejected. They could not, in fact, have exercised any influence upon Fouquet's fate, since we have just seen this prisoner pass by degrees from a very close and somewhat harsh confinement to a captivity much softened by favours incessantly multiplied. From 1665 to 1672 he is forbidden all communication, even with his relations; but from 1672 some occasional letters are first authorised, then a more regular correspondence, next daily intercourse

with the other prisoners, and, finally, the visit and the prolonged stay of several members of his family at Pignerol.
This progress, slow, but continuous, incontestably exists in
the period extending from 1672 to 1680. It is, therefore,
only in this last year that the origin of the terrible royal
anger and of the frightful increase of punishment suddenly
inflicted upon Fouquet is to be sought for. M. Lacroix has
neglected this essential distinction, and has gathered together all the grievances, real or pretended, of Louis XIV.,
without taking into consideration their ancient date and the
evident proofs of indulgent forgetfulness of the past successively shown to the offender. It was, therefore, superfluous
to remind us [7] of the secret negotiations of the Surintendant
with England, of his projects for rendering himself independent, and of retiring, in case of disgrace, to his principality of
Belle-Isle, which he caused to be fortified ; of his eagerness to
gain creatures, whom he bought at any price, by appointing
them to important offices and giving them secret pensions ;
or of his pretended love for Madamoiselle de la Vallière.
With regard to all these faults the royal resentment was
appeased, and it cannot be admitted that their recollection
may have suddenly irritated Louis XIV., when for eight years
he had been manifesting towards the prisoner a clemency
more obvious and efficacious.

"Fouquet, a prisoner at Pignerol," says M. Lacroix,[8]
"still excited hatred in Colbert and continual apprehensions
in Louis XIV.: *one would have said that he possessed some
great secret, the disclosure of which would be fatal to the*

---

[7] *Histoire de l'Homme au Masque de Fer*, p. 233.
[8] *Ibid.*, p. 229.

State, or at least mortally wound the King's pride." But upon this hypothesis, how was it that Louis XIV. authorised the frequent intercourse of Fouquet with Lauzun, and afterwards with the different members of his family? How was it that he was not afraid lest these should become participators in and afterwards propagators of this State secret? M. Lacroix enumerates all the precautions taken by Saint-Mars during the first period of Fouquet's detention, in order to hinder him from imparting or receiving intelligence. But three significant despatches show that these precautions, very minute indeed, were only inspired by the fear of an escape, and not at all by the apprehension of the spreading of a State secret. Three times, and for different causes, Fouquet's valets were dismissed. They were sent away, one in 1665, another at the end of the following year, and the third in 1669—that is to say, when the Surintendant was in close confinement. What became of these three persons, who for a long time had lived with the prisoner and been in a position to receive his confidence? Were they ever deprived of their liberty in order to bury with them this secret, which they may have had the misfortune to become acquainted with?

" I write you this letter," says Louis XIV. to Saint-Mars,[9] " to tell you that I deem it good that you should give the Sieur Fouquet another valet, and that after the one who is ill is cured, you are to let him go where he pleases, and the present letter being for no other end, I pray God to take you into his holy keeping."

" Your letter of the 28th of the past month," writes

---

[9] Order of Louis XIV., dated October 11, 1665.

Louvois to Saint-Mars,[10] " has been delivered to me, and has informed me that the valet of the Sieur Fouquet is afflicted with a very dangerous illness. It is well to continue to have him nursed, and if, after his cure, he does not wish to continue his services to the prisoner any longer, prudence ordains that you should keep him in the donjon three or four months, in order that if he has transgressed his duty, time may fracture the measures he may have concerted with Monsieur Fouquet."

" His Majesty leaves it to you," he writes to Saint-Mars in 1669,[11] " to act as you please with respect to La Rivière, that is to say, to leave him with Monsieur Fouquet or to remove him ; his Majesty counting that, in case you remove him, you will only let him depart after an imprisonment of from seven to eight months, in order that, if he had taken measures to carry news from his master, it would be so stale by that time, that it could cause no annoyance."

We see from these despatches that if, during the sixteen years he passed at Pignerol, Fouquet was the object of styles of treatment which differed greatly, it was never impossible for him to render other people depositaries of his secrets, and through them to communicate these secrets to his friends, his relations, or foreign sovereigns, as well as to the great lords of the court. He could have done this in 1665, in 1666, and in 1669, by means of his servants detained only a few months as prisoners and then dismissed without conditions. He could have done it later still more easily through the medium either of Lauzun or of all those who came to visit him. One must therefore reject the idea that

---

[10] Letter of Louvois to Saint-Mars, September 23, 1666.
[11] *Ibid.*, September 17, 1669.

Fouquet was the possessor of a dangerous State secret, and moreover, necessarily conclude from the much more humane conduct of Louis XIV. towards the Surintendant, that the King's former resentment had disappeared, and that in 1680 he no longer saw in the prisoner anything but an old man, very interesting both by his misfortunes and his resignation.

But M. Lacroix invokes something else besides reasons of State ; according to him, the last and the most powerful of Louis XIV.'s favourites was interested in the Surintendant's disappearance. Formerly the latter's mistress, when she was the wife of Scarron, at the moment of her marriage with the King she had exacted from him an increase of rigour towards this troublesome Surintendant, that awkward witness of her former weaknesses.

Will that which Madame de Sévigné calls "the first volume of Madame de Maintenon's life,"[12] always remain a mystery ? and shall we never know the exact beginning of this illustrious *parvenue* who desired to be an enigma for posterity?[13] Like all those who have had the honour to meet with eager detractors, she has found defenders, unreasonable without doubt, but who have shown the injustice[14] of the passions excited against the ex-Huguenot converted to Catholicism, and afterwards wife of Louis XIV., at the moment of the Revocation of the Edict of Nantes and the persecution of the Jansenists. It is the exaggeration of

---

[12] Letter of Madame de Sévigné, July 7, 1680.

[13] *Correspondance Générale*, Lavallée's edition, vol. i. p. 1.

[14] Let us cite amongst others, the fine *Histoire de Madame de Maintenon*, of the Duke de Noailles, unhappily still unfinished ; the labours of M. Théophile Lavallée and Chapter I. Period iii. of the curious volumes of M. Chéruel, *Saint-Simon considéré comme Historien*, which is the necessary complement of his edition of the *Mémoires*.

the attack, it is the violence of Saint-Simon, of the Princess Palatine, and of La Fare, rather than any sudden attraction, that has produced this change in public opinion, this current, general to-day and highly favourable to Madame de Maintenon.   Her rehabilitation was so necessary that every one has given his adhesion, but only from a feeling of justice.   In learning to know her better one has ceased to despise her, without loving her any the more, and one has conceived much more esteem for her mind than inclination for her person.   Never, in fact, even when looking back through ages, does one experience very powerful feelings on behalf of those who were deficient in them, and dry, cold virtue, without the passion that animates, and the struggle that vivifies it, will always lack admirers.   Madame de Maintenon not only appears austere and inflexible, but everything with her is conventional and calculated.   Her piety is not ardent in its outbursts, like La Vallière's, but restrained and deliberate, and her scruples always turn to the advantage of her fortune.   Not false, but of consummate prudence ; not perfidious, but always ready, if not to sacrifice, at least to abandon her friends; loving the appearance of good as much as good itself; without imagination, and consequently without illusions, this woman, superior by the intellect much more than by the heart, was armed against all allurements, and the fear of compromising her reputation placed her beyond all perils.   " There is nothing more clever than an irreproachable conduct," said she.   This sentence paints her perfectly, and allows one to penetrate to the bottom of her soul.   It explains and enlightens the whole of her life, and by its aid one can understand how this woman managed to live amidst the dangers of a light and frivolous society without succumbing, traverse youth without experiencing its temptations, undergo poverty with honour, hold her own at court, be constant mistress of herself, and end by irrevocably securing in the heart of the King a place which neither La Vallière, despite her disinterested devotion, Fontanges, despite her powers of fascination, nor Montespan, despite her legitimated children, had known how to preserve. To a sound judgment, to a dignity imposing, but devoid of arrogance, to that marvellous art of being queen without appearing to pretend to it, and of receiving the homage of the court with quite a Christian humility; to all these qualities, by which, as Louis XIV.'s wife, she showed herself worthy of her destiny, Madame de Maintenon had added, from her most tender infancy, that proud desire "for a good reputation," in which lay her strength. "This was my hobby," she said later.[15] "I did not trouble myself about riches; I was infinitely above interest. But I wished for honour. I did not seek to be loved privately by any one whatever. I wanted to be loved by everybody."

Nothing indicates that her firm and decided will ever failed in carrying out this proud engagement, undertaken in early life with coolness and resolution. For a Saint-Simon and for a Ninon de Lenclos, who incriminate her conduct, there are many less suspicious witnesses who come forward in her favour. "We were all surprised," says the Intendant Basville, "that any one could unite such virtues, such poverty, and such charms." M. Lacroix[16] invokes that note transcribed by Conrart, said to have been found in

---

[15] *Lettres Historiques et Édifiantes de Madame de Maintenon*, vol. ii. p. 213.

[16] *Histoire de l'Homme au Masque de Fer*, p. 244.

Fouquet's casket, and to have been written to him by Madame de Maintenon : "I do not know you enough to love you, and if I knew you perhaps I should love you less. I have always avoided vice, and I naturally hate sin. But I confess to you that I hate poverty still more. I have received your ten thousand crowns. If you will bring me another ten thousand in two days, then I will see what I have to do." But besides the fact that Conrart ascribes to Madame de la Baulme this letter, the terms of which also contrast singularly with Madame de Maintenon's style,[17] we know from positive proofs what were the relations both of Scarron and his wife with the family of Fouquet. If some doubts may exist with respect to Villarceaux, whom Saint-Simon and Ninon de Lenclos make Madame de Maintenon's lover, no one can fail to recognize the perfect propriety and the dignity she exhibited in accepting the benefits of the Surintendant. It is always to Madame Fouquet that she addresses herself; and when the latter, charmed by so much intelligence, wishes to have the wife of Scarron near her, she rejects with marvellous tact a proposition full of perils both to her virtue, and, above all, to her good fame.[18] One day, however, she was obliged, on account of Scarron's infirmities, to go herself to solicit Fouquet. "But," says Madame de

---

[17] Conrart, *Manuscripts*, vol. xi. p. 151 :—Archives of the Arsenal. The same observations apply to this other letter, likewise ascribed by M. Lacroix to Madame de Maintenon, and with as little ground : "Until now I was so thoroughly persuaded of my strength, that I would have defied all the earth. But I confess that the last interview I had with you charmed me. I found in your conversation a thousand pleasures which I had not expected ; in short, if I ever see you alone, I do not know what will happen."

[18] *Mémoires sur Nicolas Fouquet*, vol. i. pp. 448, 449.

Caylus (and Mademoiselle d'Aumale confirms the accuracy of this account), " she affected to go there in such great negligence that her friends were ashamed of taking her. Every one knows what M. Fouquet was then, his weakness for women, and how much the highest sought to please him. This conduct, and the just admiration that it excited, reached even the Queen's ears." [19]

Extreme reserve towards the Surintendant, and affectionate gratitude towards Madame Fouquet, such were, we see, the sentiments of Scarron's widow; and far from having to cause a weakness to be forgotten, Madame de Maintenon had, on the contrary, to remember the kindnesses of this family, and for her part to contribute to the alleviation of the prisoner's lot.

Afterwards, in a very vague manner, and without furnishing any positive proofs, M. Lacroix reminds us that Fouquet was mixed up in those famous poisoning trials which revealed so many monstrous scandals and implicated certain great personages of the court, in which, too, we see the audacity of the crimes still further increased by the revolting cynicism of the avowals, and which produced a profound commotion throughout the whole of France and even abroad.

That Fouquet's name may have been pronounced during the discussions, one is not prepared either to contest or feel surprised at. As his enemy, Colbert, was one of the appointed victims, and as a conspiracy seemed to have been formed to poison him, it is very natural that the accused persons should have invoked the recollection of the Surin-

---

[19] *Souvenirs de Madame de Caylus,* pp. 10 and 11 ; M. Feuillet de Conches, *Causeries d'un Curieux,* vol. ii. p. 515 ; M. Chéruel, *Saint-Simon considéré comme Historien,* p. 504, *et seq.*

tendant. But how many other names, such as those of La Fontaine and Racine, were indicated to the lieutenant of police without their reputations being tarnished by it! M. Lacroix, with reason, regrets that most of the papers relating to this dark business have not been published. They are about to be, and not one of the innumerable documents relating to these various trials authorises us to accuse the Surintendant.[20] As for those which have already been published, and which include some declarations concerning Fouquet, an attentive examination of the period at which they have been made proves that they could have exercised no influence upon the fate of the prisoner of Pignerol. "The woman Filastre said at the torture, that she had written a contract by which the Duchess de Vivonne desired the restoration of M. Fouquet and the death of M. Colbert." But this declaration was made some months after the Surintendant's death.[21] We have a letter from Louvois to the lieutenant of police, La Reynie, in which the latter is thanked for having informed the King "what one named Debray has said of the solicitation that was made to him by a man dependent on Fouquet;"[22] but this letter is dated June 17, 1681, fifteen months after the death, or, if it is preferred, the period at which Louis XIV. had determined upon causing the Surintendant to disappear. Would the revelations of the Marchioness de Brinvilliers be relied upon by preference? But her trial dates from 1676,

---

[20] This is what I have several times been assured of by M. Ravaisson, who, in publishing the documents relating to the Bastille, has come across the *affaire des poisons.*

[21] M. Pierre Clément, *La Police sous Louis XIV.*, p. 221.

[22] *Ibid.* p. 222.

and if Fouquet had been seriously compromised at that time, wherefore those successive alleviations of his punishment during a period of four years?"

In any case, if on such interested and doubtful depositions it be admitted that Fouquet's friends were the counsellors and accomplices of a crime,[23] I can understand that, struck with the coincidence,—not precisely exact, as we have just seen—between these accusations and the Surintendant's death, the suspicion might arise that the latter was not a natural one. M. Pierre Clément, in his work, *La Police sous Louis XIV.*, has expressed this idea with extreme circumspection, and has contented himself with uttering a doubt. He accuses no one, as he is especially careful to declare. But he observes that the period at which Fouquet's death occurred rendered it an untoward[24] event. He succumbed to an attack of apoplexy, and the nature of this complaint would go far to accredit the theory of poison; but there conjectures ought to stop. Let people hesitate to believe that he was really seized with an attack of this nature: I can conceive their doing so, although numerous reasons combine to make us place credence in it. But everything is entirely opposed to the hypothesis of his death[25] being simulated by Louis

---

[23] A councillor to the Parliament named Pinon-Dumartray, a relation of Fouquet's, was suspected of having been connected with the Sieur Damy, who was accused of a plot against Colbert's life.

[24] M. Pierre Clément, *La Police sous Louis XIV.*, p. 221.

[25] In support of this opinion, M. Lacroix (in the work already referred to, pp. 251, 252) speaks of a letter written by Louis XIV. to Pope Clement X., in which he requested him "to grant him a secret dispensation in order that he might rid himself, without form of trial, of a man, dangerous and hurtful to his government." M. Lacroix adds that "Clement X. was probably opposed to the death of the prisoner at Pignerol." But M. Lacroix does not give this very strange letter of

XIV.'s orders ; and whether it was natural, or whether it was hastened by a crime, it is unquestionably true that it really took place in the month of March of the year 1680.

Was it, in truth, a man in a good state of health who suddenly succumbed ? It was an old man, who had been ailing for the last sixteen years—a man unsettled by excess of blood [26]—a man whom the absence of every kind of exercise had rendered plethoric, and who, from a busy life and one given up for a long time to pleasure, had suddenly passed to the privations and the inaction of captivity.

Was it a prisoner, malignant and full of strong resentment, who was suspected of having instigated his friends to poison Colbert? No, indeed. It was the most patient and

---

Louis XIV.'s, which he terms the keystone of his theory, contenting himself with observing : " This letter, so strange that people would wish to deny its existence, is among the manuscripts in the *Bibliothèque du Roi*. M. Champollion-Figeac, who discovered it three years ago among the *papiers de Bouillaud*, told me the tenour of it at that time, at the very moment I was setting off on a long journey. But unfortunately he forgot to take a note of the volume containing this singular paper, and since my return he has in vain sought to find it again. The learned M. Libri also remembers having seen this precious document."

The following is the truth about this letter and the origin of the remarks of MM. Champollion-Figeac and Libri. It is in the *recueil Bouillaud*, Manuscripts of the Imperial Library, SF 997, vol. xxxiii., catalogue, that this seventeenth-century collector speaks of a letter " in which the Cardinal de Richelieu begged the King to demand from the Pope a brief allowing him to put to death, without any form of trial, those whom he considered deserving of it, a request which Pope Urban VIII. refused." M. P. Clément has already quoted this extract in note 2, p. 222 of his *Police sous Louis XIV.*

M. Lacroix will thus see that his letter does not concern Louis XIV., Clement X., and Fouquet, but rather Louis XIII., Urban VIII., and some unknown victims.

[26] Most of the complaints that Fouquet mentions in his letters are due to a too great abundance of blood.

the most resigned of captives, who had expiated his faults by the most admirable behaviour, who had pardoned his enemies, and whose mind, detached from the good things of the world, was raised to the contemplation of things divine, and who, offering his own life as an example, had devoted his long leisure to erecting a monument of his piety for the edification of his fellow-creatures.

Did he die mysteriously, without witnesses, save a gaoler capable of a crime? It was in the presence of the Count de Vaux, his son, and of his daughter,[27]—it was in their arms that he yielded up his breath. Saint-Mars, whom all his contemporaries represent to us as a perfectly upright man, was the sole intermediary between the King and his prisoners. Lastly, when the news of his death arrives at the court, Louis XIV. immediately causes an order to be transmitted to his representatives at Pignerol " to give up Fouquet's corpse to his family, in order that they may have it transported whither it may seem good to them." [28]

These are decisive and material considerations, the value of which cannot be destroyed by that crowd of secondary arguments which M. Lacroix has gathered up into a heap, and put forward with very great skill. But will even these resist a strict investigation? Can one be astonished that the accounts of Fouquet's death furnished by his friends, separated from him for so long a time,[29] should differ from

---

[27] Letters from Louvois to Saint-Mars, April 3 and May 4, 1680.

[28] *Ibid.*, April 9, 1680.

[29] M. Chéruel, who arrives at the conclusion that Fouquet died in March, 1680, observes, with reason, that a passage from the *Mémoires de Gourville* is alone in contradiction with other contemporary testimony, but that the contradiction is only apparent. According to Bussy-Rabutin, Fouquet was authorised in 1680 to go to the waters of

one another?   Is it astonishing that some should attribute his death to suffocation, others to a fit, when we
know that pulmonary apoplexy is always accompanied by
suffocation?   Must we consider as significant the uselessness of the researches made at Pignerol by a learned
Piedmontese,[30] when he himself explains it by the suppression of the convent of Sainte-Claire, in which the body
of Fouquet was placed for the time being, by the altera-
tions which have taken place in the church,[31] and the dis-
persion of papers[32] belonging to this monastery?   Lastly, is

---

Bourbon.   We have not referred to this authorisation, because no
document makes mention of it.   But the report was spread about at
Paris, and it is not surprising that Gourville, writing his recollections
long after the events, should have confounded the authorisation with
the realization of this journey, and have said : "M. Fouquet having been
set at liberty ——."   It is nevertheless in reference to this passage that
Voltaire writes in his *Siècle de Louis XIV.*, "Hence it is not known
where this unfortunate man died, whose most insignificant actions were
of importance while he was powerful."   Voltaire has sacrificed truth
to effect of style.   Madame de Sévigné knew of it : "Poor Monsieur
Fouquet is dead, I regret it ; I have never lost so many friends."
Bussy knew of it : "You know, I think, of the death of Fouquet by
apoplexy at the time he was permitted to take the Bourbon waters."
The family knew of it, since several of its members were at Pignerol in
March, 1680.   Gourville was the only one who was not correctly
informed ; but we have just seen in what manner and why he differs
from other contemporaries.

[30] Paroletti, *Sur la Mort du Surintendant Fouquet, notes receuillies
à Pignerol*, quarto, 24 pages.   Turin, 1812.

[31] *Ibid.*, p. 20.   Paroletti also concluded that the death of Fouquet took place in March, 1680.   There are equally the conclusions of a
work in preparation by M. Gaultier de Claubry on this special question,
and which will form part of that beautiful historical series to which for
some years past we have been indebted to the city of Paris.

[32] The ancient convent of Ste.-Claire is now a home for beggars.
M. Jacopo Bernardi, honorary grand vicar of the Bishop of Pignerol,
writes to me that in the country the death of Fouquet in 1680 is still

there anything strange in the silence of La Fontaine, in the laconism with which the *Gazette* and *Le Mercure* announce Fouquet's death, and in the absence of an ostentatious inscription in the chapel of the Convent des Filles de la Visitation, to which his body was carried? Twenty years had passed away since the fall of the Surintendant. But in how much shorter space of time are services forgotten! In the especially fruitful period from 1660 to 1680, other and more illustrious names had filled the world's stage and usurped fame. In that court which he had dazzled with his splendour, Fouquet had long since been forgotten, and only a few friends sympathized with his misfortunes. If he who has lent such touching language to the nymphs of Vaux was silent, if the death of his benefactor inspired him with no theme, it was not because he declined to believe in it. But rather than suppose him insensible to it, will it not be better to explain his silence as the result of indolence, and abandon the thought that La Fontaine was indifferent to Fouquet's death?

If the real sentiments experienced under these circumstances by the fabulist are unknown to us, if the end of him who for so long kept a portion of the court at his feet occurred almost unperceived, he had at least the honour of being mourned by Madame de Sévigné, who was always faithful,[33] and the consolation of being surrounded by his family on his death-bed; while even Saint-Mars himself must have regretted this inoffensive and resigned prisoner. A short time after Fouquet's death Lauzun was liberated.

---

a tradition. I take this opportunity of thanking my obliging and learned correspondent for the information with which he has been good enough to furnish me about Pignerol.

[33] See especially Letters of Madame Sévigné, April 3 and 5, 1680.

But a year previous to this a few dragoons, commanded by an officer mysteriously despatched to Pignerol, had left the citadel during the night and taken the road to Turin. Halting at an isolated inn, far from any other habitation, and situated a short distance from the little river Chisola, they penetrated inside the house and concealed themselves with such care that their presence could not be detected. Very early the next morning a carriage containing three persons, two of whom were priests, hastily set out from Turin. Arrived at the banks of the stream, which was swollen by the rains, the travellers were obliged to dismount and traverse the torrent by means of some planks hurriedly put together. They then entered a room of the inn. Not long afterwards the armed dragoons made their way into this room and seized one of the travellers. An hour subsequently a carriage, surrounded by a cavalry escort, quitted the inn and conducted the prisoner to Pignerol. Three days later another stranger arrived in his turn at this fatal house. Immediately surrounded and seized by the same dragoons, posted in the same spot, he was also thrown into a carriage and rapidly whirled off to Pignerol.

CHAPTER XIX.

It is almost always unwisely that the Kings of France have intermeddled in the affairs of Italy. Their occupations have never been lasting, because they have been in opposition to the true interests of France, and have violated natural boundary laws imposed upon the two countries by their geographical configurations. Charles VIII. conquered the Kingdom of Naples, but Louis XII. lost it. The latter took possession of the Milanese, but François I. was obliged to evacuate it; and by giving up Piedmont, which his father had made himself master of, Henri II. completed this retrograde movement. After having quitted the false path into which his three predecessors had dragged France, Henri II. indicated where the frontiers were to be enlarged, where national conquests were to be made, and what was the true direction to be given to her armies. He took Calais, thus pointing out the road to the Netherlands, and by becoming the master of the Trois-Evêchés he opened to his successors the glorious road to Alsace and the Rhine. While he was so happily inaugurating a new struggle, he was also establishing the basis of a new policy obscurely foreseen by François I., but the merits of which certainly belong to Henri II. The latter understood that the most effectual way of contending with the Emperor of Germany, the head of the Catholic party, was to ally himself with the German Princes and the Reformed party ; and if he was too early interrupted in his scheme by a violent death—if the minority or the weakness of his children for a long time suspended its execution—it was again undertaken, and we know with what success, by Henri IV., Richelieu, Mazarin, and Louis XIV. To assure the neutrality of Spain, to watch Italy without attempting to establish himself there, to lead all his forces towards the ·North and the East, and to extend in this direction the frontiers, which were too near to the capital : such was the glorious policy of Henri IV., suspended for a time after his death, but worthily continued by his successors.

At the same time it cannot be said that the latter were indifferent to the affairs of Italy. When, in 1627, the Dukes of Savoy and Guastalla,. aided by the House of Austria, wished to secure to Charles de Gonzaga the Duke of Mantua's inheritance, Louis XIII. loudly proclaimed the cause of this legitimate heir, and ensured the triumph of his rights. Rendered by victory master of the destiny of the House of Savoy, Richelieu did not allow himself to be dazzled by success. This incomparable politician understood that to dispossess an Italian dynasty and to establish himself on the other side of the Alps, would necessarily result in uniting the Italians to the Spaniards, in provoking against the French (who had suddenly become unpopular, even by their presence) a coalition sooner or later victorious, and creating, in fact, outside the natural sphere of action of France, incessant grounds of anxiety, jealousies, struggles, and alarms. Thus, in 1631, by the treaty of Cherasco, the skilful Minister, sacrificing many of the fruits of his victory, restored Piedmont and Savoy, contenting himself with retaining Pignerol, so as always to keep open one of the passes into Italy. To watch over her without alarming her, to be a protector of the rights of the Italian Princes without menacing their independence, to exact complete confidence from them in return, to baffle the intrigues of the Spaniards, and to allow them to accumulate on themselves hatred and resentment ; to assume, in a word, an attitude passive yet vigilant, firm but not menacing, such was the judicious conduct of Richelieu towards Italy.

Louis XIV. long remained faithful to this policy. It was towards the North and East that he led his victorious armies, and by a succession of enterprises, happily conceived and wonderfully well-conducted, he extended the frontiers of France in the proper direction ; and, arbitrator of Europe, at the Peace of Aix-la-Chapelle, and subsequently at that of Nimeguen, he inspired her with fear and admiration. In these two cities his will alone was the sole basis of the negotiations. While for every one the treaty of Aix-la-Chapelle had never appeared to be aught but a truce, that of Nimeguen combined all the conditions of a definitive peace. But even before this famous treaty was signed, Louis XIV. had conceived ambitious projects on the other side of the Alps, and the possession of Pignerol and the neighbouring valleys no longer appeared to him sufficient for the part he was desirous of playing in Italy. The influence of his government had, however, been better accepted there, when it was more dissembled, and when everything that could give the slightest offence had been avoided with the greatest care. But, when the policy of Richelieu and Mazarin, scrupulously continued by De Lionne, had ceased to prevail—when the invading and impetuous Louvois established a sort of military diplomacy, which he directed as he pleased—the sentiments of the Italians, and in particular of the Piedmontese, became somewhat modified: confiding deference gave place to restrained apprehension, and led by degrees to a hatred which burst out against France at the moment she was oppressed by coalitions and defeats.

Charles-Emmanuel, Duke of Savoy, had just died, leaving as his successor a child, under the guardianship of a mother,[1] vain, ardent, and impassioned, and whom littleness of mind, as much as hastiness of character, led to exaggerated resistance, soon to be followed by humiliating concessions. Instead of showing himself the disinterested protector and sincere counsellor of Victor-Amadeus, Louis XIV. sought from that time forward to become powerful in Italy by profiting by the weakness of this government, the vanity of the Regent, the inexperience of her son, and by the passions aroused in this court around a frivolous and capricious woman. By an altogether opposite line of conduct

---

[1] Marie-Jeanne-Baptiste de Nemours, widow of Charles-Emmanuel and mother of Victor-Amadeus II.

he might have eternally attached to himself the young Duke, who, instead, was later to become his adversary, not the most formidable, but certainly the most inconvenient, and who was to contribute, above all others, to the diversion created in the South, to paralyze the power of France, and place her within an inch of her ruin. Victor-Amadeus has been represented, and with reason, as a perfidious enemy and unreliable ally. But, in the first place, it was the conduct of his mother, and afterwards that of Louis XIV., which early disposed this prince to dissimulation. Left in retirement by a hard and ambitious Regent, with his friends watched and suspected, and himself isolated, yet not a stranger to the interests of his States, taciturn, but thoughtful and observant, more patient than resigned, he was submitting with apparent indifference to a double and oppressive guardianship, from which he only awaited the opportunity to escape or to be revenged. From this moment Louis XIV. himself prepared those disasters which were to mark the end of his reign. Whilst those audaciously arbitrary decisions of the *Chambres de Réunion* for the aggrandisement of France by conquests made in full peace, profoundly irritated the North of Europe, he was about to agitate the South by pretensions equally extravagant, for a long time concealed, then boldly disclosed, and which tended to nothing less than to place a part of Italy under his exclusive dominion.

The complacency, or at least the neutrality, which the vanity and weakness of the Regent assured to Louis XIV., in Piedmont, was rendered not less certain in Mantua by the frivolous indifference of Charles IV., its young duke. This prince, a degenerate representative of the House of

Gonzaga, which has produced so many great men, and mingled its blood with the most illustrious families of Europe, showed himself unworthy of his rank and of his name, by the most extravagantly dissipated conduct. Careless and thoughtless, he was quite indifferent to the interests of his duchy, leaving its administration to incompetent favourites; and himself a non-resident duke, was in the habit of spending the greater part of his existence amidst the pleasures of Venice, and only dreaming of returning to Mantua, when the pressing need of money called him thither. A great gambler, and lavish in his expenditure, he had soon exhausted in fêtes and adventures the remnants of a fortune and of an equally broken constitution. Anticipating the revenues of his duchy, he had just obtained from some Jews advances on the taxes for several years.[2] This sum was soon squandered, and Charles IV. deprived of resources, but not less eager for pleasure, ruined, but not less anxious to assist at all the festivals given outside his States, was reduced to expedients, and in a manner compelled to sell himself. He was not long in finding a purchaser.

Under his authority was placed the marquisate of Montferrat—that rich and fertile country, so perpetually sought after, and the possession of which was frequently contested by arms. Taken by the Romans from the Goths, then by the latter from the Lombards, afterwards forming a portion of the Empire of the West, eventually becoming an hereditary fief, several times claimed by the House of Savoy, conquered by Charles Emmanuel, then evacuated, this country had at length been annexed to the Duchy of Mantua, from which vast

---

[2] Despatch of the Marquis de Villars to Pomponne, January 8, 1677:—Archives of the Ministry of Foreign Affairs, section Savoy, 66.

States, nevertheless, separated it. Casale was its capital. This fortified place, situated on the Po, fifteen leagues to the east of Turin, was of the utmost importance, and especially to Piedmont. From very remote times the Court of Turin had coveted this natural dependency, which the defeats of Louis XIV. and the conduct of Victor Amadeus would one day secure to it.

That the Duke of Mantua should possess this territory, bordering on Piedmont, was no doubt an anomaly, but was scarcely dangerous. The King of France, on the contrary, being already master of Pignerol, on securing possession of Casale, would, in reality, enclose the Court of Turin between two formidable places, of which the one to the south-west gave access to the passage of the Alps, and the other, to the north-east, commanded the road to the Milanese. This was the project formed by Louis XIV. The intrigue was mysteriously commenced in 1676 ; but for a long time previously he had turned his attention to this important town. On September 17, 1665, a few days subsequent to the death of Charles III., the preceding Duke of Mantua, he had hastened to send to the Regent, mother [3] of Charles IV., the Sieur d'Aubeville, instructed to insist " that no change should be tolerated in the garrison of Casale during the minority of the young Duke. [4] This demand, which was very natural on account of the contiguity of the Spaniards, seemed—and, perhaps, was, at the time—ex-

---

[3] Isabella Clara of Austria, daughter of the Archduke Leopold, who was grandson of the Emperor Ferdinand III. She was married June 13, 1649, to Charles III., Duke of Mantua.—*Trans.*

[4] Unpublished letter of Louis XIV. :—Archives of the Ministry of War, vol. dcxxxv, p. 36.

tremely disinterested. In 1676, however, he no longer troubled himself with the maintenance of a Mantuan garrison at Casale, but rather with throwing the place open to his own troops.

One of the great personages of Mantua was Ercole Antonio Matthioly. He was born at Bologna, December 1, 1640, and belonged to an old and distinguished family of the long robe. His grandfather, Constantino Matthioly, had been raised to the dignity of senator. One of his uncles, Ercole Matthioly, a Jesuit father, was a very celebrated orator.[5] He himself early attracted attention by obtaining, when only nineteen years of age, the prize in civil and canon law, and shortly afterwards the title of professor at the University of Bologna. He subsequently made himself still further known by several much-prized works ; and after having formed an alliance with an honourable senatorial family of Bologna, established himself at Mantua, where his talents, dexterity, and early maturity caused him to be appreciated by Duke Charles III. de Gonzaga, one of whose Secretaries of State he became. After this prince's death, his son, Charles IV. de Gonzaga, when he attained his majority, accorded his friendship to Matthioly, whom he named Supernumerary Senator of Mantua, a dignity to which the title of Count was attached. Filled with ambition, Matthioly not only hoped to reacquire the office of Secretary of State, but also to become the principal Minister of his young master. Knowing his position to be most precarious, he was ardently desirous of

---

[5] Unpublished letter from Matthioly to the Empress Eleonora of Austria:—Archives of the Ministry of Foreign Affairs, section Mantua, 5 ; *Arbor priscæ nobilisque masculinæ familiæ de Matthiolis:*—Archives of the Empire, M. 746 ; *L'Italia regnante,* di Gregorio Leri, part iii., Geneva, 1676, duodecimo, pp. 161–173.

rendering him one of those signal services which justify the highest rewards, and an occasion offered itself during the latter months of the year 1677.

The Abbé d'Estrades,[6] then ambassador of Louis XIV. to the Venetian Republic, was as ambitious and as restless as Matthioly. Belonging to a family of *diplomates,* and anxious to become illustrious in his turn, he had the cunning to enter resolutely into the views of the Court of Versailles, and knowing very well, moreover, that his conduct would be approved, to concoct the intrigue which was to end in the cession of Casale to the King of France. Having long since been acquainted with the condition of the Court of Mantua and with the individuals holding the chief rank in it, he cast his eyes upon Matthioly as being, from his character, the most likely to embrace the project of surrender, and by using his influence over his master, to induce him to adopt it. But before entering directly into communication with Matthioly, he sent to Verona, where the latter frequently resided, one Giuliani,[7] a perfectly sure man, whom

---

[6] Son of Godefroi, Count d'Estrades, long employed in diplomatic negotiations in Holland and appointed a Marshal of France on the death of Turenne.—*Trans.*

[7] A despatch from Varengeville, ambassador at Venice, to Pomponne, July 1, 1679, given by Delort, states that Giuliani "is a little editor of newspapers, in whose shop the letters of news are written, as it is not the custom here [Venice] to print them. He works at this himself, as well as at copying for the public ; and his situation in this town answers to that of the Secretaries of St. Innocent at Paris. Therefore it would be a very improper thing to give a secretaryship of embassy to a man of this profession [as the Abbé d'Estrades had proposed to do], who, besides, in other respects, does not appear to me fit to properly fill such an employment. . . . But as he is a sort of ferret who works out and gets at all that is passing, I think it is necessary to encourage his zeal by some such gratification as forty or fifty pistoles a year, or whatever shall be approved of by his Majesty."—*Trans.*]

his occupation of journalist obliged to travel from place to place to collect news, and whose stay at Verona consequently would not excite suspicion. Giuliani had Matthioly watched, and, observing him himself, ascertained his aversion to the Spaniards, from whom he had never received anything but hopes. By degrees the connection became closer, and Giuliani was able to indicate to him without danger the plans of the Abbé d'Estrades, the pecuniary advantages which the Duke of Mantua would derive from the surrender of Casale to Louis XIV., and the security as well as the honour of an alliance with so powerful a sovereign. Matthioly leapt at the proposition,[8] and undertook to expound it to the Duke, whom he had no great difficulty in convincing. The intercourse soon became more direct. Giuliani saw Charles IV. at Mantua, and it was agreed that an interview between the latter and the Abbé d'Estrades might take place at Venice with all the more secrecy, " as, in consequence of the Carnival, every one, even the Doge, the oldest Senators, the Cardinals, and the Nuncio, goes about masked." [9] Louis XIV. and M. de Pomponne, his Minister,[10] congratulated the Abbé d'Estrades

---

[8] Despatches from the Abbé d'Estrades to Louis XIV., December 18, 1677 ; from the same to Pomponne, December 24, 1677 ; January 1 and 29, 1678. These have been given by Delort, as well as all those to which the word " unpublished " is not prefixed. Delort had seen and made use of the Mantua and Venice series, but not of that of Savoy, in which the most curious and interesting are to be found, because the Abbé d'Estrades, after having filled the post of ambassador at Venice, was sent in the same capacity to Turin.

[9] Despatch from D'Estrades to Louis XIV., December 18, 1677.

[10] Simon Arnaud de Pomponne, Secretary of State for Foreign Affairs at this epoch. In spite of his admittedly high character, he

with effusion on the propitious commencement of this delicate negotiation,[11] and on January 12, 1678, the King himself did not disdain to write to Count Matthioly, in order to
thank him.[12]

Matthioly and Charles IV., in fact, proceeded to Venice.
They first discussed with the Abbé the price of the surrender,
which was fixed at 100,000 crowns,[13] payable after the
exchange of the ratifications of the treaty, and in two sums
at three months' interval. At midnight on March 13, 1678,[14]
the Ambassador of the King of France and the Duke of
Mantua met, as if by chance, in the middle of a public
square on leaving a ball, and there, away from every
inquisitive ear, and concealed from every glance by a mask
similar to those then worn by all noblemen at Venice, conversed for quite an hour concerning the conditions of the
treaty, the payments of the stipulated price, and the manner
in which Louis XIV. should defend Charles IV. against the
effects of the resentment of the Venetian Republic and the

---

fell into disgrace in the course of the following year, mainly through
the intrigues of Colbert, with whom he was at enmity, and whose
brother was promoted to his post.—*Trans.*

[11] Letters from Louis XIV. and Pomponne to the Abbé d'Estrades,
January 12, 1678.

[12] "MONSIEUR LE COMTE MATTHIOLI.—"I have perceived from
the letter that you have written to me, and from what my ambassador,
the Abbé d'Estrades, has informed me, the regard that you show for my
interests. You cannot doubt but that I am much obliged to you for it,
and that I shall have much pleasure in giving you proofs of my satisfaction upon every occasion. Referring you, therefore, to what will be
said to you more particularly on my behalf by the Abbé d'Estrades,
I shall not lengthen this letter more than to pray God that he will have
you, Monsieur le Comte Matthioli, in his holy keeping.

"LOUIS."

[13] 12,500*l.*—*Trans.*

[14] Despatch from D'Estrades to Louis XIV., March 19, 1678.

Spaniards. Distrustful as were the Italian princes, disposed as the Venetian Republic may have been to suspect an intrigue, and prevent so dangerous an intervention as that of the King of France in the north of Italy, numerous and accomplished as were the spies who swarmed in Venice, it was in this same city, almost under the very eyes of the representatives of the different powers, that the bases of a treaty which was one of the most menacing to the independence of the Peninsula, were settled, in a mysterious and impenetrable manner.

With the same precautions, and always without attracting the attention of the other princes, Charles IV. saw the Abbé d'Estrades several times afterwards. It was arranged between them that Matthioly should proceed secretly to France, and that he should sign at Versailles, in the name of his master, the definitive treaty which would permit Louis XIV. to penetrate into the north of Italy. This journey of Matthioly's was delayed for some months, first by a rather lengthened illness, which kept him at Mantua, then by Louis XIV.'s desire to defer till the following spring, —that is, till April, 1679,—the despatch of his troops to Casale.[15] At the end of October, 1678, Count Matthioly and Giuliani, in order to avert suspicion, announced their intention of paying a visit to Switzerland, and, in fact, proceeded thither, traversed it,[16] and arrived in Paris on November 28. At once placed in communication with

---

[15] Letters from Pomponne to D'Estrades, April 13, 1678 ; from D'Estrades to Pomponne, April 30, May 21, and June 11, 1678 ; from Pomponne to D'Estrades, June 15 and 22 ; Letters from Pinchesne, Secretary of the French Embassy at Venice, to Pomponne, September 3 and 17, 1678.

[16] Letter from Pinchesne to Pomponne, November 19, 1678.

M. de Pomponne, Minister of Exterior Relations, they discussed, and drew up in the most profound secrecy, the treaty of cession, which was signed on December 8,[17] and which stated:—

1st. That the Duke of Mantua should receive French troops into Casale;

2nd. That he should be named Generalissimo of any French army which Louis XIV. might send into Italy;

3rd. And that after the execution of the treaty the sum of 100,000 crowns should be paid to the prince.[18]

Immediately after the signing of this document, Matthioly was received by Louis XIV. with the most flattering distinction in a secret audience. The King presented him with a valuable diamond in remembrance of his visit, caused him to be paid 400 double louis,[19] and promised him that after the ratification of the treaty he should receive a much larger sum for his reward, as well as a place for his son among the King's pages, and a rich abbey for his brother.[20]

No intrigue was ever better conducted or had more chances of success. In Piedmont a court divided, powerless, and almost servilely devoted to France; in the remainder of Italy, as in Piedmont, princes kept in the most complete ignorance; in Mantua a duke perfectly ready to sell a portion of his states; lastly, the two ambassadors charged with the negotiation of this affair having an equal interest in its success, since it would enrich one and assure to both the gratitude of their masters, and a high position.

---

[17] Letter from Pomponne to Pinchesne, December 2, 1678.

[18] Archives of the Ministry of Foreign Affairs, section Mantua.

[19] 760*l.*—*Trans.*

[20] Archives of the Ministry of Foreign Affairs, section Mantua, Italian Manuscript of Giuliani.

Two months after Matthioly's visit to France, the courts of Turin, Madrid, and Vienna, the Spanish Governor of the Milanese, and the State Inquisitors of the Venetian Republic—that is to say, all those who were most interested in opposing this project—were acquainted with the minutest details of it, and were ignorant neither of the price to be paid for the surrender, the time at which it was to take place, nor the names of the negotiators. In one word, they knew everything, for at different times [21] they had received the confidence of the better informed of the participators in this intrigue, of Count Matthioly himself.

By what motive was he actuated? Must we see in this treason an act inspired by base cupidity? Was Matthioly a rogue, who, after having received Louis XIV.'s money, preceeded to sell himself by turns to the Austrians, the Spaniards, the Venetians, and the Piedmontese? Or, disquieted in mind and suddenly struck by the apparition of his country in danger, was he seized with remorse at the moment of bartering her away, and did he seek the only means of preserving her from the encroachments of an ambitious King? Was he an intriguer, a low informer, or a man struggling between two opposing sentiments, whose greedy ambition had first led him to assist his master's criminal projects, and whose patriotism had then suddenly determined him to cause them to miscarry? These are questions which nobody will ever be able to answer, because nobody ever received his confidences. It is, however, worthy of remark, that if cupidity alone had been Matthioly's motive, he would have stooped

---

[21] Despatches from D'Estrades to the King, which will be referred to hereafter :—Archives of the Ministry of Foreign Affairs, section Savoy, 68.

to the execution of the treaty of Casale, since this offered
him many more material advantages than he could hope for
from a sudden change of conduct.   That Matthioly should
be designated a rogue in the despatches afterwards exchanged between the Court of Versailles and the French
representatives in Italy, is not at all astonishing; this anger
was the natural consequence of a bitter disappointment.
But the fact that there was room for a more noble motive,
and that a patriotic inspiration was possible, is sufficient to
prevent us from unreservedly condemning this man, who
perhaps thought to save his country.   No doubt he ought
to have cast aside all the appearances of knavery, to have
returned Louis XIV. his presents, to have first dissuaded
Charles IV., and if the latter had persisted in introducing
the French army into Italy, then, and then only, to have
revealed the danger to the other princes.   In this case it
would have been necessary to do it openly, with frankness,
without dissimulation, and by informing the Abbé d'Estrades
of what would have no longer been a treason, but a truly
patriotic act.   Was, however, such a line of conduct open
to Matthioly, surrounded with spies, watched over and
having to fear a power so formidable as France, and a
resentment so dangerous as Louis XIV.'s?   Must we
altogether blame him if he could not strip his character of
all its craftiness and duplicity, and if, amid the dishonouring
appearances of treason, he thought to perform an honourable
act?   To the present time people have seen in him only
a contemptible cheat, but however weak the contrary presumption may be, do not let us altogether reject it.   Let us
cease to place ourselves only in the French point of view,
and by considering the peril to which Italy would have

been exposed by the cession of Casale, let us not refuse to suppose that Matthioly, by preventing it, understood, perhaps, the interest of his country better than his own, and that, into a mind naturally greedy, a noble and disinterested sentiment was able to penetrate.

CHAPTER XX.

THE regent of Savoy was the first[1] to whom Matthioly gave
information. On December 31, 1678, she not only received
his confidence, but also had communicated to her all the
original documents relating to the negotiation, and took
copies of them. She was alike very pleased at knowing of
this intrigue, and very much embarrassed as to the line of
conduct she ought to pursue. Piedmont, indeed, had most
to suffer from the surrender of Casale to Louis XIV. To
oppose the execution of this project by arms, was far from
the wish of this princess and far beyond the forces at her
disposal. To place obstacles in the way of it exposed her
to the resentment of the 'King of France. After having
hesitated for a long time, and not doubting but that
Matthioly would, without delay, make the same revelations

---

[1] Matthioly first addressed himself to President Truccki, ex-Minister
of Finance to the Regent, then to the latter.

to the Spaniards and Austrians as he had to her, she preferred to leave to Spain and to the Empire the dangerous
task of arresting Louis XIV.'s encroaching ambition in
Italy.   But to preserve silence and prudently await the
result of the struggle, either armed or diplomatic, which
seemed likely to ensue, was not in accordance with the
frivolous character and general incapacity of this princess.
To whom, then, was she to confide this weighty and embarrassing secret?   She was too little of an Italian to
resolve to make it known at Milan, Venice, and Florence,
and thus provoke a coalition of the various interests which
were menaced.   So it was to Louis XIV. himself that she
revealed Matthioly's confidences.[2]   In this manner, she
secured to herself the merit of obliging a powerful sovereign,
whose friendship she retained without having anything to
fear from him, thanks to the vigorous measures which the
courts of Vienna and Madrid would be compelled to take.
She deceived herself, however, in a portion of her calcula-
tions; since it was not till two months afterwards that
Matthioly, on seeing the uselessness of his confession to
the regent, and learning that Louvois was continuing his
preparations for entering into Casale, resolved to inform
the Austrians, Venetians, and Spaniards.[3]   If he had not
done so, the King of France, meeting with no obstacle, and
having received the Duchess of Savoy's valuable piece of
intelligence, would have immediately taken possession of

---

[2] Archives of the Ministry of War, 686 ; Archives of the Ministry of
Foreign Affairs, section Mantua, 4 ; Instructions given to M. de Gomont,
ambassador to the Duke of Mantua.

[3] Letter from M. de Gomont to Louis XIV., May 14, 1680 ; copy
of Letter from Matthioly to the Empress Eleonora of Austria :—
Archives of the Ministry of Foreign Affairs, section Mantua, 5 and 11.

Casale. Louis XIV. was greatly moved, and with reason felt very grateful to the regent for her course of action. He expresses in his despatches sentiments of gratitude and of esteem towards the Duchess of Savoy, whilst he stigmatizes what he terms the treason of the knave. But, deceived as he had been by the one and enlightened by the other, was he in a position to judge properly the conduct of these two individuals? And, to place ourselves in another point of view to his, we may ask who most compromised the true interests of this country, the man whose information—sold,[4] it is true, but well-timed—suddenly aroused the other princes to vigilance; or the princess, who, more French than Italian, hastened to communicate this valuable confidence to Italy's most redoubtable and menacing enemy?

The regent's letter reached Louis XIV. in the middle of the month of February, 1679. The King's disappointment and wrath were so much the more lively since his plans were already in course of execution. All those who were to play a part in the *dénoûment* of this business were not only appointed, but were actually at their posts. The

---

[4] The following is the only document which establishes the fact that Matthioly received payment from the Spaniards and Venetians. It will be remarked that the information given by D'Estrades reached him very indirectly :—

"I must not omit to inform your Majesty that Father Ranzoni (a spy) *has told* Juliani (a spy) that *his father had assured* him that the Spaniards had given 4,000 pistoles [1,600*l*.] to Mattioli * as a reward for having discovered to them the whole of the Casale business, and for having pointed out M. d'Asfeld to them, and that he had also received money from the Venetians for the same reason."—Unpublished despatch from the Abbé d'Estrades to Louis XIV., March 16, 1680 :—Archives of the Ministry of Foreign Affairs, section Savoy, 70.

---

* The variation in the spelling of this name in the different despatches is followed exactly.—*Trans.*

far-sighted Louvois, who, previous to Napoleon, was, perhaps, the man who possessed in the highest degree the
genius of organization and the spirit of detail, had drawn
up—a quality in which he excelled—the whole plan of the
operation.　His orders, clear, precise, and minute, had been
punctually followed.　Numerous troops, under the command
of the Marquis de Boufflers, Colonel-General of Dragoons,
were assembled at Briançon ready to cross the frontier.[5]
The Baron d'Asfeld,[6] Colonel of Dragoons, left for Venice,
on the mission of exchanging in that city the ratification of
the treaty.[7]　Catinat,[8] then Brigadier of Infantry, arrived
from Flanders, where he had already served with distinction,
and proceeded with the greatest secrecy to Pignerol.　Saint-
Mars had been enjoined [9] to leave the postern of the citadel
open, to meet himself the mysterious traveller, and to conduct him into the donjon in such a manner that nobody
might be able to suspect his presence there.　This sham
prisoner was even obliged to change his name, and the
despatches addressed to him bore that of Richemont instead
of Catinat.[10]　Everything had been marvellously well con-

---

[5] *Mémoire de Chamlay* on the events of 1678 to 1688 :—Archives of
the Ministry of War, 1183.

[6] I am not sure whether I am correct in imagining that this was
the Marshal d'Asfeld, who distinguished himself at the battle of
Almanza, and died at a great old age in 1743.—(G. Agar Ellis.)

[7] Letter from Pomponne to Pinchesne, December 30, 1678 :—
Archives of the Ministry of Foreign Affairs.

[8] Nicholas de Catinat, Marshal of France in 1698. "He united," says
Voltaire, "philosophy to great military talents.　The last day he commanded in Italy, he gave for the watchword, 'Paris and Saint-Gratien,'
the name of his country-house.　He died there in the retirement of a
real sage (having refused the blue ribbon), in 1712."—(G. Agar Ellis.)

[9] Letter from Louvois to Saint-Mars, December 29, 1678 :—
Archives of the Ministry of War.

[10] *Ibid.*, February 15, 1679 :—Archives of the Ministry of War.

ceived, everything was prepared, everything foreseen, save what the Government of Versailles termed the treason of Matthioly.

Nevertheless, the Duchess of Savoy's communication did not entirely destroy Louis XIV.'s hopes ; so he refrained from informing the Abbé d'Estrades, who had been transferred from the embassy of Venice to that of Turin. He wished to look upon these first disclosures as only a commencement of treason,—an accident to be regretted, it is true, but one of which the consequences might perhaps be neutralized by exercising a pressure upon the Duke of Mantua, and by endeavouring to intimidate Matthioly. But the latter had become as laconic in his letters as he was inexact in keeping his appointments. The Abbé d'Estrades, very much preoccupied with the result of a negotiation of which he had been the life and soul, only suspected a treason the full reality of which he was not yet acquainted with. He sent courier after courier to M. de Pinchesne at Venice, to Mantua for Matthioly, to the principal towns of Italy for Duke Charles IV. ; and from all these different places he received the most unsatisfactory intelligence. Sometimes Matthioly declared that he was detained at Verona by the state of his health. At others, Charles IV. was attracted to Venice by the desire of assisting at a *carrousel.*[11] It was not that the Duke formally refused to execute the treaty of surrender, but that new obstacles were continually being raised by the very person who till then had undertaken the direction of this affair—by Matthioly himself; and the young prince, thoughtless and frivolous,

---

[11] Letter from M. de Pinchesne to M. de Pomponne, February 18, 1679 :—Archives of the Ministry of Foreign Affairs, section Venice.

of a very versatile disposition, and devoting himself to scarcely anything but pleasure, was very glad to endorse his favourite's views. Suddenly the news arrived at Turin that Baron d'Asfeld had been arrested by the governor of the Milanese while proceeding to Increa in order to exchange the ratifications there with Matthioly, and that he was detained a prisoner by the Spaniards.[12] However significant this arrest may have been, the Court of Versailles did not yet despair. Catinat received orders to undertake the mission at first confided to D'Asfeld, and to start for Increa, whither Matthioly was also invited to proceed.[13] The sham Richemont, accompanied by Saint-Mars, who adopted the name and dress of an officer belonging to Pignerol, left the citadel by night, and, with numerous precautions, repaired to the place of meeting. But there they awaited Matthioly in vain, and after many adventures, after having run the risk of being arrested by a detachment from the garrison of Casale, after having been compelled to appear before the governor of that place, and having preserved their incognito with difficulty, they at last returned to Pignerol, very happy at not having been recognized, but without bringing back the instrument of surrender.[14]

From this moment the doubts of the Abbé d'Estrades were changed into certainty, and it was then that he first conceived the idea of Matthioly's abduction. It is worthy of remark that it so happened with this prisoner as with

---

[12] Letter from M. de Pinchesne to M. de Pomponne, March 11, 1679 : —Archives of Ministry of Foreign Affairs, section Venice.

[13] Letter from M. de Pomponne to Matthioly, March 14, 1669.

[14] Letter from Catinat, under the name of Richemont, to Louvois, April 15, 1679.

Avedick. Louis XIV. approved the conduct of d'Estrades as he was afterwards to ratify that of Ferriol. But it is his ambassadors who have executed the project of abduction, even before receiving the authorisation for doing so. This is clear from the evidence of the despatches which we are about to quote. It is, in truth, necessary to allow the principal author of this act of violence to speak for himself, which we shall do hereafter more than once ; for, on approaching the conclusion of this work, we desire the reader to be self-convinced, and thus to participate in the pleasure which the solution of a problem affords. Having spared him long but necessary researches, we shall in future often confine ourselves to being his guide ; and by now and then putting him on the right track, by contenting ourselves with indicating the goal, and furnishing the elements of the pursuit, shall leave him all the gratification and all the merit of the success of our common enterprise.

On April 8, 1679, D'Estrades writes to M. de Pomponne :—[15]

"..... It is easy to discern, from what one learns on many sides, that it is owing to Mattioli's indiscretion that this affair has become public, for it would be impossible for the particulars of it, and even those of his journey to Paris, and of the stay which he made there, to be so well known if he had not talked about them. ...... Still I am awaiting Mattioli's arrival here in order to see if one can rely upon his good faith, and if he is in a position to perform what he has promised. I shall have him so well watched that I shall know

---

[15] Unpublished despatch :—Archives of the Ministry of Foreign Affairs, section Savoy, 68.

18

if he holds any communication with Madame de Savoy or with the Ministers, and I shall perhaps also find the means of being informed concerning what he may be treating of with them. I beg you, sir, to let me know if, in the event of there being no doubt of his perfidy, and of its being necessary to compel him by fear to put everything in train for keeping his word, the King will approve his being taken to Pignerol, which will not be at all difficult for me to accomplish without its attracting attention; because, after his arrival there, without any one knowing that I had caused him to be abducted, it would be easy to say that he had gone of his own accord. Nevertheless, I shall not think of doing this until I have received your orders, and it would only be after having lost all hope with regard to him that we should adopt these measures."

On April 22,[16] M. de Pomponne replies to him :—

" Sir, I shall commence by replying to the two letters which you have been at the pains to write me on the 8th of the present month concerning the affair of Count Mattioli. His behaviour is sufficient to make us believe that he is a rogue; but, in order to assure you the better of it, his Majesty orders me to confide to you, under the seal of secrecy, what has occurred with reference to this matter. On the occasion of his journey to Turin, he informed the Duchess of Savoy generally of the papers with which he was charged, and of everything which had been arranged with him here. He has since given the same information to the Inquisitors of Venice, and caused

---

[16] Unpublished despatch :—Archives of the Ministry of Foreign Affairs, section Savoy, 68.

M. d'Asfeld to be arrested during his journey in the Milanese, by the information which he gave to Count de Melgar. As he thinks that all this knavery is unknown, he has been in the habit of trifling with M. de Pinchesne, and you see by the letters which he writes to you that he wishes to trifle with you in the same manner. As he proposes to visit you at Turin, his Majesty does not wish you to let him know that you are acquainted with his conduct. You will continue to let him think that you are deceived, and you will make use of your apparent confidence, and of that which you will assure him the King continues to have, in order to endeavour to obtain the ratification of the treaty. He has stated at Venice that he has it in his possession. Perhaps he has it still. It is important to exert all your skill to obtain it from him. The King does not consider it advisable to cause the scandal of having him taken to Pignerol as you propose. The only case in which you could employ menaces and fear, would be if you were certain that he really possessed the ratification, and you considered these means necessary, in order to compel him to give it up to you. There is scarcely any room for doubt that, if he goes to Turin, he will see the Duchess of Savoy and will keep out of your way. You will not appear to take any notice of it, and you will not let this princess know that you are informed of this matter, although it is she herself who has given information concerning it to his Majesty."

The same day [17] the Abbé d'Estrades urges upon the Government of Versailles the necessity of granting the authorisation to kidnap Matthioly.

---

[17] Unpublished despatch :—Archives of the Ministry of Foreign Affairs, section Savoy, 68.

" . . . . . I believe that what I have already had the
honour of stating to the King proves Mattioli's perfidy sufficiently clearly; he has been here for the last four days, and
has come to see me with great precautions, as if he had much
interest in concealing himself; nevertheless, every morning he
has had conferences with a person named Tarin, who is the
man that Madame R. [18] sent to Padua to ascertain what
it was he had to communicate to her; he has insinuated a
thousand falsehoods in his conversations with him; he has
wished to have it believed that he saw me every day, although
I have only spoken to him once; and that the Duke of
Mantua had sent him here in order to declare to me that this
Prince could not keep his word to his Majesty on the subject
of the Casale treaty.   Whilst I have been writing this despatch, Mattioli has again come to see me, and the manner in
which he has spoken to me has so clearly shown me his
bad faith, that, even if I could possibly have had any doubt
concerning it, he would have left me in no uncertainty; he
has proposed to me some ridiculous schemes which would
tend only to involve his Majesty in fresh embarrassments;
he has told me that he leaves to-morrow in order to have
an interview with the governor of Casale, who was pressing
him strongly to visit him, and who hoped that the place
would soon be in the hands of the King; as he has assured
me that he would return during the present week at the
latest, and, as I know that a few days afterwards he is to
go back to Venice, I have not time to await his Majesty's
orders to arrest him.   It is, nevertheless, so important to
do this, that there remains to me only to think of the means
of executing the design without scandal, with the view that

---

[18] Royale, the Duchess of Savoy.—*Trans.*

the rumours which would ensue should not revive those which have been caused by the affair which he was negotiating, and of its not being known what had become of him. I have thought that it was impossible for me to succeed in this, except by entrusting Madame Royale with the secret, since I could not make certain of the person of Mattioli in Turin or in the States of the Duke of Savoy, without resorting to a violence at which she would show herself offended, and by whatever pretext I might have wished to attract him towards Pignerol, this Princess, whom he informs of all that passes between himself and me, would have warned him, no doubt, to take care of himself; I have seen myself compelled to act thus, from what she said to me two days ago, that since Mattioli was here, he might dwell at Pignerol or take a stroll in France for longer than he imagined, I replied she was so enlightened that I thought I ought not to neglect the idea which she gave me; that I would reflect upon it, and that, meanwhile, I begged of her in the name of the King not to mention anything which could imperil the effect of the resolution which I might take for his Majesty's service, but that I would not execute it without communicating with her. She promised me this, and, after having thanked me for having been so willing to act in concert with her, she charged me to behave in such a way that Mattioli should not be arrested on her territories, so that she might not have to reproach herself with having delivered up a man who, although guilty of a treason, had, nevertheless, confided in her. I was this morning with Madame Royale, and, after having represented to her that it was of extreme consequence that Mattioli should be put in a place where he could no longer pay his court to the Spaniards and Venetians by means of the false confidences which I knew him to be making to them every day, I have assured her that I would arrange my plans in such a way that he would be taken to Pignerol without his having any suspicion of it till he was out of the States of her Royal Highness, and on the point of entering the place ; she has shown herself satisfied with my assurance, and she has said to me that I could plainly see that she was contributing as much as possible to what would be of service to the King, since she had not dissuaded Mattioli·from the visit which he had made here, and of which he had advised her, although she had never had the smallest doubt of what would befall him through .it.

" Besides the reasons, Sir, which I have already explained to you, I have since had some news tending to determine me to seize Mattioli; first, I know that he has been unwilling to give up to the Duke of Mantua the originals of the papers relating to the treaty, no matter what pressure this Prince, who has only copies of them, may have put upon him, and that he retains them in order to show them to those from whom he wishes to extract money, and who would not believe him upon slighter proofs. Juliani [Giuliani] has written to me that D. Joseph Varano, who stands very well with M. de Mantua, and who has always manifested his desire that his master should place himself under the King's protection by means of the treaty of Casale, and to whom my letter will be delivered, and not to Vialardi, as I had informed you—having in writing used one name for the other—was to have an interview with him about this affair, and that he will assuredly not enter into any engagement whilst Mattioli is at liberty. Lastly, I have received information from Milan that the Duke of

Mantua has asked the Spaniards for six hundred thousand crowns,[19] declaring to them that not being able to fortify Casale without it, he would not answer for the safe custody of this place, and that the Count de Melgar, who was willing to give them to him, was making useless efforts to raise them, and that he will not obtain them; so that it is probable that this Prince, who is only looking out for money, on losing the hope of getting it from Spain, will listen to the offers made him on behalf of the King, and that his Majesty will find himself in possession of an important place, which will always remain in his hands, through the death of the Duke of Mantua, whose health is so ruined by his debauches, by the incurable diseases produced by them, and by the poison which it is publicly stated was given him a little while since—that according to all appearances he cannot have long to live. One may add that if this Prince should happen to die before the execution of the treaty, his Majesty would have the right of doing himself justice by producing M. de Mantua's letter, and the full powers which sufficiently authorise the articles which have been agreed on, but it is necessary for this purpose to get them out of Mattioli's hands, which cannot be done if we do not make ourselves masters of his person, since he never carries them about with him.

"Such, Sir, are the motives which oblige me not to allow him to escape, and in order to succeed in the affair, I have written to M. de Catinat that it is necessary that we should see one another at the beginning of the present week; I shall inform him at length of the state in which matters are, and shall tell him to select me a place near to

---

[19] 75,000*l.*—*Trans.*

Pignerol, whither I can proceed with Mattioli on a given day, when he shall have returned from the visit which he has paid to Casale, and to send there secretly a few men well armed, because I know that he always carries two pistols in his pockets with two others and a poignard in his belt ; I shall conduct him to this place in my carriage under the pretext of having a conference with M. Catinat, and I have already so well inclined him to it that he has testified to me his desire for it ; as I have spoken to him in such a way as to remove all kind of suspicion, and as he affects to fear lest the intercourse which we have with one another here should be discovered, he has of himself entered into all the precautions that I have wished to take, and we have agreed, in order to avoid the accidents which might happen, that we will only meet M. Catinat [at a spot] both out of sight of Pignerol and of the States of the Duke of Savoy ; it is there also that I hope to place him in good hands, and I have no doubt but that M. de Saint-Mars will be very willing to receive him on M. Catinat's report and my word, at least until it shall have pleased his Majesty to order otherwise.   *   *   *   *   *

"I am, etc.

"L'Abbé D'Estrades."

On April 29 [20] D'Estrades returns to the charge, and adduces the strong reasons which he considers ought to determine Matthioly's arrest :—

"Juliany (Giuliani) has told me that he has spoken to Don Joseph Varano, who has promised him to do his

---

[20] Unpublished despatch :—Archives of the Ministry of Foreign Affairs, section Savoy, 68.

utmost to renew the affair of Casale, but that at present M. de Mantua did not wish to hear anything spoken of except capturing or killing Mattioli, who, he complains, has betrayed him. He has learnt from this same Varano that what most disquieted M. de Mantua was, that Mattioli had made him ratify the treaty, and that he had kept possession of the ratification with all the other papers concerning this affair; so that when we are masters of Mattioli's person, we will compel him to give up this ratification together with the rest. And so, Sir, you see of what consequence it is to arrest him. I no longer hesitate, moreover, about doing it, especially since I have seen that M. Catinat, with whom I had an interview two days ago, and with whom I have taken all the necessary measures, considered, after what I had told him concerning everything, that the execution of this resolution ought not to be delayed. I hope that in four or five days' time it will be a settled affair, and I shall inform you of the manner in which it has been accomplished. It seems to me that when one has obliged Mattioli to deliver up among the other papers the ratification of M. de Mantua, if he has indeed given it to this man, the King will have the right to demand the execution of the ratified treaty, in the event of this Prince not wishing to take the ways of agreeableness and negotiations."

At length, on April 28, Louis consents to the arrest.[21] But when his orders arrive at Turin, Matthioly had already been carried off since May 2.

"I must inform you," wrote D'Estrades to Pomponne,

---

[21] Unpublished despatches from Pomponne to D'Estrades, April 28 and 30, 1679.

"in what manner I have brought Mattioli into a secure place.   I have already had the honour to acquaint you that I had been studious to exhibit towards him entire confidence, and to cause him to entertain the desire of having an interview with M. Catinat; Giuliani, who arrived here three or four days ago, and whose fidelity to speak truly deserves to be taken into consideration, furnished me with a new means which was very useful.   He told me that Mattioli had informed him that the expenses of numerous journeys, and the presents which he had been obliged to give to M. de Mantua's mistresses in order to render them favourable, had exhausted his resources, and that he was at present without money; Giuliani did not hesitate to promise that I would let him have what he might require, and on this intelligence I told him [Matthioly] in confidence that we had only to seek expedients to renew our affair; and that provided the Duke of Mantua still had the same sentiments, it would not be difficult for us to promptly execute the treaty, since M. Catinat not only possessed the power to cause the troops destined for that purpose to arrive and to command them, but that he also had a very considerable sum to meet all the expenses that he might consider necessary, that Giuliani had represented to me the state in which he was, and that I would cause to be given to him whatever he might desire. I added that there was no need to have any false delicacy about it; that it was neither my money nor M. Catinat's which I was offering him, but his Majesty's, who did not believe that he could employ it better than for so important an affair.   As he is one of the greatest rogues who have ever lived, this proposition made him extremely impatient to see M. Catinat; and he pressed me with reasons which he at once concocted not to delay the conference that we were to have with him; we made an appointment for the following day, Tuesday, the 2nd of the present month; and I gave him a rendezvous half a mile from Turin in a church, whither I was to proceed and take him up in my carriage at six o'clock in the morning; unfortunately there had been three days of very bad weather; it was still raining heavily on that day, and as the streams of this country easily become swollen, we found one called the Guisiola, three miles from the place to which we had to go, the waters of which were so high that the horses could only cross it by swimming; there was only a single bridge, which was half destroyed, and I was in despair at this hindrance. When after having perceived that it was absolutely necessary to repair the bridge with planks in order to be able to cross on foot, Mattioli worked at it with so much zeal, that in an hour we put it into a state to make use of it.

"I profited by this opportunity to leave my carriage and servants at this spot, with the view that what I was about to do should be more secret, and we proceeded on foot along very bad roads to the place where we were expected. M. Catinat had so well arranged everything that no one but himself appeared; he made us enter a room, and during the conversation I insensibly made Mattioli state what he had avowed to me two days previously, that he possessed all the original papers that concerned our affair, viz.: M. de Mantua's letter to the King, his Majesty's answer to him, the full powers of this Prince, the treaty which you had put into writing, the Marquis de Louvois' memorandum, and two signatures of M. de Mantua; one at the bottom of the treaty so as to serve for the ratification, and the other at the bottom of a sheet of blank paper, on which to write an order to the governor of Casale to receive his Majesty's troops into his town whenever they might present themselves there ; he added that this Prince had since done all that he could to oblige him to return these papers, but that he had never been willing to go and find them, that he had only sent him copies, and had deposited the originals with his wife in a convent of nuns at Bologna, called Saint-Louis ; after having invited this confidence towards M. Catinat, I considered that my presence was no longer necessary, and when I had left he was arrested without disturbance.

"I returned here with the Abbé de Montesquieu, my cousin-german whom I had taken with me for two reasons, which I trust his Majesty will approve. The first because I could not leave Turin alone without its being believed that I was not going to pay a visit as I had stated two days previously, and because I had already experienced that I had been watched during two or three drives I had expressly taken outside the town, with the view that people should not find it extraordinary when I wished to carry off Mattioli. The second and the strongest was, that all the precautions I had adopted in order to see M. Catinat at the Capucins, · whose convent is outside this town, on a mountain where there is no other house but theirs, not having prevented our interview from being known, and the Marquis de Saint-Maurice from speaking of it rather indiscreetly, I thought that I ought not to risk fresh conferences with him, and that it would be still more dangerous if I went to Pignerol ; which the Abbé de Montesquieu can do without attracting attention. Nevertheless I should not have made use of the latter, if during a stay of three years that we have made together at Venice, I had not become acquainted with his discretion, his address, and especially his fidelity, sufficiently well to be able to answer for him as for myself; it is this therefore which has obliged me to make him come here. And I have sent him this morning to Pignerol in consequence of the information which M. Catinat has given me, that he had twice interrogated Mattioli,[22] who had proposed to get his father to come to the place where he had been arrested, so that he might oblige him to go and seek the papers which we demand and bring them to Pignerol. But since it is necessary to distrust everything that he says, and as he will doubtless not be able to sustain the sight of Giuliani when he is confronted with him, in consequence of all the knavery he has been guilty of, I have wished that he should accompany the Abbé de Montesquieu to Pignerol, so as to proceed from that place by M. Catinat's orders wherever Mattioli might declare the papers to be concealed. And thus that he who should be charged with this commission might not only be a safe man, but also have a

---

[22] Matthioly underwent three examinations, in the course of which he excused himself for having confided the secret of the treaty to the Court of Turin on the plea that he had been surprised into doing so by the President Truccki, whom he described as an "insinuating and adroit man" professing much "affection for the interests of France." He admitted having received 2,000 livres from the court, and maintained that this was for services formerly rendered. He did not deny having spoken of the treaty to certain Venetians and to a partisan of Spain at Padua, but said he simply told them that the affair had failed; while as regarded the representative of Austria at Venice, he saw that he knew all about the treaty from the Duke of Mantua at Venice. In short, Matthioly pretended generally that the reason the ratification had been delayed, was on account of the unwillingness of the Duke, acted upon by his mother and the Court of Vienna, to complete the affair :—Letters from Catinat to Louvois, quoted by M. Roux-Fazillac.—*Trans.*

complete acquaintance with the country and know the language, so as to avoid any kind of accident.

"Two days after Mattioli had been taken to the donjon of Pignerol, I caused his valet to be conducted thither with all his clothing and valises by means of one of my servants whom I had already lent to M. Catinat during the journey which he made to Casale; for this I had taken the precaution to bear a letter from Mattioli which he had been made to write and in which he ordered this valet to come to him in a place where he was obliged to remain three or four days, and from which he was to depart without again passing through Turin; so that by this means one obtained all that Mattioli had brought here, without having recourse to violence. If I had made use of any other means, I should not have been able to obtain anything from him, since he would never have been willing of himself to give up to me papers which he has so much difficulty in resolving to surrender even while he is in a condition to fear the punishment of his perfidy; and if I had used towards him the least threat he would infallibly have left Turin the next day without its being possible to arrest him, except by causing a scandal which would have been very prejudicial."

Among the papers seized on Matthioly's person, there were none of those which emanated from the Government of Versailles, such as the treaty signed by Pomponne, the instructions given by Louvois, the letter from Louis XIV. to the Duke of Mantua, and the latter's ratification. It was essential to obtain possession of these, so as to deprive the other powers of the irrefutable testimony of the King of France's attempt and failure. Matthioly at first gave incorrect information respecting the place where they were to be found. But having been threatened with torture,[23] and then with death, the unfortunate Count finished by avowing that the famous papers were at Padua in a place which his father alone knew of. A letter was dictated to the prisoner, in which, without even allowing his lot to be suspected, he begged his father to give all the documents relating to the negotiation to the Sieur Giuliani, the bearer of the letter.[24] Matthioly's father, ignorant that Giuliani was a spy, delivered everything to him, and the astute messenger confided

---

[23] "I put him into the greatest possible fear of the torture if he did not speak the truth :"—Letter from Catinat to Louvois, Archives of the Ministry of Foreign Affairs.—*Trans.*

[24] Matthioly really wrote this letter, as will be seen by the annexed extract from a letter sent by Catinat to Louvois, and dated May 10, 1679 : "I have made him write three letters for the purpose of getting possession of the original papers which are at Padua, which have been put into the hands of the Sieur Giuliani, by the advice of the Abbé d'Estrades, who places an entire confidence in him ; he will make use of these three letters as he shall judge most fit, according to the disposition in which he shall find the father of the Sieur de Lestang. The first is only a letter of the Sieur de Lestang to his father, in which he acquaints him, that there are reasons which oblige him to remain at Turin, or in the neighbourhood, but that he may place an entire confidence in the Sieur Giuliani, and deliver to him such and such papers, of which I have made him give the inventory to the Sieur Giuliani. The second acquaints his father with the real state in which he is, and that it is important, as well for his life as for his honour, that his papers should be immediately delivered into the hands of the Sieur Giuliani. In the third, which is the last to be made use of, in case the first two have no effect, he desires him to come to Turin, and tells him that at the house of the Abbé d'Estrades he will be instructed where he is, and the means to be employed to speak with him. The Sieur de Lestang has no doubt of being able, in this interview between him and his father, to persuade the latter to all he may wish. I have inspired him with so great a fear of the punishments due to his bad conduct, that I find no repugnance in him to do all that I require of him :"— Archives of the Ministry of Foreign Affairs.—*Trans.*

to M. de Pinchesne, the representative of the King of France at Venice, the precious originals,[25] which were

---

[25] The ratification of the Duke of Mantua was not among them, but only several signatures in blank given by this Prince to Matthioly, on one of which the latter asserted that he was to have written the ratification.

[These sheets signed in blank were never found. The papers recovered by Giuliani comprised, in addition to the original treaty signed by Matthioly and M. de Pomponne, the instructions given to the former when he left the French Court, Louvois' written authority for Pomponne to treat with Matthioly, and a letter from Louis XIV. to the Duke of Mantua. "The ratification of the Duke of Mantua is not to be found, although the Sieur de Lestang said it was amongst them ; whereupon I interrogated him, having first obtained all the advantage over him I could, by abusing him and bringing soldiers into his room as if preparatory to administering the question * to him, which made him so much afraid that he promised to really tell the truth. Being asked whether the Duke of Mantua had ratified the treaty, he answered that he had never subscribed to all the articles, but that he had got from him four blank papers signed, one of which was a blank paper, of two sheets, at the top of which he had written, 'Ratification of the treaty made with his Most Christian Majesty.' That there were three other blank papers signed, of one sheet each, of which he intended to make use to write in the name of his master to the three governors of the town, citadel, and castle, to order them to receive the King's troops. Being asked where these papers signed in blank are at present, he answered, that they are in the hands of the Governor of Casale, to whom he sent them at the time that D'Asfeld left Venice. Being asked why he had sent them, without their being filled up, to the Governor of Casale, he answered he had sent them to him in a letter of Magnus, the Secretary of the Duke of Mantua, in which the Governor was ordered to do, without hesitation, all that should be told him regarding the execution of the orders contained in that packet,— that they were left blank, because he wished to make the ratification according to that of the King, not knowing, as he says, the exact form in which it ought to have been made out. Being asked why in his first examination he had said that this ratification was at Padua ; he answered that he had not wished to tell where it was before Giuliani,

---

* The first form of torture applied to prisoners to force them to confess.

immediately forwarded to Versailles under cover of the embassy.[26]

Louis XIV. was avenged. Arrived at the zenith of his power, arbiter of the destinies of Europe, which was submissive and mute, audacious and mighty enough to arbitrarily annex vast territories to France in time of peace, having, as yet, broken through all obstacles and triumphed over all resistance, this potentate had just been tricked by a petty minister of a petty Italian court. That one of his projects, which seemed likely to succeed the best—thanks to the weakness as much as to the division or ignorance of his adversaries—that one of his projects, on the execution of which so many important consequences depended, and which he had long dreamed over and prepared with infinite precaution and care, suddenly failed through the most unforeseen of accidents—the disaffection of the principal agent of the matter. What a natural subject of raillery for Europe was so great an enterprise as this, resulting in an issue that was almost grotesque—the first check experienced by the King of France, produced by so insignificant a cause—such disproportion between the importance of the preparations and their complete inutility—the fear of so grave a peril replaced by the certainty of being delivered from it ! Louis XIV. endeavoured to save himself by destroying

---

in order not to make him acquainted in any way with his intelligence with the governor : he added that he had never had any other ratification except that one ; and that whatever tortures might be inflicted on him, he could never tell anything more."—Letter from Catinat to Louvois, June 3, 1679 :—Archives of the Ministry of War.—*Trans.*]

[26] Unpublished despatches from the Abbé d'Estrades to Pomponne, May 13 and 27, and June 3, 1679 :—Archives of the Ministry of Foreign Affairs, section Savoy, 68. Letter from Catinat to Louvois, June 3, 1679 :—Archives of the Ministry of War.

for ever the official proofs of his attempt and failure, by causing the chief culprit to disappear, and by recalling his troops in as secret a manner as he had assembled them at Briançon. He renounced his enterprise with such promptitude, that in some degree he seemed never to have commenced it. It was in vain that D'Estrades, who was so interested in the success of the negotiation, and caught at everything in order to prolong it, begged the Government of Versailles to leave him completely at liberty in this respect.[27] The Minister's refusal was formal, and tinged both with pride and bitterness. "It is not his Majesty's intention," writes Pomponne to D'Estrades, August 4, 1679, "to follow the course you propose in this affair, nor to commit so great an enterprise to the measures you might be able to take. If he ever forms the design of pursuing it, *you may be assured that those of which he may make use will not fail him.* So you need not venture to attempt anything in this matter."[28] No doubt the Court of Savoy was fully

---

[27] Unpublished letters from D'Estrades to Pomponne, June 10 and July 1, 1679.

[28] Unpublished despatch, August 4, 1679 :—Archives of the Ministry of Foreign Affairs, section Savoy. The project for the surrender of Casale was revived two years later and put into execution, thanks to the skill of the Abbé Morel, Minister of Louis XIV. to the Duke of Mantua, and without the intervention of the Abbé d'Estrades. On September 30, 1681, Louis XIV.'s troops entered Casale. We know what this policy led to, and how, at the peace of Ryswick, he was compelled to surrender everything, even Pignerol, his father's valuable conquest. However, Louis XIV. was well advised to break off the negotiation in 1679, since Marshal d'Estrades acquainted him, on March 11, from Nimeguen, "that this new attempt was of a nature to defer the exchange of the ratifications of the treaty of general peace :"—Unpublished letter of the Marshal d'Estrades, Imperial Library, Manuscripts, *Papiers du Maréchal d'Estrades*, vol. xii. p. 1015

aware of the intrigue, but Louis XIV. was master at Turin. No doubt Matthioly's voice had made itself heard at Venice and Milan, but it was now stifled for ever; and with the recollection of his warnings was to be mingled that of his mysterious disappearance, and a salutary fear caused by the strangeness of his fate. Moreover, however humiliated Louis XIV. may have been, he still employed most haughty language towards Madrid. He exacted and obtained from Spain the immediate release of Baron d'Asfeld, who was a prisoner at Milan, and also a formal disavowal of the governor who had ordered his arrest. For Louis XIV. it was then a check, but a check in part repaired by the prompt abandonment of his projects, and compensated for by the satisfaction of having rendered powerless and carried off, as it were, from the world, of having extinguished the only being who could bear witness to the first humiliation of a great King. The report was spread abroad that Matthioly had died, the victim of an accident encountered on a journey. Those who were most entitled to doubt this appeared to believe in it. Charles IV., suspected, if not convicted, by the other princes of having wished to sell one of the keys of Italy to Louis XIV., sought to forget in fresh pleasures the shame of the enterprise. Matthioly's family, silent and over-whelmed, became dispersed. Did it believe in his death? No one knows. On its genealogical tree the date of Ercole Matthioly's end has been left blank.[29] His wife, the widow of a husband who was to survive her, shut herself up with her sorrow in the convent 'of the Filles de Saint-Louis at Bologna, the same place whither, seventeen

---

[29] *Arbor priscæ nobilisque masculinæ familiæ de Matthiolis :*—Archives of the Empire, M. 746.

years previously, Matthioly had come to espouse her.[30]
His father, who received no further intelligence after the
letter brought by Giuliani, dragged on his unhappy existence
for some time yet at Padua, ignorant whether he ought
to lament the death of a beloved son, or to flatter himself
that he was still alive. Among the members of this family,
thus plunged in the most cruel uncertainty, no one dared
to use any exertions, which, however, would have been
useless, in order to endeavour to clear it up. Feeling themselves menaced by the mysterious blow which had fallen
upon one of them, they were silent and submissive, assured of
their want of power, and certain that their inquiries would
be useless, and possibly not unattended with peril.

---

[30] Matthioly married in January, 1661, Camilla, widow of Bernardi Paleotti, by whom he had two sons.—*Trans.*

CHAPTER XXI.

Period from which the Theory that makes Matthioly the Man with the Iron Mask dates—Numerous Writers who have concerned themselves with the Abduction of this Individual—Arguments of Reth, Roux-Fazillac, and Delort—M. Jules Loiseleur—His Labours—The Supposition that an obscure Spy was arrested in 1681 by Catinat—It cannot be admitted—Grounds on which M. Loiseleur rejects the Theory that makes Matthioly the Man with the Iron Mask—Soundness of his Reasoning and Justness of his Conclusions.

PRISONERS have no history; their monotonous and uniform existence cannot be described, their lamentations remain without response, their sufferings have no other witnesses but their gaolers, their confidence is received by nobody. Poets alone imagine and sing the bitter sorrows of captivity.

The story of Matthioly's imprisonment derives all its interest from the supposition that he may possibly be the Man with the Iron Mask. Of the life of the captive in his prison, we have nothing or almost nothing.[1] Louis XIV.

---

[1] Louvois writes to Saint-Mars, May 15, 1679 : "It is not the intention of the King that the Sieur de Lestang [the name given to Matthioly after his arrest] should be well treated, nor that, except the absolute necessaries of life, anything should be given to him that would enable him to pass his time agreeably." Again, on May 22, he writes : "You must keep the individual named Lestang in the severe confinement I enjoined in my preceding letters, without allowing him to see a physician unless you know him to be in absolute need of one." In July he

has succeeded in surrounding with uncertainty and mystery the punishment of the audacious man who had deceived him. A single attempt, if not to corrupt, at least to interest in his lot one of his gaolers, the Sieur de Blainvilliers; [c] by turns the calm of the prisoner resigned to the definitive loss of his liberty, or the momentary madness of the wretched being separated for ever from all that is dear to him ; a few efforts, renewed after long intervals, to write and make known his name outside the walls within which he is con-

---

is allowed pen and ink "to put into writing whatever he may wish to say." In February, 1680, Saint-Mars writes to Louvois that Lestang "complains that he is not treated as a man of his quality and the minister of a great prince ought to be," to which Louvois replies in the July following : "With regard to the Sieur de Lestang, I wonder at your patience, and that you should wait for an order to treat such a rascal as he deserves when he is wanting in respect to you : "—Louvois to Saint-Mars and *vice versâ*, Archives of the Ministry of Foreign Affairs. —*Trans.*

[a] "Sir," said he to him, "here is a ring which I make a present to you, and which I beg of you to accept." It was no doubt the diamond given to Matthioly by Louis XIV.

[Saint-Mars wrote to Louvois : " I believe he made him this present as much from fear as from any other cause : this prisoner having previously used very violent language towards him, and written abusive sentences with charcoal on the walls of his room, which had obliged that officer to threaten him with severe punishment, if he was not more decorous and moderate in his language for the future. When he was put in the tower with the Jacobin, I charged Blainvilliers to tell him, at the same time showing him a cudgel, that it was with that the unruly were rendered manageable, and that if he did not speedily become so, he could easily be compelled. This message was conveyed to him, and some days afterwards, as Blainvilliers was waiting upon him at dinner, he said, ' Sir, here is a little ring which I wish to give you, and I beg you to accept of it !' Blainvilliers replied ' that he only took it to deliver it to me, as he could not receive anything himself from the prisoners.' I think it is well worth fifty or sixty pistoles :"—Letter from Saint-Mars to Louvois, October 26, 1680, quoted by Roux-Fazillac.—*Trans.*]

fined : this is all that we know, all that we shall ever know of Matthioly's captivity. But what prisons did he successively inhabit? Where did he drag out his existence, and, above all things, where did he terminate it? Ought we to behold in him the Man with the Iron Mask?

Roux-Fazillac and Delort are generally considered as having been the first to reveal, the one in 1800, and the other in a more complete manner in 1825, the existence and abduction of Count Matthioly. This is a grave error, and we must go back long before these two writers in order to find the first traces and the first revelations of the diplomatic intrigue relative to Casale. In 1682 there appeared at Cologne a political pamphlet [3] in which the whole negotiation was disclosed, and in which the Abbé d'Estrades and Matthioly, Giuliani and Pinchesne, D'Asfeld, Catinat, and the Duke of Mantua figured. In August, 1687, a work, published at Leyden with the title of *Histoire Abrégée de l'Europe,* [4] gave, under the head of Mantua, a French translation of an Italian letter which denounced the abduction of Matthioly. In 1749 the famous Muratori related, in his *Annali d'Italia,* [5] the story of the Casale negotiation, and the abduction of the principal agent in this intrigue. In the part of the *Journal Encyclopédique* [6] for August 15, 1770, was a letter from Baron d'Heiss, ex-captain in the regiment of Alsace, in which the whole of this affair was made known; and there is a copy of this letter in the number

---

[3] *La Prudenza Triomfante di Casale con l'Arni sole de trattati e negotiati di Politici della M. Chr.,* small duodecimo, 58 pp.

[4] This was printed at Leyden by Claude Jordan.

[5] *Annali d'Italia,* Milan edition, vol. xi. pp. 352–354.

[6] Vol. vi. part i. p. 182., Letter from Baron d'Heiss, June 28, 1770.

of the *Journal de Paris*[7] for December 22, 1779. In 1786, the Italian Fantuzzi summarized in his *Notizie degli Scrittori Bolognesi*,[8] the accounts already published on this subject. A similar opinion that Matthioly was the Man with the Iron Mask, was, in 1789, supported by the Chevalier de B——, in a work with the title of *Londres, Correspondance interceptée*.[9] On November 26, 1795, M. de Chambrier, ex-Minister of Prussia to the Court of Turin, read, before the Division of Belles-Lettres of the Academy of Berlin,[10] a memoir in which "he endeavoured to establish, by tradition alone, that the Iron Mask and Ercole Matthioly were one and the same person." Lastly, the 9 Pluviose, Year XI.,[11] the citizen Reth, the commissioner charged with organizing the national lottery in the twenty-seventh military division, addressed a long communication to the *Journal de Paris*[12] tending towards the same conclusion.[13] Thus we see that neither Roux-Fazillac, nor Delort, nor still less any writer of our own days, can claim to be first to have put forward the theory that Matthioly was the Man with the Iron Mask.

---

[7] *Journal de Paris*, p. 1470.

[8] Vol. v. p. 369.

[9] This is a collection of letters interchanged between the Marquis de L. and the Chevalier de B., in which the latter gives an account of his travels in France, Italy, Germany, and England, from September 5, 1782, to January 29, 1788. In it, Matthioly is confounded with another agent named Girolamo Magni.

[10] *Mémoires de l'Académie de Berlin*, 1794 and 1795, Division of Belles-Lettres, pp. 157–163.

[11] January 31, 1800.—*Trans.*

[12] Pp. 814–816.

[13] In this list I do not include the Hon. George Agar Ellis, whose work was translated into French and published by Barbeza, (Paris, 1830), because his book is itself only the almost literal reproduction of Delort's.

However, Delort had the incontestable advantage over his numerous predecessors of furnishing a portion [14] of the official despatches relating to the negotiation, and also of those which were exchanged between Saint-Mars and the various Ministers after Matthioly's incarceration. Since then, and in our own days, M. Camille Rousset, in his *Histoire de Louvois*, has in his turn disclosed the intrigue concocted by D'Estrades, the Duke of Mantua, and Matthioly; and contenting himself with merely giving his opinion on the Iron Mask, in a short note, [15] has declared that he sees in him the faithless Minister who betrayed Louis XIV. Depping, in his *Correspondance Administrative sous Louis XIV.*, also adopts this view. But they have neither of them endeavoured—nor, indeed, did it belong to their subject—to establish what I shall term the perfect agreement and exact correspondence between the individual carried off from near Pignerol, May 2, 1679, and the prisoner who was interred in the Church of Saint Paul, November 20, 1703.

Here is the knot of the question. We have just seen, and this, moreover, has been known since a long time, that Matthioly was carried off in 1679 by a French ambassador and taken violently to Pignerol. But it is no longer a question merely of this intrigue, which is simply a preliminary

---

[14] We have already seen that Delort had examined, in the Archives of the Ministry of Foreign Affairs, only a portion of the sections Venice and Mantua, and that of Savoy not at all. As to the despatches interchanged between the Minister of War and Saint-Mars, he had inspected the rather numerous letters in the Archives of the Empire, but not the drafts which are at the Ministry of War.

[15] " We share the opinion of those who think that the Man with the Iron Mask was no other than Matthioly : "—*Histoire de Louvois*, vol. iii. p. 111, *note.*

portion of the problem with which we are occupied. It is necessary to follow the Duke of Mantua's Minister from prison to prison, and to ascertain, not only if he may not have been, but also if he could have been, any other than the mysterious prisoner conducted in 1698 by Saint-Mars from the Isles Sainte-Marguerite to the Bastille, where he died in 1703. Delort believed he had proved it. His conviction was profound, and to many persons his demonstration seemed irrefutable. On what grounds, then, did it rest, and how has a judicious writer of our own days entirely overthrown it?

On May 2 and 3, 1679, when Matthioly and his valet were incarcerated at Pignerol, this State prison contained, besides Fouquet and Lauzun, four prisoners, incontestably obscure and of very slight importance. One, Eustache d'Auger, brought there August 20, 1669, had for some time acted as Fouquet's valet.[16] Another, arrived at Pignerol April 7, 1674, was a Jacobin monk; "a finished scoundrel," wrote Louvois, "who cannot be sufficiently maltreated or made to suffer the punishment he has deserved." The Minister recommended Saint-Mars "not to give him a fire in his chamber except when great cold or illness obliged it, and not to provide him with any other diet but bread, wine, and water."[17] Louvois afterwards enjoined Saint-Mars "not to let him be seen by any one, nor to give news of him to any person whatever." But this order was in some sort a mere form, since a like injunction had been given to Saint-Mars, July 19, 1669, at the time Eustache d'Auger was

---

[16] Despatch from Louvois to Saint-Mars, January 30, 1675.

[17] Unpublished despatch from Louvois to Saint-Mars, April 18, 1674:—Archives of the Ministry of War.

sent to him.[18] The latter, as well as the Jacobin monk, and Caluzio, brought there in September, 1673,[19] and Dubreuil, imprisoned in June, 1676, were treated in exactly the same manner and without any kind of consideration. The expense for each of them was not to exceed twenty sous a day,[20] and they were so insignificant, that when Saint-Mars was called from the command of the donjon of Pignerol to the government of Exiles, Louvois requested from him " a list of the persons in his charge, begging him to indicate, at the side of each name, what he knew of the reasons for which they had been arrested." [21] It is certain, and this has never been a matter of doubt to any of those who have occupied themselves with this problem, that the Man with the Iron Mask is not to be sought for amongst these obscure wretches, the causes of whose confinement the Minister himself had forgotten. We have seen that Fouquet, undoubtedly, died at Pignerol during the month of March, 1680; and, with regard to

---

[18] Letter from Louvois to Saint-Mars, July 19, 1669. We have already mentioned that the same precautions were adopted (*ante,* p. 234) even for the Protestant ministers who were confined at the Isles Sainte-Marguerite later. See Depping : *Correspondance Administrative sous Louis XIV.*

[19] Buticary was set at liberty at Saint-Mars' request. The following extract from a despatch proves that he ought not to be confounded with Caluzio, as M. Loiseleur has done : " In the correspondence of Saint-Mars," he says (*Revue Contemporaine,* July 31, 1867, p. 202, note), " Caluzio is sometimes called Buticary. One of the two names is a surname." Now, September 14, 1675, Louvois writes to Saint-Mars : " You have done right to give a sergeant and two soldiers to take the Sieur Caluzio to Lyons, and as to the Sieur Buticary, when the King is at Saint-Germain, I will willingly speak in his favour and endeavour to obtain his release."

[20] Delort, *Histoire de la Détention des Philosophes,* vol. i. and Roux-Fazillac.

[21] Letter from Louvois to Saint-Mars, May 12, 1680.

Lauzun, it is not less incontestable that he left the citadel April 22, 1681.

From the moment of his arrest Matthioly received the fictitious name of Lestang, as a despatch of Catinat's clearly shows.[22] He was sometimes designated by his right name, sometimes by this fictitious one. A letter from Louvois, August 16, 1680, authorises Saint-Mars " to place the Sieur de Lestang with the Jacobin, so as to avoid any intercourse between two priests ; " and Saint-Mars' reply, dated September 7, 1680, shows that Matthioly was confined with the Jacobin monk in the lower tower. In this letter Saint-Mars informs the Minister that Matthioly at first thought that he had been placed with a spy charged to watch him and give an account of his conduct. But the monk, a prisoner since several years, had become mad, of which Matthioly was soon convinced " by seeing him one day get out of bed stark naked and preach, as well as he could, without rhyme or reason." The same letter shows Saint-Mars to us just as we have always known him, and watching through a hole over the door what his prisoners were doing.[23]

On May 12, 1681, Louvois, when announcing to Saint-Mars his nomination to the governorship of Exiles, rendered vacant by the death of the Duke de Lesdiguières, " orders him to take with him *the two prisoners of the lower Tower.* According to Roux-Fazillac, Delort, and all those who have occupied themselves with this question, these two prisoners are undoubtedly Matthioly and the Jacobin monk. On

---

[22] Letter from Catinat to Louvois, May 3, 1679.

[23] Letter from Louvois, August 16, 1680, and from Saint-Mars, September 7 of the same year.

January 20, 1687, Saint-Mars, whose health had been affected by the rigorous climate of Exiles, was appointed to the governorship of the Isles Saint-Honorat and Sainte-Marguerite in the sea of Provence. He took with him one prisoner only. Reth and Delort do not hesitate to admit that, of the two prisoners in question, he who was taken by Saint-Mars to the Isles Sainte-Marguerite was Matthioly. Though unable to furnish a sure proof of it, they have no doubt. Roux-Fazillac, more circumspect and less positive, contents himself with remarking that either the Jacobin monk or Matthioly was the Man with the Iron Mask; and it is by means of general considerations, by proofs drawn from the mysterious manner in which the abduction had been accomplished, from Louis XIV.'s evident interest in concealing such a violation of international law, that Roux-Fazillac endeavours to prove Matthioly's identity with the Iron Mask.

Thus, of the very numerous writers who have advanced this opinion, some, such as Baron d'Heiss, M. de Chambrier, M. Depping, and M. Camille Rousset, have done so by only taking account of the circumstances accompanying the abduction, by invoking probabilities, and by showing a preference. Others, such as Roux-Fazillac, Reth, and Delort, have endeavoured to support their demonstrations with more precise and less general proofs, not occupying themselves exclusively with the arrest of this individual, but with the captive's existence and his changes of prison. They have, in a word, attempted to follow him without losing sight of him for an instant, from the moment of his incarceration to that of his death. How have they succeeded?

A very sagacious writer, M. Jules Loiseleur, has, for

some years past, applied the processes of a rigorous historical criticism and the qualities of a penetrative mind to some of those secondary questions which the historian often neglects or avoids, either because they would retard the rapidity of his progress, or because their exact solution would perhaps be contrary to the general theory upon which the *ensemble* of his task has been conceived. These species of minute inquiries, pursued according to a judicial model, concentrate the attention upon certain points, isolated from all others, and present, with some inconveniences, some precious advantages. For, if by such a process, we cease to take account of the necessary influence of general facts, if the marvellous chain of causes and effects be a little neglected, this method, in return, assures to him who employs it entire liberty to study the question under all its phases, and above all things frees him from any preconceived idea, from the necessity of sacrificing himself to a theory, or of obeying too servilely the conditions of art or the sovereign rules of proportion. It is thus that M. Loiseleur has studied,[24] by introducing new documents into the discussion, the question of the pretended poisoning of Gabrielle d'Estrées and of the supposed marriage of Anne of Austria and Mazarin.

The problem of the Man with the Iron Mask has also attracted the scrupulous attention and meditations of this trained mind. M. Loiseleur has not brought forward any new documents in considering this question. It is to those already published that he has directed his examination, and to the theory that makes Matthioly the Man with the Iron Mask.[25] The following is the first result of his observations.

---

[24] *Problèmes Historiques*, Paris. Hachette.
[25] *Revue Contemporaine*, July 21, 1867, pp. 194–239.

In August, 1681, at the moment when Saint-Mars is about to leave Pignerol for Exiles, of which he had just been named Governor, he receives an order from Louvois to defer his departure. The affair of Casale, abandoned, as we have seen after Matthioly's arrest, had been taken up again two years afterwards. The Abbé Morel, addressing himself directly to the Duke of Mantua to whom he was accredited, had obtained his consent, and the treaty of surrender, this time confided to sure hands, was about to be definitively executed. As before, Boufflers occupied the frontier with his troops. As before, Catinat is about to penetrate to Pignerol, in order to proceed afterwards to Casale, and take possession of the place. The following is the letter in which Louvois announces to Saint-Mars the early arrival of Catinat :—

"Fontainebleau, August 13, 1681.

"The King having commanded M. de Catinat to proceed as soon as possible to Pignerol, on the same business that took him there at the commencement of the year 1679, I write you these lines by his Majesty's order, to give you intelligence thereof, so that you may prepare him an apartment in which he may remain concealed during three weeks or a month ; and also to tell you that when he shall send to let you know that he is arrived at the place where you went to meet him in the said year 1679, it is his Majesty's intention that you should go there again to meet him and conduct him into the donjon of the citadel of the aforesaid Pignerol with all the precautions necessary to prevent any one's knowing that he is with you. I do not charge you to assist him with your servants, your horses, and whatever carriages he may have occasion for, not doubting that you will do with pleasure on these heads, whatever he shall ask."

According to M. Loiseleur the words,—"the same business that took him there at the commencement of the year 1679," signifies to Saint-Mars the arrest of a political prisoner. "Since," says M. Loiseleur, "of all the occurrences of the negotiation undertaken in 1679, this was the only one of which Saint-Mars was officially informed."[26] This interpretation is very important, because M. Loiseleur seems to conclude from it that in 1681, as in 1679, Catinat was sent to Pignerol to arrest a new individual, and confide him to the care of Saint-Mars. We are unable to share this opinion. The words in question have evidently only one meaning,—the taking possession of Casale. Catinat was not sent to Pignerol to arrest Matthioly, since Louvois' letter announcing to Saint-Mars the first arrival of this officer, is dated December 29, 1678, when there was not only no intention of carrying off the Mantuan Minister, but when his good offices were continued to be employed, without the suspicion of any treason, which, indeed, did not as yet exist. Moreover, if Catinat remained three months at Pignerol, during January, February and March, 1679, it was because the execution of the treaty of Casale was continually hoped for, and because multiplied and diverse efforts were made to obtain from Matthioly the exchange of the ratifications. M. Loiseleur says, "There was the greatest interest in surrounding Catinat's mission and his stay at Pignerol with the most profound mystery; it was necessary.

---

[26] *Revue Contemporaine,* p. 206.

in truth, to deceive the vigilance of the Court of Turin, so near to the scene of the events in preparation, and also of the Germans, Spaniards, Venetians, and Genoese, who were not less unquiet." No doubt ; and this is one of the reasons why Catinat took an assumed name. " How then," adds this writer, " is it to be explained that Louvois should have confided the purpose of this mission to so subordinate an agent as the Captain Saint-Mars ? "

The conclusion is neither searching nor exact. Not only was Saint-Mars really in the secret of the political mission entrusted to Catinat in 1679, but, as we have seen, he also helped him to fulfil it, by accompanying him to Increa, for the meeting appointed by Matthioly to exchange the ratifications, by following him to Casale, and by sharing his danger. Saint-Mars, moreover, far from being a subordinate agent, possessed, and justly possessed, the entire confidence of Louis XIV. and Louvois ; [27] and despatches which will be quoted hereafter show him to have been on the most friendly terms with D'Estrades and Catinat.[28] The pre-

---

[27] François Michel le Tellier, Marquis de Louvois, whose name occurs so frequently throughout this work, was Louis XIV.'s Secretary of State for War and Prime Minister. He is responsible for the barbarous devastation of the Palatinate, and for the revocation of the Edict of Nantes. After having served his Sovereign faithfully for six-and-thirty years, he fell under his displeasure, and was only saved from disgrace by a sudden death, which occurred in 1691, it is said from poison.

[28] M. Loiseleur afterwards brings forward two arguments which are as little conclusive as those which have just been discussed. " Saint-Mars was so persistently left in ignorance," he says, " that after having confided to his lieutenant the care of recovering the important documents concealed at Padua, Catinat thought better of it, and charged a trusty servant of the Abbé d'Estrades with this mission. . . . When Louvois requested the list of the prisoners imprisoned at Pignerol, with

cautions adopted to conceal the stay of the latter at Pignerol
were designed to leave in ignorance the officers of the
citadel, the notabilities of the town, the governor himself, the
Marquis d'Herleville—every one, in fact, except Saint-Mars,
whose presence became so indispensable, that, for this reason
alone, he delayed his departure for Exiles. In fact, in a
despatch addressed to Louvois, April 15, 1679, Catinat complains that the Marquis d'Herleville suspects his presence
in the donjon, and at the same time congratulates himself
on the precautions which Saint-Mars adopts with regard to
him.[29] Moreover, we cannot too strongly insist that the
business which brought Catinat to Pignerol in 1679 was the
taking possession of Casale. This, for more than three
months, was the appointed object of his exertions. The
abduction of Matthioly was only a second commission, much
less honourable, and much less worthy of Catinat than the
former. It was confided to him because he was on the
scene of events, and because its accomplishment required a
man who was resolute and sure in acting. But it was for
him only an unexpected and subordinate character, and

---

the reasons for which they were detained, he added to his letter,
'with reference to the two of the lower tower you need only indicate
them by this name, without putting anything else.'" If Giuliani was
charged, as we have mentioned in the preceding chapter, to seek at
Padua the papers in the possession of Matthioly's father, it was because,
being supposed a friend of Matthioly, he would inspire no suspicion,
while it would have been very different if this mission had been confided to Saint-Mars' lieutenant. As for the letter in which Louvois
requests from Saint-Mars the names of his prisoners, the dispensing
with information concerning the prisoners in the lower Tower can
be explained in a very simple manner—by the fact that Louvois knew
all about them, since a short time previously they had been referred to
in the correspondence.

[29] Delort, p. 206.

formed but an incident, and a sad incident, of his visit, which could not in any way affect the prime, essential, and incontestable cause of his being there, viz., to take possession of Casale.

M. Loiseleur insists the more upon this unfounded interpretation, because it is almost the sole pretext,[30] I will not say for the theory—he is too cautious to call it so—but for the supposition that an obscure and unknown spy was arrested by Catinat in 1681, and confided, like Matthioly, to Saint-Mars' care. Nothing, indeed—and M. Loiseleur does not deny this—absolutely nothing in the history of the resumption of the negotiations relative to Casale allows us to admit the truth of this hypothesis. While in 1679, there was uncertainty, hesitation, and embarrassment produced by Matthioly's equivocal behaviour, in 1681 everything was simple, clear, and definitive. No doubt the preparations were still concealed ; but observe the rapidity of execution and the startling revenge taken by Louis XIV. ! On July 8, 1681, the treaty of surrender is signed at Mantua by the Duke himself and the Ambassador of the King of France. On August 2 Catinat is ordered from Flanders. On the 13th Louvois announces to Saint-Mars the journey of this officer to Pignerol. From September 1 to 22 the French troops muster at Briançon. On the 27th they

---

[30] Louvois writes to Saint-Mars, September 20, 1681 :—" The King does not disapprove of your going from time to time to see the last prisoner that you have in your care, when he is settled in his new prison." M. Loiseleur concludes from this that at this period there was only one prisoner, and as two are again spoken of afterwards, he infers that a new prisoner was confided to Saint-Mars. We shall hereafter concern ourselves with this despatch, the meaning of which we shall explain.

arrive at Pignerol.   On the 30th they enter Casale with
the Marquis de Boufflers as commander and Catinat as
governor of this new possession.[31] This time there was
no intermediary between the negotiators, no obstacle to
Louis XIV.'s project ; and no employment of an embarrassing or perfidious spy.   There is nothing that is suspicious,
nothing that is obscure in the despatches relating to this
enterprise.   There is no void in them, nothing has been
suppressed.   Moreover—and this is a point upon which we
cannot too strongly insist—the King, the ministers, and the
ambassadors who penned them, could not foresee that they
would one day no longer be buried in the impenetrable
archives of Versailles, but be delivered to investigation and
comment.

Where is there anything in them about that obscure spy
whom Catinat is said to have arrested?   M. Loiseleur has
wished rather to open a new field for conjecture than to put
forward a definite opinion.   He has comprehended so well
the fragile nature of his train of reasoning that he does not
hesitate to express himself in the following manner concerning this pretended prisoner of 1681 :—" There is nothing
to explain to us his true name, his position in life, or his
crime.   The only two theories which are now current concerning the Iron Mask are both equally erroneous.   This is
all that we have intended to establish." [32]

Let us hasten to say that he has completely succeeded.
There is no need for us to return to that one of these two

---

[31] Archives of the Ministry of War ; *Mémoire de Chamlay* on the
events of 1678 to 1688 :—Archives of the Ministry of Foreign Affairs,
sections Mantua and Savoy.

[32] *Revue Contemporaine,* p. 238.

theories which makes the Man with the Iron Mask a brother of Louis XIV.[33] But with reference to the other, which represents Matthioly as being the masked prisoner, M. Loiseleur's refutation of it is very remarkable ; and the researches which we have made, as well as the new documents which we have brought to light, confirm what his clear-sighted sagacity had enabled him to discover. " December 23, 1685," says M. Loiseleur, " Saint-Mars writes from Exiles to Louvois, ' My prisoners are always ill and taking remedies. For the rest, they are very quiet.' We possess no official document relating to what passed at Exiles during the year 1686 ; but it was in this year, as we are about to establish, that Matthioly's death took place. On January 20, 1687, Saint-Mars learns that the King has just conferred on him the governorship of the Isles Honorat and Sainte-Marguerite. He hastens to thank Louvois for it, and adds, ' I shall give my orders for the care of my prisoner so well,' &c. &c."

Thence M. Loiseleur concludes that either in 1686, or in January, 1687, one of the two prisoners had died.[34] He also adduces the testimony of Father Papon, of the Oratory, who, visiting the Isles Sainte-Marguerite, in 1778, questioned an officer there named Claude Souchon, then seventy-nine years old, and whose father had formed one of the free company of the islands in the time of Saint-Mars. Now, both in a memorandum drawn up at the request of the Marquis de Castellane, governor of the islands, and in his replies to Father Papon, the Sieur Souchon said he had heard from his father that the envoy of the Empire

---

[33] See Chapters I. to V. of the present work.
[34] *Revue Contemporaine*, p. 209, *et seq.*

—the Duke of Mantua was a prince of the Empire—
carried off by order of Louis XIV., died nine years
after his arrest — that is to say, in 1688.[35]   Muratori
relates this tradition, and it is also confirmed by the fact
"that the ·name of Matthioly disappeared entirely from
Saint-Mars' correspondence previous to his departure from
Exiles."

The following despatches from Louvois to Saint-Mars,
till now unpublished, justify M. Loiseleur's suppositions :—

> "Fontainebleau, October 9, 1686.

"I have received the letter that you have written to me
the 26th of last month, which requires no answer except to
say that you should have named to me which of your
prisoners it is that has become dropsical."

> "Fontainebleau, November 3, 1686.

"I have received your letter of the 4th of last
month.   It is right to cause that one of your two
prisoners who has become dropsical to confess, when you
perceive the appearance of an approaching death.   Till
then neither he nor his companion must have any communication."

> "Versailles, January 13, 1687.

"I have received your letter of the 5th of this month, by
which I learn the death of one of your prisoners.   I do not
reply to you concerning your desire to change your govern-

---

[35] This is within a year of the date that M. Loiseleur states, and
the exactness of which we are about to confirm.   M. Loiseleur
observes with reason that the error of a year in an old man's early
reminiscences is very probable.

ment, because you have since learnt that the King has granted you one more important [36] than yours, with a good climate, at which I am delighted, and I rejoice again with you at the share which I have taken in what concerns you." [37]

Thus we see that the death of one of the two prisoners brought by Saint-Mars from Pignerol to Exiles is undeniable. Supposing that we reject the testimony of the Sieur Souchon—which, although not possessing the character of an official document, does not the less deserve the most serious attention—supposing that we are not absolutely convinced that the prisoner who died of dropsy was Matthioly, it is, nevertheless, necessary to admit that the fact of this death places in the greatest uncertainty and almost entirely destroys the value of the theory put forward by Baron d'Heiss, De Chambrier, Reth, Roux-Fazillac, Delort, Depping, and Rousset. How, in fact, can one now insist that Matthioly was the Man with the Iron Mask, who mysteriously entered the Bastille September 18, 1698, when we see that he was confided to the care of Saint-Mars along with another prisoner; that one of the two captives died in 1687; and that from this time the name of the Mantuan Minister altogether disappears from the correspondence of Louvois and Saint-Mars? After having attentively read M. Loiseleur's work, and especially after having found the despatches confirming the essential portions of it, I by no means arrived at the conclusion that Catinat in 1681 abducted some spy,

---

[36] The governorship of the Isles Sainte-Marguerite-Saint-Honorat.

[37] Unpublished despatches from Louvois to Saint-Mars :—Archives of the Ministry of War.

the fact of whose arrest or even existence is altogether devoid of proof; but I acquired the conviction that this problem would never receive a definitive solution, and that it was impossible to disperse the mysterious gloom with which the Man with the Iron Mask was surrounded.

Such was my confirmed opinion when, studying more attentively one of the despatches which I had been permitted to examine, a new direction was impressed on my researches, and led me to a result which I am about to unfold.

CHAPTER XXII.

On each side of Cannes, the coast of Provence, describing a slight curve, forms the two gulfs of Napoule and Jouan, separated by the Point of the Croisette.[1] Off this point, distant about a mile from shore, are two islands, situated one in front of the other like advanced sentinels, and affording each other mutual protection. The approach to them is rendered far from easy by the rocks and reefs with which nature has surrounded them. Both are oblong in shape, lying from east to west, and the one nearest to the shore is also much the larger. Owing to the great number of pines with which they are covered, the view from them is limited ; but if we ascend one of the highest towers, we behold the most dazzling and wonderful of pictures. On every

---

[1] Thus named on account of a cross to which pilgrimages were formerly made :—*Promenades de Nice*, by Émile Negrin, p. 273.

side is a marvellous profusion of light; just in front of us is Cannes, and its elegant villas, bathed by the waves of the sea; a little further inland lies the magnificent valley of Grasse, with its hills covered with olive-trees, its green mountain-slopes, and luxuriant vegetation;[2] on the left is the sharp and varied outline of the long chain of the Esterel; on the right, the Maritime Alps, almost touching the sky, with their snowy summits glittering in the sun; and in the background, a pile of savage mountains and gigantic rocks forms a striking contrast with this privileged spot, and provides for it at once both a sure shelter and a most picturesque framework.

These two islands, so appropriately situated for the embellishment of these peerless localities, have no share in the life or animation that surrounds them. As a rule, uncultivated, and inhabited solely by their garrison and a few fishermen's families, intersected here and there by ancient salt-marshes, and of a sad and monotonous appearance, one would say that they belonged altogether to the past. On these tranquil coasts everything tends to meditation and to poetry. Day-dreams are natural and easy here, for there is nothing to disturb the grand recollections which the spot evokes, and in which history and legend have an equal share. The Romans have occupied these islets; pious hermits have established themselves on them; the Saracens have invaded and the Spaniards have pillaged them in turn.[3] In the early part of the fifth century, Saint-Honorat founded a monastery here, which was for a long time the most celebrated of Gaul, and in which thousands of apostles were trained in virtue and

---

[2] *Visite aux Îles de Lérins,* by the Abbé Alliez, 1840.

[3] *Notice sur Cannes et les Îles des Lérins,* by M. Sardou. Cannes, Robaudy, 1867.

knowledge, of whom some became celebrated bishops, and very many martyrs.[4] Everywhere on this land of the past vestiges of ancient buildings[5] are to be perceived, and traces of savage devastation. Everywhere the uncertain and poetic recollections preserved by tradition are mingled with the unquestionable events of the history of France. Here, in the smaller of the two islands, is still to be seen the inexhaustible well that, according to the legend, Saint-Honorat caused to be dug, and from which fresh water miraculously issued forth on to a salt and arid shore till then deprived of it. Not a long while ago one used to be shown the place where the Saint, perched on a high tree, escaped the flood of waters he had called forth by his prayers, and which, on afterwards retiring, carried off with them the serpents with which the islands were infested. It was here also that Francis I. stopped when a prisoner of the Spaniards after the fatal battle of Pavia, and this was the last spot of French earth trodden by the unfortunate monarch before commencing his rigorous captivity. It was here also—a recollection at once sad and glorious—that Prince Eugène and the Duke of Savoy encountered the most obstinate resistance when they were invading the South of France, and were marching first upon Cannes and then upon Toulon by the

---

[4] Besides Saint-Honorat, there were Saints Aigulph, Hilary, Patrick, Capraise, Vincent, Venantius, and many others. See the very remarkable thesis presented to the Faculty of Letters in Paris by the Abbé Goux, professor at the Petit Séminaire of Toulouse, and entitled, *Lérins au Cinquième Siècle.* Paris, Eugène Belin, 1856. Also the charming volume of MM. Girard and Bareste, *Cannes et ses Environs.* Paris, Garnier, 1859.

[5] M. Merimée, *Note d'un Voyage dans le Midi de la France,* p. 256, *et seq.*

road bordering the sea.[6] It was from here that the cannon-shots were fired which, by delaying the enemy's march, gave time for Toulon to be defended; and after the raising of the siege, it was the attack from here that compelled the Germans and Piedmontese, on their return, to leave the sea-shore, and take refuge among the hills and mountains, where they fell under the multiplied blows of the energetic peasants of Provence.

Such are these two islands, sometimes designated under the common name of the Lerins, but better known under that of the Isles Sainte-Marguerite and Saint-Honorat, where the most varied remains abound, but which the residence of the Man with the Iron Mask has especially rendered for ever famous. Such are the spots which it is impossible to visit, pronounce the name of, or call to mind the recollection, without both the name and the recollection of the mysterious prisoner who was confined in the larger of the two islands—that of Sainte-Marguerite—immediately recurring also. Whether we follow the tradition which represents the masked man as being brought to Saint-Mars in this island,[7] or whether we think that he was con-

---

[6] A flag of truce came from the Duke of Savoy to notify to M. la Mothe-Guérin, governor of the islands, the order to cease firing. "The first person," replied La Mothe-Guérin, "who has the audacity to come again to me as the bearer of such a message, I shall immediately have hung:"—M. Sardou, work already cited, p. 111. "It was when under fire from the Isles Sainte-Marguerite," the Duke of Savoy said afterwards, "that I knew better than anywhere else that I was in an enemy's country."

[7] It is to be remarked that according to the first work which makes mention of the Man with the Iron Mask, the prisoner was conducted to the Isles Sainte-Marguerite, and there confided to Saint-Mars. This is the *Mémoires Secrets pour servir à l'Histoire de Perse*, from which we have reproduced the entire passage in Chapter VI. of the present work (see p. 69, *ante*).

ducted thither by Saint-Mars himself, it is undeniable that in 1698 the gaoler and his captive departed thence, for the purpose of undertaking that journey which was mysteriously pursued across France, exciting everywhere an inquisitive astonishment, having Villeneuve-le-Roi for its principal halting-place and the Bastille for termination. It is not less certain (and the unimpeachable journal[8] of Dujonca is evidence of this) that the individual conducted to Paris by Saint-Mars "in his litter, was an old prisoner whom he had at Pignerol."

Who was this prisoner?

It is very certain that there nowhere exists a collection of documents specially relating to the Man with the Iron Mask. Louis XIV. had too great an interest in surrounding this individual with uncertainty and obscurity for him to have been pleased to collect and leave behind him sure proofs of his identity. This interest in concealing the existence of the captive became, as we shall see further on, very much greater at the time of his removal to the Bastille. So his real name disappeared almost entirely, and he was simply termed "the prisoner from Provence." It is consequently necessary to go back long before the date of this removal, in order to establish his identity, and this can only be done by comparing a great number of despatches, no one of which furnishes of itself an unexceptionable proof, though their comparison and the logical deductions to be derived from them enable us to come to a sure conclusion. We must therefore request from our readers, especially at this stage of the argument, a close and sustained attention.

---

[8] The passages of this Journal relating to the prisoner are given in Chapter XIII. of the present work (see pp. 164, 165, *ante*).

We have terminated the preceding chapter by stating that M. Jules Loiseleur has pronounced a decisive judgment on the question of the Man with the Iron Mask, and we defy any attentive reader to study his work without becoming convinced that the problem will never be solved. But M. Loiseleur has made his inquiry merely with reference to the documents as yet published. " His demonstrations, so clear, luminous, and peremptory," a critic has observed, " have exhausted the question, and, in default of fresh documents, no profound mind will again recur to it."[9]   It is these fresh documents which I am about to introduce into the discussion, and I will proceed to state how I was led to suppose their existence, and afterwards how I became the first to establish it.

An unpublished despatch, addressed by Louvois to Saint-Mars, January 5, 1682, is thus conceived :—

" I have received your letter of the 28th of last month. You do not know what is advantageous for you, when you ask to exchange the governorship of Exiles for the command of the Château of Casale, which brings in only two thousand livres of salary.   Consequently I do not advise you to think of it."[10]

At first this despatch appears insignificant enough.   It seems to furnish but one proof more of Louvois' kindly interest for Saint-Mars, an interest which was due to the Minister's intense affection for his mistress, Madame Dufresnoy, sister-in-law to Saint-Mars, and also, which is perhaps a more legitimate reason, to the perfect devotion

---

[9] M. Baudry, *Revue de l'Instruction Publique,* June 25, 1868.
[10] Archives of the Ministry of War.

and tried fidelity of the gaoler of Fouquet and Lauzun. However, on reading it over again, I asked myself how Saint-Mars could dream, if Matthioly was one of his prisoners, of soliciting to be sent to Casale, to a town altogether Italian and even Mantuan, where Matthioly might certainly have succeeded, if not in escaping (we know that Saint-Mars' prisoners could scarcely indulge in that hope), at least in giving information concerning himself, and revealing his situation. But the sole motive of Louvois' refusal is, as we have just seen, the smallness of the salary given to the commandant of Casale. If Saint-Mars, to suppose what could never have happened, had misconceived the danger likely to be caused by Matthioly's presence at Casale, even as a prisoner, it is beyond doubt that Louvois, naturally cautious (and here caution would have been a duty) would have written to him in something like the following words : " I am astonished that you should have formed the design of removing to Casale. It is necessary to give it up entirely." But on the contrary, Louvois finds no other inconvenience in this plan than that of the inferiority of the salary attached to the duties of Casale, and he concludes with these words : " I do not advise you to think of it." It is the friend full of solicitude who speaks, and not the Minister energetically rejecting a proposal so contrary to the interests confided to him.

It was this despatch which first suggested to me the idea that, contrary to the general opinion, Matthioly was not taken by Saint-Mars from Pignerol to Exiles. As yet this was, it is true, but a very weak presumption, which was destroyed by proofs that were apparently irrefutable and had been accepted as such up to the present. We have, in fact, seen that Matthioly, a short time after his arrest, was placed in the lower Tower at Pignerol, and it was the prisoners of this tower whom Saint-Mars was ordered to conduct to Exiles. Louvois' despatch [11] of June 9, 1681, concludes with these words: "With regard to the effects belonging to the Sieur Matthioly, which are in your possession, you will have them taken to Exiles, in order to be able to give them back to him if his Majesty should ever order him to be set at liberty." This is an explicit statement, and has naturally confirmed every one in the opinion that Matthioly was removed from Pignerol to Exiles. But the doubt which the despatch of January 5, 1682, had made me conceive, was changed into certainty when I read the following letter, written by Saint-Mars, to the Abbé d'Estrades, June 25, 1681, and to be found in minute among the Estrades' manuscripts in the Imperial Library :—

"June 25, 1681.

"Sir, I should not deserve your pardon if I was certain of having the government of Exiles without doing myself the honour to inform you of it, and besides the respect which I have for you, Sir, I am indebted to you to such a degree that I should be an ungrateful and dishonest man if, during the whole of my life, I did not honour you with the utmost affection and respect. Rely on me, Sir, as being the most devoted person in the world towards yourself and bound for the remainder of my days with heart and love to your service. I only received yesterday my supplies as governor of Exiles with two thousand livres of salary; my free company is preserved to me as well as two of my

---

[11] Given by Delort, p. 269.

lieutenants, and I shall also have in custody two crows, whom I have here, who have no other names than Messieurs of the lower Tower; Matthioli will remain here with two other prisoners. One of my lieutenants named Villebois will look after them, and he has a warrant to command either in the citadel or in the donjon during my absence, and until M. de Rissan returns, or his Majesty shall have provided for this office of Lieutenant of the King by naming some other person. The Chevalier de Saint-Martin has been appointed Major of Montlouis with a salary of seven hundred crowns, and Blainvilliers, his comrade, Major of the citadel of Metz, with the same pay. I do not expect to leave here before the end of next month. I could if I chose go there from time to time in order to have the repairs made which are necessary for the good of the service, as I have received my orders to go into this place of exile whenever I please; but as nothing presses, and as it will be necessary to take up my residence in this place in order to pass the winter there with the whole of my family and the bears, it will take time for me to accommodate myself as well as possible. What consoles me is that I shall have the honour of being near to the States of their Royal Highnesses, to whom I am as much a debtor as a very respectful and humble servant."

Consequently, Matthioly was not the prisoner who died at Exiles, the commencement of January, 1687.[12] He was

---

[12] This is now placed beyond doubt, and moreover we shall find Matthioly's name occurring later in the despatches from Louvois to the commandant of the donjon of Pignerol. With respect to the testimony of the Sieur Souchon, which, following M. Loiseleur, we have given in the preceding chapter, it is rather confused in the *Mémoires d'un Voyageur qui se repose* (vol. ii. pp. 204–210 of Bossange's edition), and very clear

therefore left at Pignerol, where we shall soon meet with him again in charge of the Sieur de Villebois. Louis XIV. at first had the idea of having him removed to Exiles, as is proved by Louvois' despatch of June 9, 1681, the last sentence of which we have quoted. But it is none the less certain that this first design was abandoned, and that Matthioly was left at Pignerol.

There is also another remarkable expression in Saint-Mars' letter. He writes, " I shall also have in custody two crows " (*merles*). Now even in our own time the word " crow " (*merle*) is applied only to common and insignificant persons, of as little notoriety as importance. Up to the present, however, it is in one of these two " crows " that people have seen the Man with the Iron Mask. Is it objected that one proof alone is not sufficient to establish the entire obscurity of these two prisoners of Saint Mars? But this is confirmed also by all we have said concerning the treatment of which Saint-Mars' prisoners at Pignerol were the objects, with the exception of Fouquet, Lauzun, and Matthioly.[13] Is additional testimony required? " You can have clothes made for your prisoners," writes Louvois to Saint-Mars at Exiles, December 14, 1681; "*but it is necessary that the clothes of*

---

in the work of Father Papon, but with the signification of *the death of the servant* and not of Matthioly himself. The following is the passage from the *Voyage Littéraire de Provence* (pp. 148, 149, edition 1780), integrally reproduced : " The person who waited on the prisoner died at the Isle Sainte-Marguerite. The father of the officer of whom I have just spoken (Souchon, seventy-nine years old), who was in certain matters the man of confidence of M. de Saint-Mars, had always told his son that he had taken the dead man from his prison at the hour of midnight, and had carried him on his shoulders to the burial-ground."

[13] We shall refer hereafter to the treatment of Matthioly.

people like these should last three or four years." [14]   As usual,
the Minister's orders were punctually executed by his representative, and when Saint-Mars left Exiles to proceed to the
Isles Sainte-Marguerite, he wrote to Versailles "that the
prisoner's bed was so old and worn out" (we have previously
seen that one of the prisoners was still alive in 1687, the
other having died in the early part of January of the same
year), "as well as everything he made use of, both table-
linen and furniture, that it was not worth while to bring
them here; they only sold for thirteen crowns."[15] Assuredly
if this is the Man with the Iron Mask, and if he had that
delicate taste for fine linen, of which so much has been said,
he must have found considerable difficulty in gratifying it.

Saint-Mars arrives at the Isles Sainte-Marguerite, which
as yet had not been used as a State Prison, as they are at
present.[16]   Obeying Louvois' orders he causes some new

---

[14] Archives of the Ministry of War.

[15] Letter given by Delort, p. 284.

[16] In 1633, Richelieu had the Fort Royal built on the northern
shore of the Isle Sainte-Marguerite, but it was on the arrival of
Saint-Mars that the buildings were erected which were to serve for
prisoners of very various classes. The following unpublished letter,
written by M. de Grignan, Lieutenant-General of Provence, September 29, 1691, proves that previous to this date the Isle Sainte-Marguerite was a State Prison :—

"The guard which I had placed at Cannes have arrested a sailor,
supposed to belong to Oneglia, who was coming from the direction of
Genoa, and who, from his replies, in which he has varied a great deal,
has given grounds for belief that he has been put ashore by the Spanish
galleys and is a spy, who, under pretence of carrying to Toulon a letter
from a captain of Genoa, was going there to obtain information.   He
has been taken to the Isles of Sainte-Marguerite.

"L. DE GRIGNAN, L. G. of Provence.

"September 29, 1691, to M. de Pontchartrain."

—Archives of the Ministry of Marine, Correspondence.

buildings to be erected,[17] in which he receives in turns various prisoners, especially Protestant ministers.[18] Does the gaoler's behaviour change at this period? Is it then that we find a trace of those peculiarities which are so abundantly proved, and which form one of the characteristic features of the story of the Man with the Iron Mask? The following despatch from Barbézieux to Saint-Mars will furnish us with an answer :—

Another letter, dated July 21, 1681, from Count de Grignan to M. de Pontchartrain, shows that the island was beginning to be armed for the defence of the coast :—

"M. de Saint-Mars, governor of the islands of Sainte-Marguerite and Saint-Honorat de Lérins, speaks to me of provisions which he is obliged to fetch from the mainland, and of the twenty-five pieces of cannon which require carriages."—*Ibid.*

[17] In a despatch dated January 8, 1688, Saint-Mars hastens to apprise Louvois that his new prisons are quite ready and waiting to be occupied :—

" Monseigneur,—I will do myself the honour to tell you that I have placed my prisoner, who is generally in bad health, in one of the new prisons which I have had built according to your instructions. They are large, lofty, and light, and considering their excellence, I do not think that there are any stronger or more secure in Europe, and in like manner for everything that can concern the giving of intelligence by word of mouth from near and far, which was not the case in the places where I have had the care of the late Monsieur Fouquet from the moment that he was arrested. With a little precaution one might even allow the prisoners to walk about the whole of the island, without any fear of their escaping or of their giving or receiving news. I take the liberty, monseigneur, to point out to you in detail the excellence of this place in case you may at any time have prisoners whom you wish to put in perfect security with a fair amount of liberty.

" Throughout this province people say that mine is Monsieur de Beaufort and others the son of the late Cromwell."

[18] The greater portion of the despatches relating to the Protestants confined in the islands have been given by Depping in his *Correspondance Administrative sous Louis. XIV.*

!" At the Camp before Namur, June 29, 1692.[19]

" I have received your letter of the fourth of this month. When any of the prisoners confided to your care will not do what you order them, or cause a mutiny, you have only to [20] punish them as you may think proper."

It has been unceasingly repeated that Saint-Mars never quitted his famous prisoner from the moment that he received him in charge.   This is again one of the features characterizing the mysterious captive, and the two men are in some degree always represented as the prisoners of one another. Do we find, either at Exiles or during the first years of Saint-Mars' residence at the Isles Sainte-Marguerite, this significant peculiarity ?   We are about to see :—

"December 14, 1681.

" Nothing prevents you from going to Casale from time to time, in order to see Monsieur Catinat." [21]

" December 22, 1681.

" His Majesty does not disapprove of your sleeping away from Exiles for one night when you desire to pay a visit in the neighbourhood." [22]

" Turin, January 9, 1682.

" Monsieur de Saint-Mars arrived at Turin yesterday. *Some time ago when he passed through here* he did me the

---

[19] Unpublished despatch from Barbézieux to Saint-Mars, June 29, 1692 :—Archives of the Ministry of War.

[20] The following words are here erased :—" beat them severely, and."

[21] Unpublished despatch from Louvois to Saint-Mars:—Archives of the Ministry of War.

[22] *Ibid.:—Ibid.*

honour to stop with me.   But this time M. de Masin has the preference." [23]

---

[23] Manuscripts of the Imperial Library, *Papiers d'Estrades*.   This letter and several others in the same collection are a proof of the friendship which subsisted between Saint-Mars and the Abbé d'Estrades.

"On the first of next month, Monsieur de Catinat," we read in a letter from Saint-Mars to the Abbé d'Estrades, September 27, 1681, "will be the governor of the citadel which you have brought into the King's possession."   He refers to Casale, and these words would suffice to prove, what is already attested by the active part played by Saint-Mars with Catinat in 1679, viz., that Saint-Mars had been kept informed of all the details of the two negotiations.   Consequently, as we have already shown in the preceding chapter, the famous sentence of Louvois' despatch to Saint-Mars, August 13, 1681—"The King having ordered Monsieur de Catinat to proceed as soon as possible to Pignerol *on the same business which took him there at the commencement of the year* 1679"—has and can have only one meaning, that is to say, the taking possession of Casale, and not the arrest of a new prisoner.

But M. Loiseleur brings forward another argument in order to attempt to prove that an obscure spy was arrested by Catinat in 1681.   This is the following letter from Louvois to Saint-Mars, September 20, 1681 :—"The King does not disapprove of your going from time to time to see the last prisoner whom you have in charge, when he is settled in his new prison, and has left that in which you are keeping him.   His Majesty desires that you shall execute the order which he has sent you," &c.   And the same critic concludes, from a despatch from Saint-Mars to Louvois, March 11, 1682, which again mentions two prisoners, that, between September 20, 1681, and March 11, 1682, a new prisoner was confided to Saint-Mars.

Let us remark, firstly, that the space of time in question is much more limited still.   M. Loiseleur only made use of documents already published.   But, November 18, 1681, Louvois, in a despatch as yet unprinted, says to Saint-Mars, with reference to his prisoners : "The King approves of your choosing a doctor to visit your prisoners, and of your employing the Sieur Vignon to confess them once a year." From this it would appear that a new prisoner was confided to Saint-Mars, between September 20 and November 18, 1681 ; but, as we have already said in the last chapter, there is nowhere any trace of this prisoner, this so-called spy.   On the other hand, for the despatch of September 20, 1681, to have the meaning which M. Loiseleur attributes

"April 18, 1682.

"The King does not disapprove of your going to pay your respects to the Duke of Savoy."

---

to it, one of the two prisoners of the lower Tower must have died some days previous to September 20, since at this date only one prisoner is spoken of. Of this death or disappearance we have no proof or even trace. Thus the whole argument rests upon this single despatch, of which M. Loiseleur not only makes use in order to prove that a new prisoner had been confided to Saint-Mars, but from which he also deduces that one of the prisoners previously confined had disappeared.

This single despatch thus standing alone, and completely unsupported, would be far from being sufficient to establish this theory. Nevertheless, it is essential to discover its true meaning, so as to leave no doubt in the reader's mind, and to make every part of our demonstration clear and plain. I acknowledge having spent a considerable time in thinking over this despatch, which was contradicted by all the others, which suited no theory, and which was nevertheless authentic and very exactly reproduced, since I went several times to read the draft of it, at the Archives of the Ministry of War. Even if it had possessed the meaning that M. Loiseleur attributed to it, it would not have destroyed my conclusions at all, since the proofs which I had furnished of the obscurity of the Exiles prisoners were also applicable to this new prisoner brought between November and September, 1681, and because the superior importance of the prisoners afterwards taken from Pignerol to the Isles Sainte-Marguerite, would not have been demonstrated any the less clearly by the despatches which I am about to quote. But it was repugnant to me to leave a single point obscure; and after much reflection, and after having been for a long while of M. Loiseleur's opinion, although nothing outside of this despatch justifies his interpretation, I believe that I have discovered its true meaning.

"The King does not disapprove," says the despatch which we are discussing, "of your going from time to time to see the last prisoner whom you have in charge, when he is settled in his new prison and has left that in which you are keeping him." At first I thought it very strange that one of Saint-Mars' prisoners should "settle" in his prison without his gaoler, and connecting this fact with the numerous despatches which show that at this period, or at least at one not very remote from it, Saint-Mars still had two prisoners, I have ended by concluding that the word "prisoner" is not used here by Louvois in its ordinary sense, but figuratively. I then recollected that in 1681, as in 1679,

"March 7, 1685.

"The King is willing that you should go for change of air to the place you may think best for your health."

Catinat was at Pignerol, and treated in appearance at least as a prisoner. The following despatch from Catinat to Louvois, September 6, 1681, leaves no doubt on the subject : "I have called myself Guibert, (we have seen that in 1679, he had taken the name of Richemont), and I am supposed to be an engineer *who has been arrested* by the King's orders for having deserted with a number of plans of places on the frontiers of Flanders. M. de Saint-Mars *keeps me here with every appearance of my being a prisoner*," &c. On the other hand, during Catinat's two stays at Pignerol, with two years' interval between them, a profound friendship had sprung up between him and Saint-Mars. The despatch which we are discussing was dated September 20, 1681. Now, on the 28th, Catinat was to leave, and indeed did leave Pignerol, and on October 1, he was installed at Casale as governor. In an unpublished letter from Saint-Mars to the Abbé d'Estrades, September 27, 1681, is an expression which explains everything : "I have given your letter to M. de Catinat, and he will have the honour to communicate with you when he is *settled*. He leaves to-morrow, Sunday, with the infantry, and no one is more your servant than he is. The first of next month he will be received as governor of the citadel which you have brought into the King's possession (Casale)." —Imperial Library, Manuscripts, *Papiers d'Estrades*. Now this very expression, "when he is settled," occurs in Louvois' despatch, September 20, which Saint-Mars had just received when he was writing to d'Estrades.

But, it will be said, why does Louvois make use of the words "in his new prison" to describe Casale? Because, no doubt, Catinat had not left Louvois ignorant that a monotonous residence at Casale was disagreeable to him, and that he would very much prefer to return to the army of Flanders. Lastly, December 14, 1681, Louvois writes to Saint-Mars, who, from his excessive scruples, had probably renewed his request for an authorisation : "Nothing need prevent your going to Casale from time to time, in order to visit M. Catinat."

It is therefore to Catinat that reference is made in the despatch of September 20, 1681, to Catinat, the last of the prisoners whom Saint-Mars still had in his care, for, since the month of June, Matthioly had been confided to Villebois, and the two prisoners left to Saint-Mars were two "crows," whom no doubt he had already taken to Exiles.

" March 20, 1685.

" Madame de Saint-Mars having told me that you wished to go to the baths of Aix in Savoy, I have informed the King, and his Majesty has commanded me to acquaint you that he is pleased to grant you permission to absent yourself from Exiles on·this ground for the space of a fortnight· or three weeks."

"July 5, 1688.[24]

"The King approves of your absenting yourself from the place where you command, two days a month, and also of your returning the Governor of Nice the visit he has paid you." [25]

Thus, save the precautions taken to prevent an escape—and we have seen that these were prescribed to Saint-Mars, in the same form and with the same minute instructions, for all prisoners alike, whoever they might be, even for that Eustache d'Auger, who was turned into a servant for Fouquet—save, I say, these precautions, necessary but exaggerated by Saint-Mars' scruples, we do not find in these two captives any of the essential characteristics of the Man with the Iron Mask. Not that we accept all those with which romance has adorned him. But, however insignificant exact history may represent him, is he to be

---

It is to Catinat that he refers, and this despatch can no longer be made to serve as a pretext for the theory according to which a new prisoner was arrested by Catinat in 1681.·

[24] Saint-Mars was now at the Isles Sainte-Marguerite.

[25] This and the three preceding despatches are from Louvois to Saint-Mars, and are to be found in the Archives of the Ministry of War.

recognized in one of those two men,[26] termed " crows " by Saint-Mars, " these sort of people " by Louvois, treated in the manner we have seen ; the total value of whose effects, linen, and furniture, was only thirteen crowns, and whom their gaoler received permission to leave frequently and for considerable periods of time ?

But there is another result of our researches, quite as unknown as that which we have just set forth.

Saint-Mars is at the Isles Sainte-Marguerite, which he does not scruple to leave from time to time. All at once, on February 26, 1694, the Minister announces to him the approaching arrival at the islands of three State prisoners who are then in the donjon of Piguerol. He inquires of Saint-Mars " if there are secure places to confine them in," and orders him to make preparations, repairs, and the necessary arrangements for their reception.[27]   In another letter, on

---

[26] The " crow " taken by Saint-Mars to the Islands was undoubtedly the Jacobin monk, as is proved by the following despatch from Barbézieux to Saint-Mars: " Versailles, August 13, 1691—Your letter of the 26th of last month has been handed to me. When you have anything to inform me concerning the prisoner who has been in your charge for the last twenty years, I beg you to adopt the same precautions as you made use of when communicating with M. de Louvois." Twenty years is undoubtedly a round number, and the Jacobin monk, imprisoned since 1674, had then suffered seventeen years of captivity. A great deal of importance has been ascribed to this despatch, because it was one of the very few belonging to this period which were known to exist. We have just seen, however, that its value is very much diminished by comparison with the other letters which we have transcribed. The recommendation that Barbézieux gives in it is purely a matter of form, and similar injunctions were transmitted to Villebois and afterwards to Laprade, when charged with the care of Matthioly.

[27] Unpublished despatch from Barbézieux to Saint-Mars, February 26, 1694 :—Archives of the Ministry of War.

the following 20th of March, Barbézieux adds these words, the great importance of which it is unnecessary to point out : "You well know that they are of more importance, *at least, one of them*, than those who are now at the islands, and you ought to place them by preference in the most secure prisons."[28] Then he orders him "to prepare the furniture and plate necessary for their use, and impresses upon him that the works which he is compelled to have done should be ready on their arrival." By the same courier he forwards fifteen hundred livres to meet the first expenses.

A few days afterwards, in fact, three prisoners arrived at the Isles Sainte-Marguerite, surrounded by a very strong escort, in charge of the commandant of Pignerol, who alone gave them their food,[29] and guided by two sure men sent on in advance by the Governor ; among these prisoners, as we shall see hereafter, was the one whom Saint-Mars some years later took to the Bastille.

---

[28] Unpublished despatch from Barbézieux to Saint-Mars, March 20, 1694 :—*Ibid.*

[29] "The King charges you that no one but yourself shall give them to eat, as you have done since they were confided to your care ; "—Unpublished despatch from Barbézieux to Laprade, who, on the death of Villebois, succeeded to the governorship of the donjon of Pignerol.

CHAPTER XXIII.

Behaviour of Charles IV., Duke of Mantua, towards his ex-Minister—
His true Sentiments with reference to him—Precautions pre-
scribed to Villebois and Laprade for the Prisoners left by Saint-
Mars at Pignerol.—Change in Louis XIV.'s Position in Italy—
Transfer of the Pignerol Prisoners to the Isles Sainte-Marguerite—
Instructions given to Marshal de Tessé—Increase of Saint-Mars'
Watchfulness — Mystery surrounding the three Prisoners—Great
Importance of one of them compared with the others—It is he who
was the Man with the Iron Mask.

MATTHIOLY was left by Saint-Mars at Pignerol, and the long
silence concerning him preserved by Louvois and Saint-
Mars from the time of the latter's departure for Exiles,
receives in that manner its natural explanation. When I
had assured myself of this, I sought in the Archives of the
Ministry of War for all the despatches addressed either by
Louis XIV. or by the Minister to the Sieur de Villebois,
Governor of the donjon, or to the Sieur Laprade, who,
after the latter's death, in April 1692, replaced him in
these duties. Now, I have not only found in these
despatches the confirmation of Matthioly's presence at
Pignerol, but also fresh proofs of the very strict precautions of which the prisoners left in this citadel continued
to be the objects.

It has often been asked how it was that the Duke of Mantua should have remained indifferent to the fate of his old favourite, and not have inquired concerning him of Louis XIV., whom he ought to have known was alone in a position to furnish him with information. As the despatches from the Court of Mantua, published either by Delort or by others, do not mention Matthioly's name after the date of his arrest, people have explained this silence by the frivolous indifference of the young duke, and it must be admitted that the character of this prince rendered such an explanation very probable. Moreover, this silence has very much contributed to diminish the importance of Count Matthioly, and we have been told many times that there could have been nothing very considerable in the position of a person who suddenly disappeared without his master even thinking of inquiring what had become of him. But this is an error. However light and careless Charles IV. may have been, he did occupy himself with the fate of Matthioly; but far from endeavouring to deliver him, he regarded his release as a danger. Indeed, by breaking off the project of the cession of Casale by his desertion, Matthioly had not only tricked Louis XIV., but had also profoundly incensed the Duke of Mantua, whom he had thus surrendered to the violent recriminations, and perhaps later, to the vengeance of the other Italian princes. If Louis XIV. had not had him carried off, Charles IV. would have charged himself with this care, and would have brought about the disappearance of the inconvenient witness of his intrigues with the Court of Versailles, the agent who had negotiated the sale of one of the keys of Italy, the confidant whose very existence was a reproach, whose words were an ever-threatened accusation, and whose testimony was invaluable to the enemies of the Duke of Mantua.

"M. de Mantua," writes the Abbé d'Estrades to Pomponne, June 10, 1679, "shows uneasiness as to what can have become of Matthioly, whose conduct he blames. . . . . I inform him concerning Matthioly that, *although I do not know where he is*, and for the last two months have had no news of him, I do not hesitate to assure him that he cannot interfere at all in our negotiation, and that he will not even have the least suspicion of it; that he may set his mind at rest concerning this, and that I pledge him my word for it."[1]

Two years afterwards the Abbé Morel, the French ambassador, when about to proceed to Mantua, to Charles IV., with the view of renewing the project of surrender, writes from Turin to Louis XIV. :—

"Turin, August 9, 1681.

"I have no doubt that on my return to Mantua, the Duke will question me as to what will be done with Matioly after the execution of the treaty. Perhaps it would be as well to give me a line of information on this point."[2]

And Louis XIV. himself replies in a manner to calm Charles IV.'s uneasiness, but still without revealing the place of Matthioly's confinement :—

"Fontainebleau, August 21, 1681.

"I have already informed you that you may assure the Duke of Mantua that Mathioly will not leave the place

---

[1] Unpublished despatch :—Archives of the Ministry of Foreign Affairs, section Savoy, 68.

[2] Unpublished despatch from the Abbé Morel to Louis XIV. :— Archives of the Ministry of Foreign Affairs, section Mantua, 15.

where he is without the consent of that prince ; and if there are any other measures to be taken for his satisfaction, you will inform me of them.   On this, etc." [3]

Can one have any doubt of the true sentiments of the Duke of Mantua after reading the following despatch ?—

" The Duke of Mantua has learnt with much joy and with sentiments of lively gratitude, what it has pleased your Majesty to order me to inform him concerning Matthioli. He had intended to thank me this evening personally in an audience which he wished to accord me ; but I have found it impossible to attend, owing to a very painful rheumatism in the neck, which has forced me to keep my bed during the last three days." [4]

This joy of Charles IV. on learning that he no longer had to dread the sudden appearance of his accomplice is sadly significant.   He could again treat with Louis XIV. without fearing lest his too well-informed ex-minister should proceed to impress upon the attention of the other princes the conditions to which the Duke of Mantua had agreed, by consenting to put himself under the complete control of the most dangerous of Italy's enemies.   Everything thus combined to perpetuate the confinement of the unfortunate Minister, and the interest of Charles IV. as much as the pride of Louis XIV. required that he who had deceived the one and humiliated the other should be removed from the world for ever.

This was done ; and we have seen with what a mystery

---

[3] Unpublished despatch from Louis XIV. to the Abbé Morel :—Archives of the Ministry of Foreign Affairs, section Mantua, 15.

[4] Unpublished despatch from the Abbé Morel to Louis XIV. :—*Ibid.*

and with what an abundance of precautions and minute cares Villebois was charged to guard him at Pignerol, after Saint-Mars' departure for Exiles. Villebois never once left his prisoner. On March 22, 1682,[5] actuated by a scruple similar to those which had often possessed Saint-Mars, Villebois asked the Minister, to whom he was to confide the care of his prisoners if he should fall ill? Louvois replied, " To the one in whom you have most confidence." " The King approves," wrote the Minister, April 13, 1682, " of your lending the prisoners with whose care you are charged the books of devotion which they ask of you, taking all due precautions that these may not serve to give them intelligence of any kind."[6] " With reference to the priest whom the prisoners ask for," we read in a despatch of December 11, 1683, " I have to tell you that they should only be allowed to confess once a year."[7] " I have received your letter of the 14th of last month," writes Louvois, May 1, 1684, " from which I perceive the rage of the Sieur Matthioly's servant (*valet*)[8] towards you, and the manner in which you have punished him, which must certainly be approved of, and you ought always to act in the same manner on a like occasion." On November 26, 1689, Louvois learns " that some one had come by night to a door of the bastion of Pignerol, where the apartments of the prisoners are situated, with the intention of getting in," and he orders Villebois " to omit nothing to endeavour to

---

[5] Unpublished despatch from Louvois to Villebois, March 30, 1682 : —Archives of the Ministry of War.

[6] *Ibid.*, April 13, 1682.

[7] *Ibid.*, December 11, 1685.

[8] Here followed "de chambre," but these two words have been erased.

discover those who have done so." [9]   On July 28, 1692, when the Sieur de Laprade is about to assume the governorship, left vacant by Villebois' death, Barbézieux writes to him "that he cannot take too many precautions for the security of the prisoners with whose care he is charged." The same instructions are addressed to him on October 31 following. [10]   Despite these incessant precautions, and the vigilance of which he was the object, Matthioly still endeavoured to give tidings of himself, but it was only on the linings of his pockets that he managed to write a few words. He was discovered, and the Minister writes to Laprade, December 27, 1693, "You have merely to burn what remains of the little pieces of the pockets on which Matthioly and his man have written, and which you have found in the lining of their coats, where they had hidden them." [11]

This care in destroying everything that might reveal Matthioly's presence at Pignerol had at that time become especially necessary.   It was no longer, as in 1679, merely Louis XIV.'s pride which exacted that the greatest mystery should surround his victim's existence.   Since the date of the abduction, the face of things in Italy had changed. The King of France could no longer hold forth there as a master ; his armies had ceased to be constantly victorious, and he was expiating his impolitic and inopportune interference in the affairs of the peninsula.   That petty Duke

---

9 Unpublished despatches from Louvois to Villebois of May 1, 1684, and November 26, 1689.

10 Unpublished despatch from Barbézieux to Laprade, July 28 1692.

11 *Ibid.*, December 27, 1693.

of Savoy, whom we saw twelve years previously submitting himself, with imprecations, to the yoke of his imperious neighbour, had, in 1693, attained a position which enabled him to exercise over the progress of events an influence much greater than that due to the extent of his territories. This Prince had succeeded in counterbalancing the weakness of his position by his duplicity in changing his alliances, by his dissembling language, and by his happy promptitude in making use of favourable circumstances. In his policy he had always preferred sharp practices to honest acts, and he deceived in turn and with equal perfidy both Louis XIV. and the enemies of the King of France. The latter was anxious for peace, with the view of directing all his efforts and all his attention towards the question of the Spanish succession, just about to open; and peace depended almost entirely upon Victor-Amadeus, who, at first so humble, and for a long time so despised, was now taking his revenge. "We are proud, and wish to make use of the necessity in which we know very well that the King is placed, in order to make a general peace for ourselves," said the Marquis de Saint-Thomas,[12] Minister of Savoy, to Count de Tessé. So it was no longer the restitution of the conquests made in Piedmont, and the surrender of Caslae, that Victor-Amadeus demanded, but the possession of Pignerol, that valuable acquisition of Richelieu, a French town for the last sixty years, and whose surrender, which Louis XIV. finished by resigning himself, was a just expiation for his ambitious projects of aggrandisement. Possessing already one of the keys of Italy, he had wished to acquire the

---

[12] Letter from Tessé to Barbézieux, December 1693 :—Archives of the Ministry of War, 1271. Given by M. Rousset, vol. iv. p. 531.

other, so as to keep under his control the Duke of Savoy, who would thus have been enclosed between two formidable towns, and he was now compelled to cede him Pignerol, and to withdraw his troops from Casale.

Matthioly, who had played the principal part in the early negotiations relating to the latter place, suffered in the obscurity of his prison the consequence of this sudden change in Italian affairs; since he was one of the three State-prisoners whom the King of France caused to be transferred from Pignerol to the Isles Sainte-Marguerite, March 19, 1694. Not that his name was then mentioned. After the despatch of December 27, 1693, concerning what he had written on his coat-pockets, he was no longer named. Indeed, it was more than ever necessary to hide from every one this victim of an audacious and inexcusable offence against international law. The discontent of Europe against Louis XIV. being extremely strong, and the interests of his policy requiring him to calm it at any price, it was then especially essential to cover with impenetrable mystery an existence which recalled at once the menacing ambition, the audacity, and also the defeat of a great king. So there have, perhaps, never been so many minute precautions imposed for a journey of this nature. At the same time that Laprade was receiving the most circumstantial and precise instructions with reference to the transfer, the Marquis d'Herleville, Governor of Pignerol, and the Count de Tessé, commanding the French troops in that place, had orders " to furnish escorts and advance all the money required for the expenses of the journey." Tessé was instructed not to inquire the names of the prisoners, and to absolutely over-

come every temptation to a dangerous curiosity.[13]   The
following unpublished despatch is a proof of this :—

> "Turin, March 27, 1694.
>
> " I do not reply to you concerning that which you have
> done me the honour to write me *with your own hand*, with
> reference to the prisoners of the donjon, except that I shall
> conduct myself according to your orders and instructions
> with the greatest secrecy, entire circumspection, and every
> possible measure for the security of these prisoners, without
> having the slightest temptation to the least petty curiosity."[14]

But, no matter how great the precautions taken may have
been, no matter how reserved from that date Barbézieux and
Saint-Mars may have shown themselves in their despatches,
these still disclose something ; and, fine as may be the
thread which will permit us to follow Matthioly to his
death, it is nevertheless visible.

The prisoners delivered over by Laprade to Saint-Mars
were old captives, whom the latter had already had in
charge at Pignerol. This is clear : 1st, from a despatch,
dated January 11, 1694, in which the Minister asks Saint-
Mars the name of one of Laprade's prisoners who had just
died ;[15] 2nd, from the conclusion of the first despatch,

---

[13] Unpublished despatches from Barbézieux to Laprade, March 20,
1694, and from Louis XIV. to the Marquis d'Herleville, March 19,
1694.

[14] Unpublished despatch from Marshal de Tessé to Barbézieux,
March 27, 1694 :—Archives of the Ministry of War.

[15] January 11, 1694, Barbézieux writes to Saint-Mars : " The Sieur
de Laprade, to whom the King has confided the care of the prisoners
who are confined by his Majesty's orders in the donjon of Pignerol,
writes me word that the one who has been imprisoned longest is dead,
and that he does not know his name. As I have no doubt but that

announcing to Saint-Mars the approaching arrival of the prisoners at Pignerol : " I do not inform you of the number, persuaded that you know it;" [16] 3rd, from that significant phrase which we have already quoted from the second despatch relating to the transfer of these prisoners : "You know that they are of more consequence, or at least one of them, than those who are now at the Islands, and you ought to place them by preference in the surest prisons." [17]   Now it is quite certain, that at the time of his departure from Pignerol to Exiles, Saint-Mars had no other considerable prisoner except Matthioly, Fouquet being dead and Lauzun set at liberty. We may remark, too, that it is in Villebois' care that he leaves him, Villebois who, with Catinat, had been charged with the mission of arresting Matthioly on the road to Turin.[18]   When Villebois dies, it is another of Saint-Mars' confidential lieutenants—the Sieur de Laprade, who is sent from the Islands to command in the donjon of Pignerol.[19]   Consequently Saint-Mars—and this is an essential point to establish,—did not cease to be acquainted with Matthioly's fate,

---

you remember it, I beg you to inform me of it in cipher." The oldest prisoner was Eustache d'Auger, who was confined, as we have seen, in 1669. Anyhow it could not be Matthioly, since we have given a few pages back a despatch from Laprade, December 27, 1693, in which he mentions his name in reference to what he had written on the lining of his coat. Now Laprade would never have asked in January, 1694, the name of a prisoner whom he knew in December, 1693.

[16] Unpublished despatch from Barbézieux to Saint-Mars, February 20, 1694.

[17] *Ibid.*, March 20, 1694.

[18] Despatch from Catinat to Louvois, May 3, 1679 :—Given by Delort, p. 212.

[19] Unpublished despatch from Barbézieux to Saint-Mars, May 5, 1692 :—Archives of the Ministry of War.

and it is his own lieutenants who have replaced him for a time in guarding this prisoner.

We have shown, in the preceding chapter,[20] the evident obscurity of the insignificant prisoner brought by Saint-Mars from Exiles to the Isles Sainte-Marguerite. His furniture and effects are only worth thirteen crowns; his gaoler leaves him without scruple; he is designated as "a crow." A new prisoner, "of more consequence than the others," arrives at the Islands. From that moment Saint-Mars does not quit them; but immediately imagines fresh measures for the safety of his prisoners, which the Minister approves, July 20, 1694.[21]

It is about this period that we find, in the official despatches, the name of the Sieur Favre, whom the most unquestionable tradition represents as having been chaplain of the prison at the time that the Man with the Iron Mask was confined there.[22] Barbézieux, who previously had not been troubled with this anxiety, all at once thinks of what would happen if Saint-Mars should fall ill, and, with anxious solicitude, inquires[23] immediately what would be done if this should occur.[24] On January 15, 1696, we find

---

[20] Pp. 322–331, *ante.*

[21] Unpublished despatch from Barbézieux to Saint-Mars, July 20, 1694.

[22] *Ibid.*, December 5, 1694.

[23] *Ibid.*, December 20, 1694.

[24] A despatch overlooked by M. Topin when writing this work, but subsequently published by him, and in which Saint-Mars describes the minute precautions he adopts in order to ensure the safe custody of his prisoners and prevent them from communicating with any one, is sufficiently curious to be given at full length :—

" Monseigneur,—

"You command me to inform you how people would act when I am absent or ill, with reference to the precautions which are taken and

a new despatch from Barbézieux, expressing, in the King's name and his own, the satisfaction experienced on learning

the visits which are paid every day to the prisoners who are committed to my care.

"My two lieutenants give them to eat at fixed hours, as they have seen me do, and as I still do very often when I am well; and this is how, Monseigneur. The senior of my lieutenants takes the keys of the prison of my *old prisoner*, with whom they commence, opens the three doors and enters the chamber of the prisoner, who politely hands him the dishes and plates which he has placed on the top of one another in order to give them to the lieutenant, who only goes out through two of the doors to hand them to one of my sergeants, who receives them and carries them to a table two paces off, where is my second lieutenant, who examines everything that enters or leaves the prison, so that he may see that there is nothing written on the plate; and after everything necessary has been given him [the prisoner], a search is made in and under his bed and among the window-bars of his chamber, as well as in the whole of the chamber, and very often on himself; after having very civilly asked him if he has need of anything, they shut the doors and go to do the same for the other prisoners.

"Twice a week their table-linen is changed, as well as their shirts and the linen of which they make use, which is given to them and taken away again after having been counted and after everything has been well searched.

"One can be very much cheated about the linen when it leaves and enters for the service of prisoners who are people of consideration, as I have had some who have wished to bribe the laundresses, who have acknowledged to me, which they had little difficulty in doing, what had been said to them, on account of which I used to have all their linen steeped in water on leaving their chambers, and when it was clean and half dry, the laundresses came to iron and smooth it in my apartments in the presence of one of my lieutenants, who locked up the baskets in a chest until they were handed over to the servants of messieurs the prisoners. There is much to be distrusted in candles; I have found some which on being broken or used contained paper instead of wicks. I used to send to buy some at Turin at shops not tampered with. It is also very dangerous for ribbon to leave a prisoner's apartment, as he writes on it as on linen without any one being aware of it.

"The late Monsieur Fouquet made fine and good paper on which I allowed him to write, and afterwards I went and took it from a little

the precautions adopted.[25]   On October 29, 1696, the Minister causes the locks of the donjon of Pignerol to be sent to the Isles Sainte-Marguerite, in order to render the confinement of the prisoners more secure.[26]

But there follows a despatch more significant still.   Its existence was first revealed, then contested, and historical criticism finished by no longer believing in it, and by rejecting it altogether.   Nevertheless it exists, and I have reproduced it in Chapter V.[27]   It concludes thus : " Without explaining yourself to any one whatever about what your old prisoner has done."

These words : " Your old prisoner, " have grammatically but one meaning—that is to say, the prisoner whom you

---

pocket which he had made in the seat of his breeches, which I sent to Monseigneur your late father."

[The commencement of the second leaf has been torn ; the following only remains :—]

" As a last precaution, the prisoners are searched from time to time, both day and night, at hours which are not fixed, when it is often found that they have written on dirty linen that which they alone are able to read, as you will have seen from that which I have had the honour to forward you.   If it is necessary, Monseigneur, that I should do anything else in order to more completely fulfil my duty, I shall glory all my life in obeying you with the same respect and submission as I am,

" Monseigneur,

" Your very humble, very obedient, and very obliged servant,

" DE SAINT-MARS.

" At the Islands, this January 6, 1696."

"The above despatch, as well as the one given on p. 324, note 17, *ante*, is to be found in draft in the collection of M. Mauge-du-Bois-des-Entes.   They have both been given by Monmerqué and Champollion-Figeac.—*Trans.*

[25] Unpublished despatch from Barbézieux to Saint-Mars.

[26] *Ibid.*, October 29, 1696.

[27] See p. 61, *ante.*

formerly had in your care, and who has been again confided to you. Besides, I may remark, that if there should
be any doubt about the meaning, this phrase cannot
possibly apply to the prisoner brought by Saint-Mars from
Exiles, since he arrived at the island in April, 1687. For,
how can we imagine that the inhabitants of Sainte-Marguerite would have waited ten years, before concerning
themselves with the causes of his confinement? This
curiosity of the inhabitants of the island, this astonishment,
the prime origin of the legend which became current in the
district, is very naturally explained by the arrival of the
prisoners from Pignerol, surrounded by a strong escort,
guarded by Saint Mars' confidential men, placed, one at
least, in the most secure prison, and the importance of
whom was attested by the preparations, repairs, and pur-
chases executed at the time by Saint-Mars. There is
nothing striking in the treatment of the prisoner brought
from Exiles, nothing which could excite surprise, and, anyhow, there is the positive certainty that this surprise
would have been produced in any case during the early
years of his residence at the Isles Sainte-Marguerite.

Pignerol was restored to the Duke of Savoy a short
time after the arrival of the new prisoners at the islands.
I have carefully looked through all the despatches exchanged
between Lamothe-Guérin, Saint-Mars' successor at the
Islands, and the Court of Versailles, during the ten years
(1698 to 1708) which followed the latter's departure for
the Bastille.[28] Not one of them contains the name of

---

[28] I have read one by one all the despatches addressed during the
years 1698–1708 by the Ministers Chamillart and Voysin (successors of
Barbézieux at the Ministry of War) to Lamothe-Guérin, and nothing in
them applies to Matthioly.   [Barbézieux

Matthioly, or makes mention of an important prisoner, left behind by Saint-Mars.   Matthioly was still at Pignerol on December 27, 1693, a few months previous to the transfer of the three prisoners to the Isles Sainte-Marguerite.   They were all old captives formerly in the care of Saint-Mars. The latter, we have seen, was ignorant of the causes of their detention, *save of Matthioly's alone.*   The logical conclusion of our preceding remarks is, therefore, that these words : " Without explaining yourself to any one whatever about *what your old prisoner has done,*" are applicable to what the Government of Versailles termed the treason of Matthioly.

If this be admitted—and we trust that our readers will have no doubt with reference to it—if it be admitted that the] despatch of November 17, 1697, is applicable to Matthioly, the only prisoner, we must again repeat, whose crime Saint-Mars was acquainted with, the identity of the Man with the Iron Mask is established.

On March 1, 1698, Barbézieux offers Saint-Mars the nomination to the Governorship of the Bastille.[29] He accepts this offer, and, on June 17, 1698, the Minister replies :—

[Barbézieux, incensed at the elevation of his rival Chamillart, gave himself up to dissipation in order to drown his annoyance.   He retired to his château of L'Etang at the boundary of the park of Saint-Cloud, where he feasted and rioted with his friends, and was seized with a fever consequent upon his excesses, of which he died a few days afterwards at the age of thirty-three.   See *Mémoires de Saint-Simon.—Trans.*]

[29] Unpublished despatch from Barbézieux to Saint-Mars.   I reproduce it word for word :—

" At Versailles, the first of March, 1698.

" I commence by offering you my condolence on the death of your brother-in-law, for which you will not doubt I am very sorry, both on account of his services and of my friendship for him.   [" I

"Versailles, June 17, 1698.

"I have remained a long time without answering the letter which you have taken the trouble to write me the 8th of last month, because the King has not explained his intentions to me earlier. I shall now tell you that his Majesty has seen with pleasure that you are determined to come to the Bastille in order to be its governor. You can arrange everything so as to be ready to leave when I shall write to you, and bring your old prisoner with you in all safety.

"I have agreed with Mons. Saumery that he shall give you two thousand crowns for your expenses in moving your furniture."

"I also write to you concerning the proposal to exchange your governorship of the Isles Sainte-Marguerite against that of the Bastille. The reply which you have made to him has been handed to me since his death. The revenue of this governorship consists of 15,168 livres on the estates of the King, besides two thousand additional which M. Bezemaux derived from the shops around the Bastille and the ferry-boats depending on the governor.

"It is true that out of this M. Bezemaux was obliged to pay a number of sergeants and soldiers for the guard of the prisoners in his care, but you know, from what you derive from your company, to what these expenses amount. Having enumerated the value of this governorship, I shall now say to you that it is for you to know your own interests, that the King does not force you to accept it, if it is not agreeable to you, and at the same time I do not doubt that you will take account of the profit that is generally made upon what the King gives for the keep of the prisoners, which profit may become considerable. There is also the pleasure of being in Paris with one's family and friends, instead of being confined to an extremity of the kingdom. If I may give my opinion, it seems to me very advantageous, and I believe, for the reasons given above, that you would not lose by the exchange. I beg you nevertheless to write me your opinion frankly concerning that : "—Archives of the Ministry of War.

The 19th July following, Barbézieux wrote again :—

"Marly, July 19, 1698.

"I have received the letter that you have taken the trouble to write me the 9th of this month. The King approves of your leaving the Isles Sainte-Marguerite to come to the Bastille with your old prisoner, taking your precautions to prevent his being seen or known by any one. You can write in advance to his Majesty's Lieutenant of this château to have a chamber ready to place this prisoner in on your arrival."

We thus find, in the two despatches sent to Saint-Mars on the eve of his departure for the Bastille, at that very important moment when he is about to commence his journey across France, these same characteristic words :— " Your old prisoner." This is not all. What I have termed the perfect agreement, the exact correspondence between the prisoner who entered the Bastille, September 18, 1698, and Matthioly, is rendered more complete and more exact still by the only document concerning the Man with the Iron Mask, besides despatches, which has as yet been admitted without controversy—viz., Dujonca's Journal. If we refer to Chapter XIII.[30] of the present work we shall perceive that he too terms the prisoner who accompanied Saint-Mars "*his old prisoner* whom he had at Pignerol." At the Bastille he was called merely the " prisoner from Provence,"[31] because it was in Provence that he was confided to Saint-Mars, and Dujonca is none the less exact in terming him the old

---

[30] P. 164, *ante.*

[31] The Count de Pontchartrain to Saint-Mars, November 3, 1698 : "The King approves of your prisoner from Provence confessing and communicating whenever you think proper."

prisoner from Pignerol, since Matthioly had been two years at Pignerol under the care of Saint-Mars. Of all the captives of whom Saint-Mars was the gaoler, Matthioly is thus the only one who reconciles the two apparently contradictory features of the Man with the Iron Mask, whom an undoubted tradition represents as having been brought to Saint-Mars at the Islands, and whom indisputable documents show to have also been imprisoned at Pignerol. The general error has been to represent the Iron Mask as going from Pignerol to Exiles, the name of which was never mentioned by Dujonca, and not to pay sufficient attention to this fact, viz., that tradition as well as rare contemporary documents assign only three prisons, and not four, to the mysterious captive : Pignerol, the Isles Sainte-Marguerite, and the Bastille.

CHAPTER XXIV.

The Use of a Mask formerly very general—Frequently adopted for
Prisoners in Italy—Its Employment not difficult in the Case of
Matthioly — Origin of the Legend of the Man with the Iron
Mask—As to the Transmission of the Secret from King to King
— Louis XV. and Louis XVIII.—How it is that the Des-
patches which we have quoted have remained unpublished—
Concerning the Silence of Saint-Simon—Dujonca—Taulès' Objec-
tion—Louvois' harsh Language—Matthioly's Age—Concerning the
Name of Marchialy—Order for Matthioly's Arrest—Arrival of the
Duke of Mantua in Paris—Conclusion.

BUT what about the mask? some one will say,—the mask,
which is the characteristic feature of the mysterious prisoner,
a feature more striking than all the others, because that
whilst the latter are only known to those people who read,
the former is recalled by the very name of the famous
captive, which one cannot pronounce without picturing him
to oneself with a mask covering his face?　Need we say
that the custom of wearing a mask was formerly very general
among the great?　Need we quote the example of Marie de
Medicis, whom the exact Héroard [1] represents as going to
see the young Louis XIII., "who kisses her beneath her
mask?"　Or the Duchess de Montpensier's ladies of honour
whom she authorised to cover their faces with masks of

---

[1] *Journal*, vol. i. p. 133.

black velvet? [2]   Or, again, the Maréchale de Clérambault, whom Saint-Simon [3] describes "as always wearing a mask of black velvet on the high road or in the galleries?"   Need we recall Madame de Maintenon concealing her face under a mask,[4] when she comes seven different times to Versailles to seek the children just born of Madame de Montespan and Louis XIV., and to take them mysteriously to Paris in a *fiacre*.   Or the wives of certain rich financiers who, in 1683, dared to wear a mask even in the churches,[5] and thus provoked a severe *ordonnance* from La Reynie, the Lieutenant of Police?

But if at this period we find very frequent examples of the use of a mask in the ordinary course of life, there is absolutely no authentic example of the wearing of a mask being enforced upon a prisoner, and such a measure is altogether peculiar to the famous captive.   It has been concluded from this that the prisoner so exceptionally treated must have been of exceptional importance, and that there was some especial interest in concealing his countenance.   But, if this were the case, why was he conducted to the Bastille, where a moment of forgetfulness might cause him to be recognized by one of his fellow-captives, and almost infallibly by one of the numerous officers of the fortress?   Would it not have been as prudent as it was easy to have avoided this danger by leaving him at the Isles Sainte Marguerite?   In order to explain the removal, it has been said that Louis XIV. desired to have the prisoner nearer himself.   This is

---

[2] *Mémoires de Mademoiselle de Montpensier*, vol. iii. p. 225.
[3] *Mémoires de Saint-Simon*, vol. xiii. p. 16.
[4] *Souvenirs de Madame de Caylus.*
[5] *Correspondance Administrative sous Louis XIV.*, vol. ii. p. 571.
See also M. P. Clément, *La Police sous Louis XIV.*, p. 89.

altogether wrong.   We have just given [6] the despatches
which preceded Saint-Mars' departure for the Bastille.   Do
they contain an imperious order, unanswerable, and founded
on reasons of State?   Far from it.   The Minister informs
Saint-Mars that the governorship of the Bastille has just
become vacant, and inquires if he is willing to accept it.
Far from speaking to him of "his old prisoner" in this first
despatch,[7] he touches only upon his private affairs, and the
evident gain he would experience by accepting this very
advantageous proposition ; and it is only when Saint-Mars
decides upon doing so that the Minister charges him to
bring "his old prisoner" with him.   If this "old prisoner"
had possessed in his features any resemblance "revealing
his origin," he would not have been taken to Paris, or anyhow some mention would have been made of him in the
first despatch in which the new duties are proposed to Saint-
Mars.

In the case of an Italian like Matthioly, the use of the
mask has a very natural explanation.   Indeed, it is only in
Italy that we meet with the custom of covering the face of a
prisoner with a mask.   Individuals arrested in Venice by
order of the State inquisitors were taken masked to their
dungeons.   Moreover, we have seen Matthioly concealing
himself with a mask in his secret interviews with the Abbé
d'Estrades, Louis XIV.'s ambassador.   This mask [8] the

---

[6] Chapter XXIII., pp. 347, 348, *ante.*
[7] See Chap. XXIII., note 29, pp. 346, 347, *ante.*
[8] This mask would, however, have been of a different kind to that
which Matthioly was afterwards compelled to wear.   The latter was
no doubt secured in such a way that it could not be removed by the
wearer.—*Trans.*

Minister of the Duke of Mantua and the companion of his pleasures used always to carry about with him. It would certainly have formed part of the clothes and effects seized near Turin in 1678, and which were sufficiently valuable for Louvois to authorise Saint-Mars to take them with him.[10] In 1698, as at the time of his arrest, Matthioly was always under the ban of that order of absolute secrecy contained in a despatch which we shall shortly give; and Saint-Mars, as we know, was as exact and as scrupulous in carrying out his instructions, whether they were twenty years old or quite recent. Moreover, in 1678 Matthioly had come to Paris, charged with an official mission. He remained there a month. Supposing, as is probable, that he ran no risk, after so long an absence, of being recognized by the French whom he had visited, there was no reason why the Residents of the Duke of Mantua and the other Italian Princes should not do so. Lastly, an unpublished letter of Saint-Mars[11] and several despatches of the Minister of Exterior Relations prove that there was then in the Bastille a Count Boselli, an Italian, in whose detention the Marshal de Tallard appears to have been interested, and who, on account of his different missions, had travelled throughout the whole of Italy, and had been brought into connection with many of the illustrious families of Mantua and Bologna. He had doubtless known Matthioly's, and perhaps Matthioly himself. For all these reasons, therefore, it was necessary to preserve the absolute secrecy to which the latter had been condemned. Saint-Mars had the means

---

[10] Despatch from Louvois to Saint-Mars, June 9, 1681.

[11] Archives of the Ministry of Foreign Affairs, section Mantua, 27–29.

at his disposal—a means exceptional and extraordinary, but still very familiar to Matthioly. His face was therefore covered with a mask, and if this peculiarity was so striking to the people at the Bastille, it was principally on account of the prisoner's arriving there with the new governor, and because their attention was already excited by the expected arrival of Saint-Mars, preceded probably by a reputation for rigorous severity, and awaited, anyhow, with that impatience to meet a new chief which all subordinates display. It is this which has contributed to render so strong in Dujonca the impression of surprise which we meet with in his ingenuous journal. He has communicated this impression, thus received, to other officers of the Bastille. The mysterious memory of it is at first perpetuated within the walls of this formidable fortress. It would still have been talked about during the first half of the eighteenth century, when many men of letters were imprisoned there. These last have certainly heard the tale which, after its passage from one mouth to another, still contained a little of history and already much of legend. They have preserved profoundly engraven on their minds this story, so much more striking because it was told them on the very scene of the events, and, once liberated, they have spread it abroad amongst the public, and soon throughout the whole world. Imagination, vividly excited, has had free play. Various explanations have been proposed, supported, and contested. Great writers have taken part in this controversy, and have lent it the lustre of their talents. With the view of stimulating public curiosity, people have amused themselves with adding to it much that was extraordinary and marvellous, and thus the story of the Man with the Iron Mask has

by degrees left the grave domain of history to enter altogether into the seductive regions of fiction.

Next, various episodes have been successively imagined
and added as so many embellishments to the life of the
romantic prisoner: such as—Louvois' visit to the Isles
Sainte-Marguerite; the silver dish thrown out of the
window and recovered by a fisherman, luckily for himself, uneducated; and especially the transmission of the
gloomy secret "from King to King, and to no other."[12]
Louvois, as we have already said,[13] never went to the Isles
Sainte-Marguerite, and it was a Protestant clergyman who
threw out of the window a tin dish, covered with a few lines
of writing. As to the transmission of the secret, which thus
became, to a certain extent, an attribute of royalty, nothing
proves that this ever took place when it was possible, and it
is indisputable that it has not always been so. No doubt
Louis XIV., on his death-bed, had a private conversation
with the Duke d'Orléans.[14] That after having conversed
with him concerning grave affairs of State, he should have
spoken to him of the only two abductions of foreigners committed during his reign—those of Avedick and Matthioly;
that at this supreme hour this King, who did not at all
regret the persecutions inflicted upon his own subjects,
because, even at his last moment, he was artfully made
to consider them necessary for religion; that this King,
I say, should have understood, at such a time, that to
carry off an Armenian Patriarch, and to cause a foreign
Minister to disappear, were two extreme acts, and manifest
violations of international law; and that, acting under this

---

[12] Michelet.   [13] Chapter V., p. 62, *ante.*
[14] *Mémoires de Saint-Simon,* vol. viii. p. 66.

impression, he should have recounted them to his nephew, may be admitted. Afterwards, the question of the Man with the Iron Mask having been suddenly mooted, it is probable the Duke d'Orléans or Cardinal Fleury may have informed Louis XV. about it. All the replies of the latter, when questioned, tend to confirm the opinion we have just established, by the examination of the despatches and are perfectly applicable to Matthioly.[15] That Louis XV.

[15] Dutens, in his *Correspondance Interceptée*, relates that "Louis XV. said one day to the Duke de Choiseul, that he was acquainted with the story of the masked prisoner. The Duke begged the King to tell him what it was. But he could obtain no other reply save *that all the conjectures as yet formed concerning this prisoner were mistaken ones.*" As Madame Dubarry caused the Duke de Choiseul to be disgraced in 1770, the conversation narrated must have taken place previous to this date. Now it was only on June 28, 1770, that Baron d'Heiss was the first person in France to advance, in a letter addressed to the authors of the *Journal Encyclopédique*, as we have stated in Chapter XXI., p. 295, *ante*, the theory which makes Matthioly the Man with the Iron Mask, and this letter was inserted in the part for August 15, 1770. The abduction of Matthioly had been narrated at Leyden in 1687,* but it was only in August, 1770, that the theory began to be known and debated. Louis XV.'s reply to the Duke de Choiseul can therefore be very well reconciled with the theory.

Dutens adds that some time afterwards Madame de Pompadour pressed the King to give an explanation with reference to this subject, and that Louis XV. told her that he believed *it was a minister of an Italian prince.*

M. Giraud (of the Institute) has often heard Madame de Boigne

* In a work entitled *Histoire abrégée de l'Europe*, which, after speaking of Matthioly's proceedings with reference to the treaty for the surrender of Casale and describing his capture and imprisonment, goes on to say: "At Pignerol he was thought to be too near Italy, and, though he was guarded very carefully, it was feared that the walls might tell tales ; he was therefore removed thence to the Isles Sainte-Marguerite, where he is at present, under the care of M. de Saint-Mars, the governor."—*Trans.*

may have transmitted the secret to his grandson is also possible, although there is nothing to establish the fact of his having done so. But how was Louis XVIII. in a position to have been acquainted with it, as he is said to

---

relate the following anecdote which he has given me authority to publish. Madame de Boigne was the daughter of the Marquis d'Osmond, who held a high position at the court of Louis XVI. In one of her conversations with the Marquis, Madame Adelaide related the check which her curiosity had received with reference to the Iron Mask. She had persuaded her brother the Dauphin to question the King concerning this famous prisoner, so that he might tell her the secret afterwards. The Dauphin was then very young, and at the first word that he uttered, Louis XV. inquired, smiling: "Who has charged you to ask me this question?" The Dauphin acknowledged that it was his sister. The King refused to give a complete answer, but observed that the secret had never been of great importance, and at that time no longer possessed any interest.

The same anecdote has been related to us in almost identical words by M. Guillaume Guizot, who also had it from Madame de Boigne.

In page 47 of the *Souvenirs du Baron de Gleichen* recently published by M. Grimblot, we read that the Duke de Choiseul had vainly made researches among the Archives of the Ministry of Foreign Affairs, in order to discover the secret of the Iron Mask. There is nothing very surprising in this. These Archives contain all the documents that we have reproduced or quoted, treating of Matthioly's abduction. They also contain, spread among a number of series and volumes, the despatches which prove the evident interest that the Duke of Mantua had in the definitive disappearance of his ex-confidant. But if these documents, of which the greater portion were unpublished, have furnished me with arguments for the support of the Matthioly theory, it is not in these Archives but in those of the Ministry of War that I have discovered the despatches which have enabled me to establish the complete agreement between the individual carried off May 2, 1679, and the prisoner who arrived at the Bastille with Saint-Mars, September 18, 1698, and died there November 19, 1703. Researches made solely in the Archives of the Ministry of Foreign Affairs, would have led to nothing. It was necessary to make them in all the collections, and afterwards to compare the various results, the combination of which alone enables us to obtain a solution of the problem.

have been ? When, as Count de Provence, he quitted Paris, Louis XVI. did not foresee the catastrophe which was so near. Will it be said that in the depths of his prison, the unhappy King may have remembered the necessary transmission, and have therefore occupied himself with informing his brother ? But then, also, Louis XVII. was still living. If, therefore, Louis XVIII. has, by means of skilfully obscured answers, given out that he, too, was in the secret, it was only that he might not seem to be deprived of a privilege which some persons still regarded as a prerogative of the Crown.

Such are the embellishments with which time has adorned the story of the masked prisoner, and which, by transfiguring him, have rendered him unrecognizable. But, as has often been said to us, how is it that, reduced to his proper proportions, he has not been previously recognized in a definitive manner? How is it, too, since he has been the object of such long researches, that people have passed over so many despatches concerning him, without even reading them ? To this we shall content ourselves with replying, that these despatches are in existence, that their authenticity cannot be contested, and that any one may take cognizance of them in the Archives of the Ministry of War or of Foreign Affairs. If they have remained unpublished to the present time, it is doubtless because they have escaped notice, containing, as they do, mere indications, and no proof revealing in a direct manner the identity of the Man with the Iron Mask. It is by bringing them together, and comparing them, that light is thrown upon them. Isolated they remain obscure ; having no clearness of their own, they have not attracted attention, and have remained buried in the heaps of documents among which they are still to be found.

What objection yet remains to combat the result of this minute inquiry carefully conducted among innumerable materials ? Is it the silence of Saint-Simon [16] in reference to this affair ? But this very silence tends to prove that the masked prisoner was the victim of an intrigue concocted abroad. This immortal writer has, indeed, thrown light into the most secret and obscure recesses of Louis XIV.'s Court. None of its hidden wretchedness, none of its most secret intrigues, nothing concerning the interior of the Kingdom, has escaped this self-constituted observer. But, on the other hand, he was only acquainted with the foreign affairs of the end of the reign, when his friend, the Marquis de Torcy, had assumed the direction of them. He was as completely ignorant about all the others as he was well-informed concerning what passed within the Kingdom. His silence, therefore, which would be very strange, if the Man with the Iron Mask had belonged to a French family, is easily explained by the fact that this prisoner was arrested outside France, and in 1678.

Will it still be maintained that the slight importance of a minister of the Duke of Mantua is incompatible with the care that Dujonca [17] took to prepare the chamber in the Bastille for the Man with the Iron Mask, when in the curious manuscript notes [18] which we have found in the

---

[16] This objection has often been made.

[17] This is one of the points on which Father Griffet relies most of all in order to prove the excessive importance of this prisoner. The quotation which we have given from Dujonca's notes, establishes the fact that he was obliged to act thus for all the prisoners. But besides these notes, as yet unpublished, the *Journal de Dujonca* furnishes several proofs of what we advance.

[18] We have given these notes in Chapter XIII. pp. 167–169, *ante.*

Archives of the Arsenal, Dujonca himself states, " That on the arrival of a prisoner, it is necessary to take care to have given and brought to him all that is essential for the furnishing of his chamber, paying very dearly for it to the Governor's upholsterer, or else to the *maîtresse d'autel?* "

Is it still possible to draw an objection from the silence concerning Matthioly preserved in the despatches addressed by the Minister to Saint-Mars during the years 1680 to 1698,[19] now that we know that Matthioly, contrary to the opinion admitted up to the present time, had remained at Pignerol, and was only restored to Saint-Mars a few years before the latter's departure for the Bastille ?

People have often spoken of the severe treatment of which Matthioly was the object, and the harsh expressions used with reference to him by the Minister. But if there was indeed, for a long time, a certain harshness in Louvois' language, the despatches of the Abbé d'Estrades explain it. This harshness was caused by the cruel disappointment experienced by the Minister, when, notwithstanding Matthioly's promises, the original of the ratification of the treaty of Casale could not be found among his papers. Previously to this, Catinat had written to Louvois: " Monsieur de Saint-Mars treats the S. de Lestang [20] very kindly so far as regards cleanliness and food, but very strictly in preventing him holding intercourse with any one." [21]

Later, especially after the execution of the treaty, the old grievances disappeared, and if an incessant sur-

---

[19] Taulès was the first to put forward this objection.

[20] The reader will remember that this was Matthioly's supposititious name.

[21] Despatch from Catinat to Louvois, May 6, 1679. Given by Delort, p. 214.

veillance was maintained, useless severity was dispensed with. Moreover, these harsh, coarse, and painful expressions were only too familiar to Louvois, and in some of his despatches he has scarcely shown himself milder with reference to Fouquet and De Lauzun.

Lastly, Voltaire declares that he had heard "from the Sieur Marsolan, the son-in-law of the apothecary of the Bastille, that the latter, a short time previous to the death of the masked prisoner, learnt from him that *he believed himself to be about sixty years old.*" Now Matthioly, born in 1640, was, in reality, sixty-three years of age when he died.

He died, and the registers of the Church of Saint-Paul [22]

---

[22] The following is a literal translation of the entry in the Register in question, a facsimile of which forms the frontispiece to the present volume :—

"The 19th Marchialy aged forty-five years or about has died in the bastile, whose body has been buried in the cemetery of st. Paul his parish the 20th of the present [month] in the presence of Monsieur Rosage major of the bastile and Mr. Reglhe surgeon-major of the bastile who have signed.

"Rosarges." - "Reilhe."

In *La Bastille Dévoilée*, a work of doubtful authenticity, as also in the *Mélanges d'Histoire et de Littérature* of Mr. Quintin Craufurd, who professes to make the statement on the authority of M. Delaunay, the unfortunate governor of the Bastille in the reign of Louis XVI., it is asserted that the prisoner "was buried in a winding-sheet of new linen ; and for the most part everything that was found in his chamber was burnt, such as every part of his bed, including the mattresses, his tables, chairs, and other utensils, which were all reduced to powder and to cinders, and thrown into the drains. The rest of the things, such as the silver, copper, and pewter, were melted. This prisoner was lodged in the third chamber of the tower Bertaudière, which room was scraped and filed quite to the stone, and fresh whitewashed from the top to the bottom. The doors and windows were burnt like the rest."
—*Trans.*

bear the name of *Marchialy*.   The dissertations on this
name have been as numerous as ingenious.   Some persons
—Father Griffet,[23] for instance—have discovered in it the
letters forming the words *hic amiral* (Vermandois and
Beaufort were Admirals of France), as if the employment
of an anagram was probable under such circumstances!
Others [24] have beheld in it the word *mar*, which in the
Armenian tongue signifies *Saint*, and in the East would be
applied to the patriarchs, and the word *Kialy*, the Armenian
diminutive of *Michael*, which was Avedick's Christian name.
Is it not more simple and natural to regard this word as
standing for Matthioly's name itself, which in several
despatches Louvois writes Marthioly?[25]   No one can be
ignorant of the negligence with which proper names were
then spelt?[26]   Here there is only one letter changed;
how many examples do we not come across of much more
important modifications? No one could have any suspicion
of the date of Count Matthioly's death.   People were
ignorant that Dujonca kept a journal, and it was only afterwards, that guided by its statements they thought of searching among the registers of the Church of Saint-Paul for the

---

[23] Dissertation on the Man with the Iron Mask, in his *Traité des
Différentes Sortes de Preuves.*

[24] *Mémoires de Mallet du Pan.*

[25] The name is written in several ways.   I have chosen the orthography most generally adopted in the despatches.   We find Matioli,
Matheoli, and Marthioly.   [Also Mattioli, Matioly, and Matthioli.
Louis XIV. writes it indiscriminately Mathioly, Matthioli, and Matthioly—in different ways even in the same despatch.—*Trans.*]

[26] M. P. Clément quotes a curious example of this negligence in his
Police sous Louis XIV., p. 102, note 1.   The correct name of the
Italian, accomplice of Sainte-Croix in the] *Affaire des Poisons*, was
Egidio, but in the documents he is called Exili.

date of November 20, 1703, which he had assigned for the burial of the masked prisoner. But it must at least be admitted that at the time of this burial there was nothing which could serve to attract attention towards the registration of November 20. Moreover, all danger of his imparting any confidence, all fear of a revelation of an odious violation of international law, had disappeared with the possessor of Louis XIV.'s secret, with the victim of this violation. To inscribe his name upon the register of an obscure church, where no one had the means of seeking for it, was therefore natural, and presented no danger. Everything that was essential or indispensable had been done. The abduction was accomplished with the greatest mystery; Matthioly's presence at Pignerol, and afterwards at the Islands, was known only to his gaoler; his name merely mentioned in despatches which might be presumed to be placed for ever beyond investigations, then this name disappearing in its turn, and every trace of the prisoner, as was believed, effaced by these means; his changes of prison taking place with extraordinary precautions; all this would have sufficed to have rendered any researches useless, and to have prevented the complete identification of Matthioly, if the archives at Versailles had remained impenetrable. Louis XIV.'s order was scrupulously executed, as will be seen from the despatch,[27] which it is now time to give, and in which the King of France caused to be accorded to the Abbé d'Estrades, the authorisation which he had solicited.

---

[27] Unpublished despatch :—Archives of the Ministry of Foreign Affairs, section Savoy, 68. It is from this despatch that the motto of the present work has been taken.

"Versailles, April 28, 1679.

"The King has seen in your letter the confidence that Madame la Duchesse de Savoye had imparted to you concerning Count Matthioly's perfidy. It is rather strange that, feeling himself guilty to such a degree towards his Majesty. he dares to trust himself in your hands. So the King thinks that it is good that he should not do so with impunity. *Since you believe you can get him carried off without the thing causing any scandal,* his Majesty desires that you should execute the idea that you have, and that you should have him taken secretly to Pignerol. An order is sent there to receive him, *and to have him kept there without any person knowing about it.* It will depend upon your skill to arrange a meeting, in order to speak with him in an unfrequented spot, and if possible, in the country. But in any case, if it is true that he has had the ratification of the Duke of Mantua, and should have it in his possession, it would be good to take him and make sure of him. It is not necessary that you should inform Madame la Duchesse de Savoye of this order which his Majesty gives you, and NO ONE MUST KNOW WHAT HAS BECOME OF THIS MAN."

Our task is ended. Can it be a matter for regret that the chief and necessary consequence of our researches has been to annihilate a creature of fantasy with a particularly handsome countenance, of lofty birth, and with an affecting destiny? Is not the charm of truth superior to all others, and if it has been vouchsafed to us to introduce it into these pages, if, into a question where, as we have seen, everything was uncertainty, we have succeeded in throwing a little fresh light, why should we fear to have finished by dissipating that creation of popular imagination, that dubious and fanciful being, who, it seems to us, ought not to excite so much interest as he who has really lived, and whose existence we can follow step by step? Whilst, in fact, an inevitable uncertainty must always be mingled with the attraction exercised by the former, whilst the pity and emotion experienced must ever be restrained by the impossibility of proving even his birth; in the second case we are concerned with a misfortune quite as great, and this time real, with an individual much less eminent, but who has indeed existed, and who, condemned like the former to an unjust punishment, has really lived, suffered, and been persecuted. Wherefore, too, should one measure one's pity by the importance of those who deserve it? Are not all the victims of arbitrary power equally worthy of interest, and does not the persistence of misfortune raise the persecuted to the level of those who are great by birth and by splendour of position? Fouquet in the depths of his prison, separated from every one that he loves, but finding in his Christian sentiments sufficient strength to overcome his sorrow, seems to us a great deal more touching in his resignation than interesting from the recollection of the splendid part he had played in the court of Louis XIV. Matthioly also was torn from his family and held a high position, but in a much less important court; he too suffered the loneliness of captivity, and for him this loneliness was lasting. His wife took refuge in a convent, and thus withdrew from a world from which Louis XIV. had violently carried off her husband. His family was dispersed, powerless, and silent, feeling itself threatened as it were by the blow which had struck its chief. He dragged out his

existence in various prisons, proceeding from Pignerol to
the Isles Sainte-Marguerite, from these islands to the Bastille,
sometimes resigned, at others disordered by grief, and in his
fits of madness calling himself a near relation of Louis XIV.,
and for this reason demanding his liberty.   On November
19, 1703, his misfortunes terminated with his life.

By a strange coincidence, at the very moment of
Matthioly's death, his master, Charles IV., Duke of Mantua,
arrived in Paris.   But he—who had abandoned himself
more and more to Louis XIV., to whom he had sold one
of the keys of Italy, and had recently delivered up Mantua
itself, besides having several times permitted him to pass
through his States in order to invade the peninsula—was
fêted as he deserved to be, and was received as a true
Frenchman.   He descended at the Palace of the Luxem-
bourg, magnificently fitted up for him with the furniture of
the Crown.   Seven tables were constantly served at the King's
expense for the Duke and his suite, and brilliant fêtes were
given him at Meudon and Versailles, where he received from
Louis XIV. a splendid sword covered with diamonds.[28]   It
has been said [29] that it would have been extremely imprudent
to have inscribed Matthioly's real name upon the registers of
Saint-Paul's, at the date of the Duke's arrival in Paris, since
the latter might thus have become acquainted with his
death.   We know what kind of interest Charles IV. took
in his ex-confidant, and we have seen that he only troubled
himself with making sure of his positive disappearance.
Instead, therefore, of the fact of this death being concealed

---

[28] *Mémoires de Saint-Simon*, vol. iii. pp. 70, 108, 109.
[29] M. Jules Loiseleur, *Revue Contemporaine*, p. 236.

from him, it is very possible that he was made acquainted with it, with the view of altogether dissipating his alarms. However this may be, history presents some singular meetings, and reality often surpasses in interest the most romantic fancies of the imagination. Of the two individuals who had played the principal part in the cession of Casale to Louis XIV., the Prince who had agreed to it contrary to his duty, in order to obtain a little money and satisfy his prodigality, was the object of gorgeous fêtes; while at the same moment, in the same town, and only a short distance off, his ex-Minister, whom he had created Senator and Count, who was allied to the most illustrious families of his country, and who had once also been magnificently received by Louis XIV. at Versailles, but who had afterwards for an instant arrested the monarch's overwhelming ambition and delayed the servitude of Mantua, was dying far away from his friends, in a little chamber of the Bastille, after a captivity of four-and-twenty years; and the next day, at the fall of night, was obscurely borne to the neighbouring church, followed only by two subordinate officials belonging to the fortress.

THE END.

LONDON:
PRINTED BY SMITH, ELDER AND CO.,
OLD BAILEY, E.C.